Early Embraces II

ALSO AVAILABLE FROM ALYSON
BY LINDSEY ELDER

*Early Embraces: True-Life Stories of Women
Describing Their First Lesbian Experience*

*Beginnings: Lesbians Talk About the First Time They Met
Their Long-Term Partner*

Early Embraces II

More true-life stories of women describing their first lesbian experience

edited by Lindsey Elder

alyson books
los angeles | new york

MANUFACTURED IN THE UNITED STATES OF AMERICA.

THIS TRADE PAPERBACK ORIGINAL IS PUBLISHED BY ALYSON PUBLICATIONS,
P.O. BOX 4371, LOS ANGELES, CALIFORNIA 90078-4371.
DISTRIBUTION IN THE UNITED KINGDOM BY
TURNAROUND PUBLISHER SERVICES LTD.,
UNIT 3 OLYMPIA TRADING ESTATE, COBURG ROAD, WOOD GREEN,
LONDON N22 6TZ ENGLAND.

FIRST EDITION: JUNE 1999

99 00 01 02 03 a 10 9 8 7 6 5 4 3 2 1

ISBN 1-55583-497-3

LIBRARY OF CONGRESS CATALOGING-IN-PUBLICATION DATA
EARLY EMBRACES II : MORE TRUE-LIFE STORIES OF WOMEN DESCRIBING
THEIR FIRST LESBIAN EXPERIENCE / EDITED BY LINDSEY ELDER.
    ISBN 1-55583-497-3
    1. LESBIANS—UNITED STATES—SEXUAL BEHAVIOR. 2. COMING OUT
(SEXUAL ORIENTATION)—UNITED STATES. I. ELDER, LINDSEY.
II. TITLE: EARLY EMBRACES 2. III. TITLE: EARLY EMBRACES TWO.
HQ75.6.U5E36 1999
306.76'63—DC21   99-12132 CIP

COVER PHOTOGRAPH BY PHYLLIS CHRISTOPHER.

Contents

Introduction

*I*n 1996, Lindsey Elder's anthology of first lesbian experiences, *Early Embraces*, hit bookstore shelves. It also hit our lives, our hearts, and our desires, touching off wonderful and infinite possibilities of firsts: first love, first sex, and first lust. Readers' reactions to a book of stories written by women sharing their first lesbian experiences were so favorable, so overwhelming, that Elder decided to publish a follow-up volume.

I can understand why. The notion of firsts captivates us. Sex and intimacy grip our memory banks so much that any of us can easily conjure up a favorite moment. As you will see in this collection, the favorite moment is often the first moment.

The women's voices in these stories carry us to first times with lyrical language and sensual descriptions. Travel to working-class Eastern towns, small Southern Baptist communities, big hipster cities, and even a quaint English country house complete with a garden. Suddenly you are a nervous college student being seduced in the closet of an alluring female student. A woman sharing a surprisingly intimate phone call with her best friend. A newcomer on her first job—where the boss offers her an experience that goes far beyond what she can put on her résumé.

The stories span four decades and feature women from diverse ethnic and social backgrounds. Some experiences mark the beginnings of sexual awakening, while others are full-blown sexual encounters. All will have you reminiscing about your first time—and every time after.

So kick back and prepare yourself for more women, more firsts, more love, more lust, and, of course, more adventure.

Kennette Nicole Crockett
Los Angeles, 1999

Early Embraces II

CHAPTER ONE
The Sounds of Her Hands
Taj James

The first memory I have of her is her hands. She wrote left-handed, with her wrist curled tightly around an expensive pen, beginning her strokes from the bottom so each line began with an angry dot. I'd sit next to her in detention and drive myself crazy wondering what she was writing that required such intensity.

She was slender, tall, striking—a calculated suburban dissident with a preference for leather miniskirts to crown the pale legs that fretted under her desk while she wrote. She had already mastered the power of her arresting big browns on teacher and friends alike; I was always astounded at how easily she could get what she wanted with a flick of her brow. Recalling how entrancing she was, I can more easily admit I worshiped the very sod on her boots. We became friends, and I followed her around like a Chihuahua in tow, much to the dismay of my mother, who was sure Brit was devil spawn. We smoked cigarettes in her car at lunch, commiserating about Catholic high school and sharing teen-angst poetry. At an age at which I romanticized the Broken Home Rebel, I thought Brit was a martyr; she needed an appreciative, naive confidant. We became inseparable, and a subtle undercurrent of jealousy always surfaced whenever one of us had a boyfriend, as though one of us had betrayed the other.

It wasn't long into our friendship before we began talking over the phone for hours after our parents had gone to bed. We created characters based on our idols, spoke in voices we'd created for them, and wove elaborate stories of their

1

love affairs with one another. We devised all imaginable combinations of sexual exploits, creating vast and increasingly erotic storylines with which we explored our own writhing curiosities. On more than one occasion I'd get excited and reach beneath my sheets to investigate the slickness in my panties, but I didn't share this with her, fearing she'd be grossed out. Then one night when our adventure turned sexy, she stopped me.

"Hey, I want you to hear something really badly, but you have to promise not to freak out," and I heard a rustling of bedclothes as she pushed the receiver down under them. She held the phone for several minutes as I listened to the sounds of her fingers at work; soon I could tell by the sounds of readjustment that she'd whipped the covers off and placed the phone between her legs so both hands could be free. I heard her growling with intent; a foreign noise that was both terrifying and exciting. "Touch yourself and let me hear," she said, and I put the receiver into my own sheets. At first I just moved my fingers around obligingly, but soon the idea that Brit was on the line, listening, touching herself with me, sent a jolt through me, and I started rubbing in earnest. I heard her voice and put the phone back to my ear, and together we came, straining not to cry out for fear of being heard.

Afterward, while we lay panting, a paranoia crept into me. The clock read 8:33 A.M., and I heard the sounds of Mother in the kitchen, which was right next to my bedroom. I panicked.

"You still there?" Brit whispered dreamily.

"Yeah. Listen, I think Mom's up. I gotta go."

"Wait a sec. I think maybe you should come spend the night tonight. Will you?"

My heart skipped. "I'll try. Yes. I'll see you after class. I gotta go."

I hung up in slow motion, pushing in the lever before re-placing the receiver, afraid to make another single noise.

I spent the next day replaying all the details I could recall: her voice, the sounds of her hands over the phone. Between tiny blissful rushes, however, a sudden fear would pierce my erotic trance: *How long had Mother been in the kitchen?* When I thought of this, my heart pounded with anxiety. *Mother would have a fit if she knew I was on the phone with Brit at all, and if she'd heard me, what did she think was happening?*

When classes ended I hurried home to get ready to go to Brit's. As I was cramming my book satchel with clothes from a basket on the couch, Mother came in, muted the TV, and lit one of her foot-long cigarettes. She sat for a long time, just smoking and staring at the box, her dense silence pressing into me.

"Where are you going this evening?" she asked through a mouthful of smoke.

"Over to Brit's to stay the night."

Mother pursed her lips, her eyes still fixed on the TV. "Is her mother going to be there tonight?"

"I dunno. I guess."

"You're not spending the night over there."

"Why?"

"I think your interest in her is a little more involved than just friends," she said.

The pores in my palms burst into tears. "I don't even know what you're talking about."

"Yes, you do, my dear. You be home directly at 9 o'clock, and that's it."

I sat for a moment with my mouth agape in fake protest, knowing anything I said would only prove my guilt. She must have heard us. I suddenly felt ashamed, as if I'd been caught peeing in the flower bed. I hadn't thought that what Brit and

I had done had been disgusting or unnatural until that moment, and I was terrified of my mother's repulsion.

Brit drove up, and as I walked to her car I felt my mother's eyes on me.

"Let's get the fuck out of here," I said.

"What's up?"

"Mom says I can't spend the night."

"Why?"

"I don't know exactly. I think she heard us."

Brit squinted at the house. "That's OK. It's early. We have plenty of time."

As we drove we picked up where we left off in our story the night before. Steven, surreptitious and alluring, was my favorite character. I felt the sexiest with him. Brit played another man, Lawrence, a bon vivant with a caustic humor who was in the process of seducing Steven. We had never played the game in person before, and the added dimension of actually being near her, near enough to touch her while I felt so sexy, was intoxicating. I found myself looking at her smooth arms, following them to her long fingers, remembering the sound they had made inside her. It suddenly seemed wrong that we were playing men when all I could think of was seeing what I had heard over the phone.

By the time we got to her house, I was dizzy. Her mother met us in the kitchen, informed us she was going out for the evening, and trotted back to her bedroom to dress. Brit offered me some spiced tea and lit all the candles in the living room. I sat on the couch, on the edge of my nerves but high on hormones, and waited an eternity for her to come back. She returned with teacups trailing fragrant steam.

"Smells nice, doesn't it?" she asked, sitting next to me.

A pause. She took the fringe of my scarf into her fingers, twirling it slowly.

"You smell nice too," she whispered, leaving her lips parted after.

Another pause. I felt a tremor.

Her hand abandoned the fringe and took up my chin. "You're so beautiful as a woman," she said, and pushed the thick silk of her tongue into my mouth.

I floated. Everything merged. One single thought: so natural. This kiss was so different from the gouging tongues of truculent schoolboys; it made the whole of me quiver and float and gush, and it felt absolutely, perfectly natural. We heard her mother shout "Bye" and slam the front door; if she had seen anything, she didn't care. Brit led me into her mother's bedroom.

"I don't know what to do," I confessed. She embraced me and leaned into my ear. "You do," she whispered, licking, "whatever you want."

We rolled for a long while, trying to push our bodies as close together as we could. To my surprise I not only knew what to do, but I also quickly took the lead. I pulled up her skirt and tugged at her hose; she quickly pulled them off. I grabbed her by the hips and brought my leg in between hers, nearly swooning with the feel of her wetness on my thigh. I covered her back with desperate kisses, rolled her over, and rubbed my face against her nipples, taking them into my mouth, getting lost in my own undirected enthusiasm when she stopped me, brushed her hair out of her eyes and said, "Fuck me. I want you to fuck me. I need it. Now!"

I was so startled by her blunt demand that I faltered; she took my hand, folded down all but my two middle fingers, and pushed them into her. "Now go, baby, do it," she coaxed, shutting her eyes tightly as I fucked her slowly, cautiously. "I need more," she breathed and removed me, opened my whole hand. I faltered again, and this time she lost patience. She moved herself onto my four fingers. "Now go! Do it!" she hissed, and I pumped her as hard as I could until my hand cramped and the smell of her filled the room. I thought I was going to scream with the effort, but suddenly it was her screaming in catharsis, wailing a cat's wail of release, then subsiding into a low moan that sustained, sustained, then stumbled into tears.

I lay down beside her, my shoulder burning. "You OK?" I whispered after a while. She didn't answer but just lay there staring, breathing, tears coming out of the corners of her eyes. I was so unnerved I turned away from her and curled up. After several minutes she finally spoke.

"Hey, come back. Look at me. Please. I'm sorry."

I turned over, and she rubbed my ear between her shaking fingers. "I'm sorry," she repeated. "I'm sure you didn't expect that—I just get kind of out of control sometimes."

I tried to act cool. "No, hey—I'm just glad you enjoyed it." She buried her face in my arm. "I love you. I've always loved you, and I've always wanted to do this. Please don't be mad."

We lay there until well past my 9 o'clock curfew, finally relaxing into conversation. I didn't realize I was late until 10 o'clock or so when we panicked, dressed quickly, and departed.

"I want to kiss you good night, like normal people would," I said as we pulled up to my house.

"You think that's safe?" she said. "What if your mom is looking out the window?"

"She'll be asleep," I asserted. I leaned over for another silky kiss. "I love you too," I said, and she smiled.

I was tired but elated as I fumbled for my keys. Suddenly the door began to creak open without my help. In the doorway stood my mother in her robe.

"So. Do you always kiss your girlfriends good night?"

My jaw went slack as hot blood filled my face. We stood there in silence as she stared at me with searing contempt.

"You know what? You're going to be just like my mother. My sick bitch of a mother. You get in this house and go straight to bed. And don't you say one goddamn word to me." With that, she turned on her heel, went into her bedroom, and slammed the door. I went to bed feeling like I'd been backhanded. I tried to think of Brit, fantasize about our night together, but I only felt sick, scared, and unsure of what was next. It was a full three days before Mother spoke to me again.

In the next few months, Brit and I saw each other in secret. Her mother transferred her to a different school, not so much because she was concerned about us but to avoid my mother's harassment. When mother discovered us again, I was offered an ultimatum: Get straight or get out. Drained by the constant anxiety, I gave in and told Brit I couldn't see her anymore. It was devastating.

Years later, after my father's death, my mother and I opened up to one another. I learned where her head was at that time, and it helped me to understand why she was so terrified. She in turn found out how it was for me. I am grateful we've been able to communicate about this time in our lives — woman to woman — that she opened herself up enough to recognize me without fear as a lesbian.

I never saw Brit again, but I often wonder how she is, if our separation hurt her as much as it did me. Sometimes I still feel guilty, having left her the way I did. Sometimes I fantasize about meeting up with her in adulthood, what that would be like, what I would tell her. Usually I tell her I've always missed her.

CHAPTER TWO
Honeysuckle
Patricia

*I*t's the spring of 1958 in Cambridge, England. I sit at one of the long tables in the college dining hall, hoping my friend Sue will be able to join me. We're both 19 and in our first year at an all-women's teacher training college. As I eat, snatches of conversation from a group of women reach me:

"Well, my psychology professor said we should read it...It's called the *Wolfenden Report*...What's it about?...Homosexuality and...It says if adult males do it in private and they both want it...But it's disgusting...The Bible says...How do you tell if someone is one?...Easy, they have bleached hair, wear pink...And women...Women?...Yes, women...They have mustaches, wear trousers, smoke pipes...." Everyone laughs. I keep eating and hope no one will turn to me. I have, as we called it in boarding school, "a pash" on Jill, and I know this makes me "different."

While I eat, I remember our first meeting. A friend from boarding school had told me to look out for Sue. "You'll really like her," Mary said. I was expecting someone like us — middle-class, tomboyish (my mother constantly complains, "Why can't you act more like a young lady, Patricia?"), and with a sense of humor that makes friends say, "Grow up, won't you!" When I met Sue at the new student reception, I found she had permed hair, wore makeup and jewelry, and spoke softly with a slight London accent. But I was immediately attracted to her and glad to find out that we lived on the same floor. We were going attend many of the same lectures, and we were assigned to the same school for our first teaching practices.

I push my plate away and sigh. I don't know what to do. I'm supposed to have grown out of "pashes."

"What's the sigh for?" Sue says as she slides next to me on the bench. I turn and smile at her. "You probably thought I wasn't coming," she says. "Neither did I. The lecture ran late, and now I have to go practice the cello. But there's enough time to find out what you're worried about."

"Oh," I say, taken by surprise. "Er, well, it sounds so silly, but I'm having trouble handling those boys in Class 4."

Sue finishes her mouthful. "I do what Mother and Auntie told me. I look them in the eye and say, 'Do you want to go and see the headmaster? No? Well then, you know what to do.' You have to be firm, Pat. I've noticed…"

"Yes?" I say.

"Oh, nothing really." She puts her head on one side and smiles, then eats some more. "You think you can't do it, but I'm sure you can; just don't be too kind." She finishes eating and gets up. "Now, I *have* to go and practice or *I* won't be able to do it."

"Can I come and listen?" I ask. "I don't have a lecture till later."

"If you like, but…" she laughs again. "I'm sounding like you. I'll be making mistakes. I've only just started this piece."

We walk over to the music wing, and I sit and listen, watching her fingers move, her body filled with the music's melancholy energy. I can't believe the hour goes by so fast. As we leave the practice room I say, "Can I come again?"

"If you want to. Now I have to run. Perhaps I'll see you for a late cup of coffee. I'm going out with Ben tonight. There's a concert at his college."

"Bye." I watch her walk away. Knowing she's going to see

Ben gives me an empty, lost feeling.

That night when she comes into my room, she doesn't ask for coffee but closes the door, sits on my bed, and bursts into tears. "Ben tried to...Oh, it was horrible!" she cries. "I don't want to see him again."

The next Saturday, Sue suggests taking a bike ride. We cycle across the flat Cambridgeshire Fen Country, so different from the wooded and hilly West Country where I'm from. This place, its roads raised above the fields, seems to be without landmarks, the horizon distant. There is little sign of life except for birds crying in the bitter wind that comes in from the North Sea.

More and more, Sue and I start doing things together on the weekends. Some Sundays we spend visiting her uncle and aunt who live on the edge of town. After supper we walk in their old-fashioned walled garden, where honeysuckle clings to the rose trellises. As spring ends and summer begins, the honeysuckle flowers bloom, filling the evening air with their sweetness. Sue tells me of her dream: to have her own music school. I tell her what I've told no one else: I want to write.

One Saturday we travel to London by train with a student group to join an antiapartheid rally in Trafalgar Square. On the way back to the railway station, our bus is caught in a traffic jam. Outside a café is a group of men with bleached hair, pink shirts, and tight blue trousers.

"The third sex," someone jeers. The bus fills with laughter. I sit perfectly still. On the train to Cambridge, with all of us squeezed together, I want to hold Sue's hand so badly I quiver. I turn away from the noisy conversation, look out the window, and realize what it feels like to have a heart that might burst.

It's almost the end of term. In a month, Sue and her family are going on a tour of Europe for the rest of the summer. I am going home. One evening, over coffee, she says, "Auntie and Uncle are going away for a week and want me to look after the house and the dog. They said I could invite you." I telephone my mother:

"Who *are* these people?" she demands.

"Part of Sue's family. I've written to you about them. They have us over on Sundays. We're going to be taking care of the house and the dog, watering the garden. It's just for a week."

"Well, don't get into trouble, Patricia," she says. "They've never sounded like our kind of people. I really was expecting you to come straight home. Now I'll have to change the hair appointment I made for you."

The weather is perfect. I can't believe I have Sue to myself for a whole week. She plans each day. We get up early, have breakfast in the garden, water the flowers, do a little dusting, and walk Joey, the spaniel. Some afternoons we bike into town and go boating on the river, enjoying the quiet now that the university has gone down for the summer. Other days we lie in the garden, reading and talking. We discuss our families.

"My mother runs the house," Sue says. "My father's quiet and likes to stay home unless Mum has plans. Now David, my brother, he's another matter. He dresses fancy, oils his hair, and chases the girls. My mother pretends to disapprove, but I think she's actually pleased he's so different from Dad."

I laugh. "I need brothers and sisters. They might distract my mother. I'm the only one she has around to command!"

Sometimes, after supper, if we don't sit in the garden, listening to the night sounds, smelling the honeysuckle, Sue plays her cello, and I sit on the couch and listen and watch. We sleep in the large spare room that has twin beds. After we've put out the light, Sue talks about going to Europe and the things she'll see and do.

"I'll send you postcards," she says.

When she falls asleep, I lie in bed listening to her breathing; I'm filled with a longing I don't have words for, happy to be with her, but aching for something more.

On our last afternoon we're lying in the garden, reading. Sue puts down her book and sits up.

"I'd like to stay in this part of the country," she says. "I've heard that Ely is a pretty town and has good schools. What are your plans, Pat?"

"I don't know. Probably I should go back to Cheltenham and live close to my mother."

"Why don't you think about applying to Ely? We could share a flat. It would make moving to a new place easier."

I sit up and turn to her. She's looking at me in a friend-ly—almost placid—way, smiling, her head on one side. I keep looking at her. The whole garden seems to fall silent. As if I'd planned it all my life, I lean over, put my hand on her sun-warmed shoulder, and kiss her lips. I feel how dif-ferent it is from the kisses I've known with men; then I pull back, shocked at myself, and scramble off the blanket, turning away.

Sue catches my hand. "Don't go. I wanted that too."

I turn, my hand in hers. She must see a question in my face.

"Yes," she says. "I've kept us busy because I was feeling something, something I didn't know what to do with."

"Oh, Sue," I crouch beside her, "that's exactly what I've been feeling, and…" She leans toward me, kisses me hard on my mouth; I put a hand on the back of her head and pull her against me.

"Anybody home?" A male voice sounds from inside the house.

We separate quickly.

"It's David!" Sue says. We scramble up, turning toward the French windows that lead from the drawing room and into the garden.

Coming out of the darkness of the house and into the gar-

den is a tall young man with slicked-back hair and an amused
look on his face.

"Not expecting me? Mum said you were here, so I thought
I'd come up."

"David, this is Pat, my friend from college."

"Pleased to meet you." We all stand silently.

"Hope I wasn't interrupting anything," he says.

"Oh, David!" Sue pokes his arm. "I'm just surprised. We
were napping out here in the sun. Anyway, it's time to walk
the dog. You want to come?"

David nods. Sue and I gather up our books and the blanket, and we all go into the house.

We call Joey, find his leash, and walk to the park. We let
him run while we sit on a bench and occasionally throw his
ball for him. David gets on a swing. He starts to pump himself higher and higher.

"David!" Sue says. "Don't!"

"Bet you *girls* are too scared to swing this high," he shouts.

Sue laughs, "Don't be rude! We're *women.*"

"Oh, really?"

"I'll show you." Sue jumps up, gets on a swing, and starts
pumping back and forth. She doesn't go as high as David, but
faster and higher than I would. Joey trots over to me and
puts his nose on my knee. I pat him, reach for the ball he's
dropped, and throw it for him while I listen to Sue and David
tease each other and laugh. Finally they both grow tired and
just sit in the swings. Joey starts to pant as he lies under the
bench and chews his ball.

"Think we should go home?" Sue asks.

"Well, I'm ready." David jumps off his swing. "I'm hungry."

We put Joey back on his lead and walk home. When we
get back, David says he'll cook. "Got any liver and onions?"
he asks. "Just teasing; I'll make fish and chips. You can wash

some lettuce," he says to me, "if you do things like that."

"I think I can manage." I go into the pantry and find the lettuce.

"You mustn't mind David," Sue calls. "He's the joker in the family."

I wash the lettuce and shake it dry, set it in a salad bowl, and take it into the dining room. Sue has just finished arranging the table. "We'd better start vacuuming and dusting before Uncle and Auntie get back. Auntie's very house-proud." While David cooks, we clean.

When we sit down to supper, he says, "I want to go to cooking school, but Dad and Mum don't want me to. They look at me as if they think I'm queer or something. You know," turning to me, "one of those sick sort of people." He pulls a face. "And I've got a girlfriend and everything."

He looks at Sue. "You see any of them? Everyone at school's talking about some report that says it's all right, as long as it's in private."

"I've heard it mentioned in college, but I don't listen much. How is Jill anyway?"

"She's fine. Complains about my being gone all summer. I saw Ben one day. He's coming on the trip. Said he hadn't seen much of you lately."

Sue finishes chewing and puts down her knife and fork. She wipes her mouth with her napkin and looks at David. "No, we've both been busy. He had his finals, and I had teaching practice."

There's a silence. We go on eating, and after the meal we clear the table and wash the dishes. The evening passes somehow. David finds Radio Luxembourg on the wireless and sits in the drawing room, singing along to the Top 20 songs. Sue and I go upstairs and start packing. Without saying anything, we know we won't sit in the garden tonight. Our bedroom door is open, and David suddenly pops his head in, sits on the end of Sue's bed, and watches us.

"Pat, what'll you do this summer?"

"Oh, stay out of my mother's way, go to the seaside. Usual stuff."

"Got a boyfriend at home?"

"No one serious," I say, concentrating on folding a blouse.

Finally we're all ready for bed. We take turns in the bathroom, shout good night to David, who's in the small spare room, and close our door.

We look at each other. "I'm sorry about David," Sue says.

"I don't think he likes me."

"It's hard to tell with him."

I take a step toward her, but she turns away, gets into bed, and, saying good night, turns off the light. We lie in the dark in silence. Then I hear her crying. "Sue," I say. She goes on crying. I get up and kneel beside her bed. She's turned away from me. "Don't cry," I say. I stroke her hair.

"I can't help it," she says. "It feels different with David here. I don't know what to think." I stay beside her bed. Suddenly she rolls over. "Please hold me." I get in her bed, lie beside her on top of the eiderdown, and put my arms around her. I hold her very closely, brushing away her tears with my lips. I feel a warmth grow between us. She lies in my arms, still crying quietly, and at last she stops. I kiss her lips gently. They are soft and moist. Our mouths open, and the tips of our tongues touch and stroke; we are breathing faster and kissing harder. I press my tongue deeper into her mouth. Then Sue pulls away and buries her face in my shoulder.

"Sue," I whisper.

She shakes her head slightly. "Don't."

I keep holding her, not speaking. The words I want to say,

the questions I want to ask, are too fearful. As we lie there, her breathing grows more regular. Even through the bed-clothes I can feel the shape of her body, how round and soft it is, and how my breasts touch hers, gently moving against them with our breathing. The warmth inside me increases. I feel it between my legs in places that are frightening and un-visited by me; the warmth grows into heat, spreads, until I think I'll explode, and then it's as if I do. My whole body shakes inside, moving against my will, taking my breath away, until suddenly it's over. I lie there, catching my breath.

"Sue," I whisper again.

But there's no reply.

I sit up a little and look at her in the light of the street lamp shining through the curtains. She's asleep. I lie back beside her. I don't know what's happened, how to explain it to my-self. I keep lying there, holding her.

Later I wake, my left arm numb. I slide it out from under Sue, get up slowly, and go back to my own bed. I lie on my back and relive what has happened. I can feel the warmth growing once more in my body. Then, against all the things I've been told, I slip my hand down between my legs. I feel places that are warm and moist, soft and tender. I touch them with my fingers. The warmth increases, the shuddering be-gins again, and I hold myself till it's over. Tired, confused, I finally turn on my side and try to sleep.

The next morning I wake up to find Sue's bed empty. I lie quietly for a moment, remembering. Then I get up, put on my dressing gown, and run downstairs. I hear voices and stop, then realize *David is here!* I go down more slowly. When I reach the kitchen, I see Sue standing with her back to me, facing David, who is leaning against the counter, talking. As I come in, he stops and, still looking at Sue, pushes himself away from the counter, saying, "All right then. I'm going to walk the dog. You have an hour." Without looking, he walks past me into the hall and calls for Joey, who comes running. Then the front door slams.

"What's happening?" I ask, touching Sue on her shoulder. She turns to face me, stepping away from my touch. Her face is puffy, her eyes red and swollen, and there are tears on her face. She starts sobbing, her hands over her face. I come near- er and touch her again. "No!" she says, and I take my hand away. She lets her hands drop to her side. "He saw. He'll tell Mum and Dad if I have anything more to do with you."

I look at her, not wanting to understand. She goes on, "When he called from inside the house yesterday afternoon, he'd already been standing there watching us kiss. So last night he came into our room—we must have both fallen asleep—and…saw us."

She starts crying again. "He says you're the queer, and being friends with you would mean I'd never get a teaching job." She gestures with her hands. "I couldn't bear that. It's the only thing I've ever wanted to do." She looks at me. I see in her face my own pain and confusion.

"Please understand," she goes on. "We can't see each other alone again. David's called a taxi so you can take the earlier train. There won't be any postcards."

"You can't even *write?*"

"If I did, you couldn't write back. David would know."

"Couldn't Mary…?"

"And *tell* her? We'll…" she hesitates slightly, "get over each other."

I'm silent, too shocked and cold for tears. Still I step to- ward her and hold her. She stands rigidly, then puts her arms around me. We stand this way for a moment.

"I love you," I say, almost inaudibly, into her hair.

"I know…and I loved you. But I can't anymore."

She pulls away. "You must get dressed and finish packing."

I look at her, then turn and run up the stairs. I dress. I pack. I strip the bed. I carry my luggage down, and we go and stand outside in the driveway. Even though it's morning, I think there's a smell of honeysuckle in the air. The taxi arrives, and the driver gets out, takes my suitcases, opens the door. I turn to Sue.

"Good-bye and...thank you," I say. "I won't forget."

She nods. "Good-bye...have a happy summer."

I climb in, the driver closes the door, Sue steps away, and we wave through the window as the taxi turns in the drive. It stops before pulling onto the road. I look back. Sue isn't there; the front door is closing.

The summer passes. I return to college. Sue and I are never alone together. We never speak of what happened. We both get our teaching certificates, and I teach in Cheltenham for two years before moving to America. Finally, in 1994 I go to a group for older women who are coming out and read a poem about Sue and me. They listen, and I cry. At last, I've told someone.

CHAPTER THREE
Firsts
G.L. Morrison

*T*ime doesn't happen in the order that days line up on the calendar. It's inner chaos and small epiphanies, not hours, that we keep time by. Is this the first time just now? Or did it happen just yesterday or so long ago the details are blurred? Maybe it hasn't happened yet. This is what did happen and the dates it happened, but not the order it happened in. This is what happened to me.

In 1975 I was nine and so was she. Heidi was the first. She wasn't the first girl I'd kissed. The summer before, Heather Polson was my best friend. I spent more nights at her house that summer than at my own.

After watching the *Donny and Marie Show,* Heather and I pretended I was Donny and that we were married. Her teddy bear officiated at our wedding. I sang, "You're a little bit country, and I'm a little bit rock and roll."

We got into bed. "It's our wedding night," we told each other, then tried everything we'd heard about wedding nights. We giggled a lot, and her Mom shouted for us to shut up and go to sleep.

But that wasn't the first time. Neither was LaDonne, who took me downstairs to play house in her unfinished basement. I was the Daddy. She was the Mommy. A dozen stuffed animals and baby dolls were our kids. We spent a long time naming and feeding and spanking them. She showed me what Mommy and Daddy did when they thought all the dolls and teddies were asleep.

But that was not the first time. More than a year later,

Heidi was the first. She was the first girl I really kissed. We looked for places to be alone, not for kissing, but for talking. We talked about how we'd be together forever and how many children we wanted to have and the places we would go, the things we would do, the people we would be. We tape-recorded our conversations, our songs, and our secret messages, and played them back seriously.

Heidi lived on a farm in Provo, Utah, just outside the city. I would spend the weekends with her, planning our future and doing farm chores. I don't know which was more exotic. We got up early those weekends; I saw the sky in shades I'd never known before. I bounced along beside her in the back of the truck with a crate full of squealing piglets. I put my face down close to the crate. I was sure they were crying for their mom. Heidi and I tried to sing them something soothing. Two girls in the back of a speeding truck screaming lullabies over the screeching of angry pigs. Later, I tried to milk a goat! Heidi didn't laugh at my feeble attempts, but when it looked like the nanny might kick me for my efforts, she stepped in deftly. I didn't like goat's milk one bit, but I drank as much as I could to please her.

We were filled with a sense of destiny and each other. But destiny (and my mother) had something else in mind for us. Heidi's father was a polygamist, which I didn't realize until my mother became convinced he'd set his cap on her. She often told me men were looking at her, thinking of her sexually, and perhaps they were. All I know for certain is something shifted in my mother's thinking, and my love affair with Heidi felt the aftershock. Heidi's house became too far to drive to, and my mother declared, "All those animals affect your allergies." I was not allowed to stay with Heidi or see her after school at her house. Heidi had permission to come to my house, but she couldn't come often since her family needed her to do the work at home.

Then suddenly, without warning, she didn't come again or return my calls. Had words passed between my mother and her father? Who was forbidden from whom? I loved her. And I forgot her...as painfully and quickly as first loves are forgotten. She was the first. She was the first girl I really kissed. She was the first girl who didn't pretend I was Donny Osmond or Daddy. We knew who we were kissing.

In 1985 I was 19, and she wasn't. Lareen was the first. I had just ended my teen marriage and came blazing out of the closet in a black leather jacket covered in queer buttons with a three-year-old in tow. She wasn't the first woman I'd kissed. There had been Gidget before I decided to leave my husband. I was living in Tucson. I'd drive out at night to gay bars with a fake ID in my pocket and a car seat in the back of my Oldsmobile. I met Gidget in a bar.

"Let's get coffee or something," I'd said, thinking we'd work our way from the bar to the coffee shop to her house. At the coffee shop she showed me she carried a whip in her purse. She admitted we couldn't go back to her place because she lived with her mother. I admitted we couldn't go back to mine because I lived with my husband. We did a lot of heavy petting in my car and in the women's rest room of that coffee shop. We met there for weeks. We even had coffee with my husband. He said something so funny she laughed, spraying him with coffee. She moved to Phoenix and asked me to come visit her there. She finally had a place of her own. I flew home to my sister's wedding. When I came back, Gidget called to tell me she was getting married to a woman she met in a bar in Phoenix.

But Gidget wasn't my first. Not even my first disappointment. I left my husband and Arizona. I moved to Salt

Lake City. I went to bars where I met women. I fell in love three times a night. I met many women and chauffeured them here and there while they dated each other. I was too young or too serious or not serious enough. I knew a lot of people. I joined every gay group I saw advertised. I did AIDS activism, queer student politics, lesbian spirituality, a women's reading group, and data entry for the local queer paper.

I ran a personals ad. Lareen answered it. She was an advertising executive for ZCMI, which is like Sears for Mormons. She was 27 and almost a virgin. I say almost because two weeks before she answered my ad, she awoke with a terrifying question: *Am I a lesbian?* She answered it by looking through the personal ads and calling a man and inviting him over to have sex with her. Three days later she asked herself the same question. She called another man. The next time she asked herself she called me.

She was two weeks and two men away from being a virgin when I met her, but neither the time nor encounters had made her more "experienced." She had never dated. I took her to dinner and dancing. It was the first time she'd ever danced. The sound of her breath on my cheek and the low music as I turned her clumsily around the dance floor was intoxicating. She'd never been in a lesbian bar. The sight of women clinging to each other as they danced around us amazed her. She held me very tight.

"Is there somewhere we could go...you know?" she asked.

I took her to a popular make-out spot on a hill overlooking the city. I often went there alone to see the city lights. I was pleased to have someone to take there. There was not enough room in my car for the pent-up passions of 27 years. We got out and walked in the park. We lay in the damp grass, groping. Untucked, unbuttoned, and having shed our shoes, nylons, and panties, I licked her while she squirmed in the grass. Nose buried deep and blindly searching for her clitoris with my tongue (I knew she had one. *Was that it? Was that? Will I know it when I find it?*), we heard people rustling somewhere near. *How near?* Giggling. *That near? Can they see anything?* I was close to her, and there was not much I could see. We felt around in the dark for our shoes and dashed to the car.

We finished at my house. After paying the baby-sitter, I showed her up to my room. She lay down on my bed: a mattress on the floor covered with dirty unmatched sheets and the quilt my grandmother made. We made love until we were both too tired to move. Then she fell asleep in my arms. She was the first. She was the first woman I slept with. The first woman I woke up. She was the first woman I kissed and knew I would go on kissing. I went on kissing her for two years. After we broke up I heard she had moved in with a woman who had the same first name as mine and a daughter the same age as my son.

CHAPTER FOUR
Meine Schwulin
Veronica Holtz

*J*ust as I brought the half-litre to my lips, Bernhart elbowed me to hurry. Part of our group was already rushing out the club entrance. I left a couple pfennigs on the table and caught up to my friends back on Leopoldstrasse.

"Why did we leave so soon?" I asked, jumping in and around the sidewalk crowds. Our international group's weekend routine consisted of exploring clubs in the Munich student district. The one we had just left seemed no different than any other; maybe even *gemeutlicher*—friendlier.

Between whispered sniggers and outright laughter, I heard the word "*schwulin.*"

"You know," Uli cast over her shoulder, before she grabbed Werner's arm again.

No, I didn't know. After little over a year as a student in Europe, I was able to follow almost any conversation, whether in High German or student dialect. But I couldn't catch this private joke that my friends dangled out of my reach.

Finally, Bernhart drew in his cheeks with temporary sobriety and clarified: "*Lesben.*"

The word was much too close to its American translation for me to misinterpret. Yet it directly contradicted the definition I had established at age 14, when I had uncovered my parents' private film collection. Behind the locked door of my darkened bedroom, I collected a dollar entrance fee from each neighborhood kid. We passed around bubble gum, candy, and nervous giggles, as we attempted to decipher the great mystery of adult sexuality. After several brief and plotless het films, the television screen presented us with the shortest cinematic fiasco ever brought into existence. In a cramped and bare room, two beached female manatees, plastered with more makeup than a mime, lay together on a small cot. What they proceeded to do, none of us could comprehend. I don't recall them being able to maneuver around one another, much less engage in anything resembling sex.

As the rest of us looked on in puzzlement, the most worldly teenager in the room announced, "Lesbians."

That was enough to chill any consideration of such an existence for myself. Cuddling my pillow seemed a more exciting alternative to either the het or lesbian lifestyle. It wasn't a difficult decision to make since I was consumed by sports and music. After high school I decided to study at a music conservatory in Salzburg, Austria.

In Europe everything awakened in me. It provided a slower, yet more open way of life that fit me perfectly. Eager to learn, I absorbed every bit of Europe into my heart. And now I was determined to learn about *schwulin*. Curious and convinced of my own invincibility, I hopped on the Salzburg-Munich train and trekked back to the club by myself. Rosy-cheeked Iris, a blond-haired woman plump with diplomacy, invited me to a long wooden table for introductions. A ripple of surprise at my American origin swept through the student group because I dressed, spoke, and acted more European than Yankee ever could. And a good hour was spent on the logistics of name, circumstances, and the never-ending debate over the tastiest beer.

I didn't feel anything but a general fondness for Iris's friends, until I saw the slender frame of a woman seated at the end of the table. Marta stood out from the others, although I didn't know why at the time. Sometimes she gazed seriously through intense brown eyes. Sometimes her entire being opened up with a laugh as fresh as Alpine air. While others were unable to reconcile my adventurous musical interests with my innocent face, Marta encouraged me to speak about it.

"*Toll,*" she complimented me. "*Was fuer musik machst du?*"

"Modern," I explained.

My place in the musical hierarchy was in the group I dubbed the "explorers," composers whose passion created a personal duty to guide music into undiscovered territory. I sensed she understood instantly. As the conversation continued around the table, I began to pay particular attention to the remarks she made, the way each sentence she spoke reached out with a thoughtful balance of warmth and reserve.

My het friends had to be mistaken. Whatever glaring blemish obvious to them did not show itself to me. The women in this club looked normal in every way. In fact, they looked rather beautiful. They were students who, in my eyes, simply had a unique outlook exclusive to the region.

Throughout the evening I had only felt a gentle easing into this selective circle. True, I had observed women who were extremely attached to one another. From the conversations, one could conclude that *hubsch* or *scheisskopf* carried a more intense meaning here than "cute" or "%*$#!î" did in het land. And yes, it was conceivable that cuddling on another woman's lap bordered on the intimate. But only as the questions became more personal did I contemplate something other than mere fellowship.

"Are you with anyone?" asked a sociable Czech expatriate.

That was easy enough to answer. "Nay." I explained that Bernhart was a good friend and let me stay over on his couch when I came to Munich.

"*Weisst er das du Schwulin bist?*" voiced an inquisitive Frenchwoman.

"Nay." I laughed at the thought that he would know I was a *schwulin*. I didn't bother to add that I didn't know either.

"*Wie findest du die Lesben in Amerika?*"

As innocently as Iris asked what I thought of American lesbians, I had the distinct impression that the question did not pertain to simple friendships. All other conversation stopped. With a side-glance I saw Marta focus her attention on me. I took a gulp of beer to stall for time. I couldn't possibly admit in front of her that my only points of reference were a three-minute manatee movie and some off-color high school jokes about dykes—a species rumored to be even more notorious than lesbians.

I gathered all the bravado I could muster and answered, *"Nicht so schoen."* Not as beautiful. To my relief, this generic compliment was readily accepted. It set off a series of hilarious stories about American women who are ignorant of basic European social protocols. Intoxicated by my success, I excused myself to go to the bathroom. My taste had risen to the level of good European beer but my bladder had not. I walked down the hall, basking in my own self-congratulatory way, totally unprepared for the sight that ambushed my eyes. In a dimly lit corner, two feminine silhouettes stood wrapped in a fiery kiss well beyond the flash point of normal hormones.

The raw sexuality pinned this accidental voyeur to the spot. One woman was braced against the wall. Her breath slackened momentarily, then heaved abruptly when the other woman moved into her. Each reach of hands inspired private murmurs of enjoyment. Each tightening of bodies accelerated an erotic rhythm that fed on stroke after stroke. My balance of thought fell apart, and with it toppled my every notion of female behavior.

The bathroom door opened, spilling light into the hall, and I quickly took refuge inside. Pacing as far as one can in a stall, I tried to put things into perspective. Only now did it become obvious to me these women did not merely dance together and share affection. They made love to one another with a passion that far surpassed any heterosexual encounter.

I took this realization back to Salzburg where I immediately became afflicted by a hallucinatory sexual malady. The nimble grocery clerk, the homely string player with her knees wrapped around a cello, prim housewives on the street. I discovered all of these women had one thing in common: Underneath their dresses, jeans, and *dirndls*, they were naked. My eyes undressed each and every one of them.

Unfortunately, this new curiosity was accompanied by my inability to restrain it. Any woman remotely within my view became a mass of sexual heat in motion. I realized my thoughts had become unmanageable when I entered the conservatory choral hall one afternoon to the vision of 100 altos and sopranos rehearsing Handel's "Hallelujah Chorus" in their birthday suits.

Alarmed, I swam extra laps at the Hallenbad and changed my clothes behind the shower curtain to deprive my eyes of any opportunity to wander. I didn't feel safe from my peculiar behavior until I reached the privacy of my rented room. Even then I lay in bed immersed in images of the womanly province called *schwulin*.

My imagination sprang from one vague female form to the next. Soon, abstractions of Marta's features were juxtaposed on these strangers. This led to a thousand speculations about her entirety: the natural earthy beauty of her face, the sensuality of her slim shoulders, the smoothness in her movement. When we met again in Munich, I was conscious of being drawn to her in every way.

In public, lesbian behavior was discreet, and overt demonstrations were an unspoken taboo. Of course, it was difficult to identify the border of discretion since Europeans thought nothing of two women walking arm in arm together or sharing tenderness in the open. Most of our outings were communal amusements for students with indigent budgets: free art exhibits and lectures, picnics, or gatherings in someone's apartment.

Every now and then Marta would say to me, "Let's stop at the café first," on our way to someone's home or "Come and sit next to me," as she grabbed my hand during a performance. Her casual touch caused my brain, heart, and voice to scatter in separate directions. My behavior fluctuated wildly between effortless, inspiring conversation and embarrassing bouts of idiotic paralysis.

"What instrument is he playing?" Marta asked at a chamber concert, as she pointed at the bassist. She knew music was a subject I could talk about easily for hours on end. The lilt in her voice woke my eyes from her lips, and I glanced studiously at the last row of the orchestra.

"Uh oh." My lucidity tripped over Marta's scent. Did she mean that mustachioed wooden monstrosity that resembled a viola after an eating binge? Only a Baroque madman on too much snuff could have invented such an odd vibrating hulk.

"Cello!" I blurted out, before concluding that my foot had become a permanent part of my mouth.

Marta was amused by my ceaseless interest in her Alpine hometown and its customs. She tried to correct my idyllic vision of her childhood, contending it was nothing more than ordinary. Pampering a *kleine brauner* at a *Gasthaus* garden, I held my breadth as she mused about the American euphemism of "making love" to describe the act of sex.

"It is romantic," she said in the tone of one who had already experienced otherwise. I was willing to concede almost any point to her, but it was vital to me she understand the beauty of this particular description. She listened, sipped her coffee, and, in thought, drew her hand through the rich brown of her collar-length hair in thought. After some deliberation, she concluded she liked the idiom.

I followed every subtlety in Marta's character: the timbre of her offhanded remarks, the fullness in her tone when she spoke seriously about influencing the world, the changing tempos of her moods. This freedom to discover the intricacies of this one woman lifted, if not my reality, my fantasies to a new sensual level. Back in the solitude of my room, I could hear her resonant voice whispering in my ear. In the darkness I saw her eyes gazing at me. I could feel Marta's body as I clung to the warmth of my comforter and reached for her lips every night. One afternoon at the local *Biergarten*, our group was busy verbally recarving the world, bending and shaping theories, challenging religions. Conversation easily flowed from German to English, the common language for all foreigners, and back again. A stranger joined our table and embraced Marta with a hug born of a mutual past.

She was the political science equivalent of an opera prima donna. Exercising her eloquent vocabulary, she stretched her arms across the table and sucked up all the air in between. Her display of familiarity with Marta only highlighted my awkwardness, and I quickly became annoyed that her demonstrations prevented us from speaking together.

Somehow she just happened to mention Marta was 26. She couldn't have contrived a more devastating remark. I had thought Marta was anywhere from my age (a bare 19) up to 22. I had even stretched my imagination to 23, acknowledging my confidence to be with an older woman. But 26? The extra seven years held a wealth of experience I didn't possess. A sudden wave of melancholy washed over me. I wandered off, as I had a habit of doing when the babble of crowds grated my thoughts.

Soon the group started to break up. I assumed Marta would go with them or with the professorial diva monopolizing her attention. It was just as well, for I had a dreadful premonition that if she came near me, I would not be able to control myself. I was utterly out of my league. I hadn't learned how to hide my feelings yet had no idea how to express them.

"You're very quiet today. Are you thinking of music?" Marta asked as she approached me on the terrace. Her physical presence rattled me, and I tried not to look directly into her eyes. "Yes," I answered faintly. In reality I was thinking of her as music. And I hated her former lover for thinking only she was entitled to hear it.

"I have some studying to do. Want to come over my place for supper? About six?"

I could not refuse any request of hers. Still, this encouragement brought little expectation with it. The others would show up, either by invitation or impromptu visit, and the communal atmosphere that was a pleasure to everyone else would only increase my misery. The idea that I was being Euro-courted never occurred to me.

When I arrived she was reading the last chapter of a sociology text. I offered to make coffee and strolled over to the cupboard. Marta's one-room apartment was more spacious than most and contained an actual stove, as opposed to the usual hot plate. Beyond a few sticks of used furniture, she sat stretched out over a faded Turkish carpet with her back against the foot of her bed. Cream-colored trousers hung slightly baggy over her long legs. A pale blue shirt effortlessly framed her lean chest. Occasionally she pushed a few distracting bangs from her face or tapped her pen against her knee to better concentrate.

After a while my ears grew keenly attuned to a stillness in the room. The sound of scribbling stopped. The intermittent studious sighs fell silent. The air held the excitement of her. And the intensity of Marta's stare melted right through my back. Unnerved, I thought to throw myself between her thighs and gush out some clumsy confession of desire; or worse yet, charge out of her room under some false pretense, never to feel her closeness again. The finished coffee drew me around, and I pulled my impulses inside.

"*Das genuegt,*" Marta said, pushing her book away.

"Enough studying?" I asked, as I brought a full mug to her.

"*Ja.*" She leaned forward and gazed at me for a moment before taking the coffee.

In one gesture, she pushed her mug aside without drinking from it and placed an unpretentious kiss on my cheek. Its sweetness erased any confusion I had ever experienced with her, and I immediately met Marta's lips with my own. It was not so much boldness as it was urgency. I needed to feel her flesh against mine. A soft but brief joining became an invitation. And Marta pressed her lips to mine.

I had always believed in my instincts, although I rarely used them. Deferring to her, I followed the depth of her kisses, the warmth of her breath against my neck. She guided me down to the carpet and rubbed against me, creating a beautiful tension. Pleased with my growing replies to her touches, she followed the contours of my face with her mouth as her hands probed the length of my torso. Still enticing my lips, she unbuttoned my shirt and removed the insignificant piece of cloth I called a bra. My only worry was that if my clothes were not removed fast enough, she might change her mind and stop. Although I was barely a stick of a woman, a sensual mist covered Marta's eyes as she gazed down upon my nakedness. My breath tightened as my legs loosened. I could do nothing less than give her free reign over my body.

"*Magst du das?*" Marta whispered in my ear, as she began to stroke my breasts.

My vulnerable expression openly displayed my delight. No one had ever touched me in such a way before. Marta took possession of one breast with her lips. What I had believed until now were two bothersome bumps on my chest were now transformed into ravenous flesh. Overcome by both her sheer touch and the vision of her sucking my nipples, my thought and body instantly became inseparable from her wishes. She drew my erotic soul into her mouth at will, squeezed and shaped my every groan. Introducing me to my own tempestuous being, she aroused me wherever she met my skin. Back and forth, she kissed one breast while she kneaded the other with her hand. She moved her way up my skin and thrust her tongue deep inside my mouth again. Just as my lips begged for more, Marta seized my sensitive nipples again with an intensity that shook my deepest insides. I was soaked between my legs. I knew I had come.

Suddenly she lifted herself up. Without taking her eyes from me, she slid off her clothes. I lay awestruck. Imagining her features did not compare to the sight of her: bare breasts, larger than mine, alive and wanting; soft curves leading down to glistening and precious hair between the thighs of a hiker. Her expression was no longer sensuous and tender. She hovered above me, hungry and selfish, her desire fixed. This beautiful woman was demanding satisfaction.

Marta plunged her nakedness on mine, sending me into every color of an erotic rainbow. She looked at me with delicious triumph, knowing I was ready to light up wherever I was touched. Spellbound, I had no idea what would come next. That is, no idea how *I* would come next. I only knew it was a certainty.

Her craving sent her hand between my legs. My breasts thought it a nonessential gesture, but my cunt vehemently disagreed. A slow rhythm drew me into a heated counterpoint of harmony and dissonance. It teased me, swelled, and amplified my body until steam rose from my flesh. Marta quickened her pace, and my body greeted her every thrust. She pumped harder, deeper into my moans, stoking my sweat into her own. The grinding, inescapable pleasure threw me into sensory overload.

A primal cry was unleashed. Its unexpected force hurled us across the rug. Another explosive surge struck me, and I

lunged into Marta's body again. Then again. We tumbled together. Reeling and jerking. On top. Underneath. The animal
within me had taken control, and Marta could do nothing but
hang on. I held tight to my rider, refusing to let her remove
her hand from inside me. Unstoppable, drenching splendor!
I clung to her until every drop of carnal rage left me. Then I
finally grabbed her hand to an abrupt stop.

Across the length of the old Turkish rug, my reality had ir-
revocably changed. I had finally tasted life, and she was powerful and delicious. Gradually, the world came back into
focus. I lay close to Marta on the other side of the room and
realized how we got there.

"Are you all right?" I asked, unsure of *schwulin* etiquette in
case of rug burns or bumps on the head. "*J-a-a-a.*" The word
was stretched into an exhausted Bavarian drawl. Marta
leaned over and gazed at me, mystified that I was the un-
tamed being she had just witnessed. Apparently not every
schwulin responded the way I did.

"Are you always like that?" she asked me with a curious smile.

"No," I replied emphatically.

It was as honest an answer as I could give at the time. I
never told her I was a virgin. She never asked. A lifetime in
three months and…Strange I can't remember exactly how
long anymore. At first, every weekend was not enough. Then
our time together lessened in an aching decrescendo of
Marta's own orchestration. I told her we only needed air to
breathe. She told me I was incredibly naive and knew nothing about the realities of love or life.

Marta was the extraordinary *schwulin* who gave me my first
womanly touch. *Und nach vielen Jahren, als ich wieder nach Haus
fuerhte, wuesste ich dass es keine, solche Schwulin in den Staaten gab.*

CHAPTER FIVE
Life's Breath
Isabelle Lazar

*I*t finally climaxed that day, although it really started Christmas of '91. Simone and I both knew it, sitting there among the countless, mindless conversations going on around us at the table. We just sat and stared at each other, oblivious to everyone and everything. We knew. How could we have possibly known? Who can dare to think such thoughts?

But the visceral reaction was unmistakable. During the next four years, we limped along, writing intermittently, seeing one another on the holidays. I was constantly away: Arizona, Spain, Portugal, Austria, New York. She would later say it was strange for her to have me so far away. See, even then, it was there. For both of us.

I think I have always secretly hoped to have this type of relationship. I had hoped it would be with someone I was comfortable with—to try it out and to see if this is real or if I was imagining these feelings. But, dichotomously, I hoped also for a stranger: to be seduced, ravaged, to be sucked into it. It is so much simpler to acquiesce than to take an active part. There would, however, have been no other way with this one, not if "comfort" were to be a priority. And, ultimately, it was. It would have been too scary otherwise.

So that day I went over, as always, on my day off. Funny how we never run out of things to talk about—and she's forever feeding me!

"How about a soft-boiled egg?"

At one point it got so bad she would start boiling the damn thing from the moment I walked in the door, regardless of my reason for being there.

So that day I went over, and we lunched, as always, not talking about those things we shouldn't be talking about. When Simone's husband came home, we went outside to talk in private about those things we never dared talked about before.

"I feel so comfortable with you, Beth. As if I've known you all my life," she started.

"I've always felt that it was as if I'd known you in a different life," I answered. "As if when I saw you for the first time, it wasn't like I was just meeting you for the first time, but rather as if a recognition occurred. An unspoken acknowledgment of the previous acquaintance—and now we simply have picked up where we left off before."

"Yes," she said thoughtfully. "Perhaps we were sisters."

After some moments, I said, "I think we were lovers."

There. It's out.

To my surprise, I found the words rolled off my tongue fairly easily. It wasn't as painful or, for that matter, shameful, as I had envisioned—and from that moment nothing was. Simone didn't say anything for a long while.

Then a sigh of relief escaped her lips.

"Beth, you will never know what you have awoken in me. I was dead."

"But you're not dead."

"Yes, I am," she said out of habit, mostly. Then, looking me in the eyes, she added, "I should know better than to try to fool you. You read me so clearly."

"I read myself and hence…" That was the beginning of the beginning, if you like.

We didn't come back to this subject for some weeks, although all the while we were growing closer. One night, she came over. The conversation, although it's hard to remember word for word now, was rather coy: words to the effect of this being an "unusual bond." We dispensed with the word "friendship." It didn't fit anymore.

But clearly I remember her saying, "This can be quite dangerous, you know." And my heart leaped.

"You know I live for this stuff, unfortunately. You said 'dangerous,' and I lost my breath." She just smiled. She knew just how to hook me, although I'm not sure that was her motive. I think she was genuinely concerned about our course of action.

But I hate serious topics, and I hate being transparent, and I deplore being cornered.

"What are we talking about? Really?" I queried, pretending to be totally oblivious to the subtext.

"I don't know," came an invisible backslap. Score was love all, or check and mate, at least for the while. We established we were opponents of equal weight and class. Just then my husband walked in.

We looked at each other, each with the mischievous grin of the cat who swallowed the canary. I walked her out, and without a word she left.

Again, no correspondence for several weeks. Then one evening, my husband and I set the VCR to tape a show we were going to miss since we were going out. We inadvertently also taped the next two shows, so we watched them all the next morning in bed. I don't remember the name of the film or the actors, but the relationship was between two very atypical lesbians. In fact, they were two femme fatales. It was so hot and so sexy I couldn't help but squirm around while I lay in bed watching it.

When my husband left the room, I seized the opportunity to call her.

"Simone?"

"Yes."

"I am having 'bad' thoughts." I had been depressed for several weeks, and she thought I was referring to that.

"Oh, no. Come over. We'll talk. Maybe I can help."

"Oh, most assuredly you can help. The thoughts are about you." Long silence. And then the understanding took her.

"Oh."

"Yes."

"Come over."

I couldn't, and so the feelings were left to percolate and smolder once again.

Another few weeks passed in vain. I did not see her once in that time. I was guilt-ridden. I couldn't understand the nature of my feelings. *What can all this possibly mean? Am I gay?* If I were, then my whole life, my marriage and all the images I had of myself were destroyed. My only dream had been that when I married I would be in love with my husband. I thought I would never have cause to cheat if I were in love. *Well, I am in love with my husband, but this is different—and it is cheating. No matter that it's with a woman. It is still cheating.*

It's was all in my head, this stupid stuff. I knew where each part went, but I saw it all in such random order and at such a frantic pace that even I couldn't slow it down long enough to write it down. And isn't it so boring to go in order anyway?

OK, it went something like this: I came over. She started cooking. Craig went to say "Hi" to John. I began peeling the potatoes; she stood next to me.

As she stood next to me, I felt the beginning of the spiral. It was inevitable. It just felt too good, too warm and moist, like rich chocolate. I knew I would have her or at least I would try.

And that day, while our husbands were out smoking their cigars, that fateful day, on the cold basement floor, we *finally* got together. It was awkward and clumsy…but good…but good. I ached to taste her. The thought of it sent me salivating. I imagined it small and sleek and empty, just a black hole. When the time came it was quite a different story. It was full. It filled my mouth. It was a meal…and it was good.

She lay curled on my lap with her knees tucked into her full bosom. I looked down at her and felt impotent. What I wouldn't have done to have a dick at that moment! How could I have known that there were so many options open to women, so many different ways to love them? I think about it now, and I'm ashamed of my ignorance. But at the time I only knew of one kind of sex. In my ineptness, all I could do was use my thumb as a pseudo phallus, inserting it deeply into her again and again, feeling the depth of her all the way up to the little knob of the cervix. She was warm and luxurious, showering me with sweet liquid as I pushed deeper each time, always coming back with more and more of my reward.

I couldn't believe the fullness of her lips; there was no way to get a good angle. *How do guys do it?* Maybe it's because their hands are bigger. Maybe I just learned how to arch my back and tilt my hips and help him give me pleasure. But I couldn't duplicate the process. She had to want to receive me, and for that she had to give herself permission to want. *It's OK, you know. It's just me. I don't bite—hard.*

I angled around and felt the softness of her flesh. So thick and velvety, like molasses running over my fingers. I took out my hand and turned it this way and that, looking at what I had done. *So this is what it looks like. Funny, it has never looked this enticing before. Why now? What's changed?*

I loved coming with her. I held her in my arms, and magic happened. With a few strokes of my hand, we both collapsed, gasping, sobbing, wanting. I breathed her in and understood. My true nature. I breathe better when she is with me.

CHAPTER SIX
Pass the Hershey's, Please
Amy J. Saruwatari

"*H*ave you ever tried food and sex together?" she asked straight out. The question daunted and thrilled me simultaneously. I put my palm over the receiver and absorbed the sheer genius of the concept; food and sex sounded like a magical combination.

"Hey, Amy, are you there?" Allison's honeyed voice interrupted my fantasies before they had a chance to begin.

"I'm here—I—I just need a moment," I stammered. She didn't realize what a naughty thought process her question had started in my head. Here I was, all of 25 years of age in 1991, and had had but one lover in my lifetime—my college boyfriend. Sex with him was strictly meat-and-potatoes missionary style. Once in a while he would throw in a position that excited him, but did little or nothing to *my* libido. I had no clue what to do with food during sex, and especially no idea about the art of making love to a woman.

Allison and I had known each other for three months. We'd met through a personals ad and discovered through numerous phone conversations our common interests. We were the same age, had the same love of techno music, and loved Madonna. Like me, she also had never had sex with a woman and was intrigued by the idea.

"So what kind of food do you use anyway?" I finally asked.

"Well, I've used ice, Cool Whip, and my favorite…Hershey's chocolate syrup. Only on men though…never on a woman."

She did it again. She left me speechless, mind wandering to lustful new horizons. My imagination ran amok like a rogue elephant in an open marketplace. I loved chocolate so much I was practically born with a Hershey's Kiss in my mouth. Although I had never seen Allison naked, I pictured her without a blouse, wearing only a red satin garter and a smile. She had Pacific Coast Highway curves and a shower of blond hair that fell to the middle of her back. In my mind, I took the bottle of Hershey's syrup and swirled the chocolate sauce on her breasts.

"Amy, am I losing you?" Again her tone brought me back to the present.

"No way, baby, you can't get rid of me now." I couldn't believe the word "baby" had left my mouth. How utterly cheesy I must have sounded.

"Um, are you still interested in going to a women's bar?" she asked, and the way she raised her voice when she said "women's" made me realize we both weren't comfortable with the *lesbian* word.

"Yes, I definitely am. Want to go this Saturday? It's the long Labor Day weekend." I felt comfortable suggesting Saturday as the date since I'd gone out with Allison almost every weekend from July to September. On our first meeting we went to a movie. Then on following dates we either played tennis, splashed around in her apartment pool, had dinner, went to more movies, etc. Once we even went to a club together — a straight club. This short guy and his buddy started hitting on both of us. It was an awkward scene because I didn't feel comfortable enough to say, "Hey, asshole, leave her alone; she's my date." Allison and I were friends, but with the understanding that friendship was not the boundary of our blossoming liaison.

"Saturday it is! I read about this place called Club 22 in the Valley," she gushed. "Let's go there."

"We're finally going to go to a women's place. I can hardly wait!" I said. "I wish it were Saturday now."

It was only Tuesday. At long last I was eager to reach the physical plateau with her, and now with the date set, opportunity was dawning on the horizon of a promising weekend. I was relieved that the phone conversation with Allison had taken a flirtatious turn and that the subject of sex came up. I'd been going to her apartment for three months, and the closest we came to physical contact was a few firm handshakes and a sprinkling of embraces. On many occasions I sat next to Allison on her white couch, watching late-night television and rubbing my palms against my thighs, with three feet separating us. I wasn't even sure what my moves were supposed to be.

Oh, the weekend! The auspicious Labor Day weekend. I was going to take action this time and not let another night slip away with me driving home to my parents' house, cursing my cowardice.

During the week it was difficult to maintain any kind of concentration at work. Physically, my body was contained by three cubicle walls, but mentally, I was kissing Allison's earlobes, tasting her mouth, sampling the silky skin of her neck. I worked for a daily newspaper and the process of day-to-day business bored me to tears. My saving grace was Allison's vivacious face, her breath of fresh air in my cubicled life. It wasn't enough for me to talk to her for an hour every night; our platonic dates—although I had a thoroughly entertaining time—were not enough to satiate the intense yearning I felt to make love to her. I was beginning to doubt she would reciprocate my feelings, but the fact that she included the subject of sex in our last conversation encouraged the door to open once more.

By Friday afternoon I was climbing the walls at my mundane job. Like a high school student taking final exams, I watched the clock tick each slow tick. At my desk I closed my eyes and imagined how our evening would commence: *I'll go to her apartment, and we'll be so hot for each other that we won't even get out her front door. I'll slam it shut and look longingly into her hazel eyes and just—and just…Do what? I know. I'll kiss her and rip her clothes off, buttons flying and then…and then…* That's where my imagination cut in and said, "Look, I don't have enough data to complete this fantasy. Sorry!"

The truth of the matter was I was kidding myself. Since childhood, I had suffered from overpowering shyness. I recall being maybe five or six, at neighborhood kids' birthday parties—the kind where a piñata of some poor animal is broken open and candy pours out of a disjointed body part. Well, I never had the enterprise to dive for the candy. I stood sobbing on the sidelines till some sympathetic mother felt sorry for me and brought me a bag of treats. I couldn't expect Allison to simply offer me her bag of candy just like that.

With the impetus of lust driving my actions, I decided to make my intentions known in some way. The means of doing so came to me in the form of syrup—Hershey's chocolate syrup to be exact. When the clock struck five on Friday, I did my best imitation of Fred Flintstone jumping off the brontosaurus and flew out of the office and straight into my car. I drove to the local Ralph's grocery store and purchased a bottle of the chocolate love potion. I had the crazy notion that when Allison saw this 20-ounce bottle of chocolate sauce, she'd help me make breast sundaes on Saturday night. The Hershey's was my calling card, my invitation to something more than a handshake or embrace.

As I drove my old gray Chevy to Allison's place, I clutched the steering wheel in one hand and, in the other hand, a floral gift bag containing the chocolate syrup. My inner pessimist predicted Allison would be totally offended and never want to see me again. The wanton side of me said, "Now or

never!" As shy as I was, I knew it might take months, even
years, for me to work up enough nerve to be brazen with a
woman again. There was no turning back now.

Pterodactyls flew around in my stomach as I walked the flight
of stairs to Allison's apartment in Glendale. She had told me it
was a one-bedroom, and I had to take her word for it, because
at this point I had never seen the inside. The gift bag brushed
against my black pantyhose as I climbed the stairs. I wanted to
retreat, maybe change into an outfit that didn't make my thighs
look like tree trunks. I regretted wearing black shorts with black
pantyhose and black pumps. How was I supposed to be sexy in
a thunder-thigh costume? It was too late to back out now.

I rapped my hand against Allison's screen door, and she
answered with her usual radiant smile. Trying to conceal the
bag, I hid my other hand behind my back.

"Hey you, whaddya got in your hand?" she giggled.

"I thought I'd get you something special for tonight," I re-
torted with ease.

"I love surprises."

She reached around my torso and slid her hand down my
back. "What are you hiding? Come on." I could feel the front
of her form-fitting, eye-popping, sinewy dress graze my
chest. Had I been a man, I'm sure my erection would have
been quite evident. As Allison lunged over to see what I had
behind my back, I dodged her and scrambled into her apartment. Once inside, I raised the gift bag over my head so a
close encounter would ensue.

"Why are you being so mysterious, Amelia Jocelyn
Saruwatari?" she snickered with her hands on her feminine hips.

"You know I hate my middle name! That's hitting below
the belt. I got you a little something to remember this night by.
If you want it badly enough, you'll have to take it from me."

"I'll hit you below the belt," she quickly replied.

"Promise?" The word slipped from my lips, with my libido in full swing. "Come and get it." I waved the bag in the air, taunting my wavy-haired nymph to go further than a woman had gone before.

Instead of jumping up and down against me like I'd planned, she took a three-point stance and tackled me onto the couch. She pinned my shoulders with her knees and swiped the bag from my flailing hand, giving me a perfect view of her panties. Allison's underwear was more black lace than fabric. There it was, her seat of femininity within a breath of my breath; I was spellbound and still. The black triangle of ecstasy was ripe for the taking, and it eluded me in the blink of an eye.

"Ha! Got it!" Quicker than a Chihuahua in heat, Allison rolled over to the empty side of the couch and peered inside the bag.

"Oh-my-gawd!" She yelled, and I cringed. "You actually went out and bought the Hershey's."

I sat on pins and needles, wondering if she would be disgusted or excited.

"You little scammer, you," she laughed, grabbing the back of my neck. I was pleased she was favorably amused. "We are gonna have fun *to-night!*"

The fragrance of jasmine wafted through the open windows of Allison's apartment and mixed with her Cartier perfume. Light was fading into night along the off-white walls, and with that I could feel my apprehension fading as well. A jolt of electricity ran through the air whenever I was with her. It was unlike any energy I had felt before.

Allison hopped from the couch and darted into the bathroom. She put on Mars 103 FM (the only local radio station that played European techno music) and finished applying her makeup at the mirror.

My palms started to leak anticipation, and I had to wipe them dry on my shorts. I looked around, trying to remember what my plan was, what I had schemed on the way over. My short-term memory was failing, and I gave up any hope of trying to force anything to happen. The evening was beginning well, and I was patient enough to let it run its hopefully wild course.

As Allison put the finishing touches on her face, I noticed votive candles scattered around her apartment.

"What's with the candles? Are we going to pray?" I joked.

"That's my little surprise for later. You don't want to know now, do you?"

"Yes...mmm, no...uh, no...yes..."

"It doesn't matter. I'm not going to tell you." She stuck her tongue out at me and slowly drew it back into her mouth, curling the pink tip as her lips closed. I watched her mouth in slow-motion frames and swallowed hard.

"Want something to drink before we leave?" Allison offered, strolling toward her closet-size kitchen. "I have some chardonnay chilling."

"Uh...sure...sounds good." I was really more hungry than thirsty. I had failed to eat anything before I left my house, and my better judgment warned me not to drink on an empty stomach. Caution was left outside Allison's doorstep, and a taste of spirits would loosen my inhibitions.

I limited my intake to one full goblet, and that lasted me the hour, till we left for Club 22. I felt a little tipsy getting into my car but still coherent enough to drive. Neither Allison nor I had been to this place, and we were both a little nervous on the way there.

One daring night I went alone to the oldest women's bar in Los Angeles. This was a year or so before I met Allison, when I started my quest into this strange new world. I must have driven around the block about five times before I worked up the courage to go to the not-so-well-lit place. I paid my $5 to the masculine woman at the door and looked down at the floor most of the time. When I did look up, women who reminded me of my high school gym teachers lined the walls. I used the bathroom and left about five minutes later, too embarrassed to stay.

A green neon sign reading Club 22 lit up the night along Lankershim Boulevard. I pulled my car to the curb, and Allison and I plunged through the front doors. Much to my chagrin, a lot of the women appeared to be more butch than either of us. We stuck out like two nuns at a construction site. It was ten, maybe 15 minutes before we left. Not even long enough to finish our drinks.

"Wanna blow this place?" she whispered, and I was relieved Allison felt like bolting too. "Let's go to Rage. The music is bumpin', and we can feel comfortable there." Rage was a gay men's club Allison had been to a few times before. I had passed by it during the day but never went inside until that night.

"Cool. Let's go." I whisked us to West Hollywood in 20 minutes and even managed to find a decent parking space on a Saturday night. I has happy to travel to the gay mecca of Southern California.

Throngs of people strolled along Santa Monica Boulevard, and I felt more at ease in the festive atmosphere. The evening was still early, and I still needed to loosen up more. As I paid the cover charge, I didn't feel any eyes watching us like I did in the previous club. Instead I was the voyeur, and the dancing boys sidled up to one another. Some men were in locked trances, and others simulated sex on the dance floor. I saw Allison hypnotically swaying to the base-heavy, synthetic rhythms of house music reverberating over the mammoth speakers. I quickly ordered a Sea Breeze from the bar and carried it with me. The cranberry juice was tart against my throat but did nothing for my parched lips.

I rejoined my date, who was more than ready to release some energy. Her piercing eyes searched for mine, and we drifted to the middle of the floor. Amid flashing lights and wall-to-wall sweat, we danced in syncopated movement. The electricity did not flow through wires or circuits; it flowed through our bodies. Allison pulled me in closer, and our hips gyrated in unison to the beat of the music.

Her dress, like black skin, stretched across her figure, and I felt the swell of her breasts and the dip of her waist pressed against me. Her circling hips attracted my hands like a magnet, and I held on to her tightly. There could have been five people in the room or there could have been 500. It didn't matter. I had never been so enthralled with someone as I was with Allison.

We mirrored each other's movements for hours, and I only took short breaks to finish my drinks: first the Sea Breeze, then another, then a Greyhound. The alcohol rushed into my bloodstream, making my vision undulate. Allison drank only water, taking the role of the responsible driver. I felt this wonderful, unbridled freedom inside the club, and the alcohol seemed to enhance the mood. As midnight approached, we sat down on a cement block to catch our breath. With one man giving another man a blow job behind us, Allison leaned over and kissed me softly on the lips. I returned her kiss with a deeper one of my own. Although I was already hot from dancing, my temperature climbed another ten degrees when she put her tongue in my ear.

"Let me know when you want to leave," I yelled, trying to override the deafening music.

"How about now?" she yelled back.

We meandered hand in hand through the crowd, heading for the exit, and Allison took my keys from me as we arrived at my car.

"I'll drive because I want to get us home safely so I can give you your surprise."

Yes, I was slightly inebriated but fully awake. Allison drove me to her apartment, and as we climbed the stairs, I could feel the blood coursing through my veins. Never had I felt so thoroughly alive. She asked me to wait outside her door for a minute while she scurried inside. I saw flames flickering through the windows. The door slowly opened, and the scent of vanilla candles floated in the air. A myriad of tiny votives illuminated her living room. Somehow the word *romantic* does not do justice to the intimacy and beauty of the setting.

Wearing a silk robe, Allison took my hand and led me to a space on the floor covered with huge pillows.

"Surprise, baby," she said. "I want to give you a massage. Will that be all right?"

"Oh, yeah!" I answered, already lowering myself to the floor.

"Um, can you take off your top for me?" Allison asked, with a bottle of massage oil in her hand. I began to unbutton my blouse, and although I had never undressed for a woman before, I felt quite at ease. I reclined on the pillows and felt the warm oil pour onto my chest. She put her hot hands on my skin, and a current of energy ran through her fingertips and down to my toes. She massaged my breasts and gently rubbed my erect nipples between her fingers. Languidly, she worked her way to my stomach, then stopped at my waist. Instead of asking me to remove them myself, she unzipped my shorts and pulled off my pantyhose. My last stitch of clothing was my underwear.

"Can you slide up please?"

I inched my way up on the pillows, and she slid my panties off till I was completely naked on the shag carpet. She undid her robe to reveal her own nakedness. I loved the feel of her long tendrils of hair against my skin. Allison lay on top, our bodies writhing in passion. Cloaked in nightfall, we discovered ourselves and shed the boundaries of our human shells, with dancing moonlight our only witness. I touched the inside of her leg and further delved into languages revealed in the curve of her spine. She dived for the ripe plum of my womanhood, and I surrendered myself to her willingly and freely.

Nothing had ever felt so right or so natural. Wet with abandon, I invited her inside me, and she found her way to my ecstasy. Just as she reached the deepest part of me, I released a moan that sounded foreign to my own ears. I let out a cry of pleasure so innate, yet so different, that I was transformed into a completely new being.

An unseen force took over my body and guided my actions. I climbed on top of Allison and wanted badly to taste her womanhood as well. I nestled my head between her mountainous breasts and started to kiss her all over. Like a ship with a predestined course, I navigated my way to her center and French-kissed her feminine flower. The cry she let out was primitive and natural.

Lulled by the rhythm of her breath, I was caught in the ebb and flow of our lovemaking. As the tiny candles were burning out, I realized Allison and I had kindled and started a flame inside ourselves. The flame, though brilliant in intensity, illuminated and warmed my soul.

I left her apartment in the morning a new person, with a new life, born from our night together. On my drive home I could swear I had reinvented the wheel, but I didn't. I was incredibly happy but later remembered we never did use the chocolate syrup like I had planned. Sometimes, life doesn't go how you plan it, and in spontaneity lies the best surprises.

Our first night together was the beginning of my realization that Allison is the person I want to share my life with. We are going on our seventh anniversary, and I have never loved anyone as much as I love her now and forever.

CHAPTER SEVEN
River Rock
by Sarah Russell

*H*er entire backyard was filled with trees—mulberry, gingko, oak, pine. The grass looked as if no one had ever cut it, and there were cat paths throughout the long emerald blades. A bush of tiny white fragrant flowers appeared in the middle of the yard, as if someone had just scattered a handful of seeds. Sunflowers too! Everywhere. The foliage closed in on all three sides of her private backyard garden.

I had only briefly explored when she came out the backdoor. She seemed happy I had found her house without any problems. We were both eager to spend a restful day at the Rivanna River. We were headed to a secret place, and it was seemingly the perfect medicine for my weary mind.

I didn't really know Beth well. We had both been counselors at a summer camp the week before. I first noticed her when she was telling folktales to a small crowd one evening. We exchanged smiles and short letters but were too busy to become acquainted at the time. She was a tall woman with long dark hair and piercing blue eyes. Even on this humid August day, she was wearing her familiar attire of old bib overalls and combat boots.

While Beth got her things together, I casually took a walk through her house. Pen-and-ink drawings of trees filled the kitchen. The drawings were exquisite—even spiritual—and simply taped to the walls. The living room held many plants, and her bed was on the floor between the windows. There were hundreds of shells everywhere, all white and chalky, some broken, but all meticulously placed around the room.

Beautiful pieces of driftwood, caressed by ancient ocean waters, were placed around the room with delicate care. Her bookshelves were filled with tomes about Native Americans, Celts, Zen Buddhism, Georgia O'Keeffe, Virginia Woolf, Thai cuisine, American poetry.

I curiously scanned the titles of the hundreds of CDs arranged neatly near the books. Diverse. Yes. As I read the some of the artists' names, I thought about the power of music — Joni Mitchell, Bob Dylan, Loreena McKennitt, Segovia, Vivaldi — and I wondered with whom she identified most.

I walked into another room as her cats scurried in front of me. All that existed in this room were maps of Virginia mountains on the walls. A tiny red line ran through each map, as if an explorer had tracked her journey.

My curiosity about my new acquaintance was overwhelming. How interesting it all was! How radiant and refreshing! What a gentle woman she seemed — one truly intoxicated by the gifts of this earth! The artistry in her house was quiet but intense, peaceful but so alive. I began to envy her instantly — the way one envies an artist.

We left the house and headed west on Patterson Avenue. After light conversation and an hour's drive, we were at the Rivanna River. Avoiding the NO TRESPASSING signs, we climbed through the barbed-wire fence and walked down the steep bank to the river. It's funny, but that's when our verbal communication ended.

I simply watched her as she unlaced her combat boots and rolled up her pant legs. I mocked her as she, without hesitation, walked into the middle of the river. The slow-moving river was crystal clear, and the water cast waving shadows on the trees. I walked a ways behind her, growing absorbed in the beauty around me. Freshwater mussel shells glistened beneath the surface. When I would reach for them, they always seemed closer than they really were. Beth walked in front of me in her own world, and I just followed her around the sandy curves of the river.

I held a huge piece of coal in one hand and several rainbow mussel shells in the other. Without much thought, I climbed onto a huge rock centered in the river, and on my back I felt the smooth surface that held the day's warmth. A leaf got caught in a tiny whirlpool around the rock, swirled, and then clung to my ankle. I remember seeing a hawk gliding over-head. With a glance over my shoulder, I saw Beth at a great distance along the river. She slowly disappeared. At the time I thought how strange it was we hadn't stayed closer togeth-er that afternoon. Perhaps she just wanted to be alone in this truly sacred place and not be encumbered by other humans. I was comfortable with that, but I still wondered if she liked my company.

I had fallen asleep. When I opened my eyes, there she was, floating along with the gentle current, near the rock. She had removed her clothes and was effortlessly gliding downriver. Questions flooded my mind. *How have I come to be so intensely comfortable in her presence?* I moved into the water and surren-dered completely to the current. I walked back up the Ri-vanna and took the same beautiful ride again and again. At one point, Beth was close to me as I moved around the rock. I boldly held her calf, and my hands slid to her ankle as we floated together down the river. Silently we would walk back to the rock, as if this simple routine would continue all after-noon. A huge birch tree on the riverbank captured my atten-tion. In that moment, Beth's hand touched the small of my back. I led her to the rock, and all doubts disappeared.

CHAPTER EIGHT
Outcome
Ila Suzanne

Seventy-nine women turned up at my coming-out party. All of them did foreplay; three did me. Twenty years ago I went to Califia, a radical feminist camp, on the advice of my lesbian therapist, Mona, whom I met at a women's retreat. I was 35, a mother, and newly divorced. My radical acts included not shaving my legs, not wearing makeup, and dancing to disco music in my living room. Bra-burning and consciousness-raising groups were too far out there for me.

I fell hard for Mona. I devoured every book she recommended, listened to women's music, read women's poetry. I wondered about myself...and I waited.

Ah, but the deed—the sexual act with a woman, the only way I would know for sure I was a lesbian—hadn't happened. I had never kissed a woman, never played with my girlfriends at sleepovers. Nothing. Mona had brought me to her bed, and I had waited for it to happen with her. It didn't. She had taken me to some rebirthing place where we got naked together and hot and wet in the springs. I waited. She had given me massages. She called it feminist therapy. It was just what I needed.

When Mona suggested Califia, and when she told me it would be almost all lesbian, I didn't hesitate. She told me she would be there with her lover and that I could have a session with her if I needed. I arranged baby-sitting for my kids and transportation for myself (so I would have no way to leave if I got too scared).

I arrived at the conference center in the San Bernadino mountains, terrified someone would ask me if I was a lesbian.

I planned to keep a low profile, to observe things from a distance. After unpacking, I went to the kitchen for my first collective, an "everybody-helps-out" task. I sat and cracked eggs, 100 to be exact, and listened to the women joke around as they stirred huge pots with long-handle wooden spoons. I sat cracking one egg after the next, careful not to let pieces of shell fall into the whites, watching the yellows break and blend in slow motion. Just cracking eggs and watching women.

That night Sasha, a lesbian sex therapist from San Francisco, announced that the women in the camp needed to loosen up. She gathered all of us into a circle and taught us how to bend the circle back on itself until every woman had kissed every other woman one time. I kissed 79 women, all those mouths on my mouth. It took about 20 minutes.

Twenty minutes of full, moist lips lingering like they tasted something good…peck-on-the-cheek lips…hard-line mouths that bumped my mouth…slightly open lips…velvet lips…satiny lips and rough ones…kisses with the tip of a tongue touching the tip of my tongue…full-tongue kisses filling my mouth…deep kisses…noisy smacks…smiling blow-in-the-air kisses…hands-on-my-shoulders-plant-one-square-on-my-mouth kisses…dry, tight kisses…light, light kisses…laughing bump-teeth-on-teeth kisses…eyes open kisses, eyes closed kisses…no-nonsense mouths' hard kisses. Some kisses I remembered for a long time after.

Sleeping was impossible after that. I sat on the cabin porch with my flashlight in one hand and my pen in the other, writing about those kisses.

The next morning a woman named Betts projected slides of vulvas on a huge screen in the lodge. They looked like giant mauve irises, blushing seashells, folded lace hankies. She kept saying we were beautiful, clean, sweet-smelling, and tasty. She was a silver fox of a woman, a P.E. teacher type with clear blue eyes. One evening later in the week, those blue eyes looked my way as Betts was leaving the lodge. I couldn't believe she wanted me, so I stayed where I was. The next day she approached me and confided, "Last night I was hoping you would drop by my cabin." I was heartbroken I had missed the chance.

In the afternoon we met in small groups to process the intense morning presentations. The women in my group stroked me physically and emotionally. They gave me language for the oppression of a lifetime as a straight woman, fat, frigid, and frightened of everything. They encouraged me to be aggressive. To go for anything I wanted. To be noisy and angry. Permission for passion.

I was flattered and courted. They touched my shoulder-length hair, teased the drawstring on my blouse. They complimented me on how sexy I was. "You are *zaftig*," Wendy said. I learned later it meant full-figured and lovely.

One sweet young woman, Vonni, floated me in the hot tub. She kept telling me I was scrumptious. She touched my arms and cradled my head against her brown breasts in the water, in the sun. I was overcome. I had been so sad for so long about my body, about how imperfect I was. First the bra went, then the bathing suit as well. I walked the camp in jeans, long earrings, an open shirt, and perfume. I felt like a wild thing.

Wendy was in my afternoon group—the group to which I had confessed my secret inexperience. She was a quiet woman who smelled of patchouli. She always wore a bandanna tied around her neck, even when she wasn't wearing a shirt. She walked me down to the stream. She brought her guitar and a jay. We smoked, and she sang, "Suzanne takes you down to a place by the river...."

We talked in the dark. "Would you like to be with a woman?" she asked.

"I think so," I whispered, "I think I want to." I knew we were going to make love that night. She sang more songs while I slowly relaxed against her, drifting through her music, the shooting stars and the feel of her jeans against my cheek.

We sauntered to her bed, which was on the porch of one of the cabins, lay down, and she kissed me. I remembered all the kisses in the circle. This was different, more real. This was the beginning for me. We undressed one another slowly, slowly, one button at a time. My mouth was so hungry. Her lips were full and swollen, her mouth sweet. Her full-breasted body called my hands. My fingers crept over her pale skin. When I traced her nipples, my own nipples grew hard. When I took that very hardness between two fingers, she called out to me.

It took hours to touch all of her skin, all the soft skin on her belly, all the flesh on her hips. I moaned when I slipped one of my fingers through the hair of her mons, my mons…into her soft, soft slit…beyond the lips, my lips…through the slick entrance. I was in her tight velvet cave, the sweet circles. The rhythm was hers, mine, so slow, until she arched to pull me deeper and I curved inward to meet her last need. When she made love to me, her hands merged with my skin. There were stars, pinpoints of heat beneath my flesh, then waves, my body floating on fire. It was a long, beautiful night.

I was up at dawn, sitting under the pine trees by the lodge, writing furiously in my journal. The pine-scented crystalline sky was shimmering. As soon as I smelled coffee, I retrieved a mug, poured myself a cup, and went back to my journal, trying to find words to wrap around what had happened the night before.

Sasha came by Wendy's bed that afternoon. I was stretched out naked, enjoying the sun and the wonder of my night. She offered to rub lotion on my back, warning me about letting myself get sunburned. I rolled over, giving her my back. She spoke of my soft skin, how she liked my hair falling on the pillow. She spread the musky lotion so slowly I could follow her fingertips with the nerves under my skin; she had all of my attention. When she slipped her hand between my thighs, it seemed natural to open myself to her and her hand and her whispers, in broad daylight with women walking by on the path and the blue sky and pine trees watching — the most natural thing, to open to her.

When Wendy stepped onto the porch, I got the impression that it was not the most natural thing to be with someone else in her bed. Sasha stopped her hand, smiled at me and Wendy, and left us.

"Did I do something wrong?" I asked.

"No, no. I was just surprised to see you in my bed," she replied, touching my hair. I picked up my clothes, hugged her, and went on my way.

I ran into Sasha after dinner. We walked away from the cabins toward the meadow at the far end of camp. There was a bed in the meadow, mattresses piled in the center of the clearing. We headed toward them.

"I have no energy for making love," Sasha answered my unasked question. "But lie here with me. We can watch the stars come out, and you can tell me how you got to this place." I curled up against her shoulder, shared her joint, and told her about coming to Califia, about being afraid and excited. Shooting stars were making incredibly slow streaks across the sky. Nothing I said seemed to surprise her. Finally I was silent. We listened to forest sounds, the rustling branches, and the swaying grass.

"Make love to me," she said. "Take your hand and rub slowly and softly on my nipple." I was stunned by her request. Shaking, I turned on my side and slid my hand under her flannel shirt, felt her breast rise to the soft nipple. As soon as I touched it, it hardened tight and firm against my fingers. "Now the other one, slowly, slowly." I didn't want to leave her hard nipple, but I wanted to follow her directions, so I found my way to her lonely nipple and caressed it until it was hard. It didn't take long.

"Now little bites on my neck, on my shoulder, down my breasts—not the nipples, just your tongue on my nipples." I un-buttoned her shirt then, trying to finesse the buttons while I bit her neck. My fingers weren't working very well. I felt clumsy, self-conscious. I *needed* to please this woman. I kept going, listen-ing to the sounds of her breathing, the sighs, moans, and silences.

When she reached to unzip her jeans, I steadied myself by looking at the trees silhouetted against the sky. She took my hand and pushed it between her legs, beneath her underpants, and all the way to her wet clit. My breath burst from me wildly.

Sasha laughed, "Easy there. Easy. Take time to breathe. We have all night. Now, put two fingers there. Feel my clit? Push up and down…no, no…slower, slower, lightly…use a very, very light touch…yes, just right, keep it up…slower, slow-er…mmm…lean your body over me, put your leg on me…yes, yes…light touch, light touch, stroke me lightly…climb on me, climb on me…yes…touch lightly…keep going yes, don't stop yes…aah." She came against me, throbbing so hard I could feel her waves without being inside her.

We lay in silence. I was amazed by her directions, how well she knew herself. No shame, no inhibitions, no coyness. She rolled over, hugged me, and sat up. I watched her button and zip herself back together. "Come on. I'll walk you back," she said, taking my hand and pulling me from the mattresses.

I didn't sleep well that night. I was agitated. Sasha's odor was on my fingers, on my pillow, and on my mind. I was up at dawn waiting for coffee and writing page after blistering page in my journal.

There was a dance on the last night. By then I was high from hot sex with Wendy and Sasha, the intensity of the women, the politics, sleep deprivation, and mountain air. I put on my laciest bra (just to show off my cleavage under my thin cotton shirt), put on jeans and Shalimar perfume, brushed my hair, and walked the trail to the lodge.

I searched the big room and thought, *This is my last night, my last chance, my last time here with these wonderful women. Just what would I like to happen?* Labrys, the big and beautiful wild woman who wore scarves and flowing skirts gave me a big wink and flipped her long, long hair over her shoulder. The bad butch who kept a woman in her camper the whole week beckoned me with her rough hands. I averted my eyes. She scared me.

Across the lodge, standing alone, was Lark, dressed in leaves and feathers, her hair cropped close to her head, lit like the Madonna. She looked like a nymph, a fairy about to scurry into the forest. I wanted her. I remember watching her dance in the meadow. She had smiled at me then. I wanted her. She was so beautiful. I wanted her to want me.

I walked across the floor just as Cris Williamson began to sing "Sweet Darling Woman." When Lark saw me coming, her face changed; she looked startled. A slow blush crept up from her breasts to her cheeks. She saw me coming toward her and smiled. I held out my hand, "Will you dance with me?" She took my hand and leaned into me and the music. We didn't speak. When the song was over, we walked off the dance floor and out the open door into the dark night.

We walked the trail that took us to the boundary of the camp. She told me she had a lover, that she wasn't free, that she thought I was a wonderful spirit, that she wanted me. But she couldn't. I said I understood, of course.

"I understand. You just can't," I told her. "Let's walk back to the lodge. You can dance with me."

"OK," Lark gleamed gratefully.

When we reached the lodge, she took my hand and pulled me past the door and off the porch toward the cabins. She didn't speak—nor did I—until we were in her room.

"Have you done it yet?" she asked.

"Done what?" I asked back.

I didn't know what to expect.

"Let me show you the most wonderful thing." Lark lit a candle and peeled off her leaves and feathers. Then she helped me out of my blouse and unhooked my bra. I stepped out of my jeans. She reached to my earrings and gently eased them from my earlobes. She sat me down on her bed, kneeled in front of me, pulled my head down until she reached my mouth, and kissed me deeply. My lips, my tongue, my breath, I gave them to her. She pushed me back on her bed by climbing up my body and resting her weight on top of me. She was sweaty. She slid across my skin like a snake, slithered to fit every one of my curves.

Lark slid her tongue over my breast. Then she slipped between my legs to the floor, her tongue tasting its way down my belly ever so slowly to my mons, to the edges of my labia. Her slender fingers pulled me gently. She opened me, pulled me apart, and reached my clit. She kissed my clit, kissed my clit, and softly flicked the most tender part of me with her tongue. I was her lollipop, her ice-cream cone, her caramel. When she slipped her finger into me, I wanted to pull her into my tightness. She stroked me harder with her tongue, with her finger, lifting me into the heat of the candle. Soon I was tasting her, surprised at the strong sweetness. Instantly I was addicted to the ambrosia of this woman. I rubbed my tongue, mouth, face, and hair against her juices. I was anointed.

It was nearly dawn when I kissed her sleeping head and tucked the blankets around her. I stopped at my room long enough to pull on my jeans and grab my journal. I kept writing until the smell of coffee pulled me back to the kitchen. I hugged the cooks who were scrambling 100 eggs in a huge skillet.

I saw Lark a month later. I picked her up at her house—or rather a block from her house—in Los Angeles. She was still living with her lover. We shared a jay as I drove down Sunset Boulevard in my VW bus. Lark looked the same, except she wore shorts and a T-shirt instead of leaves. We had a long discussion about how much we liked each other and how she couldn't do it with me and how she really wanted to…really.

We went to a gay restaurant, sat down, and ordered. Later, in the women's room, Lark pushed me against the wall. We weren't even in a stall. I was scared someone would come in. She kissed me hard, pressed her tongue into my mouth, pulled my jeans open, and plowed down my panties. Hot and excited, I forgot to worry about the door. Between the cold tiles at my back and her hot, demanding fingers, I came in a quick minute. Then I grabbed her shorts. In two more minutes we were zipping zippers, washing hands, and toweling off sweaty faces. When we returned to our table, the food was cold…but I wasn't.

I ran into Labrys, the wild woman at Califia, in San Francisco. She still had her long, long hair. We went to the tubs. Naked in a private room, we settled into the hot water. She turned away from me and toward the wall, where water shot from a jet. She told me how good the pressure felt on her clit. Then, putting her head down on the rim of the tub, she closed her eyes. I tried to act casual. I stared at her broad shoulders, her hair filling the water around her like snakes. I reached down and pulled the lips away from my clit. The hot water was a shock. When Labrys came she moaned loudly. I was titillated. Later we went to her place and settled into her bed. Her hair was a canopy over our bodies. We made love slowly, her hair rippling and sliding like silk over my hot skin and the fleshy rolls of her fat body.

A year later, at another Califia, Betts, the silvery fox, sent me another look on the way out the lodge door. I was sitting on her bed when she reached her cabin. You don't have to tell *me* twice. Once I got her to stop talking about what beautiful labia I had, she let me make love to her. Betts was wild and lusty. We laughed and talked and touched and rubbed one another. She cried when she came. I held her and she cried. I was bleeding, and she painted both of us with my blood. Handprints on my thighs. She sunk her red fingers into me over and over and over until my body curled around her hand.

Remember the kissing circle? One of those kisses was so memorable that when a stranger kissed me at the West Coast Women's Music Festival, I said, "Come with me. Bring your sleeping bag to my tent now," and she did. Hers was a kiss I remembered, even though I can no longer remember her name. She stayed by my side for three nights and covered me with her down bag and her dense, muscular body. It was too cold to undress; we dove under flannel and thermal to swim in dark, hot pools. She reminded me over and over again about that first kiss and the fire that lit inside me in that circle.

I ran into Sasha at the same festival. She invited me to her tent and handed me a glass of wine. The glass was half-empty when she pushed me down on her sleeping bag. She made love to me in that same direct fashion I remembered. Sasha was a very thorough lover, taking my body like it belonged to her, giving me nothing but prolonged pleasure until I wanted everything she wanted. When she was done she wouldn't let me touch her.

Vonni and I became good friends. I see her and her girl-friend whenever I'm in the Bay Area. We laugh about old times like when she and I and Linda, another Califia woman, were playing together at my house, all naked and sweaty on my bed. My mother knocked on the back door calling, "Yoo-hoo! Anybody home?" We had one minute to get dressed. Mother smiled at my bedroom door and said—so innocently it had to be real—"Oh, you girls are having a slumber party!"

Wendy and I saw each other for about a year after Califia. I would drive to Los Angeles where she lived in a huge collective house. We put candles on every horizontal surface of the six-foot-long claw-foot tub and washed each other with loofahs, brushes, soft cloths, and oatmeal soap. It took a long time to get very clean, very dry, and dusted with talc. It took a long time to pull fresh sheets on the bed, toss rose petals on the pillows, and light incense. It took a long time to say hello to every inch of her skin with my mouth...even longer to say good-bye.

When I leaf through my journal from that summer, I am surprised it has not fallen away to scorched bits of paper and ash. The handwriting is frantic. The sheer joy of my body, my sexuality, the first real celebration of myself still rises from those scribbled pages. The words fall off the lines. After that summer I never fit between the lines again.

CHAPTER NINE
Twist of Fate
Jennifer Terrett

"*T*f I escaped from the hospital, would you come pick me up?" she had asked me, her voice barely above a whisper.

Without a moment's hesitation I responded, "Yeah, I'd be there for you in an instant."

And I meant it from the bottom of my heart. It wasn't logical — maybe even wrong in some people's eyes — but after a lifetime of waiting for Ms. Right, I had fallen head over heels in love, and I was willing to do anything for a chance at a relationship with Sandy. The only thing that stood between us was the psychiatric hospital she checked into two months prior on November 16, 1995, my 23rd birthday. I was employed as a mental health worker at the hospital and was on duty the evening Sandy checked in. She was frail and battered, but her spirit radiated a powerful energy that surrounded me that first day. Sandy had not spoken much as I helped her check in, but the unseen energy she gave off continued to draw me to her, filling me with feelings I did not understand.

The month following Sandy's arrival at the hospital I feverishly tried to bury my growing attraction for her. Always ruled by logic, I told myself it was wrong to feel what I was feeling, but my heart would launch a counterattack, saying the only thing that stopped me or any other staff member from standing in Sandy's shoes was fate. As I began to learn more of Sandy's history, I found the cards had been stacked against her from the start. As an adult survivor of child physical and sexual abuse, her life had echoed the negative self-image beaten into her tender flesh in childhood. I was no better than she, only luckier. Still, I knew to fall in love with her would be to break some unwritten law that governed relationships between people based on the roles society assigns them any given day. I was assigned the role of "staff," and she "patient." My humanity and the fact that I had more of myself to offer her just didn't seem to matter. At least it didn't seem to matter until the cold December afternoon when Sandy inconspicuously slipped a piece of paper into my hand.

Careful to not let her, or anyone else for that matter, see anything but a calm, cool exterior, I slowly unfolded the note and casually asked, "What's this?"

"Just read it," came the response. I looked down at the scrap of loose-leaf paper and read the following two sentences, written in the smallest print I had ever seen: "I have been having feelings for you. But I know there could be nothing between us because of the staff/patient thing." I looked down at her, lying on the rug at my feet, as I pretended to watch TV with the other patients and seem unaware of the message she just handed to me. "We'll have to discuss this," I said in the most serious voice I could muster. I felt the emotions I had tried so desperately to hide flooding my body. My heart had won.

The next day Sandy and I met at a secluded end of one of the hospital corridors, beyond earshot of any other patient or staff member. I confessed my attraction for her, told her how she had occupied my thoughts every day and night since the first time I saw her. For a moment we were lost in each other's eyes as we sat side by side on the couch. Voice trembling, I reassured her we would find a way to be together, to break through the invisible wall circumstance had put between us. My senses struggled to take in as much of her as I could without touching her. I stood up, simultaneously dropping a piece of paper into her lap. On it was written my home phone and calling card numbers.

"Call me tonight—collect. Make sure no one hears you say my name," I whispered. She looked at me, and I could tell she was afraid the whole thing was some sort of sick joke.

"OK?" I asked, still waiting for a response. "Will you call me?" She nodded affirmatively, then rose from the couch and followed my lead in pretending nothing had happened.

We spoke at length that night, about nothing and everything the way teenagers often do. My spirit felt light and free, and I wondered how I had lived my whole life never having known these feelings before. After we hung up, Sandy's voice echoed in my mind for hours, eventually lulling me to sleep. That night in my dreams I kissed and caressed her, waking the next morning in damp sheets with a pounding ache between my legs.

The month between that first phone call and the unforgettable night I helped Sandy escape from the hospital was a difficult time for both of us. Like lesbian versions of Romeo and Juliet, Sandy and I hid our love from those around us. Sneaking into her room as often as I could get assigned hall rounds, we squeezed in as much fondling and kissing as we could in the 30 or so seconds it takes to "check on a patient." I asked for as many overtime shifts as I could work, volunteering to work both the Christmas and New Year's holidays. I even offered to fill in on the overnight shifts, knowing that once every hour I could sneak a peek at Sandy sleeping peacefully during my hall rounds. Using my best friend's name and address as an alias, I was able to sneak Christmas gifts to Sandy, who had no family to speak of. Among the gifts was a big white teddy bear she named "T.J."—my initials reversed.

Each day it became more and more difficult for us to hide our feelings. Each night we slept apart was more lonely than the one before. The staff began to badger me, saying I was spending too much time on the unit with the patients, although they never mentioned any names specifically. Sandy endured similar confrontations in the form of lewd comments from intuitive patients who claimed she "must have the hots for a staff member." I ached to give Sandy all the love in my heart and to introduce her to my family, who I knew would accept her as one of their own. What hurt me the most was knowing the things I could offer her—love and affection, specifically,—were things she desperately wanted and had never known in her 31 years. Some nights the frustration of feeling circumstance might rob us of the chance of a lifetime would keep me awake and crying. I learned later Sandy had felt that same frustration every night.

In early January of '96, Sandy asked for a status increase, hospital jargon for permission to leave the grounds alone, which is the start of the discharge phase. She was denied this request based on a phone call to the staff from a former lover and that she had been spending too much time on the phone (with me, ironically). The former lover, an abusive and controlling woman, convinced the staff that Sandy was planning a suicide attempt, a fabrication she concocted as a final attempt to control Sandy's life. Several days after the privilege request was denied, Sandy called me, asking me if I would pick her up from the hospital if she escaped. I sympathized with her frustration and anger but mostly thought she was kidding. I was about to be proved wrong. That night, around 9:30, my phone rang again.

"I'm at the mall across from the hospital. I ran away during an escorted trip to an AA meeting. Can you come pick me up now?" Sandy's voice was trembling. She was terrified hospital security would spot her so close to the hospital, or worse, that I wouldn't make good on my promise to pick her up.

"I'm on my way." I sped past exit after exit, making the 40-minute trip in 20 minutes flat. When I arrived at the mall, I realized we hadn't picked a meeting place. I ran frantically through the mall and its many parking lots in hope of spotting Sandy. "Jen," she called out to me, and looking up, I spotted her at the corner entranceway. I ran to her, wrapping my arms around her. I felt faint, overcome with emotion. We quickly ran to my car and headed back to my parents' house, where I was living at the time. Careful not to wake my parents, who knew nothing of the escape, I quietly led Sandy up the steps to my bedroom and shut the door behind us.

For a long while we just sat there on my bed, stroking each other's hands and talking about what had just happened. Adrenaline still pumping, Sandy began kissing me with a passionate urgency that pushed me flat on my back. She covered my body with her own, running her hands over my breasts and between my legs as she continued to kiss me hungrily. The warmth of her touch made my body come alive beneath her fingers and throb with a desire I had never experienced. My lack of experience seemed to fuel her desire, and she pulled away from me only long enough to remove her clothing and my own with such force she almost ripped the fabric.

Lying back on top of me, I felt her breasts rubbing against my own for the first time. I could feel my nipples hardening beneath her fingers as she stroked them. Sliding down, she took them in her mouth, first one, then the other, drawing circles around them with her tongue, then tugging gently with her teeth. Moaning softly, I pushed her head against me, and she sucked hungrily on my tits and caressed my thighs. As my body relaxed and my legs spread open, she pushed a finger inside me. The sensation passed through my entire body, tingling from the tips of my ears to the tips of my toes. Sensing the tremendous pleasure she was giving me, she slid a second finger, then a third, inside me.

I pushed my body against her hand to feel her as deeply inside me as I could. Simultaneously, I inserted two of my fingers inside her, and we rocked our bodies against each other's probing fingers. We tried our best to be silent in the still of the night, but the room was filled with the sounds of the bed rocking and the slushy sound of our thrusting fingers. After only minutes, we both came, seconds apart, then lay in each other's arms. Neither of us could believe what had happened was real. Sometimes I still can't.

The memory of our struggle to find a way to be together taught me never to take anything for granted. Needless to say, I left that job at the hospital with no regrets. I can't remember much of what life was like before the night I first felt Sandy's touch. And now I cherish every glance, every smile, every embrace.

CHAPTER TEN
Women's Studies
Giovanna (Janet) Capone

*P*ure white snow blankets the land. Leafless tree branches are immobilized in their icy girdles. It has been snowing for three days straight. This frozen landscape is not Alaska, but January in upstate New York. This is the tundra through which I must trek, day after day, trudging to class through piles of white powder on a campus frosted with snow. It's 1978, a time when the graffiti in women's bathrooms proclaims, "Feminism the theory, lesbianism the practice."

I'm enrolled in a women's studies program, otherwise known as a den of budding and already well-bloomed dykes. We're reading lesbian books by the dozen, immersing ourselves in a world where women take themselves seriously, including their sexual desires for other women.

Novice that I am, I'm supplementing my academic reading by consuming every lesbian novel I can find in the local women's bookstore. In addition to seeking out the dykey stories, I buy these books to flip through the pages for the graphic sex scenes. In the late '70s, such scenes are few and far between—and fairly tame. Nevertheless, I rush to them first. They're jolting me from the asexual limbo I've been suspended in for so many years. I've had no interest in men and have wondered whether or not I'll ever find the guts to pursue women.

I'm one of thousands of college-age women in this era of women's liberation, a time when lesbianism seems to be spreading like wildfire and feminist college students are taking female lovers as casually as cream in their coffee. It's a hot-wheeling bandwagon rolling full tilt, and I'm hanging on the caboose with the best of them.

At 21, I'm moving toward my lesbian sexuality with a velocity I can no longer contain. Besides, as I had decided one unbearably horny summer ago, this is the year my vague and mystical lesbian fantasies will go from the impossible-to-attain to something vividly, deliciously real. I'm denying myself no longer.

The instant I meet Marcie, with her intriguing green eyes and yellow-blond, stick-straight hair, I know immediately it's with her I am destined to discover the marvels of lesbian love.

As history can attest, it was she whose heavenly body first satisfied those deep cravings for which I could barely utter the words. I met her in my gender equity class and was immediately smitten. She seemed to bask in a golden haze, like Glinda, the good witch of the North.

Fast-forward to that first morning of ours: We woke up ravenous and quietly excited, after staying up most of the night, half-clothed, touching and kissing for hours. A sensual delight to be sure, but there were definite boundaries we did not cross.

Now in the kitchen, in the light of day, we prepare a leisurely breakfast of blueberry pancakes fried to a delicate crisp, cheddar cheese omelets, and hazelnut coffee with plenty of cream. We are falling in love and inclined to lavish each other with food—a safer physicality.

Sitting at the kitchen table, we stare longingly into each other's eyes, our textbooks scattered on the counter and omelets cooling on our plates.

"You look so good in that purple shirt," I say. "It brings out the green in your eyes." It's a T-shirt with a gigantic women's symbol in black and a clenched fist bursting through the circle, screaming to the world in English and Spanish: WOMEN TAKE BACK CONTROL! MUJERES TOMEMOS EL PODER! Marcie bought it at the women's bookstore, and it certainly reflects her philosophy in a nutshell. Her mind is as sharp as a whip, and she takes shit from no one. She's also beautiful, funny, *and* politically correct. I'm fascinated.

We stare longingly into each other's eyes, and I wonder briefly whether we'll pole vault over our morning schedule and land back in bed. *Might as well,* I think. I'm already behind in my reading. I'll never finish that paper: "Feminist Strategies for Global Coalition-Building." I have to ask for an extension…blah, blah, blah…Besides, who wants to go outside and battle the cold? My spontaneous rationalizations surprise me. I'm ordinarily such a responsible student. I note my corrupting thoughts as they pass vaguely through my mind. Meanwhile, my hand moves definitively, reaching to stroke Marcie's smiling face.

Her long blond hair shifts slightly in the breeze that creeps through our drafty, non-weatherstripped windows. As usual, it's snowing again. The flakes are coming down in blinding swirls as the wind howls. My enticing thoughts return: Do you want to endure that tundra when you can have this deliciously cozy moment? The tension between us has been building for weeks.

As if reading my mind, Marcie leans into my hand, rubbing it with her cheek and pulling me toward her, eyes sparkling. "Come sit on me," she whispers, inviting me to her lap. A wave of anxiety shoots through my body. Even though she's two years younger than I am, she has more experience in these matters. I'm nervous. My face is heating up.

In seconds I'm sitting in her lap, nibbling and kissing her ears like I did the night before. My long brown hair falls on her shoulders. Slowly my hands roam her warm skin, slipping under her purple shirt to caress her silkiness.

I move to the front of her blouse, rubbing her nipples, which harden under my fingertips. She moans, breathing heavier. I bite her neck, rubbing her nipples harder and flicking them with my fingertips. "Oh!" she gasps, as her excitement builds. I suddenly slide to the floor and kneel beside her.

She looks at me and whispers, "She's not home, is she?" referring to Jean, my roommate, the chemical engineer.

Just last week after overhearing us in my bedroom late at night, Jean asked me, in stuttering words, "Are you and Marcie uh...you know..." Her hesitation and shock could have embarrassed me, but it didn't.

"No," I answer Marcie. "Jean left an hour ago." Quickly, I unbutton her pants, inching them over her ass. She raises up to help me. I pull them over her hips, underwear and all. I don't pull them off, just inch them down past her knees, far enough to gain access to her cunt.

The sight of her tawny pubic hair excites me. The night before, my hands had roamed her luscious body, but it was too dark to see. Viewing her in the light, I feel my own cunt ache with desire. I slide my fingers through her hairy mound. She moves to the edge of her chair, spreading her legs wider for me. My heart starts to pound as I separate her pubic hair with my fingers. I uncover her pink clit, swollen like a pearl. With the flat of my tongue I lick long and slow, from the top of her clit down, probing the crevices of her labia. She moans loudly, and I'm really glad Jean left early for her 8 o'clock class. The house is empty except for the two of us. I lick slowly and persistently, savoring her taste. I'm surprised at how natural this feels. Thank God for those lesbian novels. My midnight page turning is paying off. Marcie breathes harder, moving her hips in ecstasy. I recall our sensational soiree in heaven the night before, and, inspired, I lick faster and harder.

Moments later I glance at the clock on the kitchen wall and realize I'm about to miss my 9:15 class. It's too late to trudge through this furious blizzard. Too bad. I can't stop now. This flame is too hot. I'm held in its thrall, gripped by primeval forces larger than me. Echoes of matriarchy ring in my ears as Marcie comes to a shuddering orgasm, her whole body relaxing in the chair. Feeling bold, I open her legs wider and push two fingers into her cunt, my heart pounding louder in my chest as she gasps in excited surprise. "Oh, yeah!" she cries out, grabbing my wrist, and we both exhale together.

The clock reads 9:38. I've missed my class on ancient matriarchies and contemporary feminist theory, and my paper on global strategies is going to be late.

Carried away. Carried beyond the merely mystical to a concrete reality so vividly and deliciously real.

This wasn't the last time, for sure. For weeks after, my degree in women's studies hung in an abyss, temporarily suspended while I explored a more mysterious and compelling terrain—one they never mentioned on the syllabus.

CHAPTER ELEVEN
Distant Thunder
Elana Mendelson

I slide the tape in the VCR and push play. I am introducing the movie *Bound* to my housemate. I go to the bed and sit on the opposite side of her, but where I want to be. She's bisexual, and I am a lesbian who has never been with a woman. I don't know what it is like to hold a woman to my naked body. I have seen this movie a few times, but it's worth watching the seduction scene…over and over again.

Danielle and I were acquaintances when I moved into her house with three other people. The flirting began almost immediately, and the sexual tension got intense. Danielle was 25, and I was 21. I knew she was bi, and I remember how I felt about bisexuals. I had been warned against them, but there was something about Danielle I couldn't get out of my head. It could have been her blue eyes that melted me, or maybe it was the way her body moved when she danced. I ached to touch the skin that showed under her short shirt; I ached to reach out and kiss her lips.

One night we went dancing with friends in NoHo, and Danielle and I went up to the bar to get some hot shots (cinnamon Schnapps and Tabasco sauce). We toasted and gulped.

She looked at me with her teasing blue eyes and said, "You know, you're supposed to kiss someone after a shot!"

"OK," I said, smiling.

We kissed for the first time in this crowded bar. I slipped my tongue past her lips and tasted remnants of Tabasco sauce still burning. We danced closely the rest of the evening, bumping and grinding in rhythm between shots. We went home and ascended the stairs. Danielle was in the bathroom, getting ready for bed. We kissed lightly, and I began to walk away. Just then, she grabbed my arm, pulled me into the bathroom, and closed the door. She threw me up against the door and engaged me in the most passionate, lustful kiss of my entire life. As she unbuttoned my shirt, we caught hold of ourselves. We knew this was bad news. Everybody warned, "Never date someone you live with!" So we told each other no and agreed to control ourselves.

Bound is almost over now. I want so much for her to touch me, but I don't want to break the agreement. I wonder if she feels the same way. I figure there is nothing wrong with putting my arm around her and just being friendly. It's hard to be so close and not touch her. I can't help myself anymore and begin to caress her face. I am shaky because I don't know how she'll respond. Danielle takes my hand and begins to suck on my fingers, one by one. I guess she feels it too. My mind races uncontrollably as *Bound* ends — or maybe it hasn't…I really don't care anymore. We can't say no to each other. We kiss like we did that night in the bathroom. In one full sweep, she undresses both of us. She kisses and teases my nipples, touching every part of me. She spreads open my legs and kisses down my stomach. Her tongue finds my wet spot, and she begins to urgently lick and suck. My brain is in overload, not believing I have this beautiful woman going down on me.

I'm not scared, though. I completely trust this woman I hardly know. Danielle knows I am a virgin in every sense of the word, so she doesn't penetrate me.

She delicately tongues my virgin clit. An amazing feeling spreads over the rest of my body. I can't take it anymore; the orgasm is killing me. I stop her, and she gets on the bed. She lies on her back, and I am on my side just drinking in her naked body.

The TV screen is nothing but snow now. I am on top of her. I discover a tattoo over her left breast. I run my fingers over it, trying to feel the raised ink. She knows I am scared to touch her. She knows she will have to teach me. Danielle asks me if I want to "see her." I nod my head yes and go down her body, entangling my fingers in her soft pubic hair. I caress her outer lips with my right hand, not really sure what to do next. She shows me how to shape my hand to penetrate and helps me inside. It is warm and wet like a hot tub. The space inside her takes in my fingers. She breathlessly directs me, but I already know what to do. I watch her face and listen to her pleasure as I adjust the speed and pressure of my hand. I watch her facial contortions as I curl my fingers with each push.

I look up at Danielle. Her eyes are closed, concentrating on my rhythm. She reaches down and plays with her clit. I feel as if I can go on forever. It is so wet and warm inside. I don't want to withdraw my hand. She thrashes around on the bed as she orgasms. From within, Danielle clutches my wrinkly fingers. The muscle squeezes. I am stunned by the feeling, until I hear the front door open, and we quickly pull our clothes on! We stand in the middle of the room and wait to hear where the footsteps are going. False alarm. We kiss and hug a few times, and then I thank her.

We continued our affair over the next few months, with steamy sex throughout. I used to love the weekends because I knew I could sleep in Danielle's bed, holding her deep into the night. We'd have marathon sex or sometimes just a quickie by the laundry room. For a while it seemed whenever we made love, it would rain—usually a thunderstorm. We wouldn't notice it until we were sopping wet and exhausted. We'd lie on top of the sheets, listening to the rain gently tapping against the awnings above the windows, then drift off into sleep. There was something very peaceful about that rain, and it made things seem really special.

Special is definitely how Danielle made me feel. I used to think when I finally gave myself over to a woman, my "virginity" would be taken away, but it was not that kind of give-and-take game. Danielle shared something with me, as I did with her. She told me the secret, and I eagerly listened. She gave me confidence, and I supported her. It was a relationship built on lust and intellect.

We are friends now and no longer lovers. It has been a very difficult process for us, and I don't think either of us will ever make the mistake of dating a roommate again. We do, however, flirt up a storm when we're in the mood. We've slipped a couple of times but we will never be what we once were. I can't say I don't think of her whenever I hear the distant thunder, though...I love you, Danielle, and always will.

CHAPTER TWELVE
Kelly
Zoey Edwards

"Hey, girl, I'm on my way over."

"OK."

"I can't wait to hang out tonight…and just having this weekend to myself. Whew!"

"Well, I'll be here waiting."

"See ya."

My best friend. She's a free spirit. Worldly, as I call her. We met five years ago on the East Coast but have since transplanted ourselves to the West Coast. I guess you could say we're shooting for the stars. I'm pursuing a writing career, and she's pursuing an acting career. But until we make it, we are corporate slaves trapped in the system. What can I say? A girl's gotta make a living, and she has an eight-year-old son to care for. Her name is Kelly, and she's quite stunning.

Many times when I've looked at her, I've pictured Diana Ross in blue jeans. Kelly has these big beautiful brown eyes, wild curly hair, and voluptuous lips. Perhaps my favorite look on her is a torn pair of blue jeans, a cropped top to show off her pierced navel, and combat boots. I suppose it suits her youthfulness and artistic background. She's definitely a California girl.

So just as she looks like Diana "Lady Boss" Ross, I look like Pam "Foxy/Jackie Brown" Grier. My features are keen—almond-shaped brown eyes, high cheekbones, and narrow nose, all set on a rich chocolate complexion. I am a few years older than Kelly, but I feel just as youthful. I think it's a result of California livin'.

For a while I had been having dreams of a woman kissing me. It wasn't just any woman, though—it was Kelly. *But who was I kidding?* I would shake the dream from my thoughts because it seemed wrong to fantasize about my friend. I'd never wanted—or thought I wanted—to kiss her. But soon I found myself awakening to moistness between my thighs. The dream kiss excited me.

You see, there was a brief period during our friendship when we weren't communicating because of a misunderstanding. It just seemed weird for me to have a desire to kiss her without seeing or speaking to her. That particular afternoon would be our second visit since not talking. I felt like we were getting to know each other all over again. I wanted to confront her about my thoughts but lacked the courage. I suppose I was afraid of rejection. Even coming from a friend, rejection can be embarrassing.

Kelly and I made plans to visit several bars on our day together. Because I love to cook, I made us a lunch of seafood, pasta, and a bottle of champagne. I loved entertaining her. I felt so relaxed being with her and just shooting the breeze.

We were drunk by nightfall. What else could we expect, drinking not only champagne but also margaritas and beer? All we needed to top off the high was some pot. But the booze was really enough of a high. One of the bars we visited was The Palms, a well-known lesbian bar in West Hollywood. I had never ventured into a women's bar before, so it was quite interesting to be in a room filled with women who wanted other women. Kelly and I were all smiles because we were each other's date for the evening. We danced and chatted with a bartender named Billie.

There was a foreign woman at the bar staring at me. I felt uncomfortable, but not threatened. Billie introduced the woman as Helga. She looked wild and unruly, but she was not attractive. Helga just looked hard up and hard-core, dressed in black leather from head to toe. Kelly seemed to be getting a kick out of Helga's admiring me, and Helga seemed goofy because she never spoke. I wasn't planning on breaking the ice either. I really didn't need the extra attention.

Kelly seemed to think that Billie and I would have made a nice couple. It was funny how she always pictured me with other women, but not herself. I suppose she wasn't attracted to me at the time. My dreams of Kelly were my own. Still, sometimes I thought she was making passes at me—just a feeling I couldn't explain. So I got Billie's number to satisfy Kelly's curiosity.

We concluded the night closer to home at the Broadway Bar and Grill in Santa Monica where Kelly and I listened to an acid jazz band. I was absolutely amazed I had not passed out, since it's really hard for me to stay up late. Nevertheless, I hung in there, and Kelly and I finally made it home. We were completely worn-out...or so I thought.

So there we were alone in the dark at my place, and I playfully began to caress her face while she lay sleeping. She said softly to stop messing with her, but I did not retreat. Instead I tried it again. Kelly turned away from me by lying on her stomach. I seemed more determined to convince her with my flirting. I kissed half of her cheek and whispered that I wanted to kiss her mouth. She turned over to face me and began sucking my index finger, gently topping the tip with a kiss.

By now I was ready to hold her in my arms. I pulled Kelly into me. I wanted to cover her with my mouth. I think I could have devoured her. My tongue began exploring her body, gliding over her neck and down to her breasts. My taste buds were alive with curiosity as I gently nibbled on her aroused nipples.

Kelly was enthralled in the passion. I don't think she could believe this was happening with *me*. *I* couldn't believe this was happening with *her*. She had had her share of male and female lovers, but never in her wildest dreams did Kelly think *we* would be embraced in desire. I felt heat rising with every touch. It was

all so new and sensational. Even though I couldn't receive because I was on my period, I still wanted to give—and give
freely. My tongue continued on its path down to her clitoris. I
had to taste her fruit. I needed to know if it was sweet or sour,
or maybe in-between. Kelly's fruit was moist, rich, and choco-
laty-good. I couldn't believe this beautiful woman was sharing
her treasure with me. I could not get enough.

Kelly's moans were low but constant. She was in ecstasy. I
so wanted to please her with my tongue. Her pussy was so
good, and I felt so naughty. I could be myself with her. We
were enjoying each other, and my pussy dripped from her excitement. I knew later I would have to masturbate—just close
my eyes and fantasize—but I was living my fantasy. *I was eating pussy. I was eating Kelly's pussy.*

I didn't care about anything or anyone—just us. Our lives
had come to a crossroads of a special moment that no one else
could take from us. It was private and pleasurable. I felt no
shame and no guilt for being with this woman. *My first time
with a woman.* I tingled all over. It felt so right being with her.
Even though I had been with men many times, I had never
felt so uninhibited before.

"Are you having fun?" Kelly asked.

"Are you?" I returned with a wicked smile.

"I'm surprised because I never expected this. I don't approach my girlfriends because I don't want them freaking out
on me," began Kelly.

"Am I freaking out or are you?" I wanted to know.

"No, I'm just surprised," Kelly said. "I can't believe this is
your first time. Usually when girls do it for the first time,
they're nervous."

I asked her playfully, "Does that mean I did it right?"

"Yeah, you definitely did it right," she replied with a
pleased smile.

"Well, I want to do it again. Right now. I like eating you," I confessed.

"I want to eat you too—the next time we get together," Kelly said between kissing my mouth and sucking my nipples.

In the meantime, I put on Erykah Badu's *Live* CD to continue our mellow mood of lovemaking. I told Kelly to turn over and put her ass in my face so I could eat her pussy from behind. I was down on my knees on the floor, at the edge of the bed. I spread her pussy lips apart to slip my tongue inside, and I thrust deeper and deeper. Kelly scratched my arms as though she were fighting the urge to come. I wanted her to. I wanted her to feel like a little lady who deserves good loving by the tongueful.

Even though Kelly could not return the favor, she wanted me to masturbate for her. I obliged her. My clit seemed so excited that as I began playing with it, the minimal stroking was numbing. I had to rub hard to off myself for Kelly. Erykah was singing "Certainly." Kelly was sucking my nipples again. In between my moaning, she whispered softly in my ear that the next time I was with my man, I should indulge in anal sex with him, and I should let him know she would be willing to have sex with both of us. I was growing increasingly excited by the possibilities of new encounters. Wild experiences. I told Kelly I fantasized about being with two women at the same time. She said it could be arranged because she would also like to watch a girlfriend and me. *The joy of pussy.*

We awakened to the first rays of sunlight. The loving was so good neither of us remembered Erykah singing the final track, "Tyrone." I could have eaten more pussy, but I didn't want to appear too eager. Kelly had already promised another time. She said that she loved eating pussy and was looking forward to the day when she could have mine. So I wait patiently for the next time. If there is no "next time," then our one time together will forever stay with me.

CHAPTER THIRTEEN
Kiss in the Dark
Mary Marin

The party had been going strong for hours, but I still couldn't get my fill of looking at you. Laughter, sunny and raucous, carried across the room, and I followed the sound to its source: you. I drank you in with my eyes. Your honeyed brown hair was scattered in soft curls around your face. Your black eyes, melancholic and deep, were a draped window to a soul you weren't particularly eager to share with others. I watched your beautiful, lithe hands as they danced in the air, accenting a story you were telling the people sitting next to you. You wore a red velvet blouse that traced the curves of your breasts. I would have moved heaven and earth to be that velvet, just so I could lie against your softness and tease your nipples into hardness.

What was this mysterious compulsion I felt toward you? You had not encouraged it. Or had you? Throughout the evening, in different parts of the house, I felt your gaze and turned to find your eyes following me. In those moments that seemed out of sync with the night unfolding around us, our eyes met often. It was as if everything and nothing were happening at the same time. I felt as if your eyes were speaking to me, but in a language I couldn't hear or understand. And as for me, what on earth was this about? I had never been with a woman. Oh, sure, I had thought about it, dreamed about it, feared it, desired it, and been terrified by it—but never more than that. I was so young, barely out of college, barely beginning to live. Here I was in the worst of situations: You were older than I, more sophisticated than I, and—worst of all—you were my boss.

What was crystal clear was the conversation we had several days before. I had confessed—in a moment of foolish and regrettable candor—that I was attracted to you. You graciously smiled and informed me—in no uncertain terms—that you were only interested in men. How you drove that point home! "I love men. I may not like them very much as people, but I love and crave only men. And besides, Valerie, aren't you forgetting I'm your boss?" I think you went on to mention both how wonderful men were and that you were my boss no less than four times in our brief conversation. A mantra of sorts for you. What a fool I had felt like as you walked away from me down the hall. Now you knew my secret, and you would carry it with you wherever you went. All I had was an empty space inside where this truth had once been. A piece of my heart in exchange for your mantra about men—and being "the boss."

Days later, at an office party at the assistant manager's home, you were seemingly unchanged. So why did I feel your eyes trying to tell me something, and why couldn't I understand what they were trying to say? I was so lost in thought you had to call my name several times before I realized you were talking to me. Actually you were talking *about* me. You were telling your friends a rumor was floating around at work that I was an seasoned bartender and that I knew hundreds of recipes by heart. Your eyes sparkled when you teased, "So many secrets, Valerie! What else are you hiding from us?" I could have killed you for playing with me that way. How I loved you! And how I hated you! And in that way, you had come to mean everything to me. Yet, despite this whirlwind of emotions, it was at that moment the glimmer of an idea appeared in my head.

"Not only is that true," I replied, "but to prove it I will make you a drink you'll never forget."

For a split second you looked nervous, but the look was

gone as quickly as it appeared. "OK, you're on," you said, and I detected the tiniest hint of a smile across your lips. "So what are you going to make for me?" you asked playfully.

I thought for a moment, then grinned back at you. "I'm going to make you something special. It's called a Kiss in the Dark. You'll absolutely love it."

You looked uncertain again. Your friends were all talking at once, speculating over what ingredients might go into such a drink. No one but me noticed you seemed to falter, you seemed slightly off-balance. *My, my,* I thought with smirking amusement. *Now look who's uncomfortable.*

"Well, how about it?" I quipped. "Do you or don't you want a Kiss in the Dark?"

"Of course I do," you replied. But really, what else could you have said under the circumstances?

As I eased over to the well-stocked bar in the corner of the room, I felt the cool breeze blowing in gently from the open deck door. The night was dark. The deck lights had been left off since the house sat perched on a hill overlooking the twinkling city far below. It was an incredible vista. I stopped for a moment simply to enjoy it. Far below me was a city teeming with life and color. Yet just a few short miles up where I stood was a velvety darkness that filled my senses with sage and pine.

At the bar I found what I needed and began to prepare your drink. I heard you talking, and again I noticed you kept glancing in my direction. Of course, when I looked up several times, you made a point of catching my gaze just so you could look away. I smiled to myself. Even at your most petulant, you were still quite charming. First I filled a mixing glass with ice. Then I added three-fourths of an ounce of gin, three-fourths of an ounce of cherry brandy, and one-fourth of an ounce of dry vermouth. I shook the mixing glass thoroughly and strained it into two chilled cocktail glasses—enough for both of us—and emerged from the bar with our drinks.

Instead of walking over to you, however, I stopped by the open deck door and said, "Beth, come get your drink, but first come out here. I want to show you something." You stopped talking and just looked at me. There was a moment of silence, and then you slowly stood up. As you walked over to me, I saw something shift in your eyes. I think you knew what was going to happen. I tried to tell you with my eyes: "If you stop at the door and go no further, I'll understand." But even as I tried to convey that to you, I knew you would not stop at the door; you would come out with me to the deck. As you took the glass from me, your fingers lightly brushed mine. You took me in with a brief but penetrating glance and continued out the door to the deck. Turning, I asked the others to think of their favorite drink and promised to make each and every one as soon as I returned. I too stepped out the door and went to join you where you stood in the darkest corner of the deck, out of everyone's view.

The night felt lush and expectant. You turned slightly toward me as I approached you, and we stood together gazing at the distant lights, our drinks in our hands. I could smell your perfume, spicy and exotic, and that alone drove me nearly mad with desire. I closed my eyes and imagined you in my arms, my hands stroking your body, my lips kissing you, tasting you, drinking you in with an unquenchable thirst.

We sipped our drinks, each taste bringing us closer to a point from which we would not be able to return. I could feel you by my side, your curiosity warring with your hesitancy, both losing to temptation's strength.

The voices behind us grew distant as we stood silently suspended over the darkness. We were at a loss for words, both trying to figure out where this moment was taking us and who would be the first one to make a move or gesture. There is something rare and special about moments like these. You stand poised on a tightrope between everything that is and everything that might be, and there is a wonderfully reckless awareness that there is no safety net to catch you if you fall. You understand romance and passion are as much about falling as they are about keeping balance.

I'll never remember exactly who made the first move, but I heard your kiss before I felt it. I heard the movement of our bodies drawing into each other before I actually felt your lips. They were as soft as anything I had ever imagined in my life. When my arms encircled you, your lips parted, and with that simple act I dove deep into your heart. I tasted you and explored every part of your beautiful mouth with my tongue. Your smell was rich and unending. There are some moments in life that nothing can prepare you for. This was one of those moments.

Every tightrope has a beginning, middle, and end, however, and we reached the other side way too quickly. One of your friends called out for you, and you pulled away abruptly, leaving me no choice but to release you. Your face was a chaos of emotions, but you called out that we would be inside in a moment. Then you looked at me with a mixture of fear, wonder, desire, and distance.

Your words broke my heart. "Well, Valerie, as far as secrets go, I guess we're even now. Your confession in exchange for my kiss. Now we both have something on each other."

"Beth," I stammered, "if you think that's what this was about, you're completely wrong. You know how I feel. I've never done this with a woman before. How can you think I —"

"Beth!" your friends called out again. "Hurry up! We're waiting for you and Valerie. We want our drinks!"

"Val," you said softly. "We have to go. I won't pretend I didn't feel something, but there are certain limits I have, and I won't let this go any further. Let's go. They're probably wondering what's taking us so long. And what we just did— as far as I'm concerned, it never happened."

I turned away from you, and without saying another word, I walked back into the house. I felt a simple sadness come over me, like what a child might feel when a long-anticipated hug ends too quickly.

At the sliding door I turned to you, however, and startled myself by saying, "Call what just happened between us whatever you want, Beth, but no matter what you say to yourself, you'll never forget this. You, not I, will always be the one with a secret…and the secret won't be about me."

I left you out on the deck and walked back into a room full of people with requests for all kinds of exotic cocktails. I didn't disappoint. I knew how to make each and every drink. You reentered quietly and said the drink was delicious, but this time there was no teasing in your voice. You left soon after, claiming you had an early appointment the next day and needed to go home. Although I looked up when you were saying good-bye to everyone, your eyes never once strayed in my direction.

I walked over to the front window just in time to see your taillights disappear around the corner. I left shortly afterward, but first I went back out onto the deck and slipped our glasses, which we had left on the railing, into my jacket. I felt a bit foolish, but I didn't want to leave them behind. I couldn't quite explain it; I just needed those glasses. I wondered how people could walk away from the most obvious connections and still live with themselves as if nothing had changed. I placed my lips gently around the rim of your glass and knew two things with absolute certainty. One: I would quit my job tomorrow to salvage what little dignity I had left. Two: I would look for your taste in every woman I would ever kiss.

Leaving quietly, I drove down the same road you had taken when you left. The only sound in my car was the faint clinking of the two glasses on the passenger seat as I descended into the city.

CHAPTER FOURTEEN
Camp Good News
Lisa E. Davis

When I turned 18, Mama sent me to Camp Good News to become a missionary. I became a lesbian instead. Mama wasn't pleased. She was always trying to turn my life over to God.

"Now, honey," Mama told me, driving home from Sunday services, "you're gonna meet some wonderful people up there." Camp Good News was a summer retreat nestled in the foothills of the Appalachians and run by the women's missionary society.

"And if you feel the call to the mission field…" The steering wheel cut into Mama's round belly as she swung the bulky Chevrolet onto our street. "I want you to listen to God's voice and follow the leadin' of the Holy Spirit."

Plump and sleek as a breakfast sausage, Mama was on intimate terms with the Holy Spirit.

"OK." I wasn't keen on preaching the gospel, but I was happy to spend a few weeks away.

Missionaries—mostly young, single women—came to Camp Good News from all over to talk and to show slides of their outreach to the heathen. They were daring and told stories of floods, wild animals, and hostile and friendly natives.

The first couple of days at camp, I met this woman named Peggy, a college girl on the staff. She was 25, small and dark, with full lips and a classic profile like something lifted off a Greek vase. I watched her the way I used to watch a couple of older girls back home, the ones I wanted to get close to. The difference was Peggy was watching me too.

Peggy and I sat together for the Bible and missionary sessions. My leg brushed hers during the prayer. When we stood up to sing, our hands would touch under the shared hymnal. One long afternoon, we lay slightly apart on a blanket by the lake, holding hands.

I had no experience with women but had kissed and petted aplenty with the boys back home. I'd thrust my hand into flies, squeezing and tugging. The boys made no objections, sliding down in the front seat of the car to trace the stitching across the cracked plastic ceiling while I fumbled away, alone with my thoughts.

What I felt for Peggy had nothing to do with that. I wanted to share everything with her. As the days passed, to be out of her sight for very long was torture. I looked for her everywhere, listened for her voice. I waited for her and found my way to her side. I was obsessed, in love.

One night at Camp Good News, a feisty, redheaded missionary showed slides of her work in Brazil. Frothy palm trees floated over tropical, blue water. In closing, she recalled those spellbinding words about faith, hope, and a love that never failed, then sent us out of the chapel to preach the gospel to every creature.

If this setting wasn't conventionally romantic, it did have a couple of things going for it. It was an exclusively female audience. The only men on the place were the hillbilly caretaker and his sons. And there was a lot of talk about love—loving God, the heathen, and one another.

As Peggy and I filed out of the chapel that night, pressed close together by choice and by a crowd of women, a heady mixture of piety and sensuality suffused my adolescent psyche. Outside, pine boughs and honeysuckle perfumed the night. The sky was bright with stars. A mist percolated off the lake and through the cool mountain valley, thick with trees.

"Are you cold?" Peggy whispered, then put her jacket around my shoulders. Angel wings couldn't have been softer than the touch of her hand.

"I don't want to go in," I answered her. I had to leave Camp Good News soon.

"We'll do anything you want to do," she said, as she looked at me with large, brown, startled eyes.

"Let's go to the vesper garden," I said, melting with love.

I took her hand in the dark. I would have gone anywhere with her hand in mine, even in search of souls for Jesus if that was what she wanted.

Her passions were more down-to-earth. That moonless night we followed a secluded path lined with blackberry brambles. The path opened out into a woodland glade, where white benches and a rustic altar glowed opalescent. During the day we sang songs of praise in that sanctified glen.

We sat down on one of the back benches. She didn't let go of my hand. We moved closer together. Breezes hummed in the treetops and set things stirring.

"It's nice without so many people," I said.

"I'd rather be here than anywhere." Peggy's voice was like wind through the pine trees.

I put my arm around her. I felt her body soft and fleshy against mine.

"I don't want to go home," I said.

"You can take all this with you, in your heart," she replied, like a line out of some sermon. But she leaned over and kissed me on the cheek.

"It's not the place. It's you," I said. "I never want to leave you."

"I know," she answered, and looked at me with a depth of caring no one had ever shown me before. It was the kind of love I had wanted without knowing it or believing in its existence.

"Let's don't ever be apart," I said, and I kissed her on the lips.

She kissed me back, and I searched her mouth with mine. Holding tight, we kissed for a long time. We sank off the bench onto a nest of leaves and pine needles. I slipped my thigh between her legs and reached beneath her clothes in ways no one had ever taught me.

With one hand, I quested for Peggy's bra, separating the hooks from the metal eyes. Her nipples popped up as big as a baby's thumbs, and I bent over them. She enfolded me in her arms.

Luckily, no missionary stumbled over us in the dark.

I was drunk on sensation but managed to find the deepest, wettest spot between her legs. We both gasped with astonishment and joy.

Peggy said it was time to go. "C'mon, sweetheart," she murmured, my head resting on her breast. "They're gonna wonder where you got to."

We brushed pine needles off our clothes.

"I'll see you tomorrow," she promised, cupping my chin in her hand.

On that promise, I could've lived for the rest of my life.

The rest of my time at camp was bliss. Peggy and I strolled around the place each night arm in arm until we found a secluded spot to neck for an hour or two.

All my life seemed to date from the moment we'd met.

The night before I was to leave, I lay on my cold, barren cot and wondered what I'd do without her. I devised a risky plan. The cabin I was assigned to sat with others on a ridge. Peggy slept in a room down the hill and across the camp in the staff quarters. Both of us had many roommates on either side.

Long before dawn, I got up and dressed, then tiptoed out of the cabin. I crossed the campground soundlessly and let myself into the building where she slept. I climbed a flight of stairs. Down the hall and to the left, I opened her door a crack. Her bed was in the middle of a quartet of cots.

I went in, closed the door, and stood by her bed. She opened her eyes without surprise, as though she'd been expecting me, and raised the covers so I could slip in. I'd never been in a bed with anybody before. I put my hands under her nightdress. Without layers of clothes in between, we were one on that narrow cot for a few hours in the early morning.

I'd known from the beginning Peggy and I wouldn't get caught, and not because what we were doing was wrong. I never believed much in sin, although I'd been preached to all my life. I did believe if anyone found out I was happy, that happiness would be instantly taken away. Lying in the arms of a woman I loved was greater than any happiness I'd ever conceived.

We woke no one, and I stayed until light began to break outside. The smell and taste of Peggy enveloped me as I returned to my cabin on the hill.

In the morning I went home from Camp Good News. I told Mama what a good time I'd had.

"Did you get to meet the missionaries?" she asked.

"Oh, sure, lots of 'em."

Then the letters started. I wrote to Peggy, and she wrote back with a passion addressed to the furthest corner of myself. Her letters reminded me of life and sanity. I bound them together with a sky-blue satin ribbon and thrust them deep into a pigeonhole of my desk for safekeeping.

Mama never went near my desk.

Peggy wrote that she missed me, that she would finish school next June and wanted to go to nursing school.

"Who are all those letters from?" Mama asked.

"Oh, just somebody I met at Camp Good News. She's studyin' to be a medical missionary."

Mama looked wary.

"I love you," I wrote to Peggy, "as much as anybody can love anybody."

"I'll always love you," she wrote back. To die from so much joy would've suited me fine.

Separation from Peggy was like being exiled to a wasteland. I read her letters over and over. Some nights I'd take one of them into bed with me for company, as proof there really was love in the world. I sensed their vulnerability during the day — concealed behind sheaves of construction paper, scissors, paste, and rubber bands — but couldn't bear to destroy them.

When the end came it was guillotine swift.

I got home late one Saturday afternoon, and one foot inside the front door, I knew there was trouble. Mama sat massively on the sofa, an untidy heap of rifled envelopes on the floor at her feet, a pile of torn and jagged writing paper beside her.

Mama's eyes bored into me like ice picks.

I dropped my jacket and rushed to my desk. The whole length of my arm went into the pigeonhole where the letters had lain hidden and touched the emptiness.

I went back to the living room.

Mama's stout neck swelled up like a puff adder getting ready to strike. She began, "I have read the letters from that woman."

Hatred and fear froze my face. I'd never let her know how it hurt me. I'd never let her know anything again.

"Is this what they teach at Camp Good News?" she asked.

I made no reply.

Mama went on, picking up speed. I recognized a few standard phrases — defilement of the temple of the Holy Spirit, debauchery, Sodom and Gomorrah.

Spewing fire and brimstone, Mama announced, "I have called the doctor, and I'm goin' to call the police and have that woman arrested."

At that, Daddy came out of the bedroom where he listened to the radio and stood sheepishly in the doorway.

"Now, honey..." he said.

But Mama dashed past him and grabbed the telephone.

"I'm gettin' the preacher on the phone," she said. "He'll know who to call."

I watched Daddy fade silently back into the bedroom, leaving me at Mama's mercy.

"Slow down," I said to Mama. "What are you talkin' about?"

"She's a homosexual!" Mama screamed, flailing her large, flabby arms.

I thought fast. I'd heard the word *homosexual* before. I knew it devastated lives.

I remembered Mrs. Grady in sixth grade, who read to us every day from books about *Lad, A Dog*. One day she disappeared, her sweet resonant voice gone. Rumors flew thick as thieves. It filtered down that her husband—red hair and red face—who taught at the high school had been accused of something in darkened rooms with boys.

In eighth grade the ax fell closer to my heart. Our basketball coach was the kindhearted Miss MacLean. She shared duties with Miss Angus—blond, cold, and efficient.

One day at practice, Miss Angus announced tersely that her colleague had resigned and wasn't coming back. The girls were aghast and despondent.

I overheard the whole story from Mama's phone conversations with the other town gossips.

"Miss MacLean practiced unnatural love with other women who visited her from out of town," they told and retold each other.

Miss MacLean had had to make a fast getaway.

I wasn't about to let anything like that happen to Peggy. I'd tell any lie I had to, and I sensed Mama would want to believe me.

"You're talkin' silly," I said to Mama, who stopped scream-ing. "You know I'm gonna be a missionary."

Mama's face softened. "You mean that?" she asked.

"I been thinkin' about it a lot," I said.

"Well, praise the Lord," Mama said.

"I thought you'd be glad," I said. "There's nothin' for you to worry about."

Miraculously, Mama's swollen neck deflated. She dropped her broad rump back down on the sofa, *kerplunk*, on top of the pile of Peggy's letters. I knew I'd never see them again.

The next day, Sunday, I went to the front of the church and told the preacher I wanted to dedicate my life to mis-sionary work. Mama wept with joy and relief.

I pretended to forget all about Peggy. In hindsight, I could've begged her to take me with her when she went to nursing school. I could've taken any sort of job, just to be near her. I didn't. I was very young. But I carried a torch for Peggy that burned brightly for years. Sometimes I think it's burning still.

CHAPTER FIFTEEN
Marcel's Closet
Quinn Lioe

*E*veryone wanted Marcel Finley. She was tall, athletic, graceful—even at 18 when most of us were still fumbling around trying to figure out how to walk without tripping over our own feet. Her dusky skin and shoulder-length ebony hair only enhanced her long straight nose and black eyes. She was the most beautiful woman I had ever seen...and probably the most dangerous.

Even then she already had a reputation in our small enclave as being a predator. She had seduced several of my classmates—girls all. Marcel was nothing if not precocious. She was also brilliant, which annoyed me to no end.

We competed for grades in our exclusive, politically correct, multiculturally balanced private college. Most of us lived in the sterile cinder block dorms that never seem to go out of fashion. Marcel chose to stay with her parents in their home near campus.

It was November—foggy and damp in that West Coast town and nothing like my Chinese homeland. I was homesick and lonely, even though I was not close to my family. To be a lesbian in the conservative part of China I hailed from was to be a leper. I had learned early on not to discuss my feelings and to practice the fine art of deception. No one could truly know what I was feeling. No one, except by some spooky coincidence, but Marcel.

In the late afternoon dusk, the arched stone walkways on our campus seemed even more dreary and heavy. It reminded me of the oppressive European architecture we were studying in art history, not at all like the graceful curves of Chinese palaces. Feeling superior because I had scored the highest mark on the calculus exam, I pranced along beside Marcel, bragging about my physics project, which had been accepted for the science competition usually open only to seniors, not mere freshmen. She stopped suddenly and turned to me.

"What?"

She didn't say anything but backed me up against the stone wall. In the shadows, with the damp stone against the back of my head and the ever-present fog sinking into my clothing like smoke, she lifted my chin with the tip of her index finger and kissed me on the mouth.

I gasped in surprise, and she took advantage of my open mouth to dart her tongue past my lips. I felt as though I'd been shot through with electric current and that a part of me I had just discovered of late—much to my delight and sur- prise—was suddenly and almost painfully swollen. I thought for a moment that I'd wet myself until I realized my body— against my will!—had responded to Marcel's kiss.

My eyes were wide, and she laughed. "I thought so," she said.

I pushed past her angrily and strode through the fog.

"Wait, Quinn," she said, her voice even then seductive and soft. "Come have dinner at my house. Fayan is cooking, and you know his specialty is Mandarin."

I paused. I had heard quite a bit about Fayan's Mandarin cuisine—he'd spent some ten years there during his military service and was not only fluent in several Chinese dialects but also a renown chef of many special dishes. To be invited to Fayan's table was an honor one did not refuse.

I turned, my homesickness getting the best of me. "All right," I said.

Not only did Marcel have the biggest room I had ever seen all to herself, but she also had the biggest closet. Her closet was the size of my family's living room and full of the most wonderful mixture of smells—leather and cloves and cedar. The floor was covered with a thick powder-blue carpet, and I sank to my knees to touch it with my hands. I had never seen anything like it. The whole house was extraordinary, filled with gadgets and gizmos, half of which I couldn't identify. Most were from Stephen's work—Marcel's other father was an engineer who spent his spare time tinkering in an electronics workshop housed in a separate building on their property. Marcel was Fayan's biological child, and they were both the same shade of brown, a rich dark shade that begged to be tasted.

Inside the closet, she knelt beside me on the floor. I looked up into her eyes. Her generous mouth parted slightly, and her tongue licked her lips. Suddenly I wanted her to kiss me again, and I leaned forward. I could feel her breath on my skin. Her gaze was locked with mine, but neither of us would look away. Without closing our eyes, we kissed again.

Her mouth was gentle, and this surprised me. Nothing else about her was. She was aggressive, boisterous, used to getting her way. And perhaps she knew to get her way with me she had to go slowly, because at any given moment I would run away, guilt-ridden, ashamed by what I wanted. A shame made by the culture in which I'd been raised and one that would take me years to overcome.

I felt her tongue on my lips tasting me. We broke apart, breathless. She reached over and took off my blazer and folded it neatly into a pile on the immaculate carpeted floor. "Take off your shoes," she said. I handed them to her, and she put them next to the blazer. "Lie down."

When I was on my back, she instructed me to take off my underpants. I just stared at her. She raised one eyebrow and waited. Finally I complied. She slid her hand under my skirt without hesitation began to touch me where I was the most swollen and needy. I stifled a gasp. Her finger moved in slow circles. Then she stopped, reached for my hand, and put it where hers had been. "I want you to touch yourself just like that until I come back."

My eyes widened. I began to protest, but she cut me off with a sharp motion of her hand. I could hardly control my need by that point, and I complied. She watched me for a moment, then got up, walked out of the closet, and closed the door behind her.

The small room was now totally dark except for the light coming in under the door. My nostrils were full of the smells of leather, cloves, cedar, and something else—something spicy and salty and warm all at the same time. Waves and waves of pleasure were coursing through my body. I was hard and slick under my fingers. Even though I wanted to go faster, I was afraid of what she would do to me if I did, afraid of what she would do if I had come before she returned.

But it was becoming harder and harder to stop my hand from moving more quickly. My body's need was urgent, and I was young and inexperienced. I tried to think about something else—a complex equation, a science experiment, the names of all of the characters in one of Shakespeare's plays— but soon my breathing was ragged, and I was sure I had soaked through the carpet and onto the floor below. I was shaking, cursing, furious, and so aroused that I barely remember the door opening. Light coursed over me, and Marcel stood silhouetted in the doorway.

She came in, closed the door behind her, and flipped on a dim light that bathed us in a golden spill of color. She looked at me, and I saw the desire on her face, saw her own raw need, and knew something about her then that I had never seen before—a vulnerability that came from wanting to touch another, a desire as strong as the ache under my hand.

When our eyes met, she saw I knew, and something shifted between us. She knelt before me, then lay down and, with her mouth inches from the very center of my desire, said, "Do you want to come for me?"

I couldn't speak to answer her, and so I just nodded. A moment later she pushed my hand aside, and her tongue found me. Nothing was slow now, and the rapid stroke of her tongue brought me quickly toward an orgasm so powerful I can still recall the feeling of it some 20 years later. When it was over we lay together panting, the room saturated with the scent of our mingled desire.

Marcel never let me touch her. Not then. Not later. We made love twice more over the next 15 years and have remained friends. How many other girls lay on that closet floor I will never know, but I suspect I was not the only one who experienced her first passion under Marcel's touch.

For me that day marked a corner turned. I could no longer deny who I was or what I wanted, even though it cost me my blood family. And in some strange twist, the woman with whom I chose to spend my life is Marcel's adopted sister, whom I met that night for the first time at Fayan's table, eating the food from my homeland and tasting the first mark of my desire, which lingered like the memory of salt air and smoke on the surface of my skin.

CHAPTER SIXTEEN
And So It Begins
Stacy M. Bias

The day had just begun to give way to twilight, and the orange glow of the sky gave the entire outside world a scrubbed and fresh feeling. I smiled to myself as I watched the wind catch up the fall leaves and redistribute them in tiny little whirlwinds of crisp, vibrant color. It was one of those nights when a warm drink in your hand, the ambiance of a cozy little coffeehouse and the company of the woman you love is the perfect recipe for contentment.

I pulled my gaze from the window and smiled warmly across the table at her, seeing my sentiment echoed in the smile she returned. "This is a great little place," she said. I nodded and settled back into my seat. She followed suit, and soon we were wrapped in pleasant conversation. Sitting across from me was my supervisor, and we were on our first "social" outing. Outside the work environment where there wasn't the ringing of phones and the shuffling of papers to distract me, I found myself able to focus on her with an intensity I found delicious. As she talked, my eyes took in her short-cropped and barely graying auburn hair, the healthy glow of her skin (unadulterated by makeup), the adorable way her eyes crinkled when she laughed, her perfect teeth beneath her beautiful smile. She wasn't "model beautiful" by the world's standards, but she was simply perfect to me. She was doing most of the talking, and that was just fine.

I sat, snuggled into the warmth of my chair, and watched her with smiling eyes above my coffee cup. Her fingers worked through her hair occasionally and then fumbled with the handle of her mug, only to immediately wander through her hair once again. Her eyes rarely rested on mine; often they scanned the surroundings or trailed out the window. I found her unease inspired a great deal of tenderness in me. I wanted to take her flighty hands in my own and tell her she had no reason to feel uncomfortable, but not yet...not yet. After a while she stopped her nervous blathering about work and other trivialities and gave me a pointed look.

"So what's on your mind, eh? I've never seen you so...quiet," she said, assuming the listening position.

"Oh," I fumbled. "Um, well, it's nothing really..."

"Uh-huh..." she said, not so easily dissuaded.

She had me cornered. Damn my wandering mind. I couldn't tell her the truth. She knew about my "alternative sexuality," and it had never bothered her in the slightest, but telling her I was attracted to her—perhaps in love with her—would definitely push the limits of our friendship. She was not, to my knowledge, attracted to women. Still, a few of her comments had, on occasion, given me cause to wonder. I decided to play it safe.

"*Oy*...Well, it's just something silly I've done. I'm a little embarrassed to talk about it," I answered, shamefaced.

"Oh, good...something juicy. Go on."

"Thanks for taking such pleasure in my misfortune," I snickered.

"Anytime," she said with a mischievous grin.

"Well, it seems I've gone and fallen in love with an impossibility."

"An impossibility? How so?" she asked, leaning forward in her chair.

Funny, I thought, *how comfortable she is on the other end of the firing line.* Her body language had changed entirely. She gazed intently at me, and her fingers lay docile on the tabletop.

"Um...an impossibility because she's straight," I said meekly.

"Uh-oh," she said, smiling comfortingly at me. "I thought you'd decided that your rejection-junkie days were over."

"I thought so too, but this one is special," I grinned. "I've never met anyone quite like her...and besides, she's entirely too old for me, heterosexual, and not even remotely interested. It's perfect."

She laughed quietly and shook her head. "Well, how do you know that she's not interested? Have you ever told her how you feel?"

"Uh...no, I haven't. I'm not sure how she'd take it, and I'm not sure that I'm willing to chance the friendship."

"Well, does she know you're gay?" she asked.

"Yeah, she knows. And it's never bothered her...as far as I know," I said, faltering on that last bit.

"Well then?" she replied, as if that removed any and all doubt what I should do, and I was silly for not seeing it.

"Well then, what?" I asked, slightly agitated.

"Well, you're a beautiful girl. You're intelligent, funny, kind. If this woman knows you well enough to see all that, she'd be foolish to turn you away without at least giving it a chance."

I sat in silent shock. This was a far different response than I had expected, and although I was pleased, I was also confused. I decided to press a little further.

"Well, there's still the whole penis issue..."

"Penis issue?" she asked, furrowing her brows.

"Yeah...my lack thereof," I giggled.

"Well, there's that," she said. "I can't tell you what your friend will say, but I know that, for me, love is a matter of personality, not physicality."

"That's admirable," I offered, "but unrealistic. Sexuality is innate. Everyone questions themselves once in awhile — even I have had occasional attractions to guys — but those questions rarely express themselves in any more than fleeting thought. I don't believe you would really cross the line from thought into action."

"I've never been in that situation, so I can't say for sure what I would do," she voiced, "but if I knew her well and enjoyed her company, I might give it a chance. And frankly, I'd be offended if someone cared for me and never told me."

My stomach dropped to my feet. I couldn't say a word. I simply sat there, white-knuckling my coffee cup and trying to will my heartbeat into submission. I knew if I was ever going to tell her, the time was now, but I was petrified.

"We should probably go. They look like they're about to close up shop," she said, gathering her jacket and bag.

"Huh? Oh…yeah," I stammered.

My mind was racing. *Can I do this? And what if I don't? Can I let this moment pass and not torment myself forever with regret and what ifs?* This was the moment I had hoped for since I had met her. Faced with this moment, I was shocked to immobility. A sudden wave of self-reproach washed away my cowardice and pushed me into action.

"Wait!" I blurted…probably a bit too loudly. She jumped a bit and sat down again. "Yes?" she said, confusion obvious on her face. "I, uh…shit." I stuttered, trying to calm my nerves enough to speak coherently. I gripped my mug with fierce determination and began again. "It's you," I mumbled, staring into the now syrupy liquid inside the cup.

"It's me, what?" she asked, obviously determined to make this as difficult as she could.

"It's you…the impossibility, I mean. Ugh, damn it. Never mind. Let's go." I said hurriedly, reaching for my wallet.

"Hey…" she said softly, steadying my hand with her own.

I looked up at her, seeing myself through her eyes as a frightened young girl with a pained and humiliated expression. Her own face wore a combination of compassion and confusion, and her hand remained on mine for what felt like eternity.

"You mean, I am the woman you were speaking of tonight?" she asked, as if she were both accepting and questioning simultaneously.

I sighed deeply and nodded my head. "It's OK. I know don't feel the same way, but your answers made me hope. It was foolish of me. I'm sorry if this is awkward. I didn't mean for it to be."

She was painfully silent, and I grew steadily more uncomfortable with each second. The lights flickered in the coffeehouse as a man announced it was closing time. I looked at her and rose from my seat.

"We should go," I said. "If you'd like, I can just catch a taxi back to my car."

"No. It's all right. I'd like to take you if you don't mind."

I nodded, and we made for the door. The silence hovered above us like the thickest fog as we walked to the car. My courage was waning, but I gathered up the last of it and asked, "What are you thinking?"

"Oh, a million things," she answered softly. "Mostly, I am astounded...and flattered."

"*Oy*," I said in exasperation. "Flattered...that's the pre-relationship equivalent of 'It's not you, it's me.'" I chuckled despite the discomfort.

She stopped walking and turned to me, her expression gravely serious.

"No...It's not, and you didn't let me finish. I...well, Jesus. What could you possibly see in me? I could almost be your mother! I'm graying, wrinkling, damn near sagging. I'm a frumpy middle-aged woman who just doesn't understand kids these days...and you think you love me?"

Her hands were planted firmly on her hips in an almost reprimanding pose.

"No, I don't *think* I love you. I love you." I answered meekly. "And what I see in you is...You just make me smile more than anyone. You are so beautiful to me, so beautiful even with the gray...maybe because of it. I don't know. All I know is I feel something when I'm with you that makes me happier than I've been in a long time."

I stopped the flood of words with a snap of my jaws— shocked and humiliated by my own revelations. Reluctantly, I raised my head to look at her.

"No one has ever said anything like that to me before," she said softly. "Never."

"I'm sorry if I made you uncomfortable or if I've ruined our friendship."

"Don't apologize," she said, looking directly into my eyes. "Just come home with me."

My knees almost gave out.

"I...uh...I mean...you're not..." I was a stammering fool and I knew it, but my shock was far more powerful than the little voice telling me to hush. She silenced me with a look so intensely loving I could do nothing but pull her into my arms and cling to her for dear life. I breathed in her scent and grew dizzy from the reality of it all.

This was happening. I was holding the woman I had loved for so long.

I buried my face in her neck and took great breaths of her. Her arms tightened around me, and I heard her whimper softly, the air escaping her lips and brushing against my neck, making every inch of me tingle with a passion so immense could only hold her tighter and pray I wouldn't faint. "Take me home," I whispered, and then I leaned in slowly, and placed that first, frightened kiss upon her lips. She tasted sweeter than I had ever imagined.

"We don't have to do this right now, you know," I whispered, shaking.

"I know, I know," she answered, "but I want to. I'm just scared. I've thought about it before...about being with you. I never thought I'd be attracted to a woman, but you...there's just something special in you that I long for...that I love."

"Thank you," I whispered, near tears and leaning in for the second kiss.

Her lips were so soft, so warm. My hands stroked her face as she opened for me, inviting my tongue to join hers in a dance so sweet and sensual that my entire body trembled with excitement. Somehow we got to the house. I don't remember how. I only remember the first moment I lay with her, feeling her warmth beneath me, looking down into her eyes and seeing her sweet passion for me burning there. "I don't know what to do," she whispered in a soft and frightened tone.

"S-h-h-h," I whispered, smiling gently at her. "It's OK. Just let me make love to you." I covered her forehead, her cheeks, eyelids, nose, and lips with feathery kisses, breathing my desire gently into her ear. Her arms encircled me as my tongue traced a path of wetness to the tender junction of her neck and shoulder. Her flesh gave rise to thousands of tiny goose bumps as she moaned softly into my ear.

Tearing myself away from her, I gently lowered myself to a kneeling position on the floor, pulling her up and to the edge of the bed. Sliding myself between her legs, I kissed her deeply, our tongues writhing in wetness and heat, as I slowly released the buttons of her dress. She was so beautiful; her skin was golden, and her perfume, mixing with her own warm scent, filled me with an overwhelming tenderness.

I continued my trail of kisses to the soft and supple flesh encased in the silken fabric of her bra. With my teeth barely exposed, I teased the rising outline of her nipples through the fabric. She moaned deeply, her fingers tangling in my hair as

I slid my fingernails slowly up her back and released the clasp. Her breasts were so soft, nipples small and the color of roses. I took her into my mouth, rolling her across my tongue, gentle at first and then growing bolder as her sweet exclamations of pleasure increased. I felt the warmth of her sex as she pressed herself against my stomach, and the fire within me rose to almost intolerable levels.

Rising slowly, I pressed her back against the bed and crawled in, kissing her once, twice, a thousand times as I slid her dress away. I moved my hand slowly down her body, cupping her breast, running my thumb across her nipple...down the firm lines of her stomach, her side...the gentle curve of her hip...the silky flesh of her leg. Her breathing grew ragged, and her nails dug into my back. I gently cupped my hand around her sex, feeling the heat and moisture rise beneath the fabric. She let out a slow, guttural moan and raised her hips, pressing herself against my palm.

Hooking my fingers beneath the elastic, I pulled her panties away from her body and slowly slid my own dress up my body to reveal the flesh of my leg. Sliding my knee between her thighs and pressing gently against her sex, I felt her wetness and warmth against my skin.

I was indescribably inflamed.

I slid slowly down her body. My knee, then upper thigh, glided through her wetness as I dropped again to the floor. My lover spread herself wide to welcome me as I licked and nibbled my way up the velvet and musky-scented skin of her thighs, drawing closer to her sex. She smelled so sweet, so sensual. I was reborn, and she was my first breath. I raised one hand to find hers and held it tightly, her own hand squeezing mine in both fear and passion...and then I found her with my tongue. Her body stiffened, and she cried out in shock and arousal.

Slowly at first, I moved my tongue gently up and down in wide, soft motions. She tasted of forever. Her body trembled, and her moans were slow and languid. Her grip on my hand relaxed slightly as I showed her the gentle flame of a building passion. It was as if I could see the fire building in her body, spreading up into her stomach, down into her legs...and then I slid inside her. Her moan was almost primal, and I felt her muscles tighten around the fingers that filled her, as her hand tightened around the fingers that held her. My thrusts were slow, deep, and powerful and my tongue flickered across her core in a fervent and quickening pace. She was writhing beneath me, and her moans began forming my name and calling it more and more loudly with less and less breath. Her muscles squeezed tightly against my fingers, and her core strained against my tongue and, for a moment, she was simply still...and then the flood began.

I kept my tongue pressed firmly in place. My fingers locked in position until the last spasm subsided, and then I slowly took my fill of her nectar in gentle, soothing strokes. Sated, I rose and took my place beside her. Enfolding her in my arms, I gave her a long, slow kiss. There were tears in our eyes as I smiled and whispered her name for the first time — as her lover.

CHAPTER SEVENTEEN
Adjustments
Stephanie Mahone

When the phone rings at 6 p.m. at my chiropractic clinic, I pick it up myself. My last client has just departed, and as I glance at the clock, my body tingles. In 45 minutes you will be here. But when I hear your voice on the phone, distressed and full of tears, my heartbeat pounds suddenly in my ears. "I missed the ferry," you say.

I let out a breath. "It's OK," I assure you. "I was just trying to figure out how I was going to do payroll *and* the bills before you got here."

"But by the time I do get there, I'll practically have to turn around and come home." Your voice sounds so fragile, like a cracked glass that's just about to break apart.

"Have you eaten?"

Silence.

"Promise me you'll get something to eat before the next ferry."

"This is Kingston. There's nothing here."

"Then eat on the ferry, OK?" I pause, knowing you aren't complaining as much as you are asking me to reassure you that I still want to see you, that I still want you to make the 30-minute crossing and the 20-minute drive from the docks after you have already driven from Port Townsend. Even though you are only across the Puget Sound, it seems like several states away. We have maintained our friendship this way for just over a year, seeing each other once or twice a month, each trying to give the other what she needs—time to heal and time to think. Finally I add, "I promise when you get here I'll give you something sweet to put in your mouth." As soon as I say the words,

I panic. We have never made love, never done more than kiss. With these words I have opened a door I cannot close.

You groan, deep in your throat, and I feel my body constrict and open at the same time. My panic lessens as your breath rasps across the receiver.

"Steph."

"Get here soon," I say.

By the time you arrive shortly after 8 o'clock, I have pushed one of the manual adjusting tables up against the far wall and am straddling it, facing the 12-foot windows that overlook the parking lot. The office is dark except for the streetlight shining in and the one light over my desk that I leave on to tell you I am still here.

The pickup's headlights sweep across the parking lot, illuminating me briefly, and then a moment later you let yourself in, lock the door behind you, and walk to the table. I watch you move toward me with a fluid athletic grace I've admired since the first day you walked into my office, some 18 months ago. Your broad shoulders squared and determined, your expression open and friendly, your dark hair wild about your face. It touches the back of your collar now, but it is still wild, giving you a kind of rakish look that comes from continually running your hands through your hair. You say it calms you. I agree. It would calm me to touch it too. But everything about you calms me and calls to a deep place inside me I never even knew existed before.

I was attracted to you from the first, a deep physical longing that surprised me and created enormous inner turmoil. Even though my marriage made me miserable, I believed in the vow I had taken. I had promised to be faithful to him.

You sit down facing me. "I'm sorry. The whole night is ruined. Everything's closed, and we'll have to go to some bar where we won't be able to talk—"

I take your face in my hands and brush my thumbs across your lips. "Shh." I lean forward and kiss you. Your mouth is soft and sweet against mine, and I remember the first time I kissed you under the mistletoe at my house on Christmas day. It was two weeks after your partner of four years had been injured in a car accident, two weeks after they'd put her on life support, and 4½ months before you finally signed the papers to let them turn the machines off. I don't know why I kissed you then. I was trying to comfort you, trying to tell you I loved you and that no matter what happened I would stay by your side.

That morning you just stared at me, hurt and confused. You started to cry, and before I could explain, you fled my house for the sterile wing of the intensive care unit. During the next five months, you forbade me to accompany you to the hospital. But I went on my own, telling the nurses I was your partner's older sister—there was a resemblance—and I'd sit there for two, three, four hours, talking to her and begging her to return. Yes, I wanted you. But more than that, I wanted you to be happy. If I could have bargained with the cosmos—to give up a relationship with you to keep her alive—I would have. But the cosmos wanted her. And so you let her go.

It's a year after that April morning, and just a week ago you turned to me and said, "Do that again," and I knew somehow you were asking me to kiss you; you were finally coming out of the long dark tunnel that has been your life for the past year. And now it's my turn to decide what I will do.

You press into me, your mouth hungry, and I slide my hand between us to unbutton my shirt. You pull back as I unfasten my bra. Your eyes close, and you breathe out. Your mouth engulfs me, and I cry out at the unexpected pleasure of this touch. First one breast, then the other, and still your hands are on my body, your fingers like fire on my skin, and suddenly I know what I want. So I lift your face to mine, draw you up from the bench and into the back room where there is a small bed on which I have spent many nights away from my husband, lying in the dark and trying to figure out what to do.

I know you expect me to say I want to you to make love to me slowly and gently because that's who you are—every part of you is careful, thoughtful, cautious. But that isn't what I want, and I say instead, "I want you to fuck me. I want you to burn away the memory of every touch except yours."

Your pupils dilate, and our fingers fumble at the button to my slacks, which, in our haste, pops off, bounces on the linoleum, and rolls into a corner of the room. You are drinking in the sight of me with your eyes and your hands, and then you press me down on the bed, slide down my body with your mouth, and in an instant I am consumed with the most intense, exquisite feeling I have ever known. My thighs fall open, my fingers are tangled in your hair, and I rock against your mouth, knowing a woman's touch for the first time.

When I was 17 a handsome young man I was infatuated with crept into my tent one night during a camping trip I had taken with several friends. Without speaking, he unzipped my sleeping bag, lifted my nightgown over my head, ran his hands briefly over my breasts, and pushed into me. Fifteen minutes later he was gone.

Now, at 32, I am truly losing my virginity, losing myself to another, giving myself to a woman I've loved, admired, and waited for. A woman I have stood beside while she shook the hands of grieving friends, a woman who found me sleeping in my car in her driveway when she returned from the last day at the hospital. You didn't seem surprised to find me at your house, but when I looked into your eyes, you weren't there. And every time I have seen you for the past year, I have looked into your eyes to see whether or not you had returned.

It is only recently someone has looked back.

Your mouth is insistent, and I feel myself tensing. Desire has eclipsed everything. I am dimly aware of my voice calling your name, and then I come for you hard, my body arching and thrashing in your arms. Your face is beside mine before I am fully aware of time passing. I kiss you.

"So this is what I taste like," I say.

You murmur, content.

After a few minutes, your eyes flutter open and you look directly at me. You know I have wanted your touch. But we have never talked about how much I wanted to touch you. Only recently have I realized this and come to understand that once I took you to my bed, I would never return to my husband's.

You know I have made my decision when I shift on the narrow bed and slide on top of you and then down.

You lift your hips so I can pull your jeans away from your skin, and as you move under my hands, the most delicious scent rises into my face, basking me in warmth and heat. When my tongue finds you, you are already hard and open, and I delight in the sensation of you—silky, smooth, hard, soft, everything at once it seems—against my mouth. I take you gently. Slowly. A slow burn.

Tonight, time means nothing. Tonight, I know I cannot turn back. Nor do I want to.

Two weeks later I filed for divorce. The papers were delivered by mail. It was messy and ugly in a predictable way. But I didn't care. I wanted only my clothes and the photograph albums from my childhood. Everything else was simply an artifact from a time in my life before you, expendable as a broken pottery shard from an unnamed excavation. I walked away from those ruins into your arms. I never looked back. I never will.

CHAPTER EIGHTEEN
The Image in the Photograph
Bleau Diamond

*T*erese was my first. We met during my senior year at high school in the fall of 1979. It might have been love at first sight—or lust at first touch. She was tall—statuesque tall—with the longest blond hair you'd ever want to run your hands through. All of her was tall. When I first saw her, she was running from somewhere. She was on the track team. I was walking briskly to photography class. I quickly tried to get my camera out of its case to snap her picture, but she ran right by me with a smile across her face. Later that day I saw her in class and felt relieved knowing we had both English and business together. We sat by one another, traded jokes and homework assignments, and over time began to depend on one another. She was living with another woman and was "out" as a lesbian at school. I had a crush on a straight woman who lived in another state. Curious, I had spent my junior year of high school back East fantasizing about a woman who was not only straight but also pregnant. I knew hanging around with Terese would tag me as a lesbian, but I didn't care. Terese was getting laid—I knew it—and I was jealous.

During the first week of classes together I knew she was "the one"—bright and strong enough to handle the emotions we were about to face. Once I really looked at her—her mind, her soul, her runner's body—I knew she could conquer me, could make me brave enough to come out of the closet. I wanted to know what it felt like to be with a woman sexually. At 18, I was still a virgin.

She drove a '68 Mustang. *What a cool car she drives,* I thought. Since I was taking a photography class, I easily persuaded Terese to be my model. I took pictures of her and her car, but mostly her.

Taking pictures of her gave me a freedom and a liberty to stare at her, to be with her, to look into her eyes, to look at her breasts, her long legs, her fingers I imagined felt smooth. I could stare at Terese forever, biding time by telling her I was adjusting the f-stops or the focus. She was patient. I wondered what it felt like to be the subject in front of my lens. I wondered if she knew I was falling in love with her.

I never felt guilty for looking at her or for taking so long to get a roll of film shot. No, she was like candy to the eyes. I needed her—and I needed my fantasy. Mostly I needed to get over my feelings for the straight girl who never returned my affection.

Terese and other girl musicians came over frequently for jam sessions in my bedroom. There were about five of us at school who hung out together. We met at my house, played guitar, and wrote songs about being young and dealing with our sexuality. Some of the songs were about being gay, some about being straight, and some about being bisexual.

One night Terese came over by herself. We were going to develop the roll of black-and-white film I had taken of her at the park. She told me she was interested in seeing the developing process. "Us or the pictures?" I thought.

I did the usual routine with my dad and stepmother: "I am not to be disturbed because I am developing highly sensitive material." Little did they know how sensitive! I taped my hand-made "Do Not Disturb—Darkroom In Process" sign on my bedroom door and locked the door behind me. With the door closed, I was in my own dark paradise.

Terese sat on my twin bed and picked up my guitar, feeling for the strings in the darkness of the room. She cleared her throat and began to softly sing. I turned on the red developing light, which gave the room a seductive hue. I set up the three trays I needed to print her photographs: the developer, the stop bath, and the fixer. I was excited and brimming with anticipation, waiting to see if the reflection captured on the paper would be as beautiful as the image I was accustomed to seeing every day at school.

As the first picture of Terese developed, I pulled it up by the wooden tongs and said, "It looks great!" She mumbled something and continued to sing a song that was unfamiliar.

"What are you singing?" I asked.

"A song I wrote for you," she responded without skipping a chord.

My heart started racing. My hands started to shake, and I dropped the tongs into a tray of solution.

"What's the song about?" I uttered.

"You...and me. Actually it's about us."

"Oh." I couldn't say anything else.

I placed the next picture of her up to dry on the clothesline cord that ran from one end of my room to the other. The line was strategically placed so that the pretty girl in the poster of the girl band the Runaways appeared to be holding my cord rather than her guitar. Terese continued singing. All I remember now is it seemed sad. Her song didn't seem like a celebration of life, but rather a love song for love gone unnoticed, unreciprocated.

I pulled up a picture and exclaimed, "This one is my favorite!" It was a picture of Terese sitting on the trunk of her Mustang. She looked butch with her flannel shirt and boots, and yet femme with her long hair flowing all the way down her back, right down to her belt.

In another picture Terese's long blond hair rested to the side of her face and flowed down her chest. I wondered what it would be like to be entangled in her hair. I thought, *If I develop one more picture, I am going to pass out.*

My breathing was irregular. Her singing and strumming in the background stopped. She came up behind me, and I froze. "I just wanted to see a professional at work," she said, as her voice cracked a little. "Oh, I'm no pro, Terese. I have a lot to learn," I responded nervously.

Maybe my raw talent was seducing her. Maybe her ego was lifted by someone wanting to take her picture, someone who cared enough about her to make a lasting imprint.

"You look good. Um, I mean your work looks good," she explained, pointing to the developing pictures.

"Thanks. I liked your song too," I said.

Scared to turn around and face her, I looked down. I pointed my gaze toward the image developing in the tray.

As she reached up to grasp one of the dangling pictures, she lightly touched my hair. "You smell good," she said softly. I didn't respond. "I want to kiss you," she stated with a gush of emotions that made her voice rise and fall. She was both nervous and excited. I should have expected that our flirting would lead to this, but I was actually caught off-guard.

"No, that's not a good idea," I answered with a hint of confusion.

But Terese was persistent, and as I turned around she leaned into me and we kissed. It was passionate, stimulating, soft. Her tongue was the softest I have ever felt in my mouth.

"She kissed me!" I exclaimed to myself.

Her mouth: so exciting, so new. She kissed me again and pulled me onto the squeaky bed. I threw my stuffed animals to the floor. Having someone in my bed was a strange sensation. For 18 years I turned to my stuffed animals for comfort. Now I had someone to hold me, to touch me. I was trembling.

She was aggressive, although I am sure she had to be. I had never been with another woman and knew nothing about how to please one. I knew I liked her, and I knew she aroused me. My hormones were stormy and alive.

She kissed me and unbuttoned my shirt and my jeans and reached inside. I didn't know if I was supposed to reciprocate or just feel it. I didn't think I could concentrate on doing both, so I just relaxed and enjoyed myself. She made the bed squeak each time she thrust her thigh into the crease in my jeans where my clit began to harden. I don't remember who pulled off my jeans. I do remember how she balanced her body and weight upon me, how she wrapped her legs around me, how she leaned up with her hand protruding from her and into me as if she were inside me. She thrust the weight of her body into me. With hand, fingers, and thumb, she rode me like a wild stallion, thrashing and bucking. I clutched patches of her long hair as if they were horse reins and pulled her into me and my wet pussy.

My cherry broke and blood squished out and down my leg. *I was devirginized by a woman,* I thought. I never thought it would happen that way. Me, a virgin, and another woman takes it away. It seemed so pure, so goddesslike.

We were both embarrassed, but it didn't stop us. I didn't want to stay on the sheets. Now that I was no longer a virgin, I wanted to move on to discover my sexual maturity. So I wiped myself, and we retired to the floor. I pulled the NFL blanket and pillows from my bed, and we lay on top. This time I straddled her, trying to model her moves, but mine were a little different. She had a natural lovemaking style, while mine was more uneven. It was my first time, so I was nervous, and I kept trying not to concentrate on the pictures I left in the developing solution—becoming as overexposed as I was, as full of liquid as I was.

What I remember most was slippery, hot, passionate kisses. Terese drew me in deeper. She ran her hands across my body and lifted my soul into her own in the ecstasy of the blanket. She was my soul mate. She was the one, and I needed her to feel alive. I felt more self-confident with her loving me; she made me feel special, important, and beautiful. Her love seemed to wipe away all the bad memories and experiences of my coming-out as a lesbian at school. Lying there in her arms and allowing her to please me made me feel content, but still vulnerable. *How can I ever survive without her?* I was in heaven. *Where can I ever find these feelings again?* We lay there for several hours. I had found a new dependence on her.

Terese left her lover, and we lived together right after graduating from high school. We stayed together as lovers for more than two years and then broke up, going our separate ways. She was a great lover—giving, passionate, and nurturing. I had lost my innocence and my youth with her.

That was almost 20 years ago. Today, we are still friends. She is a part of my history. She knows me, and it feels good to be with someone who knows me. The history she and I experienced remains an imprint in my heart and in my soul. When my mind needs reassurance that true love really can be true, I look at the image in the photographs. Her beauty is captured forever in black and white.

CHAPTER NINETEEN
Away From Home
Ashley Robbins

I couldn't help noticing the way Jaime tossed and turned in her sleep. We were sharing a dorm room at an out-of-state university. The two of us had been invited to tour the campus. Our parents had been reluctant to let us travel alone, even though we were both 18 and would be leaving home soon. But we had convinced them this was a necessary part of growing up.

A fluorescent light from outside poured through a crack between the heavy beige drapes and lit the room. I looked toward Jaime. She had pushed her covers off, and her baby-doll nightgown was twisted around her slender body. One of her round breasts peaked seductively from beneath the blue nylon fabric. The nipple was hard and pointed in my direction. I imagined what it might be like to caress her smooth, pale skin and to tug on the stiff, pebble-like bud.

There was a familiar tingle between my thighs I could not ignore. I reached down and caressed my own smaller, firmer breasts. I squeezed and pinched the pink nubs with one hand, while the other trailed down my flat belly to the throbbing area between my thighs. I pushed my finger down my wet, slippery slit, teasing and tantalizing my hot sex. I couldn't suppress a low moan when I pushed a finger into my warm, slick, virgin pussy.

I had never had sex, never even got past first base with any of the boys I had dated in high school. I was uncomfortable with their urgent needs, their demanding attitudes. The thought of their hard bodies, consumed by animal lust, was frightening. I didn't want to be possessed, deflowered by some boy who would just move on to his next conquest.

I knew Jaime was different. Her soft, fleshy breasts had felt Aaron's touch. She had told me so, the morning after it had happened. I envied him; he was free to explore her hot, sexy body. His fingers had explored her most private parts— teasing and tantalizing her until she was nearly ready to surrender herself to him. At night, alone in my bed, I fantasized about her. I wanted to run my fingers through her long, dark hair, to bring her body to the brink of ecstasy.

My breathing was loud and ragged in the silence of our room. I rubbed my throbbing clit, pretending it was her fingers bringing me closer and closer to a powerful climax. My body was on fire. I imagined how it would feel to be naked with her, to have her pale, soft skin pressed against my own. She would smell like baby powder, like she always did—soft, feminine, and innocent. I could almost taste her kiss as I lay there alone.

When she moaned and rolled onto her back, her legs spread wide, I could no longer contain my desperate desire. I gathered my courage, rolled off my bed, and crept toward her in the near darkness. I kneeled down on the floor and pushed her nightgown up, exposing those luscious breasts. I let my fingertips brush across her nipples. She moaned again and thrust her breasts upward, seeming to seek out my touch in her sleep.

I lowered my lips and captured a swollen bud. My tongue flicked against her tender flesh. Then I closed my teeth, letting them scrape against the captive. She squirmed and thrashed, tilting her head back as her body arched off the mattress. I sucked slowly, gently, wanting her to experience each tiny sensation.

My hand moved between her thighs, my fingertips pushing through the dark curls that covered her swollen sex. The throbbing between my own thighs was becoming nearly unbearable. I ached for her touch, wished she was caressing my body.

I was becoming more daring, bolder with each passing second. I released her stiff nipple from my moist, warm mouth. I rose from the floor, leaning over her and admiring her perfect features. She was so beautiful as she lay sleeping that I could no longer contain my yearning. I pressed my lips to hers, softly at first, then with more urgency.

As I kissed her, her eyes opened. She seemed startled and turned her head away. But she didn't protest. Although I felt her body stiffen, she didn't resist as I slipped off my nightgown and lay on top of her. The feel of her warm, silky skin against mine was more exquisite than I had imagined.

Once again I kissed her lips. This time she kissed me back, parting her lips slightly so my tongue could slip into her mouth. She thrust her hips upward, grinding her body against mine and making her needs known. I had not expected her to be an active participant in my fantasy come true, but she was.

She wrapped her arms around me. She caressed my back, rubbing gently, then let her hands slide lower until she was holding my fleshy ass cheeks in her palms. She tugged the two creamy cheeks apart, causing erotic shock waves to shoot through me.

I was becoming more and more aroused as she let her fingertips explore my moist crack.

My lips blazed a trail down her neck, once again seeking out her large pink nipples. I repeatedly drew the hardened nubs into my mouth, teasing and tantalizing her heated flesh. She was slowly surrendering herself to me. Her muscles had relaxed, and she was obviously enjoying the erotic contact.

I ran my tongue downward, certain she would allow me to treat her body to the forbidden pleasure I had fantasized about so many times. I crawled between her parted thighs, using my fingers to separate her swollen pussy lips. Her horny clit protruded like a tiny penis, throbbing and hungry for attention.

My heart pounded in my chest as I lowered my lips. Although I had imagined this moment many times, I had never actually done it. I hesitated, then planted a soft kiss on her quivering flesh. I let my tongue slide lightly, carefully down one side of her slit, then let it flick around the rim of her tight chamber.

"Oh, that feels so good," she groaned.

With that encouragement, I pushed my tongue inward so it was engulfed by the heat of her body. I nuzzled her pulsating clit, kissing and licking and sucking until she was moaning and thrashing. She rested her hand on the back of my head, guiding my efforts as I guessed Aaron must have done to her.

I used one hand to pinch and tweak her right nipple while the fingers of my other slipped into her warm, wet chamber. Her body stiffened, every muscle contracting. She shuddered uncontrollably, and a low, guttural moan escaped from deep down inside her. But I was unrelenting. I didn't stop kissing and sucking on her sensitive clit. I just slowed my pace, making each contact light and deliberate. I wanted her to come again and again. Her body had responded to me in ways I had only dreamed about. I didn't want this special moment to end.

She didn't push me away; she just lay there allowing me to coax her body to a second climax. Each moan of satisfaction fueled my desperate hunger. The heat spread slowly from between her thighs, then her body convulsed. Once again I shifted my pace and position of attack. This time I let my tongue press lightly against her throbbing clit, then slithered into her creamy slit. Slowly, methodically, I again brought her to the brink of ecstasy. "No more," she pleaded, squirming beneath me.

I looked up at her beautiful face. She gazed at me, obviously exhausted, and smiled. I lay down beside her, my body still on fire with my own unsatisfied yearnings. I wanted desperately for her to bury her face between my thighs to feel her lips on my quivering flesh, but I knew she would not reciprocate.

I spread my legs and let my fingers creep down to the wet, throbbing area between my thighs, knowing I would have to be satisfied with a little self-stimulation...but at least she was there with me. I was shocked when she rolled over onto her side and let her hand lightly stroke my hardened nipples. She pinched and tweaked them before drawing one into her mouth. I moaned as her teeth scraped the tender flesh.

Her fingers probed my slit knowingly, spreading my swollen pussy lips and seeking out my own horny clit. She stroked the sensitive tissue while her mouth continued to pleasure my nipple. I came in one sudden, overpowering burst. My body trembled. I gasped for air, then relaxed back onto the bed.

"That was so good," I whispered, turning to face her.

Our lips met once again, for one brief, fleeting kiss. Then she turned away.

"I know. No one's ever done that for me before."

I smiled to myself, satisfied I had given her something Aaron had not.

We drifted off to sleep together, our bodies entwined and

our souls momentarily joined.

She was just returning from the shower, her sexy body covered only by a skimpy towel, when I awoke. I lay there, watching her as she let it fall to the floor. She set out a pair of pink panties and a matching bra, then searched her suitcase for jeans and a sweater. I was glad she still felt comfortable dressing in front of me. Last night had not seemed to alter our friendship.

"You better get up," she called. "We've got that meeting this morning."

I rolled out of bed, still stark naked. I approached her, letting our bodies touch intimately as I wrapped my arms around her waist. Her body tensed as I kissed her neck. "Not now," she snapped, pulling away from me. I was hurt by her sudden rejection, and tears formed in my eyes. I turned away and began to search through my own suitcase.

"Last night was really different," she said softly. "I had never even thought about what it might be like, you know, with another woman." I wiped away the tears as I listened to her.

"It really felt good, and I'd be lying if I said I didn't enjoy it." She pulled on her jeans and sweater as she spoke. "But it was a one-time thing. I love Aaron, and I can't cheat on him like that again." There was a knock on the door. I grabbed a robe while she went to answer it.

"Who is it?" she called.

"It's me, Aaron. Open up."

She threw open the door and wrapped her arms around his neck. "What are you doing here?"

"I knew you'd be coming home today. I really missed you, so I thought I'd drive up and give you a ride home. Save you the long, boring bus ride."

"We've got one more meeting this morning."

"Can't you skip it?" he pleaded.

She looked at me, then back to him.

"Sure, why not?" she replied. "Come on, Ashley. Let's get packed and get out of here."

She tossed her clothes into the suitcase. I stood motionless, understanding that despite last night Jaime belonged to Aaron. He was the one she loved, the one she fantasized about when she was lying in bed alone. It was his touch she hungered for.

"Aren't you coming?" she asked, suddenly aware I was not packing.

"No. I think I'll stay for the meeting and then take the bus home. But you go ahead, and I'll fill you in later."

She took my hand and looked into my eyes. An unspoken understanding passed between us and she smiled.

"I'll see you tomorrow," she called as she and Aaron left the room, hand in hand.

I stood alone for a while, not moving. The realization of what had happened began to slowly sink in. This trip had been educational in more ways than one. I had finally come to terms with my own sexuality and as a bonus had lived out my fantasy with Jaime. I would no longer try to deceive myself, and there would be no need to lie to my best friend. She knew and understood.

CHAPTER TWENTY
Cathy
by Jody Ekert

I was 19 and miserable. I had been questioning my sexuality for about a year, but I still hadn't found an identity I was comfortable with. I thought I liked women, but I had no experience with them. I was pretty sure I liked them sexually, but I still didn't know how I felt about men. After a number of disastrous experiences with various men, I decided the only way for me to decide was to sleep with a woman and compare my feelings. I was sure this would settle the question. Then I would live happily ever after. It wasn't quite a easy as that—but then I had never expected to find Cathy.

I was at a gay nightclub having a big night out with a friend, when I first saw Cathy. I was really drunk, and I couldn't keep my eyes off her. She was gorgeous in a very feminine way—dancing in a little black dress and heels. She was slim, with short black curly hair and chocolate-colored eyes. I had been going to this particular club for months in hopes of finding a woman to sleep with—or at least kiss—to prove to myself I was gay or bisexual. I'd never really had any success. My desire was cruel. I didn't want emotions or talk. I just wanted to have sex to finally solve my identity crisis. Looking back, I see several women were interested enough to make a move on me, but I had been too naive to realize what was happening. But not this time.

It wasn't love at first sight; it was uncontrollable lust. I tried to keep my gaze off her. She was dancing with another woman, and the last thing I wanted was to create a scene in the middle of the dance floor...but she was looking back. I thought I was imagining it, so I glanced again, then quickly turned my eyes away. It was real. She was definitely looking at me. I didn't know what to do. I thought maybe I should pretend it wasn't happening. *What if her dance partner is her girlfriend?* I thought. She looked pretty big. She could probably do some real physical damage!

Cathy must have said something to the woman. They swapped places on the dance floor. She was dancing only meters away from me now. Slowly she moved closer. My heart was racing. She danced closer until she was next to me. I turned around and soon we were dancing together. My hands were on her body as we moved to the music. I was seized by the desire to kiss her...so I did. After a brief hesitation, she responded. My mind reeled. I was kissing a girl! I didn't know what to do next. This was about as far as my fantasies had taken me. It was up to her to make the next move—and she did. She grabbed me by the hand and led me from the dance floor. We went outside, away from the thumping music. She introduced herself and told me she was 25. Now I was really surprised. I thought she was around my age—19 or 20. She asked me if our age difference was a problem. When I shook my head, she gave me an invitation I couldn't resist: to meet her at the nightclub next week. I agreed without a second thought. Just like that, and then she was gone.

The next week was torture. It took six of my friends to persuade me to meet her again, and they all came with me. She was there, just as she said, and I noticed she also had a large number of friends with her. We spent a couple of hours awkwardly talking, and I tried to show her I was interested. It was by no means easy since my younger sister was present and had no idea what was happening. Nevertheless, we exchanged phone numbers. The evening ended—not a complete disaster, but not a resounding success either.

We organized a date, and then the nerves really set in. By then the "Am I gay?" fears had turned into worries about sex—even kissing was a issue for me. I was going to the movies with a girl who seemed to like me, and there would be no alcohol to make the process easier! I didn't eat for a week. When the night arrived I could barely function. Somehow I survived the pre-movie coffee conversation. We found ourselves in a nearly empty cinema, and I started to sweat.

I could feel her body next to mine. Our arms touched slightly. I could hear her breathing. I glanced sideways. She was wearing red lipstick (flawlessly applied), perfume, and a leather jacket. I squirmed in my seat, trying to focus on the movie. *Should I make a move? Should I let her make a move? How can I do it subtly?* Our hands inched closer until eventually I lifted mine and placed it on top of hers. Her hand felt cool and reassuring. For the remainder of the movie, our hands remained intertwined. After the movie Cathy offered to drive me home. I considered what to do when we arrived back at my place. *Invite her up for coffee? Kiss her?*

I decided to kiss her good night. A big mistake. I leaned across the car, and somehow the kiss just didn't work. Our lips didn't connect properly, and I fumbled. I was so embarrassed I got out of the car without looking back. I was heartbroken.

Nothing could have surprised me more than when Cathy called the next day. She asked me on another date. And then another. And another. Over the next three weeks, our dates became more and more intense until one day she asked me to her house to help her with her computer. I knew she had the place to herself and that she had even bought some alcohol. I was nervous. *Could this be the moment I've been worrying about — and yearning for?* I wondered. We discussed our relationships; she revealed she had only last year broken up with a woman she had been involved with for years. *Great,* I thought. *Now I'm going to look completely inexperienced if anything sexual happens!*

As we got drunker and drunker, we moved closer to one another. I don't know who kissed whom first, but our desire was ignited. Cathy kissed my neck, my ears, my eyelids, and my mouth. My hands found her breasts, and I slowly caressed them. She pushed me gently and soon I was lying on the couch while she kissed my stomach. I undid her bra and she took off her shirt. She forced my bra over my breasts. It was an amazing feeling. I wondered what would happen next. Then I remembered, *My period!*

"Um…Cathy," I tried sheepishly to get her attention.

"Mmm." She was still kissing my body.

"I've got my period…and…I wear pads."

I was so embarrassed. It's probably the most unglamorous thing I've ever said. *Isn't this supposed to be like the movies?* I wondered. But my words had no effect on her. Cathy kept kissing me, and as I moved to a more comfortable position, I felt a tug at my hair. I gasped in pain. It seemed to get her attention.

"There's something in my hair," I said.

She stopped and sat up to have a look. "Oh, my gosh! I'm so sorry."

"What? What's in my hair?" I yelped.

"It's gum. It's my fault," she confessed. "I put it on the arm-rest before we kissed."

"What should I do?"

The romantic mood was ruined now.

And that was how our evening ended. Two drunk women, one brandishing a pair of scissors and the other moaning in despair as chunks of hair, mixed with green gum, fell to the floor.

It grew pretty obvious that my task wasn't going to be as easy as I thought. By now I had gotten to know Cathy pretty well, and I was beginning to wonder if I was falling in love. Every time I thought about how we met I was ashamed. I had just wanted to sleep with someone with no strings attached, but here I was with a wonderful woman and feelings steadily growing. I wasn't unhappy with the situation. I really did like her, but I hoped she wouldn't get too upset if things didn't work out.

I put all my fears aside and found the courage to ask her to spend the night the following Saturday. We both knew that this would be the night. A new set of fears took hold. I'd never had an orgasm before. *Does she expect me to? What if I can't? What does it feel like? Should I fake it if I can't have one? How can I fake an orgasm if I don't know what one is like? Will I like oral sex?* My friends asked me whether or not I could go down on a woman. *What will she taste like?*

I wanted it to be special. I spent $70 on a matching bra and underwear set—black with white lace. I fretted and again I lost my appetite. But it didn't go quite as planned. Earlier in the week we went to see a friend sing, and I decided to wear my new underwear set to see if it was comfortable. The evening passed uneventfully, and when Cathy dropped me home I invited her up for coffee. This was standard by now. We'd drink coffee in the lounge room and kiss on the couch. This time, however, one of my flatmates had a visitor who was asleep in the lounge.

I suggested we go into my room. I flicked on the lights and we both stood there, unsure of what to do. The only place to sit was the bed. Trying to ignore the bed, I moved to kiss her while standing, wondering what to do next. I didn't have time to think because as I leaned in to kiss her I tripped on the corner of the bed and had to make a quick decision: *Do I stagger and try to regain my footing and look like I'm afraid of the bed and its implications? Or do I fall and act nonchalant?* As I fell backward I opened my arms, and Cathy joined me, smiling.

We started kissing. I ran my hands down the length of her body. She was wearing her favorite black dress and knee-high black boots. My hands slipped under her dress and brushed lightly over her underwear. I was unsure of what to do next. I was completely out of my comfort zone.

Cathy paused and sat up.

"Is it OK if I take off my boots?" she asked.

"Sure," I replied unsteadily. She undid the zippers, and the boots fell with a clunk to the floor. She lifted my shirt, and slipping her hands under my new black bra, she ran her hands across my breasts. "I think I should take this off," she said as she unclipped my bra.

I was wearing only jeans now, and I realized this was the first time she had really seen me naked. I tried to ignore the butterflies in my stomach as I unzipped her dress. I tentatively kissed her stomach and then her breasts. Her nipples hardened immediately. She tugged at my jeans. She fumbled with the zipper, and I started to pull them. For some reason they wouldn't come off. As Cathy tugged at them harder, I nearly fell off the bed. Then I realized. They wouldn't slip over my eight-hole Doc Martens. I let out a giggle.

"We have to undo my Docs," I said. I sat up and fumbled with the laces. Cathy tried to help, and when she thought she'd undone them, she pulled. I fell back laughing.

"They're stuck. Is there a knot or something?" she asked. Now Cathy started to laugh as well.

"S-h-h-h," I whispered. "Paul's asleep in the lounge, and Tracey's bed is on the other side of this wall." I was frantic, sure that the whole house was now awake listening to our laughter.

After minutes of frantic maneuvers, we got the Docs off and they joined the growing heap of clothes on the floor. My jeans and our remaining underwear were the last items tossed onto the pile. Cathy moved toward me and placed her body on top of mine. She kissed me passionately, and I responded. I could feel every inch of her body against mine. I ran my hands over her back, her bottom, and, as she rose above me, her breasts. She moved and kissed my breasts and then my belly. My stomach jumped in anticipation and nervousness. I gasped as she finally buried her tongue within me. Her gentle lapping made me squirm with pleasure. And just when I thought I couldn't stand it any longer, she stopped and kissed my thighs and then moved back to kiss my neck and face.

I didn't know how these things were meant to proceed, but I thought it only fair I reciprocate. I pushed her onto her back and ran my tongue around her belly button and then with only a brief hesitation, my tongue reached to stroke her clitoris. She moaned as I explored her body for the first time. She reached down and gently tugged on my chin, encouraging me to stop. I sat up as she reached for me and whispered, "I want you," before she positioned me on my back, gently pulled my legs apart, and wrapped her arms around my thighs. My mind was racing. I loved the sensations but was worried about climaxing. *When does it happen?* I wondered. I was considering faking when suddenly I felt like I was on fire. Everything seemed too intense. I gasped and then pulled back breathing heavily. Cathy stopped, and it was all I could do just to get my breath back. She wrapped her body around me and held me. I had finally done it. Sex with a woman…and it was fantastic.

We celebrated our six-month anniversary at the beginning of this year. It hasn't been all smooth sailing. My family reacted well to the news I was a lesbian, and both my mother and sister treat Cathy as a part of the family—she even got her own Christmas stocking! Cathy's mother didn't take the news she had another girlfriend well; it ruined her "just a phase" theory. But I love Cathy more than anything, and the lust hasn't died. For our "half-anniversary" we bought a set of imitation-fur–covered handcuffs and the alcohol needed to make a drink called a Quick Fuck. Let's just say life will never be boring with her, and that, I guess, is the closest you can come to a happy ending in the '90s.

CHAPTER TWENTY-0NE
Arms of an Angel
Linda A. Boulter

"Mom, Mom," a little voice of reality broke my reverie. As a homeschooling mom, I was always on call. My world consisted of meeting the needs of my children and moments of daydreaming about the possibilities of an encounter with the woman who would become my first lover. In my mind, the kisses would be deep and lingering; our touches, soft and gentle; our connection, real and meaningful.

In my day-to-day life, the neediness of three children loomed. My eldest daughter was eight; her sister, five; and the little guy, 2½. I had never been away from them for more than a few hours. I had done all the socially expected things: settled down with a man and had a family. I played the "earth mother" role to perfection. I homeschooled, home-birthed, and then I nursed each for more than two years. By heterosexual standards I had it all, but I still felt empty; I desired the tenderness of a woman.

D. was that woman. From the moment we met, we had a connection that was spiritual and intimate. We both had a passion for life and love. The intimacy I felt for her became the seed for a desire to experience her sexually. I longed for a closeness that could be only filled with her breath on my cheek, her body in my arms. Women loving women—it felt so right at the time…and still does. I never once questioned why or how I felt this way. I know in my childhood I had been attracted to girlfriends, and in my 20s I had been approached by women. It never occurred to me I might just be fooling myself in this heterosexual role. But now—with me at 37—my world was about to change.

The woman of my dreams and our friend B. were house-sitting a beautiful bed and breakfast on an island only 20 minutes away by water taxi. They had invited me to spend a weekend; all I needed to do was convince my common-law husband that I deserved a break from the children and that he and they would be fine without me for a two days and a night. He had no idea I was feeling this way about our mutual friend. He and everyone else in my life had no inkling this "earth mother" of three was really a lesbian waiting to come out. He agreed to be the main caregiver while I spent a weekend with the girls.

On the dock, D. and I waited for the water taxi and spoke small talk—what we would cook, what we would do. The weather, warm and sunny, matched the elation I felt at the freedom, the possibilities, and D.'s closeness. Sunshine gleamed off the water. Our eyes squinted from the brightness. Our laughter and smiles welled up into a joyful closeness. I hugged her.

I remember the clarity of small waves dancing in the wake of boats on the harbor. The water taxi was dwarfed by an oceangoing freighter. My desire for D. grew. On the other side, off the dock and onto the path, D., our friend B., and I held hands and laughed like small children. We pushed a wheelbarrow loaded with supplies and my day pack.

We were going to watch *The Grateful Dead Movie* and eat Leary biscuits, which are crackers topped with cheese and a fragrant bud, then nuked for ten seconds to bring out the THC. Then we would enjoy the euphoria that eating marijuana can bring. We talked about every cosmic thing under the sun, about no coincidences, about our passions and pleasures.

As the evening progressed, the three of us decided to share body rubs. Nothing is as sensual as two sets of hands rubbing a well-oiled and naked body. Time stops, and body and hands merge into a pleasure of not knowing where hands end and body begins. The house was warm, and our nakedness felt natural and comfortable. I savored every caress. My hands explored the curves of D.'s body, the firmness of her muscles. I felt her melt under my touch. My lips wanted to kiss her graceful shoulders. My mouth wanted to nibble her ears and follow the nape of her neck. But we were not alone, and I believed my feelings and desires were a product of my imagination.

The euphoria of the night, the closeness, and the drugs began to mellow into the need for sleep. First B. said it was time for her to sleep. I sat up with D. for a while longer. We were enjoying each other's company and not wanting to call it a night. Finally we said good night. I went to my bedroom upstairs and she to hers, also upstairs.

A few hours later I woke up covered in sweat. The next thing I knew I found myself sitting at the top of the stairs where it was cooler. D. must've heard me come out because she called, "Are you OK, Linda?"

I said, "I'm hot…just really hot."

"We must've forgotten to turn the heat off after the massage," she replied. "Why don't you come and sleep with me? It's cooler in this room."

I took a deep breath. Although I had fantasized about this moment, I never suspected it would come true. She didn't have to ask a second time. I found myself slipping naked between the sheets, since I never wear pajamas—nor does D. I felt the softness of her skin against mine. She gave me a hug, and we rolled over to go back to sleep. I lay there, almost afraid to breathe at being in bed with her so close. I must've dozed off, because I woke with a start. She reached over and pulled me closer.

I put my arms around her. The next thing I knew, our mouths were touching. Our lips passionately explored each other's faces. Her hands caressed my shoulders, and I responded with gentle strokes. I heard the panting of my voice echo in her open mouth. I couldn't remember the last time I had felt so turned on. It felt as if I was in the arms of an angel waiting at the gates of heaven.

My tongue traced the curve of her breast and encircled her nipple. I felt her shiver as I gently sucked that brown jewel. At moments, I would feel like a babe at the breast; then I would feel the passion of a lover at play. It was all so new to me. This sensual femininity was as heady as fine wine. I rolled the other nipple between my fingers, pinching, pulling, and knowing all the while exactly how she felt. I knew the motions would send sensual charges from nipple to clitoris. The rocking of her hips confirmed my intuition.

I smelled the fragrance of her pleasure. As I reached between her legs, my fingers were rewarded with a slippery passion that beckoned me further. My tongue traced down between her breasts to her navel, where I lingered to probe and kiss. My fingers massaged her inner thighs, and I felt her legs spread in anticipation. I touched the lushness of her pubic hair, cupped it with my hand, and heard her gasp. I paused, my head on her belly, savoring the softness of her skin, the smell and wetness of her pussy. I wanted to dwell forever in this intimacy.

She gently touched my head, beckoning me to pleasure her. My tongue easily found her swollen clitoris. For the first time, I kissed a woman's delight, licked and took it gently in my mouth. I was surprised to find she tasted so much like I did. Her hips once again started rocking in my face, my tongue flowing from vulva to clitoris. I heard her staccato breathing whenever her hands paused from rubbing my ears.

Her hand reached down and gently pushed my fingers toward her pussy. They easily slipped inside, movement of tongue and fingers complementing each other. I felt waves of relaxation and tension; her back arched, her hips rocked, her fingers ran through my hair. She came with a huge sigh and a shudder I felt on my fingertips and my tongue. I rested my head on her belly and moved up to kiss her long and deep, giving her a taste of her pleasure.

After a while, without a word, she made love to me. I was in heaven. As the world woke up bathed with the pinkish tinge of the morning sky, I watched her sleeping. I saw a constellation of birthmarks on her back. In my mind I traced them. I lay loving her with my whole being. Quietly I rose, got pen and paper, and wrote her a love poem. When she woke we shared a bath together. I savored every moment because I knew my family would be arriving soon to spend the day.

When I met the children and their dad at the dock, I was forever changed. There was no turning back. In the guest house, I took my husband up to the bedroom and fucked him fast and furious as if it were the last time. It wasn't, but it was the beginning of the end of our relationship.

D. told me in clear terms this was a one-time thing, just for fun. She'd slept with a couple other women in the past, but she did not want a relationship with a woman. She had just enjoyed making love with me…and that was that. We still continue to be friends.

I kept the secret of my one-night affair from my husband. Through E-mail, however, I shared my experience with friends on a bisexual list. Eventually he read the E-mail and confronted me. I confessed. He was very hurt. Our relationship was rocky for two more years and a few more affairs, and then it was over. Three milestones mark this past year: I came out, I became a single mom of three, and I turned 40. Life has just begun.

CHAPTER TWENTY-TWO
Honeysuckle in November
Kyes Stevens

I waited almost two years after coming out to have any intimate contact with another woman. I knew there was a really good reason for me to wait, and on October 31, 1994, I found out why.

Jennifer and I had a blind date of sorts to go to a Halloween party. We knew each other from the university where she worked and where I was a student. I'd seen her during the previous two years when I'd go to the humanities department administration office. She was always there; her deep penetrating eyes knew things about me even I didn't know yet. During those two years, we flirted—unconsciously I guess—trying to figure each other out. I remember thinking it odd she knew my name out of the 25,000 other students at the school. She also mysteriously knew I didn't go by my first name, but I chalked it up to my association with the women's basketball team.

The Halloween party was sponsored by the university gay and lesbian organization. I, being prone to extreme shyness, had been having a difficult time asking someone out for quite some time, so a mutual friend set Jennifer and me up. When she walked in she took my breath away. I know it sounds like a cliché, but I now know where that cliché comes from. I remember just standing there thinking, "Oh, my god. There she is." She was dressed in a white wedding dress for the costume party, and I was decked out in my firefighter's gear. I was afraid she wouldn't sit next to me because my gear was covered in soot and grease, but she walked up, shook my hand, got me a beer, lit a smoke for me, and pulled me to a corner of the room before I knew what had happened.

We talked about what most Southern lesbians don't discuss on the first date: religion. I initially thought my agnosticism and her Southern Baptist upbringing were bound to cause friction. But we sat right next to each other on a chair not really big enough for two people and philosophized about how Southern culture is rooted in religion. I remember sweat in my hands, an intense burning, a longing to kiss her—wanting just a peck at first, wanting to feel her in my mouth, to taste her lips laced with nicotine from the last cigarette and the whiskey on her breath

She and her friend got up to leave, so I walked her to the car. She asked me to dinner the following week. I tried not to anticipate our date, tried not to fill my mind with the hope that she would take me to her bed and make love to me. I knew she was the one, but I didn't know when we would come together.

I changed clothes three times before going over to Jennifer's place. I opted for butch attire: dark blue Wranglers with a good stiff crease down the legs, boots, and T-shirt that showed off firefighter shoulders—hard, yet feminine.

The cat sitting on the washer noticed my nervousness. He'd stare as I'd light a smoke, take a drag, then crunch it out, only to reach for another a minute later. I paced through the house....*Don't want to be early...Don't want to be late.* Finally, after fixing a stiff drink to take off the edge, I got in my truck and drove the 25 minutes to her house.

I knocked, then waited. "Hello," I called in through the screen door. "Hey," she said, "come on in."

The smells of good ol' Southern comfort food—greens, ham, corn bread, and sweet potato pie—drifted around me and out to the back porch. Through the pines at the back of the lot, the sun was setting—golden with an unmistakable streak of fire right through the middle.

We talked, drank wine, had dinner, then went for a walk. There was a smattering of houses around. Through the calm night air I heard crickets and frogs chiming from the nearby cat-fish pond. We talked of family, of writing, and the passion it takes for both. I remember looking at the sky, the position of the big dipper, knowing it was getting late. We walked back to the house, where we sat on the back porch and looked at the stars.

The relationship questions started to come. I remember thinking shyly that Jennifer might not want to date me if she knew I'd hadn't been with a woman before. Jesus, I hadn't even kissed a woman before.

"Tell me about your last girlfriend," she said.

I looked out in the distance toward the pines. "I haven't dated anyone before."

"But surely you've been with a woman."

"No," I said again, "I haven't."

The silence that filled the space around us was almost too much to bear. No matter how hard I strained I only heard my last words reverberating through the air. Jennifer was think-ing. She got up, went inside, and emerged with beers and blankets. Music flowed through the backdoor: the Cowboy Junkies, a band I was not familiar with yet. The CD had just started when she wrapped a blanket around me, then around herself, and leaned over and kissed me. There are points in a person's life where all that is familiar—words, descriptions, and feelings—just fly out the window. This was one such mo-ment. Quiet...stars overhead...and the words "Is that OK?"

I think I remember trying to say yes but merely shaking my head in timid and shocked approval. I thought, *She kissed me. She touched her beautiful lips to mine and kissed me.* Despite the un-certainty of my next move, I leaned over and kissed her back, our eyes meeting right before contact, right before a passion-ate gasp for air. I was nowhere I had been before, and it ex-cited the hell out of me. When her hand touched my face and we lay down together with the shining stars overhead and her hand stroking my hair, I knew I was there at last. After long moments of deep kissing, her hand moved down my stomach and worked its way under my shirt, caressing—gently and passionately—my virgin skin. While one hand was under my sports bra, the other moved to the belt, steadily and adeptly loosening my pants. No words passed between us; we didn't need any. Her hand moved beneath my underwear and touched me. A life formerly unknown to me filled me.

I remember feeling so like a woman, so alive that tears came to my eyes as she moved her hand up and down. Her words mixed with the words from a Junkies song: "Oh, you are so wet."

Her fingers slipped inside, bringing light to uncharted darkness. Almost as quickly as she was inside me, her fingers were out and she pulled me to her face. Her tongue, my clitoris, met in a junction of two souls that had longed for each other for many moons and seasons. Being compared to the taste of honeysuckle, with a bit of dew is a gift—it is gentle and comforting. She stayed there for a while—the fire building within me—as a plane moved slowly and purposefully across the night sky.

The November air was cold. Chills set in through the heat rising off me and surrounding her. She moved her fingers down and penetrated me and—with a burst—I almost exploded. She crawled up and lay on me, breathing into and out of me, gazing into my eyes, saying it all without opening her mouth.

Jennifer took my hand, and we moved inside. I guess I must have still looked a little shy. Maybe I was still glowing. We stood before the bright orange and red heater and I pulled her close to me. My hands touching, moving, learning about the shape of her body. I pulled her shirt off and put my hand on her left breast, softly. My other hand slid down the small of her back, almost lifting her smaller frame to mine. I wanted to feel her everywhere on me. Slowly the rest of her clothes fell to the floor. A grand gift stood before me. I kissed her everywhere. I wanted to taste and savor skin, soft, yet rugged with her age. I remember staring—almost dumbly—watching her move, watching her sit, watching her smile at me, smoke trailing from a cigarette she had just lit.

As Jennifer and I lay in the bed, my mouth quickly found her breast. I gently moved my tongue around the hardened tip that peaked from a dark peach-colored center of firmness. My tall frame covered her, my hands filling her whole back with touches, my mouth exploring her. She grabbed the nape of my neck as my hand moved between her legs, slow and steady. Alive with want, I thought I could stay there, feeling the new terrain, searching for the hardened clit to rest my finger on. She whispered, "Go inside," and I positioned my forefinger at the entry to her vagina, slowly caressing the outer layer, waiting to plunge inside. As her body lunged for mine, trying to pull me into her, I slipped in, feeling a rush of warmth and wetness. She tightened around me, keeping me attached to her, moaning and moving rhythmically with my hand. As she built heat and screamed for me to fuck her, I pushed harder, finding parts of a woman I never imagined. We worked together, growing tired and wet with sex and sweat. Hot with passion, she came to me, hard and long, digging her nails into my shoulders, drawing blood.

We curled together on her single bed, hot from sex and the heater blowing across the room. She lit a smoke and handed it back to me, where I was wrapped into her back. She said, "I loved making you scream." Blushing, afraid of what to say, I just moved closer, kissing her gently. I answered, "Thank you."

We saw each other for a few months after that first night. I graduated and went out West to hike, leaving behind a fabulous first experience with a woman. As the years have passed, we occasionally see each other when I return home. I often wonder, in the middle of our conversations, if she is remembering what we were like together and how our bodies intertwined—a fusion of sorts—and if she ever yearns for that again.

CHAPTER TWENTY-THREE
Creamy De-Lite
Lisa C. Stanton

Wearing nothing but a pair of white bobby socks, primly folded at the ankle, she answered the apartment door. She didn't even look to make sure it was me, or seem to care if any neighbors were in the hallway. I saw somebody in the living room, which was also technically the bedroom, since that's where she kept the bed so she'd have someplace to watch TV. She didn't have a couch or much other furniture. She had a couple of ratty chairs, but on the whole she preferred to be horizontal. When I moved in later, I made a bed with some blankets and a camping mattress in the back room. The room was empty except for a closet filled with frumpy clothes and a dresser with this big, bright makeup mirror that she stood in front of for days while she got ready for work. Makeup was a big deal for her; sometimes she'd even put on fake eyelashes and glittery silverish eye shadow pulled all the way out to her eyebrows. Then she'd climb into her favorite set of gray sweats and I'd drive her downtown. You could never find a place to park at that time of night, so I'd just pull up in front and let her out by the sign that said LIVE NUDE DANCERS.

There was a person in the bed in the living room, and that person turned out to be Greg. Joanie had originally introduced him to me as a jeweler at a poetry slam near Queen Anne Hill. He was so strange. Whenever he got the chance, he'd show off this incredibly intricate platinum and ruby ring he'd made for a woman who had dumped him months before. He carried it around in his pocket because he still planned to give it to her if he ever ran into her again.

"Greg was just going," Joanie said. "Do you want a drink?"

"Sure."

"Well, there's vodka in the freezer, but I think I'm out of Kool-Aid. Will you make some?"

I wanted to do anything to get out of the living room, although technically the kitchen was the same room since the only thing separating them was a counter covered in dirty dishes, animal-rights magazines, and empty ice-cube trays. I opened the cabinet and flipped through packets of dye and artificial flavorings. "What kind do you want?" I called out with my back to the bed. "We've got grape, cherry, tropical punch, and lime." She giggled from under the covers. "You pick," Greg said. I tore open the foil and tapped the powder into a seemingly clean plastic pitcher balanced on top of a pile of coffee cups in the sink. I found an almost-empty bag of sugar smashed into the bottom shelf of the fridge and used a wooden spoon to swirl the mix with cold water from the tap. The spoon soaked up the purple. I was cracking ice into three glasses when Greg, smoothing down the boxers inside his open Levis, hopped over to the counter. "Don't make me one," he said. "I've got to get to work." Besides being a jeweler, he was the night attendant at a U-pump gas station.

Joanie kissed and giggled Greg out the door and snatched a drink from the counter. She sank into the chair next to mine and kicked her feet up onto my knee.

"Sorry about that," she said. "I tried to get rid of him before you got here, but we got distracted."

"I noticed," I said back. "Do you still feel like going out?"

I hadn't expected to spend the evening like this. I mean, I hardly even knew her really. We'd studied together for economics a few times at her place and gone to see a movie together on campus, but I wasn't even sure if she wanted to be friends or what. I couldn't understand why somebody like her would want to hang out with me (although I am pretty good at monetary theory). "Just let me finish this drink, and I'll get dressed," she smiled. So we went out, and you know, I don't even remember where. Does it matter?

While I knew her we went a million different places, and the one thing I remember is that every single time we went out, men were hanging on her, drooling. One night when we were on our way home to watch videos, a guy asked her to marry him in the salsa aisle at a convenience store. She always wore this same baggy gray sweatsuit, which I guess brought out the blue-gray in her eyes. That must have been what made men flip out for her—that and her wavy, dirty blond hair.

Joanie was cute and everything, but she was so down on her body. She always made a big deal about being flat-chested. She went on and on about it. Before I met her, she got pregnant and had to wait to have the abortion. Her boobs really filled out, and she didn't fit into any of her bras. Her boss at the strip joint said he'd give her more hours if she could keep her breasts that huge. She had a certain way of moving too. I watched her. She seemed oblivious to the attention and to the fact that the two of us were so completely different—me in my tomboy cutoffs, Doc Marten combat boots, and short hair. My one touch of femininity was the tube of lip gloss in my pocket. She borrowed her stage name from a lip gloss package, actually: "Creamy De-Lite." Gross, huh?

Anyway, when Joanie and I left wherever it was we went, it was late, and we smelled like smoke. I'd maybe had too much to drink to have been driving, and we were back at her place, which was still her place and not yet ours. She got me to drink another vodka with that godforsaken Kool-Aid, and then she really got going. She was on a rampage about her job and all the creepy ways the customers touched themselves in front of her.

"The men who come in there would shit if they knew all the strippers were fucking each other," she said with a little snort. "They're paying all this money to watch us touch ourselves, and they actually think we want to see them jerk off."

"I thought you were dating Greg," I said, a bit confused.

"Yeah, well, sometimes we go out and stuff, but he's so hung up on his old girlfriend. He's just waiting for her to take him back. Working at the club has just gotten me so turned off by men. They act so fucking disgusting! I don't know. I've fooled around with some of the dancers. It was all right. I mean, the whole place is just one big love triangle, and I'm not getting into the middle of that, but sleeping with women is pretty awesome. Have you ever done it?"

"Uh, no. I mean, I probably would if I had the chance, you know, just to see what it's like, but..."

"That's funny," Joanie said. "I thought you seemed like a lesbian."

Well, I've gotten called dykey since before I even knew what it meant, but it never really hit me that dating women was an option. Up until then, I'd fumbled along the best I could with men. I guess it seemed like the thing to do.

Anyway, sometimes Joanie would say or do anything, but she acted funny other times. Like she actually got under the covers to wriggle out of her pants, then batted those eyelashes at me and said, "Don't you want to get in?" I crawled into the sheets, and we lay there in the blue glow of the TV set, stripped to T-shirts and underpants like two kids at a slumber party. After a while she slid one leg over mine, her gaze still on the TV. I lay there pretending to watch this old *Mary Tyler Moore Show* rerun, sneaking sideways glances at her and woozily wondering what the hell was going on. Then she flopped herself onto me and reached for my mouth with hers. She pulled herself up by my shoulders, elbows in my ribs, as she climbed on and dug in, going into sexual attack mode, probing with her tongue in drunken, grape-flavored wet kisses. I was too shocked to respond at first. Energy flooded my body—especially my crotch, of course—and I kissed back, grasping, pulling her into me, onto me. I had no idea what to do with myself. I mean, I was so shocked part of me wanted to run screaming from the room. The first thought that went through my head was, *What if my mother finds out?*

I couldn't figure out where to put my hands, and when I felt hers reaching past the elastic of my sensible cotton underpants, I felt a clench in my stomach. Her fingers crawled around for a minute before they found moisture. She dove in. With her free hand she tugged down my underwear and squirmed down the bed. "Is this OK?" she asked me, her chin brushing my pubic hair. My brain was busy overloading on sensation, I think I grunted or maybe moaned. She took it as a yes. Her fingers beckoned inside me and stroked my spongy inner walls. Her grape tongue flicked at my clitoris, and I told myself to calm down. I tried so hard to relax but I couldn't. I thought, *Is this legal?* I felt my shoulders creeping toward my ears as I lay back on the bed with my back arching spasmodically. Writhing, I gripped the twisted blankets and begged her with my convulsing body to pump her entire hand, arm, and body into me. She pushed deeper and deeper inside, and I felt a ripple of electricity growing at my core.

Behind my closed eyelids I saw the ruby from Greg's ring swirling in creamy black liquid. It worried me a little bit. I'd never felt like this before. My body was levitating off the bed. I lost track of my arms and legs, melting into the feelings coming from deep inside my body. I felt Joanie's finger tickling the tight pucker of my asshole. She traced its outline a few times. I gasped as she gently pushed it inside. That was it. Bliss tore through me in waves. I felt stars and vast expanses of outer space sucking into the vacuum of my gasping vagina. The feeling rippled up my spine and out the top of my head, and through my shoulders and down my arms to my fingertips. My torso contracted, pulling me into a fetal position.

I opened my eyes and saw a tangle of sheets hanging off the bed. I tugged at a blanket, drawing a corner of it over my chest, and sank into a pillow. A bead of sweat trickled down my forehead to my temple. Joanie rested her head on my thigh. Absently I combed my fingers through her damp hair. Blood pounded in my ears. I heard myself panting from what seemed like miles away, my throat raspy. She picked up her head and looked at me with those eyes still shrouded in glitter, lashes thick with mascara. Her lips were moist and rosy.

"Hey," she said. "Could you hand me that drink?"

CHAPTER TWENTY-FOUR
A Miss and a Hit
Miriam Carroll

I felt intimidated coming to a lesbian rap group for the first time. I was here to help myself accept that I might be "that way" too and begin to understand the consequences of my desire to be one of them—a l-l-lesbian.

I knew nothing of their lives, what set them apart, how they recognized each other, and most importantly, how they made love. I sat quietly for once, determined to listen carefully, as I had nothing to contribute. Besides, they might get upset if I had said I'd been married for 22 years and had three kids. Lesbians didn't have children, as I understood it. I had recently discovered my new, confusing attraction to women. I'd barely been able to say "gay," never mind the other absurd word, and here I was in the middle of a room filled with them. I was enthralled. *Where did they all come from? Did they tell their mothers?*

What I did know was lesbians had sex—lots of it, anywhere, any time, any place. Here I was, fresh meat. Surely, one (or more?) kindly woman would approach me. I searched for a likely candidate. *Will she take me to a warm place, undress and bathe me, then lead me through the initiation rites? What part of me will she touch first?* I mused, as the conversations faded from my ears. *Will she lick me all over, and how much is "all?" If my imagination plays out true, can I actually put my mouth on her sex?* I tuned back to the fully dressed women. Just talking. No kisses. No fondling. No undressing. *Are they all inhibited by my presence?* The meeting was ending, but nobody came forth to address me, except to say I was welcome to come back. I realized how overdressed I was in the heels, suit, and gloves I might wear to a ladies' gathering. Little did I know about butch and femmes—and femmes were not de rigueur in the '70s.

I am the optimistic sort, so I kept going back to these meetings. Finally someone noticed me, suggesting to a member who lived midway between my home in New Hampshire and the rap in Boston, 50 miles south, that we might carpool. I got a letter in the mail, inviting me to dinner. Her name was Ginger, she wrote, along with other introductory matters. She lived with her diabetic mother and, platonically, with Isabelle. *Some platonic,* I thought. I, however, decided to meet her and let her awaken my body to whatever the hell women did to each other. This was going to be *it*!

Dormant juices began to flow.

I rummaged for some easy-off clothes and raced down the pike to her home. The door was opened by a friendly reddish-haired woman, some years older than I. Isabelle was present; Mother left, taking a tray to her room. Isabelle proved to be a fussy sort: picking something up, putting it down, nervously twitching, not making eye contact. I realized Ginger could not possibly have a personal relationship with this masculine type. A feeling of elitism gorged my throat. It wasn't nice not to feel at ease with this type of lesbian—butches, as I now knew the term to mean. I had learned they were good to have around, as they could fix things. With my husband on the way out, she might be handy to keep around. In my mind, this candlelit dinner was as good as an engagement ring.

Ginger invited me to stay the night, as the streets were covered with ice. *Here it comes!*

She handed me a pillow and blankets, then pointed to the sofa. *Oh. She's waiting for Isabelle to disappear upstairs. Hey, wait a minute. She's going up too! Do they sleep together after all?* What a predicament! I took off my clothes in the darkness, wrapped myself in the cocoon I made of the blanket, and waited. Surely Ginger would be down any minute. Ten of them passed in silence.

Well, maybe I'm supposed to be the aggressor and seek her out. I thought I'd try that. I put the pillow in front of me, and, shivering, tiptoed up the stairs.

I was confronted by two closed doors. *Which is Ginger's? Lady or Tiger?* I tried to figure it out logically. *Now, Ginger seems to be the boss of the house, so she would take the room closer to the bathroom. Makes sense. This door.* I tentatively knocked, as my mind went into a void. The door opened a crack.

Isabelle in a flannel shirt and long johns. *Tiger.* She said nothing but hooked her thumb toward the other door, then shut hers with a finality that could not be mistaken.

Whoops! OK. Knock on the other. Silence. A bit louder. Nothing. I dared to open the door.

"Ginger, it's me. Will you show me how women make love?" Where did I find the chutzpah to say *that?*

"CAN'T YOU SEE I'M SLEEPING?" was the violent retort, shattering my fantasy, along with my ego, to smithereens. *There goes my lesbian,* I thought, struggling into my clothes in the dark, tiptoeing out the door, and slithering into my car for the icy road home. *Oh, well, there seem to be a lot of them. Maybe another day.*

I sent her a short note thanking her for dinner, to which she replied with a short note. Hmm. The door remained open a crack, I surmised.

A month or so later, still celibate, passion unspent, I attended an all-night consciousness-raising session, quite popular at the time. As the event was near Ginger's home, I impulsively drove there after it ended. I boldly knocked on the door. Again, the Tiger. Oh, shit. She mentioned Ginger was shopping, and, yes, I could snooze while I waited a short while. I awoke, feeling her presence at the edge of the bed, watching me.

"I could love you," she said, "but in the end you'd hurt me. I do not have your education, capabilities, or economic status."

I didn't know what she was talking about. What did class differences have to do with this moment of awakening love? *It* was going to happen *now*. I opened up for her like a steamed clam. Her fingers flew beneath the covers as I reached for her breasts that swung over my face. Hastily pulling her sweater off, I was delighted to touch in wonderment that soft object forbidden to me my whole life. *Yes*. This was what I wanted, for my tongue knew just what to do. In released passion I allowed her to penetrate me and slice through my opening, a buttery rose melting to her ministrations. I had no problem returning the joyful climax, with nary a thought to my inexperience in this matter.

"Are you sure nobody has ever seduced you before? You're a natural, baby," Ginger told me, as we plucked little foreign things from between our teeth. That lady taught me almost all I ever needed to know, but the rest of what I learned is another story.

It didn't take long for the U-Haul to move me in. I had to get out of my previous home because of my upcoming divorce. Twelve anniversaries later, I did hurt her, leaving her to move to a warmer climate, far away. Eight years after that, I found my wife-for-life, and now that we've been together more than six years, I, at age 68, know that a loving home is more important than daily sex.

Ginger lived with her dog and numerous cats, never had another lover, and died at age 72.

CHAPTER TWENTY-FIVE
Complex Equations
Jennifer Lindenberger

I was 19 and living on my own in a small town in Pennsylvania a few miles from where I grew up. Nothing much ever happened there. Like every other single female my age, I was working retail at the mall. The alternative was child care, and I realized quite early neither of these things would lead me far. I wanted out, and I set my sights on a college in Maryland. Maybe a degree could help me get what I wanted, because folding flannel shirts sure wasn't.

To help prepare for school, I set aside a few of my off-work hours and hired a tutor from a newspaper ad at the local community college. It's ironic I now work in accounting because math frightened me the most. My grades weren't a problem, but like many young overachievers, self-doubt followed me wherever I went. Still, I'm glad I hired her. She helped me to discover part of who I am.

It was raining the first night she arrived. I didn't see her car pull up because I was living in an apartment with only one window, which was in the bedroom, and the forceful knock at the door startled me. She was early. I ran around frantically picking up clothes and books from the floor. I wanted to make a good impression. After all, this was a college woman. Maybe she was only a year or two older than I was, but I thought of her the same way as I thought of teachers when I was a little kid: always out to impress. I answered the door out of breath. My heart pounded, so maybe that had something to do with the tingling I felt between my legs. Her appearance took me totally by surprise.

"I'm Nicole," she said. "Your tutor."

"Jennifer," I said absently. I looked her up and down. She appeared quite stunning in the ambient light of early evening, the rain in her hair and her face glistening with fresh, dewy drops. It wasn't the first time this had happened. Although I'd grown up dating boys, women had a way of taking me off-guard. They looked so good, so inviting. I'd had sex with males, even sort of enjoyed it once or twice, but I never thought about the way they looked or smelled or felt. Their purpose was functional, and the less I thought about them the better. But women...

With women, I wanted to know more.

"It's damp out here," Nicole said, smiling just a little, and I came to my senses, apologized, and let her in. I smelled her as she passed. She smelled good, soft but smoky, like incense or a fire, and I took in her shape through her long jacket. I hurried to help her remove it, my hands lingering over her bare arms beneath her short-sleeved blouse. Unlike a lot of lesbians I now know, I never fantasized about women. But I liked being close to them and secretly touching them when they least expected. When she turned around, her nipples formed prominent pearl-shaped circles under her nylon blouse. No bra. Very unusual for any respectable woman in this small town. Maybe she wasn't so respectable. And even as I hung up her coat, I'd already decided I liked her.

We sat down on the couch. I had to move a few more things aside to do so, but I was happy to show her I had a notebook and pencils ready on the coffee table, along with some tattered old books I'd kept from high school.

"We won't need those books," she said, sounding somewhat aloof. Maybe her words struck my pride, because I hid behind a smile as I studied her face. How naive I was then, how unsure of myself. She looked so smart with her wire-rimmed eyeglasses suspended over her soft cheeks by a longish and bony nose, her lips drawn up like a tight red bow. She had the most incredible lips, and I wished I could kiss them.

"How will I learn without books?" I said.

"If these books had taught you anything, you'd already know it." Her eyes remained stern as she settled back in her seat. "I need for you to explain to me what you don't know."

How awkward! Probably the hardest thing in the world is to explain what you don't know. The task frustrated me. I forgot all about her smell and her appearance and the way her leg brushed against mine—denim against denim—I stared at the coffee table for a good ten minutes, my thoughts stumbling through four years of high school math. I told her bits and pieces, fragments that made almost no sense to me and certainly couldn't to her, and I finally gave up with a shrug.

Nicole put her hand on my shoulder.

"Look here," she said, pulling me with her as she leaned over the table. She picked up a pencil, wrote down some long-forgotten equations and such, and said, "Does this look familiar?"

"Does it?" I laughed. "That little job right there gave me six weeks of hell!"

"It's not that difficult," she said reservedly. "Not as long as you really understand what comes before it. Unfortunately, teachers can't always tell whether you grasp something or have just remembered it for a test. Let's say we go back a few steps."

And so we did. As papers with scribbled numbers and notes piled up, we became lost in this little world of complex numbers and equations. Pretty soon nothing else existed; I became absorbed in her voice and the lesson. It must have been around midnight before we stopped and I realized how quiet it was. My eyes burned, and my back ached like crazy from sitting for so long. I was tired, and my head swam almost like I was drunk, yet more vivid. Her bright eyes were vivid, that's for sure. I looked at them, and I looked again at her mouth. Her lips parted, and something urged me to touch them with mine. I moved into her arms, and I kissed her. She kissed me back.

OK...

I got up. I headed for the kitchen, then back again, running my fingers through my hair. I felt like a fool, and I felt like even more of one when I realized I was making noises that weren't really words, just scared little syllables with no meaning. Nicole watched me, expressionless. Smart woman. She looked like she was studying me. I stopped and took a breath and said, "Should I pay you?"

So young and inexperienced!

"Pay me?" she said back to me, emphasizing the words so that they came out like a joke.

"I mean, for the tutoring," I said.

"Of course," she said with frown, "but not until after the third lesson."

Well, she was right. That's what we'd agreed to over the phone. I was nervous. I think maybe I wanted her out of there without any further commitment. I could either call her for the next lesson or not. But Nicole wasn't about to give me that liberty. Instead, she got up, gave me a peck on my frozen cheek, and told me to call her the next day if I wanted to cancel my lessons.

"Otherwise," she said, "I'll see you Friday."

The next thing I knew, she'd put on her coat and was gone.

It would be easy to say I didn't sleep at all that night, that I stayed up late soul-searching and whatnot. The fact is I was probably snoring before my head hit the pillow. I was exhausted. I went to work late the next morning, and on the drive

I remembered having the strangest, most wonderful dreams.

I didn't call to cancel the next lesson.

Well, Nicole wasn't the first female I'd kissed. She was the first woman, but I'd kissed girls back in school. It was a somewhat innocent pastime, but maybe less innocent than I assumed. We made believe we were each other's boyfriends and that we were "practicing" for the big kiss. We'd close our eyes and imagine, but I kept a secret: I never imagined anyone else. I just liked to kiss them, and I wanted to kiss again. This time, I wanted a grown woman.

Each day passed more slowly than the last. I was eager for Friday to come. I wanted to see what would happen next, and late that afternoon I readied myself as though I was preparing for one of my high school dates. I wore a tight cardigan and a short plaid skirt with white knee-high socks. I looked like a girl at private school, but I was used to dressing for male yokels who all enjoyed schoolgirl fantasies, whether they knew it or not. I was fixing my hair for the seventh time and deciding I hardly looked sophisticated when I heard a knock at the door. I ran over to open it, stumbling over my clumsy long legs, and took a breath to gather myself. I opened the door. It was dusk. Nicole looked like the silhouette of some beautiful statue against the gold- and rose-colored horizon.

"Hello, Jennifer," she said.

"I remember everything we went over," I told her

"I'm glad you didn't forget."

I brought her inside. This time she was dressed in a businesslike jacket and skirt, snug but very professional. I looked her over as we walked back to our familiar (and today, much cleaner) place on the couch. I searched for meaning in what she wore. What was she trying to tell me? That tonight was all business? That the last time we met was a mistake and now she wanted to keep focused on work? How people dress can really set a mood, and more than ever I felt like I was the young, girlish student and she the refined, sophisticated teacher. Looking back, I wish I'd simply enjoyed her beauty: the way her jacket held her otherwise bare breasts and exposed her deep, sweet-smelling cleavage. She started going over our notes from the last the session, but my mind was elsewhere. My heart was pounding again, my mouth gone dry. Curiosity got the better of decorum, and I asked her bluntly why she'd let me kiss her.

"I mean, I seemed more surprised than you were," I said, and she looked up and held me with her bright green eyes. She smiled. Such a soft, sweet smile. That was all it took for her stern face to melt into something altogether warm and inviting.

"You're right," she said. She put her hand on my shoulder. Her touch felt comforting, but I couldn't deny the sexual undercurrents. I felt uncomfortable, yet *wanting*. She said, "A gay woman can't live safely in a town like this without learning the signs."

Gay? I thought. *As in lesbian?* Well, if I felt uncomfortable before, now I was doubly so. Sure, I'd dreamed about her. I'd even fantasized about her a bit in the past couple of days. But what did that have to do with being a lesbian? Lesbians were women in big cities. They were worldly and tough and *different*. They weren't real. They existed in the movies and magazines my parents never let me see, and certainly I couldn't possibly know one. I couldn't possibly be one, and yet I felt a strange sort of relief at hearing the word.

I put down my pencil. I looked into her probing eyes and my hand was on her bare knee. "What made you feel safe here?" I asked. "What made you think...?"

"That you wanted me?" she finished.

"That I was curious," I corrected, and as I adjusted my

seat, my hand slipped over her thigh. Her skin was cool and hard with muscle. An active woman. I liked that.

"Look around," she said. She motioned to things I had in my apartment, things I'd bought over time and had never really looked at as a whole: femme statuettes and prints, a lamp in the shape of a woman, and wax figurines. "You appreciate the female form and all its variances," she said. "You're a very sensual woman."

A woman. No one had ever called me one of those before.

I must have had tears in my eyes because everything sort of blurred. I knew what I wanted, and that confused me even more. My hand moved further, sliding to the softer upper part of her leg. I leaned toward her with yearning and hot breath. Our breasts touched, and my hair fell over her shoulder. I kissed her neck. My body, the room—everything seemed to pulse. I crawled deeper into her, but she seized my hand and halted my penetration beneath her skirt. The hidden hair between her legs brushed against my knuckles. I wanted to go further. I wanted to lose myself in this dream and experience it and then never think about it again. But Nicole wouldn't let me. I could tell by her breathing she wanted it, but she just wouldn't let me.

"You have to know who you are first," she said.

"I already do," I lied.

"No. You don't."

I felt angry. Angry and aroused. Her warning sounded like a taunt, and I pushed against her. Her body yielded, succumbing to the soft, deep cushions around her. Her hand yielded too, and my fingers reached the soft warmth between her legs. She moaned consentingly and closed her eyes. I opened my hand and rubbed her, my palm moistening with her juices. Yes, she was excited for me. She wanted me, but not in the curious way that I wanted her. She wanted me because she already knew how good it could be. Her legs opened wider. Her arms wrapped around me, and I slipped my finger inside. She felt so warm and full of little ripples. I wasn't even sure what I was supposed to do, so I felt every part inside her with delicate care.

"Here," she said. She lifted her hips, and together we pulled her skirt up around her hard belly. Her thick, dark bush ran almost up to her navel. She slid her hand through her mound of hair and squeezed her pretty clit while I stroked her inside. I watched like a scientist, moisture forming at the corners of my mouth. I wanted to lick her. I wanted to put my mouth on her and taste this attractive young woman.

"Does this feel right?" I asked, meaning the sheer mechanics of my act. Nicole found deeper meaning.

"Does it feel right to you?" she asked, looking at me deeply.

Well, of course, it felt right. I eased my fingers in deeper. She closed her eyes again and tore at her suit jacket with her free hand. Her buttons came undone. One of them popped across the room, and her breasts fell out, nipples erect and burning with lust like mine. I ran my tongue down her neck. I sucked her nipples, sweet with summer sweat, and licked the curves of her breast. My hand gained momentum in her pussy. I slipped down to her belly. I teased her navel until she giggled and kicked, and while she was distracted I dove upon her femininity.

Forgotten dreams flooded me. She smelled divine, tasted even better. I licked her clit as she squeezed it into a little ball between her thumb and finger. I spread her labia with my tongue. I didn't know it then, but she had the thickest labia of any woman I would ever touch—soft as velvet, like her mouth. I kissed and nibbled them. She squirmed beyond control and pulled at my hair. I licked in long, forceful strokes, my fingers still inside. I sucked her. I drank in her wetness and her aroma. I relished the taste more than I could imagine.

I must have feasted on her for close to an hour. Sometimes I went mad with passion and burrowed deep, delighting in her groans and the way her thighs quivered around my head. Other times I slipped into my scientist mode, backing off and touching delicately, exploring her soft folds and playing with her red little clit with my sticky fingertips. Nicole pulled at my cardigan. She wanted my clothes off, but I ignored her advances. I don't know if I wasn't ready or if I was simply too content with my own explorations. I wanted to make her come, and I did. She screamed so loud I wondered what the neighbors would think. I got off on the things they would think about me, the things they would say to each other and the funny looks they'd give me in the morning. I wasn't like them. I never was.

Finally, Nicole and I were both so tired that I collapsed on top of her, my ear against her belly. I breathed deeply, inhaling the smell of her sex and feeling content. Her fingers remained in my hair, stroking more gently. I felt happier than I had ever had after a sexual encounter—so much more at peace and not feeling like I'd done something wrong or had missed something. I even started to doze, listening to her rhythmic breathing and feeling her gentle touch. I awoke, suddenly aware of how badly I needed gratification.

"I think I should be alone," I said, not even sure why. I looked up, and Nicole looked almost angry. I know she wasn't. It was just my own confusion setting in.

"You want me to go?" she said.

"I just…" I couldn't finish. I got up. I brushed down my clothes and went to the kitchen. I told myself I was thirsty and got a glass of tap water. I was hiding from her—and hiding from myself. I stood against the stove and drank slowly.

A few minutes later I heard the door open and close again. She was gone, and I cried.

Words played again and again in my head that night and through the next day. Words that had made me feel so good before now just scared the hell out of me: *Lesbian. Woman. Lesbian woman.* I was supposed to see Nicole again Sunday afternoon. I called and left a message on her machine. I told her not to come.

In my life I have few regrets. Still, I regret all the times I felt fear of myself. As much as I denied it, my conservative upbringing had influenced me. I felt I'd done something wrong with Nicole. I'd expected the experience to be another new thing to try, another experience to chalk up to my experimental nature like my various hairstyles and makeup. But it was more natural. It felt so right, and that's just what scared me.

When the phone rang I didn't answer. Midweek I called an old boyfriend. We went out that night, and I fucked him. Later that same week, I fucked some other guy, one I hardly knew. I fucked a lot that summer. I cried a lot too. I know I'm not the only one to act that way, to act like a slut to shut away a part of myself. It's so silly and sad to see others act out my past. I didn't think about Nicole, but I dreamed about her. I dreamed about tigers, sleek and smart, playing rough with paws and fangs. I'd always dreamed about tigers, but I'd never before realized the sexuality behind those dreams. Relationships with friends and family began to fall apart, and here I was, ready to go off to college. I couldn't leave things like this. I had to get my shit together.

One hot day in August the phone rang. I was watching television and eating. My bags packed and ready for Maryland, I was sad and thinking how alone I'd be. After all, I was about to go somewhere new and strange, and I didn't even know what I wanted. I picked up the phone after three rings, expecting to hear my mother offer more words of wisdom. But it wasn't her this time. It was Nicole, and my stomach flipped like a pancake.

"Come over," I told her, my palms sweating like mad.

"I shouldn't. I just want to tell you good-bye."

I shook my head. "No. Tell me in person. Meet me somewhere." I tried not to beg but begged anyway. She finally agreed to meet me at a café in town. When I got there she was waiting at a table. She looked the same, but somehow more real, not like in dreams or musings. This was a real person, and I felt awful for the way I'd treated her. I sat down, and we talked over coffee. It was the easiest and most comfortable conversation I'd had in a long time.

We decided to go dancing. The club was small and the music terrible, but it was the best our little town had to offer. We got a lot of funny looks. We ignored them. We were just into each other, and we ended up back at my apartment. This time the barriers were down. We took things slow, and we made love. She showed me what it felt like to touch the body of a woman, not just her parts. It felt like freedom. For the first time, I remained myself during sex. I didn't turn off and hide behind my body. We talked and laughed and joked about the most meaningful and meaningless of things. She licked me inside and out, and I came for the first time in my life.

Nicole and I lost touch soon after I arrived in Maryland. We both expected that. I'd always seen her as the woman and me as the little girl. Now I was somewhere new, discovering all the things she had before me. College wasn't nearly as intimidating now that I knew who I was. How lost I might have been if Nicole hadn't helped me to discover myself! Instead, I was confident and ready to take on anything—even math and the most complex of equations.

CHAPTER TWENTY-SIX
Friends for a Lifetime
Wenona Susan Church

*I*t wasn't a particularly auspicious occasion, our first meeting. In fact, we were only seven. I was the new kid in town, a fresh, confused face in the classroom. I had moved to Ohio from New York, and it was January, so I could not hide in the chaos that normally marks the first day of the school year. I walked into the classroom after lunch, and science was beginning. The teacher had grouped the class into groups of four. I was the fifth wheel in my group as we began a unit on transportation. My group had two other girls and two boys in it. How brave of my teacher, Mrs. Yohi, to mix the genders. I immediately aligned myself with the girls, thoughts of solidarity flying through my mind. Any alliance I sought was a bad idea since I had failed to notice that the girls were divided. Crystal had a crush on Kevin, and Jimmy was Kevin's best friend. I looked to the other girl, Kris, and she smiled at me. A partnership was born.

It was a partnership that lasted a lifetime. We giggled under the covers during sleepovers. We went to camp together in the fourth grade. In the fifth grade we played spin the bottle with the boys from one street over. The summer before sixth grade began, Kris told me she didn't like boys. Like any best friend, I immediately agreed with her. Boys were icky.

She looked away from me and said, "Wendy, I think I like girls."

"So do I. Girls are cool," I replied.

"No," she said. "I mean I want to kiss girls."

I looked at her, astounded the words came out of her mouth. I couldn't understand the full implications of what she said—she was always ahead of me in maturity. But I did know there was no way I was going to be different from the rest of the girls in the sixth grade. I didn't want to be ostracized, so I never entertained the thought that I might like girls too. But Kris was my best friend, so I kept her secret.

Every once in a while she confided in me about a crush she had on another girl, someone's mother, a teacher. I listened with interest but wrote off my own dreams of kissing girls as an extension of her fantasies. The rigors of teenage heterosexuality were already too complex for me to even consider whether or not I was a lesbian—even if I had known what the word meant. So I stayed with the safe, the familiar, and the accepted.

Kris and I remained the best of friends even after we separated to study at different colleges. She stayed in our home state of Ohio, and I moved to East Lansing, Mich. She pursued her life's dream of art, and I pursued my father's dream of mechanical engineering. She was gloriously happy, and I was gloriously miserable. After three years of semi-torture, I moved back to Ohio, and we spent a wonderful year together at the same college. We went to football games so she could ogle the cheerleaders and to baseball games so I could indulge in my baseball camp fantasies. At the end of the year, I moved to Washington, D.C., and she moved to Cincinnati.

Working as a nanny in our nation's capital should have been exciting, but it wasn't. The family I worked for was large and held unrealistic expectations of what a 22-year-old could accomplish in a 24-hour day. Couple this with the fact that I had left my boyfriend of two years back in Ohio. Kris remained in Cincinnati until she graduated the following May. Then Kris moved to Streetsboro, Ohio, where I now lived. It had been almost a year since I had last seen her when she invited me over for an inaugural dinner in her new apartment. I arrived with wine and rang the bell. She came to the door in a dress that could melt Antarctica and bring the water to a boiling point. I, of course, didn't notice for any other reason than friendship. I was merely being observant.

She gave me the grand tour of her new apartment, but I didn't really see any of it. I spent my time wondering if I was getting sick—I felt flushed, and my heart was racing. Each time her arm, hand, or any other part of her anatomy brushed against me, I jumped a bit because it felt like electricity. I was walking through a Harlequin romance novel, bombarded by every lust cliché ever written—except that this was *me*, and she was *Kris*. My best friend, my confidante, my heart, my soul, my love. My love? That couldn't be. This was the woman to whom I had confided all my dating woes—dating woes with men, not women. I was *not* a lesbian. I was even considering marriage with my longtime boyfriend. I couldn't be gay.

Or perhaps I could. I sat down on the couch, totally oblivious to anything Kris was saying. I couldn't look at her. If I did, she would know exactly what was going on in my mind, and I wasn't sure if I was prepared for that. I needed my best friend who I could talk about everything with, but currently she was the object of my confusion and my desire. Desire? Did I mean desire? I did. I wanted to kiss Kris. I wanted to do everything to her she described her girlfriends did, and I wanted her to do those things to me. But what if she didn't want to do those things to me? What if she felt...nothing?

I couldn't look at her. I just sat there with my eyes glued to the piece of carpet that had been pulled up a bit, perhaps by a previous renter's pet. I tried to think about that pet: *Was it a cat? A dog? What color was it?* I felt her hand touch my cheek. Her cool fingers left hot streaks where they brushed my skin, as she pushed my hair out of my eyes. "What's wrong?" the touch asked. I took her fingers in mine and held them against my cheek. I could feel her pulse melting into mine. With my other hand I gripped my thigh to help me hold back the tears I could feel threatening my eyelashes. I looked at her wonderful, beautiful face, her face with the green eyes that sang into me with love. Love! Love! I could see it there. I smiled as big as my face would allow.

She looked at me and had the nerve to say, "It's about time."

I did the only thing I could do. I kissed her. This wasn't just a kiss between good friends, but a down-deep-to-her-soul-why-did-it-take-me-so-long-to-do-this kiss. And she kissed me back: a deep-down-to-my-soul-I-thought-you'd-never-get-it kiss. Her hands followed the contours of my body, and I allowed her hair to flow over and over again through my fingers. Soon our clothes were the next day's laundry, and our bodies breathed life and pleasure as they found new places to make contact with each other. When her soft lips found my nipples, I nearly exploded with the raw emotion they created. Her fingers touched me in places I never knew had meaning until she found them. When my mind and body finally erupted under her attention, I was exhausted but in a state of bliss. Kris lay on her side slightly panting, her eyes sparkling with tears in the corners. When I could speak again, I asked her why she was crying.

"I thought you'd never figure it out," she exhaled.

"What? How to make you come? I tried, honey, I really did," I breathed back.

"No, Wendy. I thought you'd never figure out you were in love with me."

"Why didn't you tell me?"

"You had to figure it out for yourself."

Kris and I were together for the next seven years. We took our own paths, thinking we would always have the rest of our lives together. Kris moved to New York to pursue photography. I moved to Rhode Island. Then I moved back to Ohio, and she moved back to be with me after I was raped. That was a hard year. I kept pushing her away. I couldn't let her touch me. I couldn't let her in emotionally. She patiently supported me until I was able to allow her back in.

When I was able I went back to being a nanny. She went back to New York to renew her career. I would move to New York as soon as I finished my degree in psychology. I had trouble getting back to school for a while. Some of it was financial, but most of it was emotional. Kris came back to visit me as often as she could, and I went to New York as often as I was able. Kris came home for a leave of absence from her job in March of 1995. She was chronically tired and lacked inspiration; a sabbatical would be a good thing. I had some time off from my position, and we decided to take a long weekend and go camping up by our lake.

Ever since we were teens we had been making pilgrimages to a lake in central Ohio. We found it one weekend when we got lost on the way home from Columbus, and we always tried to make it back about the same time each year. We packed up our gear, shopped for some grub, and were on our way. I could tell Kris was tired — her usual high-spirited banter was replaced by one-syllable grunts and a lot of sleeping. By the time we got to the lake, however, she had revived enough to help me make the trek through the woods to the shelter. We made camp, made love by the shore at sunset, and fell asleep in each other's arms with firelight creating soft shadows on our faces. In the morning we awoke and went fishing, eating our catch for breakfast. As we washed the dishes, Kris turned to me suddenly and said, "Let's get married!" I stared at her. We had talked about it before but had decided we would tell our parents first that we were gay and, when the uproar had died down, that we were getting married.

"I thought we were going to do that later," I said. "You know, after we told our parents."

"I want to get married now. Here."

"Here? But we have no friends here, no minister."

"We have us. Please, Wendy. We have all we need."

When she used her eyes to plead with me that way, there was nothing I could do but say yes. All day long we collected branches to weave for an arch, for garlands, for our hair. We created a little table from a flat rock and two logs. We found gifts from nature to place on it: a bird's nest, a peeper frog who definitely didn't want to stay on the table, and pieces of fern for the green of the life we were beginning together. When the light said good-bye and the stars appeared, we pledged our love to one another. The peeper frog called out to his friends to join our wedding song, and the fireflies twinkled their greeting as we kissed for the first time as wife and wife.

When we got back to civilization, I went back to work, and Kris went to the doctor to deal with her chronic fatigue. The chronic fatigue turned out to be acute leukemia, and after the first two months of treatment, we were told she didn't have long to live. It was now June. She moved into my apartment for a while until I was to move to a house near the college I was attending. Kris decided she would tell her parents about her lesbianism and tell them about me. She thought I would be the easy part—after all they had known me since I was seven years old. I was as much a part of their family as she was.

We told them together, in August. It was horrible. They blamed everything on me. I turned her to lesbianism. I prevented her from getting cancer treatment sooner. It was my fault she would die in sin, my fault she would die at all. Kris pleaded with them and told them it wasn't true. She tried to explain, but her parents were stubborn assholes. We left for home.

When Kris was hospitalized in September, they came around. They were loving to her, civil to me. They never quite apologized, but I felt they had finally accepted her, me, and us. I was wrong. When she lapsed into a coma in the beginning of October, they took me to court to revoke my power of attorney and—most seriously—my durable power of attorney, the document that gave me the legal right to make her medical decisions. They forbade me to see her.

I didn't listen to them. I went in to see her on off hours. The nurses knew me and how much she loved me, and they let me sit with her. I held her hand, read to her, and sang the silly camp songs we sang as children. And I prayed. I prayed to any and all deities I could think of, hoping one of them would see what we had, know it was just beginning, and give her back to me.

I went to the hospital the second week of October. She was gone. The nurses told me Kris had been moved to another hospital where her parents felt she would receive better care. I immediately raced over there, but the nurses' faces were unfamiliar, and they had strict instructions to not let me in. I begged. I cried. I tried to sneak in, but the closest I came was looking through the window at her in the ICU. I called her parents. I called the judge who made the ruling. I called my lawyer. Nothing. I was denied. I did the only thing I could do: I worked with a vengeance. I worked 50-hour weeks, had 16 hours of classes, and still drove to the hospital every day to see if someone would relent.

In November I came home to an empty house and a light blinking on the answering machine: "Uh, Wendy? This is Mark…Kris's brother. I, uh, just wanted to let you know Kris died a week ago. I'm sorry I didn't call you sooner, but we thought it best. Anyway, call me. I have something I know you would want." My world shrank. I walked through a void. I regained awareness later in my room. It was dark. The house was quiet.

I went to work. Studying, going to classes, working two jobs, holding a position on the PTO, singing in the choir...and this. I slept little, ate everything. I, too, was no longer alive. I merely existed.

About two or three weeks later, Mark showed up on my doorstep with a carved wooden box. He told me it was her ashes. He had taken them from her parents without telling them and replaced them with fireplace ashes. He said I should have them. I stared at him. Ashes. They weren't Kris; they were bits of carbon and charred pieces of bone. They did nothing to erase the pain and guilt I felt for not being able to be with her at the end. Mark read my expression and said, "Say goodbye. She will hear you."

The next month I gathered a group of our friends together and we drove to the lake. We hiked to the remnants of our bridal sight, and I explained to them how Kris and I had joined our souls as one. As one friend played the flute, we created a funeral pyre and barge out of branches. As notes echoed over the lake, we lit her pyre. For a time it was silent. Then our flute player began to play soft, random notes, joined by the guitar of another friend, and the drum of yet another. The joyous cacophony lifted our hearts, and we began to dance—first just slight movements, but then full body expressions of our collective love for the extraordinary woman that touched all of our lives with her passions, her fiery temper, her spirit. Abruptly the light of her pyre died out as the barge sank to the depths of the lake. Although the night was dark, we hiked out from the lake. None of us wanted to be there in the light of the morning. At least not for a long time.

It's three years later now—they have been rough years, but they are getting easier. I have slowly opened my heart to other women. With each woman, I heal a bit more, and my life is enriched by each in her own special way. There will never be another Kris, but I have come to understand that although my life will never be the same without her, it did not end with her. I can celebrate again with another.

CHAPTER TWENTY-SEVEN
Star-crossed
Elisa Ross

"Estelle! My glancing stream! My crystal!" I cried. "Your crystal?" she sneered back at me, disgust dripping from her voice. "It's grotesque. Do you think you can fool me with that sort of talk? The crystal's shattered, but I don't care. I'm just a hollow dummy, all that's left of me is on the outside—but it's not for you."

I knelt on one knee, instinct telling me to amp up the drama. "Come to me, Estelle. You shall be whatever you like—a glancing stream, a muddy stream. And deep down in my eyes you'll see yourself just as you want to be."

She rolled her eyes. "Oh, leave me in peace. You don't have any eyes." She spun off the sofa and whirled away from me. I jumped to her, tried to grab her hand. "Oh, damn it. Isn't there anything I can do to get rid of you?" she snarled, shaking herself free. "I have an idea."

She reared back and spit in my face. "Oh, man! I'm so sorry!" she exclaimed.

I blinked, trying to clear my vision. The shot was a little too good; she hit me right in the eye. She reached out and brushed the saliva off my cheek.

"Are you all right?" She touched me.

"I'm fine," I snapped, feigning anger. "You missed a line."

"Well, at least I had the juice where it counted," she joked. "Which one did I miss?"

"Everyone knows by now what I did to my baby," I said.

"Oh, yeah, that. I don't consider it relevant," she lilted in sotto voce, waving her hand. "Let's just take that out."

"Jess, it's relevant to your character," I sighed. "Why else would you be in hell? It's the justification."

"Oh, please," she laughed. "I'd be in hell for a hundred other things anyway. You want to try it again?"

"I guess so." I threw my hands in the air. "Just don't aim for my eye this time, OK?"

"I could punch you instead," she offered generously.

"Not the ladylike Estelle!" I laughed. Maybe she'd touch me again.

"'I'm not polite,'" she quoted impishly, her eyes going darker blue.

"That's my line, thank you."

Jessica and I were rehearsing for our community theater workshop; this was our second course together. The teacher had partnered us on dialogue exercises, and we were attacking our project with determination. We were assigned to take ten lines of dialogue every week and interpret our scenes a different way each time. So here we were, rehearsing, as we did three nights a week.

The prospect of working with Jessica had horrified me. She adored the limelight, and I had already become familiar with her center stage monopoly. In our group of would-be prima donnas, her dedication to stardom reigned supreme. Jessica's gift for performance was not so much for playing a role as it was for playing herself playing a role. The overkill annoyed me, but her relentless antics inspired me to new heights of impatience. To tell the truth, I was kind of bitchy about it. We commonly broke out in strings of petty arguments during class meetings. This didn't make us very popular with the rest of our group.

Our rivalry, however, did have one benefit: The tension between us was fantastic, and the room crackled with electricity when we performed together.

For this particular exercise, Jessica and I were working on a scene between Estelle and Inez from Sartre's *No Exit*, a short play about three mortals stuck in an existential hell where they each torture one another for eternity. Jessica played Estelle, a vapid, baby-killing seductress whose unavailability tortures Inez, a taunting, venomous lesbian. I was uncomfortable playing Inez since I didn't understand her attraction to Estelle or her disdain for convention. But her relentless goading of the other two characters came more naturally to me than I would have liked to admit.

To be fair, Jessica was a perfect Estelle: She was a dreadful flirt. No man, woman, or child in the class was safe from her calculated attentions. She was tiny and vivacious, with a glorious mane of curly red hair that she knew exactly how to play with to lure the gazes of others. Her well-honed charms filled me with scorn, and I had initially resolved to ignore her as much as possible. My contempt was probably a thin veil for my deep envy of all the doors I subconsciously knew her gorgeous red hair opened up for her. Her rippling tresses constantly reminded me of all the men she surely must be holding captive. Her beauty silently reproached my painfully awkward and seemingly perpetual bachelorettehood. I knew I should be interested in men, and the fact that I wasn't didn't keep me from being jealous over her horde. She had to be the one who was preventing me from getting a boyfriend.

In short, Jessica was the enemy, and I was condemned to work with her. At least I wouldn't have to act very hard to seem tortured by her presence. That's how things were until we actually started rehearsing together. Once we did—as much as I tried to fight it—I secretly started to enjoy Jessica's company. We never really got a lot of work done. She was always looking for an audience, and when we were alone I naturally became her victim. She would digress from our rehearsals every other minute to fascinate me with outrageous tales of her job at a local tabloid. She'd intrigue me with yarns about her time harboring fugitives from the KGB. She'd inspire me with stories from her days spent in an Indian tribe out West (A diamondback bit her. She had to be evacuated). Jessica *was* entertaining, so I easily warmed up to her, even though I knew she was merely playing to a captive audience. As I basked in her good graces, I speculated again about how many men she must have left in the wake of that red hair — such luscious red hair. Men are such clowns.

We whiled away many weeks rehearsing together, and as time passed, Jessica and I laughed and talked more. Our sessions got longer: They turned into dinners and movies and all kinds of things I treated like dates without realizing it. I was always painfully nervous and self-conscious, always checking my clothes, my hair, my makeup, my smile. I was constantly tongue-tied around her; fortunately, Jessica was so caught up in her one-woman show she never noticed. My heart would start to race when I saw her, but I didn't really question it. Wasn't it a natural reaction to feeling like we were always performing? A kind of stage fright? I couldn't be interested in Jessica; I understood her too well. I was far smarter than all those silly men.

I smiled at her. "I have your taste, my dear, because I like you so much," I flattered. "Look at me. No, straight." I lightly touched her chin with the tip of my finger. "Now smile. I'm not so ugly, either. Am I not nicer than your glass?"

She shifted uncomfortably. "Oh, I don't know," she answered. You scare me rather. My reflection in the glass never did that, of course. I knew it so well. Like something I had tamed..." She gave me a wink no one else could see. "I'm going to smile, and my smile will sink down into your pupils, and heaven knows what it will become."

I leaned close. "And why shouldn't you tame me?" We fell silent. The class, which had been squirming with unease, burst into applause.

Jessica and I had chosen another scene from *No Exit* to perform, and it was a hit. We bowed, grinned, bowed again, then ran off the stage. She caught me in a hug. "Let's go celebrate," she crowed. She hugged me. I was suddenly afraid to go with her, but I couldn't stand the idea of not being close to all those charms, all that red hair. So I agreed.

"Where do you want to go?" I asked.

"I know just the place," Jessica said, winking devilishly. "Perfect for two thespians out on a Friday night!"

She dragged me to this dive bar in an unfamiliar part of town. "It's fun and it's close to my place," she smiled. "You can stay over if it gets too late." I cautiously agreed. Who's to say she wasn't secretly planning to abandon me once she met some guy? In the car her chatter eased my fears a little. "I'm over guys," she chirped. "They're an inferior species."

By the time we got to the bar, my spirits were soaring, and I was ready to have some fun. *Who knows...maybe I will meet someone this time.* Bursting through the door, we were promptly engulfed in a swarm. Laughing, we squeezed through. "Let me buy you a drink," Jessica offered. Before I could answer, she bustled off to the jam-packed bar, where it appeared—from the length of the line—she'd be gone all night. I grabbed a table and waited.

Once I settled down, I looked around and began to notice something different about the bar. There was something subtle, and I couldn't quite put my finger on it. The crowd seemed unusually well-behaved for its size. People were actually having real conversations. Then it hit me: This bar was full of women!

My head spun. I hadn't considered the alternatives to "sick of men," and now I was in a mob of them. *Us? Sure, I'm female,*

but... There was something else going on here. A new realization slowly dawned on me. I was stunned. *Was Jessica...?*

"Miss me?" she teased, leaning in from behind. Somehow
she had gotten two beers in no time. All that red hair has its
advantages. I sat puzzled, and then deadly panic gripped me
as the final piece clicked. There was a new hint of flirtation
in her voice. *Does she think I'm...? Oh, no!* All the old suspicion
I had ever held for Jessica melted away, to be replaced by
utter terror. I stared at her. On the surface she seemed to vi-
olate every lesbian—*oh my God, lesbian*—stereotype I had
ever held. But who's to say there wasn't a demon gym
teacher lurking underneath? Someone who would try to lure
me into unspeakable temptations?

Suddenly when she smiled brilliantly at me, my fears evap-
orated. She was just Jessica, my diva costar Jessica, and I
was still her captive audience. But now she was seeking my
attention in a whole new way—the idea was very appealing.
Without the buoy of competition between us, I found myself
feeling quite shy. My shyness worsened when she started
telling me about how hard it was to meet women "for romantic purposes," as she put it. Jessica, whom I had always assumed to be so straight, was blazing the Lesbian Trail. She
had been with a few women before and was exhausting possibilities I had never even considered in trying to find men. I
was intimidated by her experience, but I decided to play
along with it. Happily, her love for center stage kept the conversation safely focused on her. She was, however, curious
by nature and did ask me a few questions. I answered as non-
chalantly as possible, keeping the details vague—as much to
cultivate an air of mystery as to hide my inexperience.

When our conversation lulled, Jessica asked me to dance,
and I realized I had played the part too well to back down
now. It was quite awkward...that is, until she saw two old

women outside glaring scornfully through the window. This excited her; Jessica grabbed me close, and we began dirty dancing. Holding her this way, dancing this close, was electrifying—there was a tantalizing danger to it. For the first time, I felt giddy with possibility. Something could happen. She was not going to spit in my face again. There was nothing to stop it.

As if to prove this, when I later let Jessica led me onto the dance floor for a slow song, she kissed me—right on the mouth, for longer than a peck. It was such a quick, sweet, innocent, girlish kiss it almost didn't register. Almost. Oh my God, she kissed me! All sorts of alarmed voices began shrieking in my head: *Lesbian! Unnatural!* The scariest response of all, however, was the quiet understanding that overpowered everything else: Jessica had kissed me, and I had liked it. It was the softest, most sensual kiss I had ever experienced. It was glorious. Perhaps I was more like Inez than I had thought. Perhaps I could understand this attraction after all.

I got out as quickly as I could. I needed to think. I needed to go back to a safe place where I could shield myself with the usual dose of spite. I needed to go to a haven where Jessica couldn't affect me like this, and—as badly as I needed to get away from her—I cursed her for not following me.

Maybe Jessica let me leave that night because she already knew what I soon found out: a sanctuary away from her didn't exist. I went home and tried to sleep, but she kept prodding my brain. Without talking to her, I heard her voice around me. Without seeing her, I imagined her in front of me. Without touching her, I could feel her red hair in my fingers. When I finally did fall asleep, I dreamed about her: She played Estelle, she played Inez, she played the drama teacher calling all the shots. I had to face the facts: I was attracted to her in a way I didn't understand.

I guess she understood it, though, because the next morning I woke to her knocking on my door.

"I'm sorry," she said in a rush the moment the door opened. "I didn't realize you weren't interested. Can I come in?" I couldn't look at her. "Huh? Oh...sure."

Jessica jostled past me, surveyed the apartment, and then looked me up and down with an appraising eye.

"You don't look like you slept well," she pronounced.

"Call it my penance for being a jerk," I muttered.

"Oh, I'll think of a better penance than that," she threatened. "Wanna go for a ride?"

I reached a hand out to touch her cheek. "I want to kiss you," I whispered. *What am I doing?* She floated into my arms without hesitation, and our lips met shyly. I felt myself spinning at the lip of a dark whirlpool, welcoming the wave of her smile that kept pushing me closer. Slowly, softly, wonderfully, as the morning sun played through the windows, we kissed again...and again...and again.

An hour later we were on my couch, still kissing. She finally got up and walked over to the window.

"I do have to go out, you know," she said. "I have to find a pumpkin for that Halloween skit. Wanna come?"

"Sure," I smiled.

Ask me why we didn't go to a grocery store...I'll never know. Instead we went out looking for a pumpkin patch. We never found one. Wandering around for hours in the country, we admired the foliage, the burning orange-gold autumn landscape that hinted of all that red hair. I tried not to listen to the thoughts that kept nagging me: *How will I ever know what to do? How can I possibly compete with all those women in her past? Am I a lesbian? Do I love her? What if I'm not perfect? Will she laugh at me?*

Eventually we found our way back to her place, but the journey left us exhausted. We opted to spend the evening lounging on her couch. Couches were a good place for us, it seemed. She turned on the TV, and we settled cozily down, she lying easily in my arms. I marveled that it should be so easy. Soon we were too comfortable even to talk, soaked to the bone with contentment, as I breathed in the scent of all that red hair and felt myself drifting in some shapeless, wordless paradise. *This is what it's supposed to be like.* Gradually I became aware her fingers were tracing a light pattern over my chest, over my stomach, through my hair, over my face, and back again, always returning to trace a rune over my heart. I felt waves of a new, sweet ache begin to wash through me. The feeling surged, stronger and stronger, to an unbearably wonderful point that left me on the verge of drowning, where I could not move, could not breathe. My heart thudded painfully as if it were following the wake of her fingers.

"I'm feeling very vulnerable right now, Jess," I finally said stupidly, not knowing how to handle the tide of feelings she had stirred in me. "You could kill me." *Why'd I say that?*

"I could never hurt you, babe," she answered softly, close to my ear. "I'm not really Estelle, you know." She shifted to look up at me, and kissed my cheek. "And you're not Inez, either."

I sighed as I turned my face and sunk it into all that red hair, a luxurious pillow of aromatic softness. As her hands moved gently over me, I felt my heart crack open, and she just poured in. We held each other like that all night, and when the sweetness of being with her brought tears to my eyes, she tenderly brushed them away. It was an intimacy so gently erotic I will always remember that night as our first, when she stirred this strange new desire in me, when I lost myself in all that red hair.

The next morning it seemed the most natural thing for Jessica to lead me softly into the bedroom. When she wrapped her arms around me, and I felt her hands undressing me, I felt I had at last found myself. She wrapped me in wonder. It was so easy to touch and explore her; her skin was the color of the pale harvest moon, her body all curves and softness—a sensual delight. I wondered at how responsive she was to my touch. I marveled at the lovely feel of her wetness on my fingers. I basked in the sound of her every breath. When she came I felt I was feeling the orgasm with her. When she touched me I thought I would die from the pleasure of her fingers and her mouth.

After I came she kissed me, and the taste of sex fired things up again. I don't know how many hours passed while we bathed in lust; it was so easy to make love physically once we had already crossed the emotional terrain. All through that morning and over the next several weeks, Jessica touched me in a way no one ever had: She wove charms around my heart, spun visions of bliss over my eyes. Her sorceress hands summoned my hormones to do her bidding.

Perhaps that's the most dangerous thing—to be touched by the hands of a sorceress. It's one thing to dare to touch a woman; that's perilous business in itself. When you brush away the taboos, when you touch her—really touch her—you touch your own essence, and you become completely vulnerable. If she touches you that way, there can be no barriers.

Alas, too much heaven has a way of painfully bringing you back down to earth. After a few months things subtly began to change. My hopelessly romantic penchant for writing love letters hopelessly annoyed Jessica. Her constant flirtations with everyone around us constantly tortured me. She quickly lost interest in sex; then she got very busy. Hurt by this, I pretended to be equally busy. Jessica didn't notice, and I grew even more hurt. Our basic incompatibilities should have warned me, but I doggedly persevered. Finally I persuaded her one weekend to clear her schedule so we could spend some time together walking around the harbor.

We walked until there was nothing left to see, finally stopping to relax near the water. The winter sun shone brightly, a torch setting fire to all that red hair. I watched the play of light splash over her and wondered idly why something felt so wrong. On the dock, we sat silently, looking at each other's feet, listening to the sucking sounds of the brackish water lapping relentlessly.

"Whatcha thinking about?" Jessica finally ventured, a little too casually. A strange premonition bubbled through me:

Estelle drowned her baby in the water.

I felt a cold smile play over my lips. "I have this funny feeling you want to push me in and walk away."

She nodded emphatically, avoiding my eyes. "You're right," she confessed brightly. "I'm fighting it. It's really bad." She smiled wanly. She didn't have to tell me. I knew.

An hour later at lunch, that weird feeling washed over me again, and this time it nearly carried me right out of the restaurant. I couldn't eat. I knew.

"Honey…" She wouldn't meet my gaze.

"Don't," I said.

"I know you've been picking up on this," she started.

"Don't. Don't say it. I know."

Jessica looked at me out of the corner of her eye. "You know how incompatible we are," she continued.

"Just don't." I got up to leave.

And I ran, the unspoken words still heavy in the air. I wanted to go anywhere, do anything, as long as I didn't have to hear the words. Jessica's words? Estelle's words? They would be different, but it didn't matter. The end result would be the same. "I just need to end this," she called. "It's not your fault!" *You know too much about me. You know I'm rotten through and through.*

It was a year before we spoke. It was a long year, and I spent a good bunch of it hating her, then dating others once I stopped hating, then coming out to my family once I stopped pretending she and the women who followed her didn't mean anything. I finally decided I was going to be a single lesbian—and I was going to enjoy it, damn it. I was going to be sure everyone else enjoyed it, too. I threw a party, a big 30th birthday bash, and spread the word to all my friends that their lives would be made permanently miserable—by regret or by me—if they failed to attend.

People took me seriously, and the party grew crowded quickly. It was noisy and boisterous—for every one guest that left, five more wandered in. Late in the evening the doorbell rang. This was unusual, since PARTY! COME IN! signs screamed from everywhere, and the door was left open. I tore myself from my guests and ran to answer it, uncustomarily looking through the peephole to see who was there. I barely made out a dark feminine figure with short dark hair and a confident pose. My heart began to flutter. I didn't recognize her, but her silhouette affected me.

She was a stranger...she was the woman I had been waiting for.

I threw open the door to find her there—no more long red hair, dressed very differently, hands jauntily propped on her hips. I should have known it was Jessica. She *had* to make a dramatic entrance. *My glancing stream! My crystal!*

A glance can be a quick look...or a flash. It can also be a physical blow. Seeing her was all three. She knocked the wind out of me. In that endless second of recognition I had time to objectively wonder who cut and dyed all that red hair, while simultaneously suffering a knee-jerk hormonal rush and remembering my agony. I knew right away I still adored her. *I'm going to burn, and it's going to last forever. Yes, I know everything. But do you think I'll let go?* She was still a vision, but she had now switched off her own narcissistic spotlight.

"Hi," she smiled. "Still love me?"

What a lovely play it would have been had we left it at that. Life, however, never places the curtain calls where you want them, and we stubbornly tried to salvage our passion. I wanted to be cautious, to act as if it didn't mean anything, but I couldn't dampen the fire she lit in my heart.

Unfortunately, Jessica and I were even more incompatible than before. I couldn't walk away from the ensuing rounds of sex, tears, and accusations—but she could. I waited for a long time, hoping if I left the first time, and she left the second, then there would be a third and final time when we'd have to just walk off somewhere together. I was tragically half-right. For years we kept up an endless game of now-you-want-me-now-I-don't. I finally became exhausted and decided I could only win by exorcising her permanently with a long, angry, vicious letter. Even then there was probably a hidden fault line in my heart Jessica could have flowed through, had she spoken just the right liturgy of desire—or regret. I suspect I even harbored a secret wish she would call my bluff. She took me at my word, though, and the game ended.

But the show must go on, and endings always bring the prospect of beginnings. I have a wonderful partner now. She has taught me over the years to find my own words, to tell my own stories, to become my own center-stage diva in the spotlight of our shared masterpiece. I know I would not have been able to build a home with her had I not played out my earlier scenes with Jessica. I rejoice that Jessica once shared her spotlight with me, even as I wonder how I could have floundered so badly in all that red hair. Women are such clowns.

CHAPTER TWENTY-EIGHT
Hot Summer Night
Juliana Harvard

*T*he night was steamy hot. Even the welcome cloak of darkness did not dispel the sweltering mugginess of the long, lazy Texas summer day. Outside the motel door, Sharla paused, then thrust the key into the lock. I stood slightly behind her, lightly fingering the back of the ribbed tank top that caressed her smooth ebony shoulders. Suddenly, as the door opened, a burst of icy coolness hit our faces, and we disappeared inside the room.

When my hand flipped the light switch, only the dimness of the small lamp by the bed filtered into the darkened room. I let the small leather purse drop from my shoulder onto the floor beside the bed. I sank into the flowered quilted bedspread, my face buried deeply into the pillow, as a persistent migraine continued to throb across my forehead.

Why, now, of all times? After many months of communicating through E-mail and more recently by telephone, Sharla and I had finally been able to arrange this special time together, just the two of us, away from husbands and kids. We knew it was a moment of fantasy we could indulge in perhaps only once in our lifetimes…at least for me.

For the past 19 years, I had been married to Capt. Denny Harvard of the United States Air Force and had no real intentions of changing that. My two teenage children had no idea their "perfect" mother had been harboring secret fantasies for the last two decades. Denny knew, before we were married, about my sexual attraction to women. It was, however, only a fantasy (much like his fantasy of having a threesome with two women) I never acted on. Although Denny had had two affairs during our marriage, they did not include me.

I had always considered myself to be inherently bisexual, although I had chosen the more pragmatic path of heterosexual relationships and finally marriage. My lesbian experiences had existed totally in my fertile imagination—until several months ago. I had activated the modem on my new computer and found a whole gay and lesbian community on America Online; I discovered the meaning and practice of "cybersex" in private chat rooms for $6.95 an hour. Then I switched to Prodigy.

That was the summer of 1993, before live chat was available on Prodigy. The "Alternative Lifestyle" bulletin boards, however, were plentiful and available with unlimited access for a monthly flat fee. I encountered many lesbian and bisexual wives and moms, but Sharla Highland piqued my interest with her wry wit and the common bonds we shared. Besides having a husband and children, Sharla and I each had a "straight" girlfriend whom we had been trying desperately—but futilely—to get into bed for a long time. Sharla finally succeeded in her quest with the beautiful blond Lani, and through E-mail I shared her celebration. I, however, never did get my best friend, Megan, into bed.

Sharla and I had established a solid E-mail friendship before I finally asked, "What do you look like?"

She both startled and fascinated me with her answer.

"My friends tell me I'm a Whoopi Goldberg look-alike."

I suddenly became obsessed with seeing Whoopi Goldberg movies and collecting magazine articles about her. Sharla began to have dreams about me, which she described to me in luscious detail. Online and on the phone, without any consciously deliberate agenda, we were beginning to fall in love, although she was more than a decade younger than I was.

Sharla had been involved with several women before—a total count of nine. But because of whatever pressures she faced as a young black lesbian growing up in the straight, white rural community of Podunk, West Virginia, she eventually married a half-white man and had three children. Like Denny, Jerry Highland was fully aware of Sharla's attraction to women long before they were married. Unlike Denny, however, Jerry had encouraged his wife to indulge in girl recreation—which often included him. One time he even brought home a bisexual woman to Sharla as a birthday present.

Both Denny and Jerry knew their wives were too fully committed to motherhood within a stereotypical nuclear family framework to leave the structure of heterosexual marriage. Still, both men had agreed to our spending a week together in a motel three miles from my house in Fort Worth. They were certain we would "get it out of our systems," and our lives would continue along status quo lines.

Now Sharla sat beside me on the bed and touched the side of my head.

"How's the headache, pretty lady?" she asked softly.

Without stirring, I moaned pitifully. Sharla ran her fingers through my short, straight black hair for a few moments. Then she stopped and bent down to kiss me lightly on my forehead. I turned over, opened my eyes, and started to sit up.

"No, hon, that's OK," Sharla protested. "You don't have to get up."

I smiled, closed my eyes, and let my head fall back onto the pillow, this time with my face turned toward Sharla. I reached a tired hand toward her shoulder and let it slowly caress the length of her arm, momentarily brushing against the side of her rounded breast, before finally falling onto the bed and resting against her hip.

Now Sharla touched my face with both her hands, at first outlining it. She caressed my cheeks and my slightly parted lips. I sighed, opened my eyes, and gazed lovingly into Sharla's sparkling dark eyes. I started to speak, but she placed a soft finger onto my lips as she bent down once again, this time her lips touching mine in a soft kiss.

I reached up again, with both arms around Sharla, and pulled her toward me. Her full moist lips were parted now, and her tongue searched the warm openness of my ready mouth. I responded quickly, my own tongue finding Sharla's warm succulence.

My hands found the lower edge of her shirt and then slipped inside onto Sharla's bare back and up toward her bra fastener. With a quick motion of my nimble fingers, the back strap separated, and Sharla quivered slightly. Sitting up, she quickly pulled the shirt up over her head, and at the same moment her bra fell onto the bed.

I was quick to find Sharla's erect chocolate nipples. I caressed both lightly, then more intensely, as I alternated gentle squeezing with holding each full breast in my cupped hands. Sharla reached for the snap on my jeans. "This is too tight," she said in a matter-of-fact tone. "Doesn't help the headache." As she unzipped my jeans, I raised my hips slightly and freed my abdomen from the denim. Sharla pulled on the jeans until my legs were bare.

"Don't you think it's getting warm in here?" I panted. "Maybe I don't need this shirt."

Sharla smiled, helping me free from the cotton T-shirt. "You don't need this either," she whispered, reaching around my back to unfasten my bra.

I unsnapped Sharla's jeans in almost the same instant, as I murmured, "You can relax too, you know." Sharla stood, letting her jeans fall to the floor. She stretched out beside me on the bed, with one arm under my head and the other hand reaching for my tiny breasts. I placed one hand gently on her upturned buttocks and tugged at the bottom elastic of her panties, then lightly stroked her inner thighs. Sharla's breathing quickened slightly, as her parted lips once again found mine in a growingly passionate deep kiss. She moved her body over mine so our breasts were touching and her legs were spread apart over me.

After several intense moments in the embrace, I mouthed the words I had said a thousand times before in my fantasies.

"Oh, Sharla! Do you have any idea what you're doing to me?"

I squirmed visibly, moving my hips in a rhythmic motion.

Sharla grinned. "Oh, yes…I think I have some idea!"

"But I'm so…so wet!"

Sharla laughed. "And you think I'm not?"

I reached around, this time bravely placing my hand between Sharla's legs onto her very soaked panties. "Wow!" I whispered. "You are! Well, you really don't need these now." With that request, I used both hands to pull off her panties as she accommodated by lifting her hips.

Now Sharla sat up, still straddling me, her dark pubic hair glistening with ample moisture. "Well, you don't need yours either, you know." She winked mischievously as she playfully pinched the crotch of my panties, also fully drenched with my love juice. Without further words, Sharla removed my panties quickly, then placed her hand once again between my legs as she lay back onto the bed beside me. Nothing had ever felt quite so nice *and* naughty—and amazingly natural—at the same time!

Trembling, I placed a timid hand on Sharla's fuzzy labia, feeling her profuse wetness. I cautiously ran one finger from the very front, across her swollen clit, the full length nearly to her anal opening. She found my clit and methodically circled it with a short-nailed finger, then stopped to gently roll it between two fingers. Both Sharla and I were breathing harder now.

"What are you like inside?" I ventured.

"Why don't you find out?" she invited, and I slowly drew one finger back through her soft crack until I could explore deep into the slippery opening. Unsurprisingly, it felt much like my own, except it was Sharla's voice groaning now and not mine.

I wondered what her finger would feel like inside me. Almost as if reading my thoughts, she suddenly slipped her finger deep inside me. It seemed as if someone had cranked up the room temperature a thousand degrees. I sensed electricity surging nonstop through my heated body. I felt her finger exploring my depths as I explored hers, searching for an inevitable magic accelerating at warp speed.

Suddenly, like a million fireworks in a velvety black sky, we both felt explosions inside and moaned audibly at nearly the same time. I was breathing rapidly, and my mouth found Sharla's, kissing her passionately until my quickened breathing began to subside. I sighed a long contented sigh, although my hand still remained on the soaked lips between her legs.

Vaguely aware Sharla had pulled her hand from my wet opening, I watched with fascination as she placed her dripping fingers into her mouth, licking my juice from them.

"Sharla!" I wrinkled my nose. "O-o-oh, how can you do that?"

Sharla smiled. "Mmm," she teased, holding her hand toward me. "It's delicious. Want some?"

"Yuck!" I protested, "Not mine, anyway." Then I tilted my head in a wry smile. "But maybe...yours." Gingerly, I pulled my hand from Sharla's cunt and looked for a long moment at the dripping juice. I sniffed cautiously at first, then licked the end of one finger. My eyes widened. "Wow!" I licked again, this time the full length of my fingers, then sucked hungrily. "It's all gone!" I whimpered.

"Well," Sharla teased, "there's more where that came from, you know."

I sat up straight now and turned Sharla onto her back. Straddling Sharla's body as she had done to me earlier, I kissed her neck as my hands fondled her breasts. Soon my mouth covered her nipples again, and I began to suck gently, first one, then the other. Sharla's hands lazily stroked my hair and shoulders until I had moved down out of her reach, my tongue tracing her navel for only a moment. Then I reached the warm, still-moist love nest between her legs.

Sharla's spread her legs, trembling in anticipation. I glanced up long enough to see her closed eyes and her slightly open mouth. My fingers parted her labia and traced the outline of her rosebud clit. Unable to resist the ultimate act of my lifelong fantasies, I covered her pink button with my warm mouth, tracing it with my tongue. I sucked it slightly, then moved my tongue along the path my fingers had taken earlier, to the very source of Sharla's warm, sweet nectar. Losing track of time and space, I lingered, drinking deeply of ecstatic delight, only faintly aware of my own juices dripping down my thighs.

Sharla moaned with an erotic sound that until now I had heard only in my secret fantasy world. Her hips moved in a definite rhythm as they pushed her mound into my face, then subsided as I swallowed. I continued to explore with my tongue, caressing her hips and legs, and feeling an unexplained oneness with her. Again the intensity increased, accelerating rapidly beyond all control, until Sharla's ecstasy exploded into a million new fireworks all at once.

Keenly aware my arousal had not yet subsided, Sharla sat up and reached to pull me toward her. Wordlessly, she turned me onto my back, sucking momentarily on my erect nipples as her own breasts fell onto my tummy. I reached to touch her breasts again, but Sharla had already moved quickly to my inner thighs, which were totally covered with the juices that had flowed down moments earlier.

Sharla licked my legs as she massaged my swollen clit. I felt a new surge of heat as her tongue penetrated my moisture-laden opening—sucking, licking, and exploring more expertly than I had never dreamed possible. I didn't want it to ever end! Even after the fireworks had again exploded more fiercely than I could have imagined, Sharla's tongue and hands continued to caress every crevice of my body.

I felt Sharla's ardor build again, her breathing quicken, her rhythm accelerate. "OK," I whispered, "your turn again."

Sharla would not let me pull away. "I can't stop making love to you," she breathed. "I can't let you go!"

"OK," I acquiesced. "But turn around. Put your bottom up here."

"Are you sure?" Sharla hesitated.

"Sharla, sweetheart, I've never been more sure of anything in my life!" Of all my fantasies in all the years, nothing was quite as exciting to me as imagining the classic 69 position with another woman. I knew doing it just once for real would give me enough memories to fuel all my fantasies for the rest of my life!

Sharla turned her body, now straddling my face, as I reached up and pulled her cunt down onto my open mouth. "Mmm, yes!"—and then the sounds were muffled. Sharla once again buried her tongue into my warm, sweet juice. We both became totally immersed in the other's embrace, as if we were one body. We lost track of how long we lay locked together and how many times ten million more fireworks exploded inside us, until we both sank from exhaustion into the damp bed.

The first rays of the morning sun peeked through a needle-sized slit in the heavy curtains as Sharla awoke, her face on the bed still inches from my upper thighs. She smiled, eyes closed, remembering. I had been watching her for several minutes without stirring. I reached around to touch her still-naked bottom with a light pat. She giggled, then sat up and turned fully around to put her head near mine.

"Good morning!" we both cooed, almost at the same moment.

"I think it's cooled off in here a bit," Sharla observed.

I grinned. "Yeah, but probably not for long."

I turned back the quilted bedspread, crawling under it and motioning for Sharla to join me. Our arms encircled each other, as our faces touched on the pillow. We kissed lightly, then rested together in a comfortable snuggle. Although our legs entwined around each other, we were not feeling the physical intensity of a few hours before, but rather strong, emotional warmth, unexplained and undefined.

"So," Sharla spoke at last, "how's the headache, hon?"

I smiled broadly. "You know what? I think it's gone!"

Sharla squeezed me just a little tighter. "Let's take a shower," she suggested. "Not a cold shower, though!"

"Are you kidding? How could it be cold with us in it?" I quipped. "It'll be hot before we even turn on the water!"

"OK, OK," Sharla closed her eyes, still smiling, not moving for a long moment. "And then...and then what?"

"What?"

"And then what?" Sharla repeated.

"And then...we'll do it all over again!"

Sharla hugged me but still repeated, "And then what?"

I looked into Sharla eyes, knowing neither of us really wanted to answer the question. The look spoke thoughts of children, of our children's fathers, of conventional marriages and "respectable" American families. It spoke of a sadness, of unfulfilled dreams and desires. It spoke of resignation poorly disguising the dare to hope somehow, someday things might be different.

For now, Sharla only returned my longing gaze. She started to speak, but I put a finger on her lips, then my own lips on hers. "Let's think about that tomorrow."

We spent the next eight glorious days acting like foolish tourists in the sunshine of the Dallas/Fort Worth area. We luxuriated in eight more nights like the first, all filled with passion and tenderness, explosive fireworks, and utterly unexplained contentment. Then Sharla went back to Podunk. As I watched her car pull away from the parking lot and disappear in the bustling traffic of Interstate 35, I felt a hollow, gnawing emptiness. I sensed strongly that life could never be quite the same again.

Not wanting to go back home to Denny immediately, I wandered aimlessly in Wal-Mart for an hour or two. I hummed softly to myself, making up a tune that formed inside in my head:

> *Love knows no color,*
> *Love knows no race,*
> *Love is the star dream*
> *I see in your face.*
> *Love knows no distance,*
> *Love crosses miles,*
> *Love is the reason for*
> *All of my smiles.*
> *Age doesn't matter,*
> *Makes no difference what size,*
> *All that really matters*
> *Is the love in your eyes.*
> *Love knows no gender*
> *But what's meant to be,*
> *Love is this special thing*
> *Between you and me.*

In my wildest dreams, I couldn't have imagined what would transpire within the next year. Neither Sharla nor I could have foreseen how our normally sane and responsible husbands would become unreasonably insecure and completely hysterical; would threaten divorce, suicide, and homicide; would lose their jobs; and would molest their own teenage daughters. Neither of us could have predicted to what extent our own feelings would change and how our long-range plans would ultimately include more than an annual summer visit with each other.

Sharla and I would, in reality, plan to live together, to raise our children together, perhaps even have a baby together. Those plans, however, crumbled, even before beginning to be built; separate new paths opened up for our well-deserved emancipation from patriarchy.

Moving to Dallas/Fort Worth brought Sharla a whole new world of opportunities she might never have had otherwise, even if those options ultimately did not include me. For me, a "half-breed" Asian who grew up in a sexist-racist European-American culture, falling in love with a beautiful African-American lesbian stripped me of any vestige of prejudice I unknowingly might have had. Even our breakup, as painful as it was at the time, gave us both much needed independence and strength. We were able at last to take control of our own lives, to protect and nurture our children, to realize personal and professional growth, and to bring to our relationships with other women the richness and warmth that has made us exactly who we are.

CHAPTER TWENTY-NINE
Coming Out at *The Rocky Horror Picture Show*
Bonnie J. Morris

*O*nce there was a moment in time when teenagers did not spend their Saturday nights drinking or smoking dope or looking for fights; instead, we were all down at the Varsity Theater shouting ritual innuendoes—and throwing rice at a transvestite movie icon. Those who think transgender posing is a '90s phenomenon weren't at my high school in 1978, when my then-boyfriend won first prize at the Halloween screening of *The Rocky Horror Picture Show* for showing up in his mother's dress and jewelry.

The Rocky Horror Picture Show offered three terrific opportunities: You were actually invited to talk back to the screen instead of accepting a passive audience role; you were enjoined to show creative contempt for restrictive gender codes of behavior and dress; and you were likely to have gay people in the audience, thus enjoying a nonthreatening social mixer with gay adults. The picture was superbly successful in bringing together two historically hostile adolescent groups—punks and queers—as united dramatis personae in an authentic theatrical rite. Never mind that the film customarily ran at midnight or—for kids under 17—presented the usual R-rated hassles. This was a place where we toyed with the notion that it was more hip to cross-dress than to be square. And cross-dress I did, binding my breasts flat with an Ace bandage, pulling my hair into a male-hippie ponytail, and jogging down to the Varsity Theater in male garb, delighting in the freedom to pass.

For full participation in *Rocky Horror*, one had to bring the following accoutrement in a paper bag: rice, to throw during

Brad and Janet's wedding; a newspaper, which was worn on the head during Janet's rain walk; a flashlight or cigarette lighter to hold up during the song "There's A Light"; toast, to throw when Frank N. Furter proposes "A toast!"; a deck of cards, a bell, and sundry other props used when such objects were mentioned in songs. It was a gleeful enactment of the scavenger hunts we'd all played out in childhood. One's status increased notably with each additional prop brought to the theater and used correctly. And, of course, the props were but one part of intimately knowing the screenplay; real troupers knew *every* line of dialogue and responded accordingly, with group back talk that was known coast to coast ("Asshole!" "Elbow sex!"), and also less frequently heard replies ("Magenta, don't let your mind wander; it's too small to go outside by itself.").

We who set our minds to memorizing this routine of foolery were the despair of parents who yearned for the same studious care to be focused on SAT preparation and college applications. Perhaps that was why we so joyfully returned, again and again, to see *Rocky Horror.* Our senior school days were crammed with preparation for the adult academic world, our parents clutching us close for the last year. But up there on the movie screen were all the personalities we'd never been allowed to gaze on before: transsexuals and mad scientists. "It's just a movie," we'd say, proud to justify time spent not on drugs or sex or junk food—just a movie, at the Varsity.

When I began college in Washington, D.C., I was a drama major, and I quickly found in the drama department a clique of gay and punk and New Wave students who had cars and drove down to the Key in Georgetown to see *Rocky Horror* every weekend. We competed with one another for the most outlandish costumes, the most cleverly memorized lines, and the most daring skill: to get out of one's seat during the film and lip sync in drag in front of the screen. In the company of such friends, I was very well cared-for and gradually hovered on the verge of coming out. But I was a commuter student who lived at home with my parents.

And my parents, ever game, asked cheerful questions about this cult movie I dressed up for almost every week. What was all the fuss about? Could they go too some time? They still enjoyed dressing up in costume. Why should *I* have all the fun? Amused by their tolerant inquiries, I agreed to "chaperone" them to a midnight showing of *Rocky Horror* on April 26, 1980. It was a night that changed my life forever, but not because I went to the movies with my parents.

My movie date with Mom and Dad wouldn't begin until 11:30 that night. I expected to spend the afternoon and evening studying for spring semester final exams. I drove my parents' Buick Skylark over to the university dorm where my new friend, Angie, lived. A fresh drizzle plastered green leaves against her window while we quizzed each other, paced, flipped pages of heavy first-year tomes, compared notes, and, finally, settled into a cozy bitch session about every personality in the drama department.

At 6 o'clock we realized we were hungry, so we drove down to the Roy Rogers at Tenley Circle for milkshakes and fries. Angie spewed on hilariously about the various college men she'd had, was having, wanted to have, had let herself be tied up with in a storage closet, or had given up on entirely because they were gay. Suddenly, I thought I might be able to trust this freewheeling sister, this 18-year-old wild thing.

"I think I'm gay," I heard my own voice announce through a mouthful of fries.

"Like, wow. Really? Have you, like, *done* anything?" Angie stared at me with considerable interest. I looked down at the lonely blobs of ketchup on my tray. She launched into the

who-do-you-like parade, mentioning the few bisexual or lesbian students we knew. Did I like that one? Was I attracted
to that one? Had I had any of them?

Mortified by my lack of experience, my poverty of anec-
dotes, I shrank back into the yellow plastic light generated by
the imitation lampshade, curled my feet in their Birkenstock
sandals, and chewed the end of my long braid indecisively.

"No...nothing...nobody," I finally whispered. "I like
Leslie, and I like Gillian, but it's no use, and I've never even
kissed another girl."

"How long have you been thinking about this...or, I guess
I should say, having feelings?"

"All semester," I admitted. "I mean, um, since around the
end of eighth grade actually."

I crunched a mouthful of crushed ice between my teeth,
hoping it would cover up the grating sound of my thighs, in
blue corduroy Levis, pressing together.

Angie leaned forward to say something, but at that moment, seeing our empty trays, a harried counter worker
whisked over to us and demanded, "Are you ladies through?"
It was the start of Saturday night; the place was filled with
hungry college students and families with crying toddlers.
Clearly, Roy Rogers wanted us to leave so another group
could have our table.

"Look, let's just go sit in my parents' car," I said.

"Cool. I'd like to keep talking."

In the Roy Rogers parking lot, we had just settled into the
Buick and picked up the thread of the conversation again
when a car, light beams glaring, pulled in behind us and sat
idling with a kind of aggressive patience.

"I think he wants this parking space," said Angie.

"Jesus, this is impossible! Look, I'm going to go park
somewhere else, or I'll never finish telling you this stuff. I'll

just drive around the fucking block." I peeled out and turned into the first quiet public driveway I saw, which led into the enormous, empty parking lot of the Home Mortgage Association on Wisconsin Avenue.

Now it was dark; it was the very last night before spring daylight saving time began. Trees edged the silent lot, guarding our sudden privacy. We were alone, fresh spring rain drizzled on the steamed-up Buick windows. "Have you ever wanted to kiss *me?*" Angie asked.

"Oh…no, n-no," I stammered, lying through my chattering teeth. "I didn't mean for this conversation to make you feel like I'm after you."

"So you don't think I'm as pretty as Leslie?"

"I…sure you are. Yeah, I do. I mean, I didn't bring you here to…"

"Well, I feel like someone's waiting to make the first move."

"Oh. Um…"

Angie picked up my palm and traced her soft fingernails around and around on the back of my hand. I felt both of us trembling. The steering wheel vibrated. Look at her she is so she is so she is so…I don't know how to *touch* her I…

"Will you kiss me?" Angie finally asked, interrupting my free-range chickenhood.

"Yes," I avowed, not moving an iota, feeling her hand caress my hand like a blessing. "I just don't know *how.*"

"Oh, it can't be that different from kissing a guy," she smiled, and wrapped her arms around my neck. Then, the warm rain and her warm mouth and the soft down above our lips and the digital clock on the dashboard flashing 9:30.

"Mmm. O-o-oh…" she moaned.

"That wasn't so bad," I managed to say, casual-like.

"It's gentler," decided Angie, "than kissing a guy."

We kissed again. "You're beautiful," she said.

Much later, after more kissing, after the discovery that a woman's tongue in my mouth was a *really great thing* and *heaven on earth* and the *total cat's meow*, I suddenly awoke to the stark realization that in a short while I was supposed to take my parents to the movies. At about this same time, Angie remembered that she was, in fact, heterosexual.

"You'd better take me back now."

"I know."

In silence we drove the long mile back to her dorm at American University. I thought of and bit back many things to say. Next to me, her pretty seashell eyes were closed.

I took her to the front door of McDowell. "Good-bye," she said, and that was the last look, the last word I had from Angie for some time.

Now I was driving home, taking the loop around Westmoreland Circle like a condemned cowgirl, dashing down Massachusetts Avenue without playing my usual game of counting lucky green lights, and composing my face so that my parents would *see nothing, suspect nothing* when I walked through that rectangle of light at our front door. I mentally went through my usual habits of arriving at home: Turn off car. Turn off lights. Pull out keys. Walk down front steps. Push open front door, say "Hi," hang keys up on hook.

Now I was in my parents' driveway. *I had kissed a woman.* We were 18, no longer girls, but women. I'd left my girlhood—my girl reel—unwinding all over the front seat of the Buick.

Now I was turning off the ignition; *I had kissed a woman.* I was turning off the lights and pulling out the keys; *I had kissed a woman, had a woman's tongue caressing mine.* I was down the front steps; *I had kissed a woman.* The rectangle of light gave way against my fist as I pushed open our front door; *I had kissed a woman.* I walked into my house, said

"Hi," hung the keys up on their hook, and marveled that no one stopped me, no one saw anything different about me. *I had kissed a woman.*

My parents were in pleasant spirits, preoccupied with dressing up for our outing to *The Rocky Horror Picture Show.*

"Did you have dinner?" my mother asked from her make-up table. I stood transfixed by the sight of my own face in the mirror. *Does it show? I am a real lesbian now. When will the lavender "L" start to glow in the middle of my forehead?* I inspected my lips closely. They felt tender but looked like any 18-year-old's lips. I turned my jaw this way and that.

"I said, did you get anything to eat?"

"Huh? Oh, yeah, we—I—I went to Roy Rogers with Angie." I disappeared into my room and slammed the door.

For 40 minutes I lay on the floor of my room in the dark, playing my Roches albums over and over, and letting my stomach twirl on the image of Angie's mouth.

At 11:20 my father knocked on the door. "We'd better get going, or we'll never find a parking place." Numb, I rose and put on my usual *Rocky Horror* gear, collected my props, and climbed into the backseat of the Buick. I could still smell Angie's perfume.

My mother sat down in the front passenger seat that was still warm from Angie's body. I choked back a scream. "Movie candy!" Mom announced brightly, showing the gummy bears and Hershey chocolate she had secreted inside her purse; my parents never bought movie candy, only popcorn. The smell of Angie dissolved into the sickening sweetness of gummy bears.

"OK, where are we going again?" asked my father, who lived in a world of his own and often had to be pointed in the correct next direction.

"The Key."

I could barely believe that on this solemn occasion, my formal initiation into the tribe of Sappho, I was not in some nourishing nook reading Adrienne Rich but, instead, was on the pavement outside the movie theater with my *parents—* both of them dressed in their old costumes from the 1960s California Renaissance Fair. I turned my eyes heavenward in supplication as we joined the usual midnight *Rocky Horror* throng and pushed inside for seats. *Why am I here?* I wondered. I wanted to be alone, to hold myself steady, cradle into my body the new language of sensation.

Not that the Key Theater, in Georgetown, wasn't gay space of a kind. Here my lesbian cousin, Shannon, (not yet out herself, then, either) had taken me to see *My Brilliant Career,* a film about a real-life Australian lesbian writer (whose sexual orientation is never mentioned in the film). The Key Theater was where I went to *Rocky Horror* with all my gay and lesbian pals from my college drama department. Now I had brought my parents into this gay lair on the very occasion of my own coming out. Perhaps it *was* an acceptable place to hide while I contemplated what had just happened with Angie. After all, there was no moment of my emotional life that I had not subjected to a nice long bake in the light spill of a movie screen. I let my reel spin out.

Punks were dancing in front of the screen during the warm-up music, which was always the same: "I Want Money," played while assorted cartoons ran upside down and backward. "Look at that guy," my mother marveled. "He's dancing like he's mesmerized, hypnotized; he could easily be a Hitler Youth."

"Lips!" shrieked several impatient audience punks, wanting the picture to begin.

I saw my beloved gay friend Jim saunter past, wearing a wig, garter belt, lipstick, and fishnet stockings. "Oh, hi, Jim," I said, indicating my parents. "Mom and Dad, this is Jim; he used to go to St. John's Military Academy." Jim, in character, gave us a Frank N. Furter lip curl. My father began to shrink into his I-am-invisible pose.

Finally the movie began, and I automatically threw rice and yelled out dialogue with the rest of the crowd. Inwardly I was tingling, my mind returning again and again to Angie's mouth and my stomach soaring. Outwardly I felt myself small and possum-like, wedged between my parents as I had always been at movies, but suddenly in possession of a lesbian silhouette they could not see. I was different now; I had done what they had not, in their lives.

What is Angie feeling? What is she thinking? Is she asleep? Here at the movies, it was 1 o'clock in the morning, already tomorrow; our kiss already yesterday's dream. I thought of the many movies I had seen that spring semester with Angie at my side, the blue light from the screen illuminating her terrific profile and half-moon eyes; would we ever sit side by side like that again? "Two women, touching, just at the knees, but connected, extending each other like halves of an oyster's shell," my poet friend Ronna Hammer had written. *Will I be Angie's oyster again or cast off forever to tumble in the surf?*

On-screen, the cast of *Rocky Horror* was singing, "Don't dream it—be it." I would have to go on with this thing, this being a teenage lesbian, whether or not Angie continued kissing me, whether or not any movie reflected this life in all its bittersweet discovery. And sooner or later, I would have to come out to my parents. Maybe the next day, when we set ahead the clocks: fitting imagery—no turning back for me now. Spring forward. Don't dream it—be it. I started smiling, thinking of Angie calling me beautiful, and I kept on smiling, although my parents could not see me, in the dark.

CHAPTER THIRTY
The Dream
Marti

*O**h, my God. What is happening to me? What is going on? I've
got to stop this. How can I? I don't want it to stop. No, this is
wrong. No, it's not wrong; it's not. I love it. Oh, God, I'm so
scared. I want to sleep again. No, sleep brings her back. I don't dare. I
don't care. I want her back. Oh, dear God, I want to dream again.*

The dream returned every night for more than two weeks.
I couldn't wait to go to bed each night. Sometimes I tried
napping during the day. I craved the feelings from the dream.
The dream was kissing her: a kiss that always started gently.
Our lips touched lightly, the passion built, gradually, delight-
fully, fabulously. The kiss deepened and did not stop. I woke
trembling with desire, a physical, sexual need beyond anything I had ever experienced.

It terrified me. My marriage was already falling apart. This
sure as hell wasn't going to help anything. *I've got to make this
stop. No, no, no—I want it. I need it. I have a right to feel like this. I
cannot let it go.*

We had met at church. Our friendship was instantaneous.
Over the year, we worked and played together, at first a little. It quickly became a lot. And then we were doing everything together. We started our day at 6 o'clock every morning, walked a mile, then two, followed by quiet talks over
coffee before parting for work. The day didn't end until we
shared our thoughts, our plans, and our dreams. Most of that
sharing took place on my rec room sofa. Sometimes we
shared a blanket against the chill of the downstairs room. I
liked her touch, her hugs, her laughter. Our husbands com-

plained about how much time we were spending together. We didn't care. They were boring, demanding, and they were men—incapable of understanding real friendship. That's what Jayne and I had, and we were not about to let it go.

I knew the problem in my marriage was my fault. The once dutiful wife—devoted to dinner promptly at 6 o'clock; laundry always clean, ironed, and put away; kids always bathed, appropriately quiet or playful, always my first priority—had now begun to think about herself. It scared him, and it also made him angry. It scared me too, but there was an excitement now in my life I just could not resist. I took a job without asking his permission. I opened by own checking account. The world was turning upside down. I was free-falling and soaring all at the same time. And the desire to be with Jayne kept growing.

Something was happening to me. I met a lesbian at work. First time in my life I'd talked to one. I found some books about lesbians and devoured them. I was coming alive. *No! This is stupid. I've been married 15 years. I've got kids who need me. I've got a family to nurture and protect. I can't throw that away. This is just crazy. I am a responsible person, a mother, a wife.* In desperation, I arranged a marriage encounter weekend for Joe and me. An attempt to hold things together. I was never so miserable my entire life.

Eventually I told her about the dream. And she was gone. My confidante, my friend was gone. My life changed forever. I didn't know what to do; I didn't know which way to turn. I made up my mind to push it away. It was just a phase I could get over if I tried hard enough. Then I changed my mind. I had given and given and given. It was my turn. Goddamn it, it was my turn. One day I was positive I could push it away; the next I was certain I couldn't. *Should* and *shouldn't* jerked me back and forth like a car rear-ending me into a concrete wall again and again.

Everything changed when Diane came into my life, first as a new neighbor, then my friend. Soon we were sharing the problems of our marriages and our lives. She told me about the lesbian experiences she'd had in college. I shared with her the thoughts haunting me about my own sexuality. Sometimes we talked far into the night. Sometimes our talks began in the middle of the night and lasted till dawn. The talking was accompanied by casual touching, holding hands, and comforting hugs as we provided support for whatever problem faced us for the day. Truth: I loved her problems. The more she had, the more I got to touch her. The more I touched her, the more I wanted to touch her. I felt guilty that her tears brought me such joy. When she cried, I got to hold her in my arms; I held her close. I felt her tears against my cheek, and I wiped them tenderly away. Sometimes I kissed them away. She didn't seem to mind.

She didn't mind but allowed nothing more. I told her I wanted more. That shocked me. Shocked me that I could admit it to myself. Shocked me that I could take the risk she wouldn't run from me too. By then I knew for certain I was a lesbian. I knew I wanted her. My dreams had stopped, but daytime fantasies had taken over. I wanted the feelings the dreams had given me — and I wanted them for real.

It made sense to me. Who better to have sex with for the first time than my trusted, dearest friend? She said no again and again. She wouldn't risk our friendship for a fling. And she'd never brought anyone out. At 35 she did not intend to start. I was very frustrated. What was to risk? We both knew what this was about. And if everyone had her attitude about bringing someone out, I'd never have sex with a woman. The situation was driving me nuts. In the meantime, she started visiting her old friends, returning to share with me how wonderful it was to have sex with women again. I hated her for that. Why not me? I was almost 40 years old. Old enough to know what I wanted.

Why couldn't she understand?

I filed for divorce and told the kids as much as I dared at the time. Joe knew. He had found and read my journal. The threat was constant that he would charge me an unfit mother and take away the kids. That part of my life was hell. Another part, however, had set me free. That part gave me happiness and courage beyond any I had ever known. Maybe I never would have sex with Diane. Maybe I never would have sex with anybody. All I knew was I would not have "pretend sex" again. Not pretend to be orgasmic, not pretend to like it, and most important, not pretend I was heterosexual. I was a lesbian. It was my turn. I was free at last. Free at last.

There is no doubt I was always a lesbian. Society's expectations; homophobia; a sheltered, hick farm girl—all trapped me in a vice so tight that my brain was stuck. I have to laugh when I recall the torture of dating, the fear of being touched, the relief I found being married to a man who prematurely ejaculated. But my marriage wasn't too bad. At first I buried myself in my job. It was important to put him through school. Then kids. They were my life. I stayed focused on my responsibilities. I just couldn't do it forever. The dream released the vice that had trapped my brain and my feelings.

Diane and I were having a rare afternoon get-together. Normally school and work prevented our talks from starting earlier than late evening. I complained about yet another deposition Joe was dragging me through. Diane filled me in on her last semester of classes. I was propped up on her bed, pillows behind me. She lay beside me. We heard the laughter of our children as they played in the front yard. "I learned a new technique called visual imagery," Diane told me. "Want me to show you?"

I knew that would allow us to be close, to lose ourselves in some strange wonderful world, whatever I invented. I felt my heart skip a beat in anticipation. "I'd love it," I told her, my voice much calmer than I felt. I didn't know where it would go. But I knew what I wanted.

"OK, lie down flat. Now close your eyes." Slowly she led me through the relaxation exercises. Hands, fingers, arms, toes. I faked that really well. My heart was racing. I was a spring ready to explode. I wanted her. Her voice was quiet, soft, soothing.

"You are completely relaxed and drifting lightly somewhere."

My mouth is drifting over your body.

"Where are you?"

Too soon to tell her the truth. "I'm on the beach. A secluded beach. We are alone."

"What are we doing?"

I am devouring you with my tongue. "We're lying on a blanket, talking, drinking wine."

"What do you hear?"

I let the imagery build. *Ecstasy, the sounds you make as you are about to come. Oh, God, how I love my tongue on you.* "Your voice. An occasional gull squawking as she spots a fish. The waves caressing the shore."

"What do you smell?"

I smiled. *You smell and taste like dewdrops. You're salty, slippery, and full of honey.* "Your perfume. I like the way you smell."

"Just keep imagining you are on the beach. Tell me now, what you see."

I see you naked, your legs pulling me to you, your thrusting hips pushing into my face. "I see you lying next to me. I see myself taking a bottle of lotion from you, and now I see myself slowing bathing your skin.

Diane's voice was barely audible. "What do you feel around you?"

I feel you. I want to go down on you, put my tongue in you, eat your pussy till I can't breathe another breath. "Heat. The sun, maybe. The sand. A breeze. You, Diane, I feel you. Do you feel hot too?"

She got up from the bed.

"Don't disturb the ambiance, Diane," I suggested softly. "The stage is set. Lie back down beside me. Continue what you started."

"I don't think I started this, and I think you know just what you are doing."

"Yes, I do. Now let's continue."

She hesitated briefly, then locked the door before lying down beside me. We turned facing each other. I kissed her on the lips. Not like those we had shared before. The kiss was from my dream. I knew just how to do it. This time as the passion built, I didn't have to wake up; there was no fear, no hesitation.

"Are you absolutely sure?" she asked.

I began to unbutton my blouse. "Absolutely."

Within moments her lips were enjoying my breasts. This was the most heavenly feeling I had ever known. The divine was yet to come. And it did as I felt her mouth slide down between my legs. If she had any lingering doubts about whether I was ready, they disappeared. My body responded to hers—the aching, longing need met at last. With every kiss, every touch, her hands, her lips, her tongue gave meaning to my body.

When I make love to her, all that had been bound and hidden, buried, and denied for so long flooded from of me. I took her breast into my mouth, let my tongue caress her nipple. I sucked it gently at first and then with all the passion I felt. Her sounds excited me even more. Her body pushing into mine took me to an even higher level of desire. When my tongue dipped between her legs, I found her pussy wet and juicy and eagerly awaiting my need to please her. I teased her with licking, light kisses, playful touches, my tongue across her clit, in and out of her vagina.

I felt her passion reaching mine, soaring. I waited until she was almost there. I slipped my finger into her hot open hole and let it go deep inside her. I lowered my mouth and tongue to her clitoris, sucking, stroking, devouring it and her. She came as if exploding in my mouth. I came as if her body was mine. I kissed my way up her body to her lips. "The dyke has burst wide open," I told her with a grin.

"Great God," she said laughing at my pun. "I'll say. And I must also say I would never have believed this was your first time if I hadn't been with you every step of the way. How'd you get so good without any practice?"

"I've practiced in my mind a million times. I have wanted this for a very long time. Thank you."

We laughed and hugged, got dressed. Suddenly we were shaking as we remembered our kids, how close they were. Thank God they stayed put. "Good clean living, Diane. That's why we got lucky. There's just no way anything could have ruined this day for me."

That was 17 years ago. We are still best friends. That was the first and last time for us together. Rarely have we told anyone. She and I talk about it, but not often. We laugh about how it happened; sometimes we tease each other about her resistance and my aggression; sometimes we get very serious as we recall my coming out. We each moved on to other relationships, and neither of us has any desire to repeat what happened between us.

But visual imagery—I'm sold on that for life.

CHAPTER THIRTY-ONE
The Diamond
Robin Lind

*I*t was well past midnight on that memorable evening in September of 1994. I said good night to my best friend, Michael, and his lover, Leonard, in front of their house. Then I crossed the street toward my upstairs studio apartment at the foot of Twin Peaks in San Francisco's Noe Valley. I paused for a moment at the top of the hill to look down over the beautiful city I had grown to love over the past few years.

Tonight my life is perfect. After nearly 20 years of being married to the wrong person, I found a lifelong treasure I had been waiting my whole life to find but had never known to look for. I had found a diamond, the most precious and sought-after jewel in the world.

A sudden cool breeze sent a chill through my body, but I knew it was caused by more than air temperature. I tightened my hug slightly around the petite woman who was with me and sighed softly. "This is almost heaven!" I whispered, my lips barely brushing her ear. I marveled all over again at how this weekend had come about.

When I was 17 my parents sent me to Orchill Hills, an exclusive boarding school snuggled in the green mountains of North Carolina. That year, Michael Diamond would change my life forever. He was the new music teacher—a young, quiet, sophisticated, and extremely talented musician from Los Angeles who at once recognized and appreciated my own musical talents. Out of all the sopranos in the whole school, I was chosen to work as Mr. Diamond's student secretary in the music department. Mrs. Diamond was the girls' dormitory dean. But being a good girl who didn't get into trouble, I didn't get the opportunity to know her very well. At the end of the school year, Mr. D.—as we called him—and his shy Filipino wife disappeared. I grew up and got married.

Two decades and two babies later, I knew my life had to change. Through persistence and ingenuity, I found Mr. Diamond again. He and Mrs. Diamond had divorced many years before, after Michael had come out as a gay man. He had moved to San Francisco where he became a prominent organ performer at a theater in the famous Castro district. Since I was in charge of the Orchill Hills alumni homecoming, I invited Mr. Diamond to be our guest concert artist one year. There was an instant bond, a rekindling of an old relationship in a new setting. I had found the best friend my heart had always longed for. I visited him in San Francisco and knew immediately I had to move there. It felt more like home than anywhere else in the world.

Despite an insanely jealous husband who nearly killed both Michael and me with a shotgun, I managed to leave my dysfunctional marriage. I quit my factory job of 19 years, sold most of my personal possessions, and moved across the country to San Francisco in the summer of 1992. Together Michael and I started Diamond Music Enterprises so we could record and distribute his exceptionally popular movie music, as well as publish the printed arrangements that were in great demand from his adoring fans.

For the next year Michael and I spent long days—and nights—building Diamond Music Enterprises in recording sessions, computer music engraving, and endless advertising and promotional endeavors. Our efforts were well rewarded with the increasing sales revenues and contracts that began to pour in.

Then Leonard Starr, a brilliant young actor, came into Michael's life. He and Michael went to Guerneville for the

Fourth of July weekend. For the first time since I had moved from North Carolina, I was alone with my thoughts and feelings. For the first time I had to face some options. *If I do not spend the rest of my life alone, then with who will I spend it with? Not with a man, not ever again! But with…a woman?*

I allowed myself to indulge in fantasies I never before dreamed possible. I rented videos from Good Vibrations and bought magazines I had never noticed were for sale before. I began to date JoAnn, a gorgeous alto with long curly brown hair that drove me wild. When we sang together in the Lesbian and Gay Chorus of San Francisco, I nearly could not contain the intensity of passion growing exponentially inside me. Unfortunately, JoAnn did not share the same level of fervor.

One day, in a rare moment of idle time, I found a lesbian bulletin board on America Online. A woman who posted as Jewel Stone caught my attention. We began E-mailing. She was so much like me—a musician, a computer user, and now an ex-wife and single mom who also had recently come out. She lived several states away and was dating a local teacher named Jean Roberts. I was intrigued.

"Jean must be a very, very lucky lady!" I told Jewel. "And I feel just as lucky to have the chance to be your friend." Jewel sent me MIDI files of some lesbian music she had written, with the lyrics in E-mail. I *knew* I had to talk to her on the phone. Although we were total strangers, we exchanged phone numbers.

After our first six-hour phone conversation, I felt a rapidly growing affinity for this woman whose face I had never seen. I told Michael, who was unquestionably my best friend, about it all. I showed him printouts of our E-mail.

He studied for a long moment. "She writes so much like *my* Jewel," he observed thoughtfully.

"Your ex-wife?! Do you know where she is now?"

"The last I knew several years ago, she had moved to Texas, married some military man, and was rearing several children." He shrugged.

"Jewel Stone *is* in Texas! She's divorcing an Air Force creep and has two children. Do you suppose—?" My mind began to race, and my heart beat even faster. "We *have* to meet her!"

"Diamond Music will fly her here," Michael offered, a wry grin spreading across his face. "We must audition her lesbian songs. Perhaps I can even do arrangements of them." He winked.

When I confronted her, Jewel did not deny that she was the long-ago dean of my adolescent years. "Our mutual friend Allen Rodgers told me about you several months ago, after he met you in person on Michael's last concert tour to Iowa," she confessed, "but I never expected to find you on an AOL lesbian bulletin board. How could I know that the astute entrepreneur Robin Lind was the Robin Jackson of Orchill Hills? But when you said you were a musician in San Francisco, I figured you *had* to know the illustrious Michael Diamond. Then I checked your AOL online profile and found out that you're his business partner!"

With my help, Jewel Stone and Michael Diamond were reunited via E-mail on America Online the very day that would have been the 30th anniversary of their wedding and the 25th anniversary of their divorce. I was overcome with joy at their happiness in discovering they both still shared a brother-sister kind of family love that had never diminished through their years of separation. When Jewel's divorce was final a few weeks later, she had her name legally changed back to Jewel Diamond.

Jewel shared one of her fantasies with me. For several years it had been her wildest dream to work with and for a woman executive in the music industry. The executive would be a demanding woman who was harsh and exacting of her employees but who would take a special liking to Jewel because of her superior computer and music skills. Eventually this tough and elite sophisticate, who was a few years younger than Jewel, would ravish her after hours in her private studio. In Jewel's fantasy the woman was a blond with voluptuous breasts and wore a red business suit with a white silk blouse. *Perfect—absolutely perfect!*

When Leonard and Michael and I met Jewel at the airport, I made sure I wore my red blazer with a white silk blouse and black suede pants. Coincidentally, I had just been to Dennis, my hairdresser, for my twice-yearly coloring to keep my coiffure as blond as it had been when I was 17. Before Jewel arrived, Michael had asked me if I thought I could be physically attracted to the woman who had once been my boarding school dormitory dean.

"I'm not ruling out anything," I responded, and as I had said to Jewel in an E-mail before her trip, "I'm not assuming or presuming anything." But when I watched her emerge from the plane, my whole body and soul leaped with a indescribable fire I never knew possible. Leonard and I watched with genuine delight as Jewel and Michael hugged, long and hard, with giggles and tears of joy. Then it was my turn. After weeks of E-mail and phone calls, with not even an exchange of GIF file photos, I had fallen in love with Jewel Stone, now Jewel Diamond. As we ate dinner at the Sausage Factory on Castro, I did not allow her to leave my embrace for the rest of the evening. I ate my whole meal entirely with my left hand.

My arm was still around her as I unlocked the outer door to my apartment building. I felt Jewel cringe at the sight of the long carpeted staircase. I placed my hand gently under her arm as we ascended in silence. I instinctively pushed aside all other thoughts except the awesomeness of a more-than-two-decade-old acquaintance renewed. There was an undeniable ease between us, as if we had never lost touch with each other during all those years. Now, as two adult women, we shared many common bonds—not the least of which was our mutual love for the famed Michael Diamond of the Castro Theatre.

With Michael's expertise I had carefully cleaned and decorated my little apartment. Everything was meticulously arranged—from the few but exquisite pieces of furniture I had managed to acquire to my mother's china and crystal displayed in the glass case in the entryway. With Michael's help, too, the room lighting was perfect. Jewel's sigh of obvious delight pleased and flattered me.

She grinned mischievously as she turned toward me now.

"I'm looking forward to that back rub," she said, reminding me of my casual E-mail promise. "Of course, my dear!" I grinned back, with a smile that had not left my face since the moment Jewel arrived at the airport. I had already taken off the red suit jacket.

"But if you're too tired tonight..." Jewel chuckled easily.

"Not at all," I quickly replied. I slipped out of my shoes and unzipped my black suede pants.

Jewel didn't seem comfortable with undressing in front of another woman for the first time, and I tried hard not to stare. Still, I noticed she removed *all* of her clothing, then put on a long T-shirt. I removed my blouse and bra and slipped on a T-shirt but kept my panties on. Jewel lay down on the freshly made-up futon where she and I would sleep.

The lavender silk sheets were smooth and soft, and Jewel stretched out on her stomach and buried her head in the fluffy pillow. I turned off the room lamp, and only the faint glow of the streetlight outside filtered into the quiet room. This room, where I had heard Jewel's voice on the phone for so many hours over the past few months, now took on a new reality. In those late hours, when we were each struggling to stay awake, we had talked often of how nice it would be to go to sleep together, in the same room.

My hands began to gently knead the stiff muscles in her neck and shoulders. "Mmm," Jewel murmured, "that feels *so* good." Eased into comfort by my hands, she removed her T-shirt—after all, it was dark—so that I could reach her back more easily.

"Beverly and I gave the best back rubs in the whole dorm at Orchill Hills," I boasted, reminiscing about an old friend from boarding school. I realized now that the tall, square-faced 14-year-old girl and I had been two baby dykes who had had little idea about our own sexual identities then but shared an unspoken camaraderie. We had given each other back rubs for free, while charging 50 cents each to all the other girls in the dorm. There had been rumors that year about Beverly and Mrs. Diamond being secret lovers, although nothing was ever proven. *Perhaps that's why the Diamonds disappeared so mysteriously at the end of that school year.*

Suddenly—totally unaware of Jewel's ticklishness—I let my hands stray to the ribs on her sides. Jewel squealed with a start and in one motion squirmed and flipped onto her back, exposing her bare chest.

"Oh, I'm sorry. Are you ticklish?" I chuckled in surprise.

Jewel was silent, as if she were not sure what to say. Did she think I did this deliberately to make her turn over? But she lay still, not turning back over. She reached up, touching my shoulders, drawing me gently onto the bed. Wordlessly, I took off my shirt. Jewel began to massage my neck and shoulders from the front as we lay side by side. I wondered—but somehow knew instinctively—how I would respond to more intimate caressing.

Jewel's first touch was light, almost reverent, as her fingers encircled my now-erect nipples and cupped the roundness of my very large breasts with both of her hands. I did not pull away.

"This is nice," Jewel murmured, "not having to...phone long distance."

"Yes," I whispered, now caressing Jewel's small but firm breasts. "Very, very nice."

As our hands explored each other's bodies, we both marveled silently—as always—at how soft and smooth a woman is. *How very nice to touch and be touched by another woman, to lie side by side, to hug, to kiss, to caress.*

"I love to hug and kiss and cuddle," I had confessed to Jewel in E-mail. Now my hungry lips found hers: warm, succulent, slightly open. Our tongues entwined easily and naturally.

"It's hard to believe you've never kissed a woman like this before," Jewel teased. "You certainly couldn't have experienced this level of enjoyment kissing a man."

I couldn't answer. *How do I know exactly how to kiss her, how to respond so perfectly and instinctively, how to touch and caress her delicate body?*

Jewel, in growing ardor, began to tug slightly at the elastic of my panties. I eagerly assisted in removing one of the last garments between us but felt myself draw away unintentionally as she placed her hand on my inner thigh.

I cleared my throat, almost imperceptibly, and Jewel pulled her hand away. "I'm sorry, I didn't mean to offend you," she spoke quickly.

"No, no," I insisted. "You didn't offend me. It's rather nice. I just, er, well, uh, all my life I've had a problem with...dryness. Even my doctor concluded there was just no solution to my problem." I paused. "Please...it's OK. Really!"

Jewel continued her exploration silently as I began to reciprocate. My trembling fingers slipped through her thick pubic hair and into the silky wetness of her labia. *How does she get so wet?* After a few moments I spoke softly. "You don't seem to have that problem."

Now Jewel could not restrain her grinned chuckle. "Guess what, Robin," she said jubilantly, "neither do you—now!" I realized with a great deal of surprise that I was just as wet as she was. We both relaxed and now embraced even more fervently.

Her fingers continued to probe the depths of me, of what I never imagined could be so moist. I had never experienced this with my husband. I grew aware of Jewel's lips caressing my belly, her tongue exploring the creases between my legs. In the faint glow of moonlight that had found its way through the upstairs window, I gazed at the beautiful contrast of her dark hair against my pale skin. I reached down to stroke her soft curls. At the same time, her hands reached upward to my breasts, now grasping my aching nipples, squeezing them harder than before. Her expert tongue soon found my swollen love button, alternately encircling it, sucking it, and licking the juices that now flowed freely from my throbbing cunt.

After some time had passed, the initial throes of passion blossomed into an inevitable crescendo of orgasmic explosions that left me gasping for breath but satisfied beyond anything I had ever before experienced—or even imagined. Before the fireworks in me had a chance to subside, I gently changed our positions so I could have the aphrodisiac of tasting *her* nectar, of stirring her deepest feelings, and watching her respond to the ultimate pleasure that only women can give each other. As she reached that absolute peak of total physical and emotional climax—and then sighed in contentment—I knew we both felt a deep sense of bonding, of caring more than either of us had anticipated, of secretly wishing this fantasy weekend would never have to end.

Jewel fell asleep first. I covered her exquisite naked body with my purple down comforter, then slid beside her into the bed. Although she was sound asleep, she snuggled up to me, put her head on my shoulder, and wrapped her arms around me. Nothing I had ever felt before—or will ever feel again— could have prepared me for the small, soft, and oh-so-warm body pressed against mine. If I live to be 100, I'll never forget the ecstasy she brought to me that night. *She is incomparably beautiful, erotic, soft, huggable, and intelligent. She has given me the gift of herself in the most beautiful way possible.*

Jewel and I had not had very many hours of actual sleep when the phone rang early on Friday morning. It was Michael of course.

"It's 9 o'clock," he informed me.

I groaned sleepily. "We aren't even awake yet."

"I have a lot planned," he reminded, almost impatiently. "When do you think Jewel will be ready to leave?"

Ah, yes. I had promised Michael that he could have this entire day with Jewel, to tour her around San Francisco, to spend time catching up on the last 20 years.

I looked at the still-sleeping form just beginning to stir under a rumpled sheet. "Soon," I yawned. "I promise." At 10:30, Jewel and I stepped outside into a characteristically overcast San Francisco morning. Michael was just coming down his front steps, dressed casually in black slacks and a white turtleneck under a gray textured cardigan that had the word "Provincetown" stitched neatly in small purple letters. One look at my face told Michael all he needed—or wanted—to know about what had transpired in that second-story apartment across the street from his house.

After the red VW Jetta disappeared down the hill, I somehow managed to go to my day job in the financial district. I felt a blushing glow all day, certain my office coworkers could see my sudden change. But no one said anything. I could hardly wait for Michael to bring Jewel back that night.

Michael and I had a full schedule of activities planned for our weekend with Jewel. We drove to visit friends and music business acquaintances in Napa, Larkspur, San Rafael, and San Jose. One evening we wined and dined her at the celebrated Tonga Room, and another evening we had an intimate supper at Pachas. We took her to breakfast at Baghdad Café, known for its strikingly good-looking lesbian waitresses. And, of course, Jewel was able to hear Michael play nightly on the "Mighty Wurlitzer" at the Castro Theatre. She and Michael even performed a duo on Sunday at the legendary Golden Gate Club, one of many places that booked Michael on a regular basis. But the nights, as short as they seemed, were ours—mine and Jewel's, spent on my futon. We packed an unbelievable amount of pleasure into that weekend.

When I said good-bye to Jewel at the airport on Monday morning, I felt as if my heart were being ripped from me. We hugged through drenching tears and promised to keep in touch. "How can I leave you here?" she asked softly, as she kissed my cheek. *I don't know how I can let you go. But I have to. My body is aching with the desire to hold you against it, and my heart is about to explode with joy.*

As her plane taxied down the runway and began to soar into the sky, I felt an agonizing emptiness. *I now have a new fantasy—one I will likely never realize—that I can go to sleep every night with her beside me and wake up every morning with her tongue and lips on mine. I love her more than I knew it was possible to love someone.*

It was almost impossible to fall asleep alone that night. *This bed never seemed big before, but tonight it is huge and empty. I cannot face doing laundry. I don't want to wash the smell and feel of her off the sheets and towels.*

I didn't ask for or expect miracles, but I wanted nothing more than to share her life, every little piece of it, on a day-to-day basis. The very thought of her hand touching mine, her lips pressed against mine, her body held close to me, sent all of my senses into high gear. The mere memory of licking her lips tasted sweet, and caressing her body in my imagination started fires in me only she could quench. But even greater than the dynamic physical love was the positively explosive intellectual and spiritual eroticism she sparked. I became possessed by a complete and eternal love for her.

For the next two years, we E-mailed daily and phoned nightly, except on the weekends Jean Roberts spent at Jewel's house. We visited as often as we could, each saving up money for plane tickets between Dallas and San Francisco. I loved her so much I was willing to "share" her with Jean. I was torn between the ecstasy of loving her and the panic that I would lose her.

Through some miracle, the day came when I flew to Texas for the last time. Jewel had completed her contract as a Service Engineer at Microsoft in Dallas and was ready to pursue her career path in California's Silicon Valley. I helped her pack her four-bedroom house into a 27-foot U-Haul truck, drove it across the formidable 1,800 miles, and moved our combined earthly belongings into a charming Victorian flat in the quaint town of Alameda across the bay. From the stretch of beach that runs the length of the island where we walk hand in hand, we can see my beloved city that sparkles like a thousand diamonds over the black night waters of the bay. Michael and I are still business partners and best friends, and Jewel has now become everything Michael is to me—and much more. I know a lifetime will not be long enough to live with—and love—my most priceless treasure, Jewel Diamond.

CHAPTER THIRTY-TWO
Rock Rattle
Jane Eaton Hamilton

We met because I could not find an auditorium. The opening ceremony of West Word's summer school for women writers was there. Somewhere. We would have met regardless. We were to be in residence two weeks, in monastic rooms of one's own on the fourth floor of the Iona building at UBC in Vancouver, Canada. Aubrey said later that the Iona building reminded her of the building in which she had been a nun.

"A nun!" I exclaimed almost biting off her Dairy Queen dollop of a left nipple.

She said, "Don't stop," and settled my lips against her breast again. She had fabulous knockers, big and floppy as hell. If she'd let me try the pencil test of my adolescence, I could have fit a dozen.

I slurped in mindless veil-taking obedience, covering her body with mine like a habit, my eyes scudding over her face, her pretty face.

"During meals," she told me grinning over bell-shaped teeth, "I had to sit next to this fat old nun named Sister Mary DeChantal."

I snorted.

"True," she said, nodding to convince me. "A hundred and eight years old. She made suck-suck noises through her teeth. Like this." Aubrey demonstrated an obscene whistle-like noise and I, oh I, oh this woman, laughed off the loftiness of her mountain breast and landed — *ker-plunk* — in her armpit.

She danced her straight fingers across the spine-bones of my neck. "After a while," she said, "there got to be a rhythm to it, like a percolator, this steady suck-suck."

I climbed back up, piton by fingernailed piton. I smacked my lips against her, grossly.

"Mmm," she breathed. Her hands tattooed my back. My hips rocked against her legs gently, piously. "Picture five hundred nuns."

Five hundred nuns.

"A refectory."

Five hundred nuns in a refectory.

"Eating."

This is the body of Christ.

"Silently."

The blood of Christ. Oh my Christ. Oh my woman funny woman.

"No noise."

"No noise," I agreed surfacing, trailing mesmerized fingers across her forehead, the ridge of her eyebrows, her ears.

"Sacred silence. No unnecessary movement. Jaws chewing."

Sacred, sacred. Oh Aubrey sacred.

"'Suck-suck,' Sister said then forked boiled potatoes between her teeth. My habit got tighter and tighter against my forehead. Tighter." I kissed her.

"Tighter."

Oh little nun. Oh big woman tight. Tight dyke cunt, pretty small cunt washing Pacific Ocean strong against my loins, seashells dropping from Aubrey like amulets. Mary, mother Mary. Five hundred nuns. Tighter. The habit drawing tighter against Aubrey's forehead. The quiet refectory. The five hundred masticating nuns.

Aubrey licked my face, the buck of my teeth, tongue-tip of

a wave. "You guessed what's next?"

I was beaming but I shook my head. I wouldn't have told her yes for the world.

"I couldn't resist. I did it too. 'Suck-suck,' I said. 'Suck-suck.' Into the silence, deadpan. 'Suck-suck.'"

Into the breasts of five hundred nuns. The crucified Jesus. Crown of thorns. Mea culpa. Mea maxima culpa. Red coral laughter snuck in wild astonishing branches up my gullet.

Aubrey said, "Everyone heard. Sister Mary's eyes bird-slid my way. Oh, old and bleached and watery but sharp as beaks. Puckered old woman's lips clamped over those jaundiced teeth. No sound but the horrified nerves of five hundred nuns crackling. Oh, oh, and my face was hot and my habit black and white itchy. I waited, ate vinegar peas speared on my fork, a mouthful of baked cod, chewed, swallowed painfully, waited. I crossed my ankles. At last I laid my fork aside to finger the cross that choked my neck. As I did, as I bowed my head, Sister Mary DeChantal winked at me. One eye surreptitiously. Then she said, 'Suck-suck.'"

I guffawed.

Aubrey crowed. "First I did penance eating breakfast on a stool in the refectory for a week. Then Mother Superior reconsidered my application. They kicked me out of the convent."

"Amen!" I cried.

"Praise be to God," Aubrey whispered.

A sign on the washroom cubicle door down the hall said, about flushing: IF THERE IS SOMEONE IN THE SHOWER PLEASE WARN HER SO THAT SHE WILL NOT BE BURNED BY A LACK OF COLD WATER.

Between her thighs was hot and milky. I twisted around on the slim cot creaking and slid my electric pudenda against hers. The way sand fell away under our feet as we stood, hands clasped, in the foam of the Pacific Ocean, the bottoms of our rolled pants sodden, so we now gave way to the tug and push of different waves. I clasped Aubrey's right ankle. I hardly thought. Just jubi, jubi, jubilation!

It was sunny that first July day at West Word. Twenty women gathered for courses of poetry or fiction or in simple retreat from places as varied as Nova Scotia, Winnipeg, and the Yukon. A grand achievement of hard-ass work, we woman would stretch creative muscle beyond endurance into torture and yes, with guts and gall we would produce. But I didn't know that as I stood befuddled by the lobby blackboard wondering where the hell I really was, and why, and what audacity, what bravado, what shining tomfoolery to be at West Word at all. They'd find out, too quickly, that I was actually an avocado. Not a writer. Thick-skinned, green-tinged, and soft delectable insides. But not a writer. I didn't even know, for heaven's sake, when 'who' was 'who' and when 'whom.'

"Going to the opening ceremony?"

My head moved around lazily. When I saw her, my neck elongated like a giraffe's. I nibbled at crazy bursts of spring foliage sprouting out from around this woman's head—then I got excited and jerked a whole tree limb into my mouth. I fed myself. Privately I said, *This is love.*

Out loud I said properly, "If I can find the damned auditorium."

"I think I know where it is," she said.

"Then can I be your puppy dog?"

She smiled diamonds. "Follow me."

"What's your name?" I asked shyly.

"Aubrey. What's yours?"

"Jane."

"That's lovely," she said.

You're lovely, I said but not out loud. I'd follow you anywhere. And I did, slavishly and dazedly through mazish halls to the banquet.

A drab room. Strangers. Women strangers. My nerves popped. Strangers who wrote. Chrome and vinyl chairs. And me not a writer. Veneered tables. Too many strange women writers. Fluorescent lighting.

"Coffee?" I asked. "I'm going to sit outside." Because out double doors was a garden of lolling hills—the full pot of summer stewing, flowers and sunshine and benches kelly green. Escape. Here I was not so uncomfortable, my literary inadequacy could burble and steam to its heart's content without my attention.

She sat beside me.

"The sun feels good," I said pointedly. "Good on my skin."

We spoke with others—exotic others at ease, beautiful, articulate and real writers—but I assimilated not a word. In an hour Aubrey was still seated beside me, by this time unnecessarily close. The sun grew long-limbed with evening and because of the glut of tree-leafery was dappling against her hair, kaleidoscope on white-brown brindle. I knew it but didn't look her way, and I knew other things too—that her face was lightly tucked into middle age, that her eyes were chestnut under unpolished eyebrows, that her lips were thin and at their corners curled down, that in her right ear were two earrings, an etched silver cuff halfway up and an ordinarily placed—that is, on the lobe—gold ring. Her other ear was naked. I knew that her very pale face was either scantily sunburned or scantily ruddy. She was delectably overweight. I couldn't look at her anymore. I couldn't look because if I looked I would have even more trouble than I was presently having with my farcically burlesque groin. Oh vigour.

It took precisely 31 hours before we were in each other's arms, minds, hearts. I counted. Then she seduced me.

"So," she said.

"Well," I said.

"So…" she said. "Do you have a partner?" She was lying belly down on her cot while I sat in her floral armchair, primly smoking.

"No," I said. Did I have a partner? Did a bear use toilets? Was the ocean fresh water? I was 31 and I'd never even slept with a woman. "You?"

"Nope. So… You want to come over here and smooch a while?"

My breath caught. Suspiciously I said, "I don't have casual sex."

She said, "Woman, I want to leap on your body. We can be serious."

We became lovers. What would be best next to say? Or not to say? Secrets? Little secrets: On Wreck Beach I overheard a man say that a summer ago—accidentally—he pissed on a peeping tom hidden in a bush. On Wreck Beach I saw a woman, brown nude, pink lipstick in cowgirl hat. Big secrets: That dusk arranged itself around Aubrey and me with sun hands orange and magenta, climaxing globe screaming her descent into her night grave, that gulls perked on rocks with the waves smashing toothpick legs, silly group rituals in the stiffening color of the night water, classical wave notes. Oh rock-rattle of our shoes on the cluttered stones walking: that at last I climbed a boulder to cheer my thanks, Oh thank you for this one week Stop I can stop could stop now die or I can on I can go on—Oh dancing!— and I leapt down, a stupid leap to insecure footing before strolling Celebration with Aubrey by the capsizing Pacific Ocean shoreline. Big secret raw as a mother's womb: The muggy blood salt smell—moss no longer green in the suck of disappearing light on rocks and rotting seaweed, fruity kelp.

"Oh, look!" I cried and clutched pinching fingers to Aubrey. One little log, more debris, the licorice hang of a thin dead tree branch curving to the long pencil beak of a bird.

Dark. Was she really there? In the deepening dusk, the profiled mountains, the wash of waves, the screaming gulls? Or was this just emotion's jest? A bird but not a bird. It didn't know it was not a bird but I did stock still 15 feet away, this was no mere bird. It couldn't fool me, not fool Aubrey either frozen under the drape of my arm.

Blue, but it was not blue. Heron, but it could not have been heron blue heron. But heaven, yes, some orchestration our goddesses prepared, a night-woman's hallucination (but no voice), a witch assessing her own Pacific Ocean with bead black bird eyes.

When I realized we had been born again as trees in Annie Dillard's Tinker Creek looped chase of the coot, I nudged Aubrey and said, without whispering, "She won't care." She did not seem to, as in stupid coot Tinker Creek she could not have, but our shoes were wet and scratchy inside with sand and we clung dangerously and noisily fell over rocks in our approach.

How close would she permit us? Her neck was like Aubrey's arm stretching out to reach my body, sensuous. On her belly was a punk tuft of hair; her beak was a forward thrust, a swift dance. I saw the shimmer of the grail under the sloshing waves. Did Aubrey? Did Aubrey? The bird oh non-bird did, she placed her webbed foot on my body and kneaded me where Aubrey had.

We did walk closer made careless by the imprudence of Annie Dillard's coot, flirting. How close to the heart? And our fierce invasion sent her to flight at four feet, an awkward spreading of wings, an effort of lift and our swift intake of breath and her huge wingspan and unbridled passion power against the soot-blue sky forever, she was flying. She. We. Someone was flying.

We were accomplishing nothing. I had run out of clean

clothes. Wreck Beach and sun were becoming as vital as underpants in some former life. Naked Pacific Ocean, unfolding herself and challenging our rhythms, cycles. Like swamp frogs Aubrey and I barely slept. We hardly ever ate and then, tasted little but the pepper of love, the cayenne sting of eye to eye.

I had only two simple pragmatic goals for the weeks of West Word. I wanted to buy a fuse for my car so I could use my directional blinkers and wouldn't have to ask Aubrey yet again, "Which hand movement means left? Quick! Which right?" I wanted to buy the Sunday *New York Times*. I wanted to read the Book Review in bed.

In the gas station I bought five fuses, a box of five fuses. It took me five days to remember to stop there and the effort proved devastating. Out the office to my open hood, but I passed Aubrey in the front seat first. "You know what I'm thinking," I said suggestively. She did and suddenly I did not and I could not open the packet of fuses and my lunatic laughter and bumbling fingers and a service station attendant said, "I'll do that," and I said, "No, I'll do it." I did it, wrenched the plastic violently and the fuses fell out, rolling against black concrete and I considered the havoc when women cannot make men hear language, hear No and No never. "No charge," he said diving upon them, and I squalled with the delicious humor of one besotted with love and reverently he replaced my fuse.

Oh Aubrey, my fuse. In there, deeper, where my ridges are the floor of the Pacific Ocean, made of sand that molds your fingers.

Little secrets: She liked baseball, snooker, poker.

The *New York Times* purchased sedately. Measuredly. But we could manage no more that was practical. We said, "Coffee, we need coffee" in our throats I wanted her throat that cleft there between her shoulder blades and we dashed the four lanes to a restaurant. And then brunch and romance crazy romance I had never known romance like this I had short-circuited romance. I had a startling burst of pride as I fingered the *Times* beside me under a potted palm.

I almost didn't want to go on with her because it would alter, had altered hour after hour until days were like perfect strangers to their next-door neighbors. West Word created an artificial construct because my own life was sometimes bone cold hard, strict and severe, and Aubrey was never bone, never cold, never hard except sometimes during lovemaking, arousingly. But I say artifice. Which life was the more artificial? I almost didn't want to go on with her, through the changes in love that I knew would hurt preciously. I did not want the next dawn, or the next. In cowardice I longed to rope time, lasso it inhumanely its hooves bound four-in-a-knot and hold it prisoner. *But yahoo!* I thought.

Ooh la la, I thought.

We went on, forward, on forward for five more years.

Six a.m. not-gone-to-sleep laughter, chortling with covered mouths trying not to be annoyance to orchestrally sleeping writers through rice-paper walls. Hopelessly unsuccessful.

Toujour gai. Toujour gay.

Oh, ooh la la. "A little less head," she said a few minutes later and drained my IQ out my vagina.

We never did read The *New York Times.* Aubrey stacked it on the dresser and reached for me. Listen, our list was love, what can I say? Words fell into me and I was a typewriter. But I couldn't keep up. I lost conversational treasures for typing too slowly. Keys clacked in the other writers' gray-stuff, too, I could tell. Eighty WPM and gaining.

"Sister DeChantal," Aubrey told me, "held me when I was leaving the convent. She was the only nun who ever touched me, who cared that I was being sent away and was sorry."

Someone flushed without warning us.

CHAPTER THIRTY-THREE
My Liberal(ation) Arts Education
Debra K. Dekker

I went to college to open myself to all that life could offer. I didn't think that would include opening my legs to the hands and mouth of another woman.

I am one of those dykes who knew from birth (well, almost) I was homosexual; don't ask how, I just knew. While living under my parents' roof, I neither talked about it nor had any sexual experiences with girls or boys. No kissing, hugging, no holding hands. I grew up in a rural farming community in the middle of the Midwest in the middle of nowhere. The pace of life was about as fast as corn growing in the fields. Folks followed a strict and narrow Protestant lifestyle that taught if it felt good, it had to be a sin. This included sex. My mother never talked to me about sex, but she made it clear that genitals were dirty and not to be touched. Even in the shower I had to wash "down there" last; once soiled, the washcloth could not come in contact with other body parts. I wonder how I got past stuff like that and chuckle to myself sometimes when I am "down there" having oral sex with a lover.

I was a complete fledgling when it came to sexual behavior, knowing little except for what I read in magazines like *True Romance.* I secretly bought them at the Piggly Wiggly a few towns away when I was old enough to drive. One time Mother found some hidden beneath the Kotex in my bottom dresser drawer and said, "Good Christian girls don't read these kinds of things," trying again to suppress my sexual curiosity.

I dated a few guys during my college years, not for sex but because I wanted to be with my straight girlfriends on the weekends. Disco was popular, so we danced; after the bars closed, my date and I would find some place to fool around, going as far as heavy petting. A guy ate me out once. It was strange, surprising, and a little bit nice. Fortunately, I did not return the favor. I never had intercourse with a man; I had paid attention in high school biology and knew the consequences. I didn't enjoy fooling around all that much either, but I did learn what it felt like to become sexually aroused. I got extremely wet, always soaking through my panties.

In college I looked at female classmates as dates and possibly more, but I lacked the nerve to ask anyone out. I was convinced I would remain a virgin lesbian until graduation. The college hired a new director for our women's dormitory at the start of my senior year. She was around 30 years old—far too young for that grandmother stereotype—and she hung out with the student resident assistants, most of whom also comprised my circle of friends. Early interactions with her consisted of group activities like going to movies. I did get to know her better in small group situations whenever I spent time with one particular friend. Early in the first semester, this friend and I were constantly together, studying for GREs, filling out graduate school applications, and drinking cheap wine. The new director lived in the dormitory with the rest of us, and the door to her apartment was across from my friend's room. When she came out of her apartment and saw the two of us, she often invited herself over. We didn't mind. She had finished grad school recently and had some good advice, but it pissed us off that she always drank all our wine!

It didn't take long for me to run into her alone. She asked whether I played backgammon. I didn't. She taught me how, and that began our relationship—albeit platonic. For months, we played nightly and talked. I was surprised at how natural it felt to be with her. I was certain I was not attracted to her in a romantic way; she was more self-confident than I, outspoken, much older, and overweight (not that I was overly judgmental about looks). After I spent time with her, however, my friends would always say to me, "Girl, from that grin on your face, you look like a cat who swallowed a canary."

One evening she passed by my room and undoubtedly heard me slam down the telephone receiver and curse loudly. I had had a frustrating conversation with my mother. From the corner of my eye, I saw her peering around the open door, as she innocently asked, "Is everything all right?" I shook my head slowly and started to cry. She came in, closed and locked the door (I had a rare single apartment and no roommate to worry about), sat on my bed, pulled me down next to her, and wrapped her arms around me. "No," I cried, bawling into her shoulder while she rubbed her hands up and down my back, massaged my neck, and messed with my hair. It felt like she lightly touched her lips to my forehead too. *Wow, did she just kiss me?*

I sat up after a while, wiping away tears and snot with the back of my hand. She put one of her hands in the middle of my heaving chest, grabbed my face with the other, looked me in the eyes, and asked, "Are you OK?" I nodded but thought, *How can I be? Your hand is precariously between my tits, I think you kissed me, and now I want to kiss you back.* She must have read my mind because she leaned over and gave me a full kiss on the mouth, with slightly parted lips making those small chewing motions. This time she left no doubt it was a kiss.

Kissing—and the more explicit stuff we would get to later—did not alarm us. We had had many conversations about homosexuality. She did not have a problem with it. I talked in theory, never confessing my inclinations.

Shocked at my brazenness, I slipped my hands up the open sleeves of her robe, caressing silky smooth skin of arms and shoulders. I sat back, and she unbuttoned and took off my worn flannel shirt. I opened her robe, let it fall down to the bed, and we mutely sat there, staring at each other's naked chests. Her luxurious and tender hands held my entire breast while her thumb rubbed over the nipple. I was barely breathing, my eyeballs rolling back in the sockets, but my mind was shouting, *Yes, this is it, what I've been wanting for so long! My God, it feels so good.* I reached over to touch her large breasts. I brushed the back of my fingers over her taut pink nipples, and she moaned low in her throat. We squeezed together on my small single bed and proceeded to kiss, taste, touch, caress, and make love to each other's bodies, staying above the waist. I have no idea why or how we resisted going any farther down, but we did.

She left at 5 o'clock that morning, and I doubted a night like this would ever happen again. I dozed but couldn't sleep, so I got up, showered, dressed, ate breakfast, and arrived on time to my 8 o'clock organic chemistry class. I even went to my work-study job but left early to take a nap. Walking across campus and lost in thought, I glanced up, and there she was with some other people, walking right toward me. I almost peed in my pants. Everyone exchanged greetings; she remained quiet but smiled.

Later on I was embarrassed by my behavior, convinced she thought I was an idiot, convinced any relationship with her was history. I made it to my room, exhausted, and ready to flop down for that nap when the phone rang. It was her. A sharp, tingling wave rapidly descended my body. I broke out in a sweat and felt my sphincter muscle snap shut like it does when you creep over the crest of the roller coaster's first hill, and *wham,* you're down at the bottom again. "I wanted to make sure you were all right about last night and all," she said sweetly.

Huh? I thought. *Is this what caring is all about?* No one had ever called me the morning after a date. I didn't know what to say, but she fortunately did.

"Hello, are you still there?" she laughed.

"Yeah, sorry," I mumbled. Jeez, I was being such a dork.

"Don't be sorry," she calmly replied. "I wanted to talk to you but couldn't with everyone around today. I enjoyed last night, but I realized it was probably quite emotional for you."

My psychology major kicked in as I thought, *Shit, she's attributing everything to an emotional release. I thought we were just plain horny.*

But I said, "No, I'm fine. I'm glad you were there last night. I didn't sleep much after you left. I remembered how nice everything felt."

"Um-m-m, me too," she crooned back. "Could you come to my place tonight? Maybe we can talk more." *Oh, my god. She wants to see me again,* was my first thought, but luckily I gave a much more casual reply.

"Sure," I said. "What time is good for you?"

"I'm having a meeting in my apartment tonight. It'll probably last all evening. Is 10:30 too late?"

"Fine. I'll see you then."

I hung up the phone much more delicately than the previous night. The words *She wants to see me again. Oh, fuck. Oh, wow,* raged through my head while I jumped up and down like a human pogo stick. I tried to take that nap, but my mind kept racing around and around while my body tingled and floated all over the place. I gave up on everything but light reading.

Absentmindedly watching TV all evening, I glanced at the clock every few minutes. I made numerous trips past her apartment for a bottle of pop or a candy bar from the snack machines, checking the progress of her meeting on every trip. At 10:30 P.M. sharp I stood outside her door, waiting and shifting from one foot to the other, as the meeting dragged on and on. When the last person left, I gave it an extra minute, then slipped into her apartment, anxious and scared shitless. I found her in the kitchen making a cup of tea. She looked up and smiled as I peered around the corner and said "Hello." We embraced, and our lips met again, as soft and tender as last night. I finally let out a sigh of relief. We kissed until the kettle whistled, and more while the tea was steeping.

"So what did you want to see me about?" I murmured against her lips.

"Why don't you go on back to the bedroom?" she grinned. "I'll be there in a minute."

Was this an invitation? What next? Should I remain clothed, strike a casual pose, and wait? Undress and hop into her bed? Something told me it was now or never, so I took the second option and undressed and slipped between the sheets. I was stark naked and trembling.

I heard a noise and looked up, startled to see her so suddenly in the doorway. Then, sitting on the edge of the bed, she stroked my face and whispered, "You are so beautiful." I desperately wanted to be sexy for her, propped up on an elbow, the sheet pulled up to just my waist. My nipples were buzzing, standing on end, and I had a delicious throbbing "down there." I managed to say (almost begged), "Please come to bed. I want to make love to you all night." She started to unbutton her blouse, and I relaxed, but she stopped all of a sudden.

She glanced toward the window and whispered, "I'm not sure I can really do this." I wanted to think I heard wrong but knew I didn't.

My heart stopped and inwardly I groaned, *Oh, shit.*

I knew I couldn't just let it end; being the only one so bold and so naked embarrassed me. I reached up to touch her cheek gently, turned her face toward me, and said, "Yes you can...It'll be OK." I was so proud of myself! That simple line actually worked! I undid the other buttons and removed her blouse, then reached around the back to unhook her bra and seized on the opportunity to nuzzle her neck. She stood up and pushed down her slacks and underpants. My eyes were riveted by her crotch; I saw pubic hair in the bathroom every day but never red pubic hair like hers.

I lifted up the sheet, scooted over, and she slipped in next to me. I had never been naked with anyone before, so when the length of her body touched me with full skin-on-skin contact and she pushed her leg between mine, I let out a long "O-o-oh" and forgot to inhale until I turned blue.

Making love was everything the erotic lesbian fiction said it would be—electric, luxurious, hot, wet, sensual, sexual, desirable, wonderful, languid, ecstatic, delicious—and so much more. Once together, we were eager to explore and please. She removed her leg from between mine, then lightly traced down one leg and up the inside of the other to end back at my cunt, cupping it in the palm of her hand. All the while she nibbled on my nipples, sucking and licking, gently at first, then growing fiercer. I squirmed, wiggled, and arched my body upward, wanting more. She massaged all over between my legs, then parted my labia with her fingers, and hummed, against the top of my ear, "You are s-o-o-o wet." She slid around some more, then let one finger glide ever so slowly and gently inside as far as she could, moving her entire hand in a barely perceptible circular motion. It felt wonderful. I wanted it to last forever. I wanted to give her pleasure too, so I gritted my teeth, rolled over, and pushed her onto her back.

Here it was, my culmination—a naked woman underneath me—all I had fantasized about since puberty or before. I didn't know what to do. I tried to recall some *True Romance* stories, but that failed me too. She put her hands behind my neck and pulled my face down to hers for another kiss. *This is good*, I thought, and proceeded to lay kisses over her face, eyes, ears, forehead, chin, nose, then down her neck, chest, and between her breasts. I finally took each nipple, in turn, in my mouth. I knelt, my knees astride her thighs so that my hands could caress the sides of her body, and gently pulled the pubic hair on top of her mound. I pushed her legs apart to touch her soft, wet silkiness with the back of my hand, moving back and forth to absorb the texture. She was as wet as I was as she reached (almost begged) for me with her hips. I turned my hand over so my fingers could slide in her wetness. I entered, becoming wrapped in velvet, going in and out to match her rhythm. I came out for a slow and tantalizing rub on her clitoris, wanting to feel her for myself and delay orgasm for her. It didn't take much to bring her over the edge. She was so ready and beautiful when she came. I was astounded at the power I had, that I could make someone feel this good.

She barely caught her breath before I felt rubbing from underneath. I was still straddling her. It felt so good from this angle that I had to brace myself against the wall so I wouldn't collapse. She rubbed my clit with one hand, fucking with two or three fingers from the other. I immediately exploded in orgasm, a release of more than 20 years of pent-up tension. I kept coming and coming.

We made love until dawn and did everything I imagine all new couples do: fuck, cuddle, talk, giggle, fuck some more. I flinched the first time she shimmied down my body for oral sex, recalling that awkward boyfriend experience.

It shocked me when she rested her head between my legs and just looked for the longest time, her fingers gently touching and rearranging my lips. Over and over she said how beautiful I was, and—despite my shyness—I found this extremely sensual.

From that point on, we spent almost every night at her place. Afraid of scandalous rumors breaking out on campus, I would sneak back to my room early in the morning. On weekends we slept late. When I woke up before she did, I watched her sleep, feeling content and peaceful. If she woke up first, she made breakfast for me. I had never fantasized about this, how good it could feel to love and be with someone.

Graduation came, and I was accepted into a number of graduate schools. She decided to come with me; she was too much a feminist for the staff at this small college. I chose a school in a large city on the East Coast, wanting to get as far away from the Midwest as possible. We found an apartment, she found a job, and we began a life together.

I thought our relationship would last forever, but I also had a hunch that things could change. We started to meet other lesbians, and when they gave me those full body hugs instead of "diamond" hugs around the shoulders, I began to appreciate the different shapes and sizes of women's bodies. I was fascinated by women and curious about what they might feel like naked since I had never really "dated." I watched us slowly grow apart, partly because of my curiosity. I thought I would eventually be the one to make the move but was dumbfounded when she dumped me for another woman. There was a lot of hurt and anger; I'm not sure I'll ever be completely over it. Our relationship lasted five years, and she and I have not spoken since the breakup.

I've been in my second long-term relationship for more than 11 years now. My girlfriend and I live on the East Coast, but we're farther south from where I originally started. We have an adorable four-year-old daughter, a beautiful house with a yard to play in, two cats, a dog, and a minivan. We joke that we have become the average American family, something I think my first lover never aspired to. I finished graduate school with a Ph.D., worked for a while, but now stay home full-time to care for our daughter who is usually more of a woman than I can handle.

I had many lovers between my first and present relationship. I enjoyed them all, but some were definitely better than others. When I think back to that first time, first touch, first kiss, and first sex, there was something special, something unique, and something electric that never did and never will happen again.

And that is the story of my first embrace. It may not be exotic or earth-shattering, but it was for me because it truly changed my life. That sounds sentimental, but it's not why I wrote this story. I wanted to make you wet. I hope I did.

CHAPTER THIRTY-FOUR
My Butch Baby
Laurie Kay

I must have been searching for Marie all my life. How else can I explain why I had sex with 40 men while I was married? Unenjoyable, meaningless sex. No orgasms with any of them. I was with some of them more than once. My sons were in college; I wasn't the hockey mom anymore, which was kind of a shock to my system. Hockey had filled every waking hour of every winter for 15 years. Even in the summers, my youngest son would play hockey in Canada, a hop, skip, and a jump from our small northern New York town.

Time, once a luxury, suddenly hung heavy on my hands. I started spending a lot of it on my computer. One would think my husband of 24 years would have been a tiny bit curious to know what I was doing, but he was content watching television while I scanned chat rooms. First I chatted in rooms about pets since I'm such an animal lover. Then I found the rooms with married people in them. That's how I met Coy from the Midwest. We shared a few months of hot, sexy talk over the computer and on the phone, but he knew I needed more. He suggested I needed a woman's touch. So I began looking in lesbian chat rooms.

At first I was shocked at what I read, but I soon grew interested. A few women wrote to me. One in particular always sent me pictures of naked women. I was beginning to get really curious about what a lesbian was. So I kept writing to her and a few others. In the past, I had done some fantasizing about masculine women making love to me, but I never thought it was anything I would really want to happen. It was almost a rape fantasy. She would be this Joan Jett type who'd overtake me completely. It was a real turn-on.

Fate brought me to Marie. I had been writing to a woman in Boston who was having problems with her boyfriend, who had attention-deficit hyperactivity disorder. My youngest son has the same problem, so we had a lot of notes to compare. She told me she had found a personals site and was looking to see if she could find a man in her area she could have dinner with. I went to the personals site and subscribed for a free ten-day period. I searched New York State and found the ad Marie had posted. She was 46, three years older than I, not into the bar scene, and looking for someone who was quiet but knew how to let loose at the right times. I wrote to her, and she answered. For the next two weeks, we talked on the phone and wrote E-mails to each other. I became so comfortable talking to her that we decided to meet for dinner since I had to take my son down to Long Island for an evaluation and Marie nearby.

My son and the friend who had made the trip with us both wanted to see New York City. While they were gone, I waited for Marie to show up at my hotel room. I'll never forget how nervous I was. The room became very hot, so I opened the door, only to find Marie coming toward me down the hallway. She had told me she was a soft butch, whatever that is. She sort of scared me at first, not smiling, herice-blue eyes raking my body boldly. *If this is a soft butch, then what the hell is a hard one?* I thought apprehensively.

We had made plans to go to dinner at a nearby restaurant. She was wearing jeans and a T-shirt; I had on jeans too, but I was having a problem with my low-neck sweater. It needed a pin, and I couldn't find one. I nervously ransacked my luggage, looking for one, when suddenly Marie whispered,

"Why don't you take it off so I can see your sexy bra?" She was sprawled casually on the bed, head propped up on her elbow. The intensity of her gaze made me want to surrender to this confident, mysterious woman. I didn't hesitate; I quickly pulled the sweater over my head. (A few months later, I told her that I had wanted to seduce her and that the sweater was all part of my devious plot.)

"Nice," she murmured. "Now why don't you take that off and show me what's underneath?" Her tone was teasing, but when I looked into her eyes, I saw a burning hunger in their depths. Never before had anyone been so aroused by me. It was getting me hot…and not the kind of I hot where I needed to open a door.

Slowly I unhooked my pink satin bra and let it fall onto the bed. A look of awe sprang into her eyes. I had warned her I had huge nipples. "They are absolutely exquisite," she breathed. When she patted the mattress next to her, I lay down, excited and scared at the same time. I mean, this was my first time with a woman. I didn't know what to expect.

She began to suck on my nipples, pulling them with her teeth, licking them. She made small noises, letting me know how much she was enjoying my body. Suddenly she gently kissed me, half lying on top of me with her knee between my thighs. I'd never been kissed by a woman before. I was stiff at first but loosened up after a few minutes under her expert hands and lips. I began kissing her back . Somehow we reversed positions, and I was on top of her, taking her jeans off. She lay back with her hands behind her head, an amused expression on her face. "What are you doing?" she asked when I started pulling her underwear off. Although I am really a shy person, I was so eager to see, touch, smell, and taste her pussy that I couldn't hold myself back.

"You told me eating pussy is an acquired taste. I want to start acquiring it," I smiled.

She looked at me for a few seconds and then said, "Rock on." She was impressed by my natural ability. So was I. I really enjoyed what I was doing. But I got scared when I heard talking outside the room. I thought it was my son coming back, so we quickly jumped up and started getting dressed. We soon figured out it was a false alarm, and Marie took control again. Before I knew it, I was up against the wall, and she was kissing me, plunging her tongue deep inside my mouth while she slipped her fingers deep inside my wet cunt. Her hands knew just what to do. I was very turned on. But it had to end there. My AIDS test results weren't back yet, and Marie was adamant about not being with me until I had them.

We went to dinner and stopped at a bookstore on the way. (Marie's only vice. Well, it was her only vice until she met me.) During dinner she kept undressing me with her eyes, making me so nervous that I could barely eat. No one had ever done that to me before. When I showed her pictures of my family, she just shook her head in wonder. My husband is handsome and so are my boys. My husband knew we were meeting and encouraged me to "Go for it or you'll never know."

After I got back home upstate, Marie and I continued to E-mail each other and talk on the phone. She invited me to see *The Wizard of Oz* playing in Madison Square Garden in May. When I drove down to her new house in Staten Island, I had my AIDS test results in my hand: negative. I knew I was going to feel Marie's mouth between my legs.

"I've missed you," she said when she opened the door. "A lot," she added huskily. We walked down a long ceramic-tiled hallway, and then she pushed me back onto the deep carpeted stairs. "I can't wait one more minute," she said and began kissing me. I was at first shy and stiff, but as her kisses grew in passion, I started warming to her touch. It seemed as if we kissed for hours, but eventually she led me into her bedroom and slowly undressed me. My knees trembled with nervousness, with anticipation. When she held me in her arms, I felt as if I knew what letting go and being myself meant.

"Just lay back and enjoy yourself, baby," she advised. "I'll make all your fantasies come true." When we were first getting to know each other, I told Marie I didn't kiss and that I'm very quiet and reserved during sex. I was soundless even while having orgasms with my husband. But that first weekend with Marie was so completely different. I never knew sex could be so soft, gentle, passionate, and rewarding. She's brought out a passion in me that surprises me. I never knew I could have that with someone. Sometimes I become the top and bring her to pleasure in a way she's never experienced before. I still can't believe how easy it is to make love to her. She loves to go down on me, gently tugging and sucking on my petals, telling me with her moans how much she loves to watch them open for her. My Marie loves the way I taste. My husband always complained that I was either too wet or that my scent was too heavy. Marie tells me I never taste too strong. She gets excited by my wetness. "It's all mine, baby. All mine," she says. And when she lets her fingers trail gently along my hips, I want her so much I wish I could fuse my bones into hers.

Oral sex is the only way I can come. I think that's why I was so intrigued with being in bed with a woman, because if anyone knows how to eat pussy, it must be a woman. My husband is too rough, and I have to block out the pain during our sessions. Sometimes I'm very sore after sex with him. With my Marie I never want her to stop. In the months we've been together, I've become more verbal during lovemaking. My butch baby doesn't want me to just lie there. She wants to hear me, hear my enjoyment, hear my passion. It never was important before, but now, letting my lover know how I'm feeling means a lot to me.

"Make love to me, honey." I never thought I could say those words, but I know how much my Marie wants me. She's always horny for me, always lusting after me.

"What does my Loree-girl want? Hmm? Does she want me to tug on her?" she asks in a breezy way, her baby blue eyes alive with desire.

"Yes, baby, please," I moan. But she doesn't rush. She just takes her time. She kisses me, long and slow, teasing my tongue with the tip of hers. Her fingers drift lightly over my body, but they feel like live flames. I anticipate what will happen next, hungering for it, needing it, but when she finally plunges her fingers inside me, I still gasp with surprise. Pleasure. Joy.

"Does my baby like that?" Marie asks. I can only moan in response.

"Mmm, I love the way you moan, baby," she whispers throatily in my ear, as her fingers churn inside me. I can feel myself, as I arch my hips to get more of her hand inside me. "Tch, tch, tch, you're being a greedy little baby, Loree-girl," she chides, sliding her fingers slowly out of me. "Oh," I cry in disappointment. "Please, baby, don't stop." She just laughs, letting me know that I'm there for *her* pleasure as much as for mine.

"Please, baby, please," I beg. "Eat me...please." I open my eyes and look into hers. "Please, baby," I whisper. I know how excited she gets when I whisper like that. She says my little girl voice goes right to her clit. She parts my legs with one of hers and gently traces her fingertip along my cunt. "

You're lips are so swollen, baby," she praises. "They are so fucking big for me." Marie loves how my inner lips reach out to her. I watch as she gets between my wide-open legs and sweetly kisses my pussy. "Is this what you want, baby? Huh?" she says.

I feel her fingertips pry my cunt open, and then she takes my lips into her mouth. "Oh, Marie!"

Her mouth works on me, her lips tugging on my swollen pussy lips, her tongue licking my wet slash. She teases me, rubbing her nose on my engorged clit as she laps at my cunt. I'm on fire with desire! I can't wait!

"Please, Marie, please," I moan as I pull the hood away from my clit. "Please let me come." She looks up, just to let me know who the boss is. "Please," I moan. I know how hot my moaning makes her.

"OK, baby," she says low and sexy. My legs jerk, and my hips buck when I feel the first snakelike flick of her tongue on my burning clit. I can't restrain myself. "Fuck me, Marie. Fuck me!" I scream.

I feel her tongue through my growing frenzy. I hear her noises of enjoyment as she sucks on my button, strokes me, plunges her tongue as far inside me as she can. "No one has ever done that to me before!" I manage to gasp out, as her tongue wantonly explores my drenched opening. My butch baby is an expert lover. As I lay under her hungry mouth and tongue, my clit jumps. She makes me feel things I never have before. My body reacts wildly—legs tremble, hips buck, fingers entwine themselves in her short blond hair. "Oh, baby, oh, baby," I chant through short gasps of breath. "Don't stop! Her tongue moves faster, whipping my clit. Everything builds up until I can't hold it in anymore. "O-o-oh," a long drawn-out wail bursts from deep within me as my powerful orgasm flops me around on the bed.

Marie moves up next to me and softly kisses my lips. "That's what you taste like, honey."

No one has ever done that to me before. "Do you like it?" I ask shyly.

"I thirst for you," she whispers before laying her head on my heaving breast. We fall asleep sleep like that, holding each other.

She tells me I'm her one true love, that she's waited her whole life for me. And I believe her. I'm the only one who's seen her femme side, the side she shows me when I bring her pleasure, when she completely surrenders to me. She's the first one to lavish me with compliments that I believe. She loves to look into my "incredible green eyes," loves my red hair, loves that I'm a femme. She desires me. This is the first time in my life that I truly feel like a sexual woman. I buy sexy bras and panties for her. I had never realized how unhappy, how unfulfilled I was until Marie came along.

I had always been one of the "guys" to my husband and sons. My husband, the one who said "Go for it," freaked out when he saw the bond that developed between me and Marie. He demanded I end the relationship. But I won't. I can't. He simply cannot understand what she does for me, how she boosts my self-esteem, how I'm her equal. She is the one who makes me look forward to the future. Without her in my life, I don't have one.

I don't know how to really put it in words. I'm not a lesbian, bisexual, or any of those labels. I'm in love with someone who just happens to be the same sex as myself. It's who I want and who I feel safe with. I've never before felt so happy and secure with who I am.

I'm looking forward to the day when I can wake up next to my butch baby every morning and find her nuzzling between my legs. I have found my soul mate, my pride, my joy.

CHAPTER THIRTY-FIVE
First in Line
Margaret Bradstock

I was always a tomboy. By the time I was nine I had cut off my hair and usually ran around in khaki boys' shorts and a Bond's singlet until people's glances began to tell me what I didn't want to know: I was beginning to develop a "chest." If I ever fantasized about a future partner, it was a faceless, genderless person (who enjoyed reading with me at night!), although for a long time I firmly believed I would grow up into a man, the patriarch of a family. By high school, peer group pressure and compulsory sex-role socialization had taken over, and I put these ambitions behind me.

In 1959, I went on to university and Women's College and managed to break most of the seemingly pointless rules in my first year there—including climbing the college drainpipe on a dare. My dreams were split. I was always in love with one or another of the Women's College girls, dark Jewish-looking girls or blond ethereal types with passionate faces. But I never talked about it to anyone, and possibly didn't acknowledge fully to myself what I was thinking. Lesbianism was something we laughed about or discovered surreptitiously in the pages of Havelock Ellis. "Lez be friends," girls joked, going through the motions of seduction, assuring themselves and each other that it *was* a joke. It was something I'd never heard about before—exotic and impossible. *The Well of Loneliness* was whispered about behind closed doors.

In bed at night, I fantasized about women, but I went out with boys. Sexuality meant boys, and in spite of a nonpermissive society, sex was what we were all groping toward. The doublethink of the early 1960s involved never acknowledging what you were really doing, even with the opposite sex. There was a price to be paid for petting beyond the point of respectability. We went around singing "It's Now or Never," but fended the boys off to preserve our virginity (technically, at any rate) for that never-never land of the future. Possibly it was the very distancing of male sexuality and companionship that made it seem the ultimate goal. To be home on a Saturday night or to have to go out with the girls was a personal failure. I became a man's woman with a vengeance.

Little wonder, then, that I was married by the time I was 21 and soon had three children. I won't go into the disappointments and loneliness of that relationship—they are the story of many housewives both straight and gay. Once the pleasures of a regular supply of sex had lost their first excitement, I began to think about women again. When Rick, my husband, had sex with me, I imagined it was a woman's body against my own. We were living in the country at that time, the last bastion of the heterosexist imperative, where even electric plugs and sockets have male and female parts. My imaginings were a secret life.

After we moved back to the city in the early 1970s, I went through a period of affairs with other men, in search of I'm not quite sure what, finally ending up with long-haired boys who seemed an ideal compromise. My longest affair was with Ted, a man whose wife I was really in love with. She was one of a line of what Kate (of whom, more later) had christened "lizard ladies," with dark hair, Jewish looks, and almost boyishly slender bodies. I enjoyed talking to Ted about Lynda and whether she might one day be persuaded to indulge in sex with women.

My best friends at the time were male; most of the women I knew were busying themselves with Tupperware parties and conversations about children's school lunches. Still, I continued to be fascinated by the concept of women together. There was a lesbian bar at the Vanity Fair Hotel (now bulldozed flat) where we went drinking. Here was the prospect of a whole different lifestyle. I sometimes saw the women in passing and felt strangely drawn, still denying that this could be *my* reality.

I got a job at university and met a new breed of women, mostly younger. I began to have erotic daydreams, indulging in all kinds of sexual behavior with them (in a male persona, of course). That was where I met Kate, a fellow tutor, 24 years old and fresh out of a master's degree. Our first encounter wasn't at all promising. I was drinking whiskey as a cure for a summer cold, and she advised an all-grape fast. I thought she was some kind of health nut, and she thought I was "mad, bad, and dangerous to know." Still, it was like a body blow when I looked at her. Her different faces had crowded my dreams for years. Her long eyelashes and pre-Raphaelite lips suggested a hidden sexuality. When I discovered she was a lesbian, that was it!

She was unconsciously flirting with me, wandering in and out of my office on the vaguest of pretexts, and I felt I had to make a move before someone else did.

"What would you say if I propositioned you?" I asked, kicking the door shut with my motorcycle boots. I tried to be casual in case of rejection. She was affronted by the word *proposition* and thought I was an opportunist looking for ways to revivify a flagging marriage.

"No," I said, laying myself on the line. "I can't eat, I can't sleep for thinking about you."

"How medieval! Does it often get you this way?"

She was amused at my desperation, but she came home with me anyway, without making any promises. The ostensible reason was that her flat was infested with bedbugs and she had nowhere else to sleep.

The whole night was like an absurd dream. The house was in chaos, furniture in the process of being shifted to make way for that suburban status symbol — a new Berryman bedroom suite. We drank wine, sitting on whatever we could find. Voyeuristic, not believing he was irrelevant, Rick rushed out to buy more wine. Kate's arms were around me, her mouth pressed hard on mine. The shock of her tongue! When she kissed me, the earth didn't just move — it disintegrated and fell away completely. We made love that night in spite of Rick snoring drunkenly in the same bed. I guessed my way blindly through that unfamiliar country.

"I love you so much," I said to Kate.

She laughed, rejecting the possibility. "You're drunk."

Then I lay wakeful all night with one arm around her. Kate's body curved away in a taut bow. She wasn't very communicative the next morning.

"I'm being caught in my own toils," she said briefly, lower lip curled down, soft and vulnerable.

Good Friday. The sky was a plastic dome imprisoning air still warm from the summer. The bridge spread its steel tentacles across the city. I drove her to the train that morning. "I'll be glad to get away from the city," she said. "It's just the weather for riding, especially along the beaches." I glanced sideways at her long eyelashes, her suntanned hands, felt again the body blow; excitement punched at my nerves in closed-circuit. In many ways it was like looking into a mirror that reflected some other, younger self. "I wish you could come with me," she added, face suddenly animated, shamelessly coquettish.

I tossed the long, dark hair out of my eyes, a noncommittal gesture. "I can't. I'd like to. There's a party this afternoon that I don't want to miss…and the pub tomorrow." Not to mention the kids and the whole messy lifestyle.

"I'll see you when I get back, then." Her lips brushed mine and she was gone. Jeans and a tight denim shirt open one button too many, the figure, the walk, flamboyantly female.

I watched her go out of my sight, then drove back past carefully tended suburban lawns, shaved like priests, and Italian gardens lined with chrysanthemums. I drove into my own unruly yard and sat for a while, the memory of her voice, darling that's lovely, playing over and over in my head.

On Tuesday, Kate dropped by my office briefly. "How was your weekend, Margaret?" She flirted outrageously with her eyes.

"Fine. I had a great time at the party. How was yours?"

"Lovely. It was hot enough for swimming and sunbaking. I didn't take any bathers, but that didn't matter. An inspector chased us along the beach."

I pictured her running along the water's edge, hair wet and stiff with salt, laughing manically, her life running away from mine like sand. I remained carefully distant. "How were your friends?" I asked

"Fine," she said. "I told them about you. They were a bit surprised. You'll have to come with me next time. You'd like them."

She was back again the next day. "I thought we might have lunch together."

"That would have been nice, but I'm having lunch with Geoff. He's the trumpet player in Rick's band. I've always rather fancied him. We're going to a place called A Different Drummer. He thought that would be appropriate," I laughed.

"You're very predatory."

"No, I'm not. I just want everything, I suppose. Opportunistic, if you like. I don't intend to grow old gracefully, you know."

"Well, I'll walk down to your car with you."

We were already on the stairs. I was glad to appear busy, in demand. Fearful of seeming too eager, too possessive, I didn't realize I was building up walls, brick by brick.

"I was talking to Ted on the phone this morning. I said to him, 'I've got a husband and a boyfriend and a girlfriend now. What more could I want?'"

"How did he take that?"

"He laughed. He thought it was funny."

Kate didn't laugh. "Who is he, anyway?"

"An old friend. I've been going out with him for years. We have an understanding."

"I'm glad," she offered. "Because your marriage doesn't seem very good."

Kate's voice was gentle despite her words. She leaned against my car, barefoot, wearing a long Indian skirt and an old opportunity shop blouse. For a moment her eyes held mine. "Well," I said, half-reluctantly. "I've got to be going or I'll be late. I'll see you."

I didn't see her for over a week, but on Friday I went to a staff welcome for A.D. Hope, the grand old man of Australian poetry. At the last moment, Kate came in. She had a rose tucked into the buckle of khaki overalls and a bemused, slightly quizzical smile on her face to cover self-consciousness. I drank and re-filled my glass, watching and not watching. Eventually I wandered over. Kate, wary, cornered, leafed rapidly through books.

"Look. I've got to talk to you," I said. "Can you come to my office for a minute?"

"All right. Not for long, though." Again Kate's wry, paranoia-producing smile.

We sat down side by side on the hard, black chairs, totally separated. "You've been avoiding me," I accused. "I've got to know what's going on."

"Well, I've been thinking over what my friends in New-castle said, and I've decided they're right. You're not good for me. Your lifestyle's all wrong—all those lovers. It's sick. Trendy bourgeois. I don't want to be part of it."

"That's pious. Moralistic," I jabbed back. "You're such an idealist. You don't live in the real world."

"Of course I do. If anything, I'm a cynic. But I believe you have to have ideals to strive for. You're empty inside, Margaret. That's your problem. And as long as you remain that way you leave yourself open to all kinds of corruption." She grinned suddenly, irrepressibly, undercutting herself, "Said the high-flying ace to her faded rose."

"Well, then," I answered, ignoring the mixture of metaphors, "that's it." My instinct was to grovel, subservient, like a courtly knight, but I sensed the futility. "I'm afraid so," she answered. "I have to be true to myself." We walked down the stairs together. "Cheer up," Kate added. "It's not the end of the world. We can still be friends."

I gave her a lift to the station, and again Kate's lips brushed mine in a farewell gesture—this time, unyielding. "Curse you, Red Baron," I said softly, attempting to match her humor. I drove recklessly, shot down in flames, seeing my collision written on every brick wall.

Denying myself dinner as a kind of flagellation, an emotional hair shirt, I poured a double whiskey and sat down at my desk. I couldn't concentrate, though, listening to the silences, staring at the blank wall like an immured nun...waiting to be buried alive.

What was it I really wanted? Basically Kate had refused to go to the wall because of my other relationships, which she saw as destructive. For the first time in years I went inside my own head, endeavoring to face what I found there, no longer relying on the excuse of drunkenness to put it off until tomorrow. The region I entered had become a frightening, impenetrable forest. If I succeeded in forcing my way through, what deadness would I find at the center? What I do and what I am are two separate things. Inside I'm untouched by it all. But how to get back to that imprisoned self? At the center of it all stood Kate. The self became other, merged into her. I had treated her as an object. "Learn to know me as a person," Kate had said. "Maybe then we can salvage something."

She came back, and I wooed her with poems and stories until she believed me (though she could never resist criticizing my style). Those were halcyon days, days of intense passion. I was so turned on by Kate's presence I would come the moment she touched me sexually. We learned to make love with eyes wide open, seeing into each other's souls—perhaps too much so.

At first Rick was tolerant and excited by the whole idea, as long as I kept sleeping with him too. These were the swinging '70s. He was prepared to baby-sit once a week while I spent the night with Kate. But she demanded I make a choice, and that was when the trouble began. I moved a double mattress into the spare room, and Kate came over whenever Rick went out on the town, which was often. If he didn't score, he'd be home beating on my door, shouting, "What about my conjugals?" We would cower there, mattress pressed against the door, wondering whether he'd take an ax to the pair of us.

"Bloody lezzos," he'd shout. "You don't know what real sex is anyway."

They were lonely days too, without a context, without others like ourselves. The acceptability I'd worked so hard to achieve was gone. In spite of my closeted existence, the neighbors all seemed to know.

Why didn't we leave? Kate wanted me to, but I was afraid the kids would be miserable in rented accommodation, afraid that living with them would place impossible strains on the relationship I had with her. There was also the constant shadow of a court case and loss of the children altogether. I stayed on in a marriage in name only for six years. They were years of violence, of sexual harassment, of being sent to Coventry by outraged in-laws. Again it's the story of many married women who've changed horses midstream.

These things erode love, and eventually Kate went away overseas. Both of us had other affairs and learned the value of separateness in togetherness (though, for me none of the others ever really mattered). But this is a true story, not a cautionary tale. We sorted out our early differences and decided to live together. For a while it was an open relationship (in theory, at least), although that didn't work out very well. While rejecting the possessive, hypocritical concept of monogamy projected by a straight, Christian society, I'm afraid I don't welcome the disruption and misery that often accompany a freer lifestyle. Nor does Kate, now that she's had two children by insemination and knows, firsthand, the responsibilities of parenting. The boys bridle at any hint of my infidelity or dereliction, and in any case, commitment to their welfare comes first in this family.

Where do we go now? Twenty-four years down the track, five children and two Ph.Ds later, we sometimes wonder what there is left of "us," the "relationship." She said today she thought we were rather like the survivors of the *Titanic*, clinging to the wreckage. I laugh, surveying the flotsam and the jetsam. But being an incurable romantic, I think instead of the words of that old Elvis Presley song, as outdated and clichéd as they may be:

> When they gave out eyes like diamonds,
> that would shame the stars that shine,
> my darling, O my darling,
> you were the first in line,
> the first and the last in line.

CHAPTER THIRTY-SIX
Venus Rising
Sara Eclevia

*I*t is not advisable to have sex for the first time with a cunt. Michèle was a cunt; I was the ass. Or as they say in my missionary country: *Elle était le con. J'étais le cu.* It is perverse to judge what led me to kiss those moist lips and take in their sweet stench—she bolder than I—in the damp tent. It might have been desire for her, nostalgia for old sexual games, or submission to fate. I will not see clearly. But I was there of my own design and still am today. Paper flowers in the mud, a WANTED poster flapping in the desert air. Enough to give me the shits. Lordy, lordy, hair on my fuckin' swordy.

I seduced her. I had to seduce her because I was too old for patience. I'm going to seduce her, this very night, in front of the woman I want because, baby, I can't wait for you no more. We will return to your games after I have myself a woman. I see your panic, growing with an appreciation of charms that are not enough to keep me biding my time. But I will come back to you, and you will have one less fear about sleeping with me because you won't be my first. It won't be you that I suffocate with the rabid desperation of which you are so piously certain. So go dance another dance while I drink another drink to numb the twattle of a brewing lay. It could have been you, baby...it could have been you. But you believe in karma, your just desserts.

Hélène Fouquet was a pretty little French bitch. A perfect pink-lipped *poupée* with golden hair and eyes of blue that turned to glass when I dumped on her dollhouse. It was on her high bed under our Alice skirts that I wanted to play. But she would shake her fairy-tale curls in distress before *l'obsédée d'Américaine* and soon left me flat. She was a virtuous innocent (as all little girls should be), a genuine ingenue; I, for all of my five years, was already a sheepish wolf in angel's clothing. I will mourn her bright crib, skippingly drenched in cigarette smoke and *objets d'art* that sparkled and swirled around the fay Hélène, ice nymph of my censured dreams.

It is time to go, my dear. My friends have left, the lights have gone up, and I'm not sure I want to see you this clearly too long. I need you, I want your body tonight, and I'm going to have it. Surely you know that by now. Of course, we will share a cab; we live in the same direction. Yes, I know. You have made enough half-heard twattle, and I have told enough fish stories to smooth through a seduction's coral heads. You have filled the night's silence with nonsense while I have ornamented its darkness with smiles.

"Perhaps you would like to go out to dinner with me sometime," you say quickly as the taxi slows.

"Sure," I smile. "Would you like to come up for a bit? " I can already taste your sex. It is torn open and glistening in my hands.

My first orgasm with a woman soaked through my jean shorts and made me sob with desolation. I hadn't wanted it to happen with her—me, the closet

romantic. I certainly had not wanted that first female-to-female orgasm to happen for her. It was an
A-bomb, out of context, inappropriate, uncivilized.
How could it have happened? She forcefully pawed
at me after she had undressed. How did I end up in
bed with her tugging at my T-shirt, soft mounds of
flesh partially hiding the stretched-out G-string that
had to be riding up her ass and dripping lips, holding me down, pushing my arms into the mattress? *I
really don't want this, just stop. Why?* On the couch
again, she's still groping, pulling me back when I
struggle to get up and away. *Just...Let go...Don't do
that...Stop...Why?...Because it's not going to happen...Why not?...Let me go...Relax, honey...Come on,
turn around... No...Don't...You've got to stop...*But it's
too late. She is finally still. She holds me, my back
cushioned against her softness, drenched and shuddering, until I fall asleep and grieve. The air-conditioning has turned the wetness cold against my
thighs and cheeks.

Silky music, sensual wine, the soft glow of hair and skin.
Next to me on the love seat, you have actually stopped
talking to me, and I am surprised by the silence. "I want to
sleep with you," I say quietly. You are still. I am years
younger than you, and your innocence is almost sweet. But
it is not a quality I can ponder for your sake; it is too late
for that my dear. Let me say instead that I am sorry. I will
try to make it worth the pain. I must have you. Surely you
must understand. Surely you would if I made it clear. But
I cannot. You mean nothing to me, nothing and everything
in a moment.

"How old are you?" you question.

I laugh and ask "Does it matter?"

"No, but...I'm older than I look," you warn.

Moments pass while I watch your fog. "Where would we go from here?" you shimmer.

"I don't know. Carefully? I don't know that this attraction is anything more than...physical," I answer gently. But I do know, and I won't risk your running out the door. You are already poised to go, but I can't let you. Surely you know that by now, my sweet. You are rigid with fear because you feel the deepening cold of the pit you will not see, even as you roll up your sleeves and whet the sword. I cannot show you mercy, my dear. Maybe I could have, had I known. Maybe I would have, had I seen before now the black chasm in your eyes.

The first time I stroked the flesh of a splayed woman, I was with a man. I did not know my hand would creep out below my stunned vision and touch her there, so close to her swollen red vulva stretched between white thighs and black hair. But I knew suddenly the moment she said, clearly but gently, "No, Sara." And the man I so despised, but had needed to get this far and needed now desperately, mocked my disappointment with his own.

You put your arm on the back of the couch behind my head, like a teenage boy on a date in Dad's car, and I smile again, amused and repelled, before I turn to you completely and kiss your mouth. Your lips and tongue are shy, but you will follow my lead; I know how I like to be kissed. You sink to the floor before me on your knees, and the kiss takes over my brain. I am so damn hungry. I touch your face, your soft hair, your gentle arms and shoulders, and it is all very nice; but it is your breasts—your breasts and your cunt—that I want before they slip away from me again. I'm sorry, my dear. I hope you are old and wise enough to understand. Please be strong this time, just this once.

I touch your breasts through their expensive knit sweater and close my eyes heavenward. I unhook your bra because I must touch your skin, your tanning-booth skin that I trace like folds of drapes with the tips of my fingers, not knowing yet how to grasp its distended texture. So you do have enormous strength, my sweet—yes, you do. That power must still be there, love, and you will draw upon it again when I am through with you. "Is there," you breathe against the skin of my neck, "any place we can go? The windows…" *Of course! How remiss of me!*

You are a woman of obvious experience, my dear, and I am a creature of instinct. My nose is sticking out from beneath sheep's clothing, and you look a little frightened. But there is no need for that, no need at all. My eyes are unfocused, yes, and there is drool dripping off my chin from my hurry-scurry lust, but you are not a woman to back down after you commit. Oh, how I know that now—how you thrived on my need, how you kept it blazing. You would fuck me so easily and all night, and then wake me again with numbing sex—day after day. The more you fucked me the more I wanted it. And then, when I finally tore my body back from you, the torture really began: Your claws ripped past me, again and again, and left me dripping. But I was not sucked in with you. I could not be snatched up, taken in, and plundered. Because I could not help you, darling, I knew that from the beginning, and so did you.

Caffeine is a drug. When you're not used to it, it gives you a high as breathless as cocaine. The mind, eyes wide, jittery and spare, goes clear and disjointed as a bell. And the sex is economical, mind-blowing, bone-crunching. The first time I saw a man whipped in a dungeon against a wooden cross, I had an epiphany, chemically induced, since my body was born again. The blood dripped from his back into my cunt and I saw through gold.

Are you muddled from too much alcohol, baby? I am not; all I feel is you, your body and mine, the way it should be, the way I always knew it could be. Who am I kidding? It's me I'm kidding, because I've never had this part of the picture, the part that is now making it almost whole. I've only had it in my dreams…vivid, but less perfect…not like now…not like feeling your tongue on my nipple and your fingers between my legs…sliding across my pumping clit…over, across, and down toward my vagina…fast, slow, fast…tonguing my tongue wetly across my face—Jesus Christ! "Sh-h-h," you whisper. "It's OK. It's OK." But your fingers don't stop their rhythm, and I suck on your mouth to quiet my howling. Jesus, this is what I've been waiting for for so damn long, and I didn't know it would be so damn fucking good. Everything: your hair, the smell of your neck, those beautiful curves of your hips and thighs under my hands, the heat of your skin, the look in your Byzantine eyes, the texture of your tongue, the movement of your fingers. Woman, beautiful woman, I am yours. In this moment I am open and completely yours.

My first kisses—down and up and back again— took me out of my fucking mind. The first brown nipple I tugged between my teeth, the first girl who kept me panting week after week. Making out for hours but too shy to come. Her smell, the fucking smell of her. She doesn't screw white girls; sex is too spiritual. She preferred to watch me fuck another. But I'm not done with her. She believes in karma.

"Sorry, honey, I should have warned you." I ejaculate, horrifically. "I bet you haven't experienced that before. I'll get some towels." You giggle that damn giggle and pull me back into bed. You kiss me again, licking your lips. You are already addicted to my orgasms.

But I want the juice between your legs, so spread 'em, baby. Let me at you. Let me see how things have changed since the last time when I barely had breasts or a will. I want inside, darling, and you're going to let me in. I will kiss your body on my way down, but I've got to make it quick. I've got to get at you. That's it...spread them wider...oh, honey...oh, darling...look at you, look...oh...the smell of you...oh, God I want to taste you...look how open you are to me...oh, baby, you have a beautiful pussy...but you already know that, don't you? You probably hear that all the time.

Devouring a cunt for the first time is a feeding frenzy, pure physical hysteria. With a soupçon of skill and a dribble of control, add a sip of patience and a smack of attentiveness. I'm not all bad, baby; I like to bring my victims to the height of ecstasy so they may behold nirvana with tired mortal eyes before I let them plunge and self-destruct. Isn't that right, baby? Isn't that the way the bitch operates? I lick, I tease, I penetrate you with my soft tongue, instead of scraping you raw and eating you whole, instead of sucking your blood with my fangs.

When my hot fingers slip deep into your vagina, I grasp the ridges of your cervix. I am home. I am finally home. Why did it take so many men to find my way here when you, woman, were sitting at my kitchen table all along. Light a match and the whole block will go down.

"Harder, hit me harder," she cried and cried. Rhodora was the first girl I belted for pleasure. I almost cried later because when the flat of my hand snapped her head back, I came hard. She is dark-skinned, and I am white—snow white, fluorescent green-tinged white. She rolled her eyes with contempt. I'll hurt her again. Make no mistake.

Maybe pleasure knows no more than the quantifying and qualifying of multiple orgasms. There is always another one around the corner, greater than the one before. Weeks later, in bed with you again, my sweet, I directed with my hips the minutest movement of the pad of your finger inside my cunt. The bed was soaked in a matter of minutes: great astonishing ejaculations—mere seconds apart—building and building until I had your brutal fist inside me. One finger from the other hand pumped my ass simultaneously, your tongue on my clit. I thought I would go insane from pleasure and frustration, climbing toward a release that would maim. But that elusive orgasm—the really big one, the one you can work toward hour after hour, advancing to the limit before turning back abruptly—is one I have not achieved. Maybe it really will blow out my brains when it rips through them…Oh, miracle of sex, you have taken me over completely.

Save me, strong Claire, like you saved me in your pubescent dreams. You were my first great

love, but you never knew it. "They called you to
the teacher's hall," you said, "where they were all
assembled, all those who wanted to destroy you
because of your beauty, *ma belle Américaine*. I had
to pound down the door to get you out, and everyone was yelling, and you were crying. I carried
you out, past the gates and into the forest. And I
took you in my arms *et je t'ai emballé*." We kissed in
your dreams, deep, heart-drenching kisses, and
you told me every dream. You told me about that
boy you fucked in the horse stables. I told you it
was wrong, that the Bible told me so. You left. Ah,
Claire, where are you now? Did your drunk father
finally beat you to death after puking his guts out
in your filthy toilet?

My heart is asleep and dreams, far from the mind's glass
eye. My sex feeds on its casualties. So be it. You have taught
me, baby, that someone must always suffer the pleasure of
another. I combust while the other writhes in pain. I am
guilty, alive, and guiltless. Look into my eyes when I fuck
you, and I'll tear out your soul.

CHAPTER THIRTY-SIX
The Bath
Jill Fontenot

"With an accent like that, you must be from New Orleans." French class had just let out, and I was behind her on the staircase. She turned and looked up at me with a startled expression. Almost immediately a smile crept across her face.

"I'm from there also," I said. But I've been away long enough that I've lost mine."

"Not quite."

I laughed.

We stood at the bottom of the stairs while students pushed past us from both directions. She studied me for a moment.

"Do you have another class right now?"

"Nope, not for two hours."

"How about a cup of coffee at the Union?"

"Sure."

We crossed campus to the student union, exchanging information about growing up and schools and the flavor of old New Orleans. She was easy to talk to. I had noticed her accent in my French class almost immediately. That wasn't all I noticed. She was very attractive, with long brown hair and very dark eyes. She had a cleft in her chin that made her look sexy or stubborn—depending upon one's point of view and maybe her mood. She looked to be around my age (25), although I later discovered she was two years older. Her name was Susan.

"So what brought you to the University of Oregon?" she asked. We had managed to locate an empty table out of the line of traffic.

"I wanted to go to a West Coast school, and this one seemed as good as any. And you?"

"Well, they were the first to accept me in their graduate program. So here I am."

"Studying what?"

"Experimental psych. You know, the basic rat runner."

As the semester wore on, we had many chats over coffee. I found myself more and more attracted to her in every way. I had no idea if she were a lesbian, but I knew I was drawn to her like a moth to a light. By this time, I knew I was a lesbian, but what kind of lesbian was I without sexual experience? Oh, I had had attractions and a few kissing scenes, but nothing really sexual. OK, nothing sexual at all!

Spring pushed into summer, and then she was gone. She had a summer job out of state. I continued into summer school. At least I tried. I found myself dreaming about her in my classes, and she invaded my homework at night. Missing her was a constant awareness that shocked the hell out of me. I had never been in love. Maybe infatuations, but those were easy enough to dismiss. Suddenly here I was in a state of pathetic disarray. I was falling in love with a woman who could very well be straight. Good God! Meanwhile, I plotted how we could advance from coffee chats in the union to something more interesting.

I didn't have to wait much longer. Mercifully, the fall semester started, and we met again the first day. I sat in the cafeteria munching a rather dry tuna sandwich when I felt a hand on each shoulder. No need to turn around. The electricity in my body would have made me glow in the dark.

"Hey, I've missed you," was the first thing she said. "Be back in a minute." She went off to fetch her own dry tuna sandwich. Meanwhile, I practiced the mechanics of normal breathing.

That first day of the fall semester brought our relationship to a different level. Although nothing was acknowledged beyond "I missed you," there was an urgency in our need to be together that wasn't present before. We began studying together and taking weekend drives to the ocean. We shared pizza and Chinese. We listened to music and talked about our dreams. We laughed and cried at movies while sharing a large popcorn. We argued about things from politics to the proper way to boil an egg. And through all of this I knew I had fallen completely, totally in love. Yet, not even a kiss.

One day that changed. We were taking one of our Sunday drives to the ocean. She was at the wheel, and I was staring out the window trying to focus on something that would help me stay out of her lap. The sexual tension in (my) air was incredible this day, even though I wasn't certain about hers. Suddenly she reached over and took my hand, and I still remember the feeling. Every cell in my body sang. We held hands the rest of the way. Hungrily and tenderly, stroking and grasping. Months of feelings came gushing through in fingers and palms.

The rock ocean is always gorgeous in Oregon. That day, it was spectacular. We scrambled along the rocks until we found a comfortable spot. We sat down, leaned back, and took each other's hand. We sat in silence for a long time. Usually we brought a book and would read to each other. Today the book stayed in the car.

"I guess you know I want to kiss you," she said.

I nodded. I couldn't speak. My heart was pounding, and I could hardly breathe.

She looked at me. Her eyes were incredibly soft and scared. She was as afraid as I was. I released her hand and put both of mine on her face. I leaned over and pulled her to me. Slowly our lips met, tentatively at first, but becoming very quickly a hungry, searching kiss. And then in the middle of exploding passion, she pulled away. I said nothing. She stared at the ocean. We left shortly afterward.

I rode home in a kaleidoscope of emotions that ranged from ecstasy to panic. We had crossed the barrier and could never go back to the relationship we pretended to have. But what now? What was she thinking?

"Have you—uh—had any experiences with women?" she asked.

"Sort of. Attractions, kissing. That's all. Have you?"

"No."

Then a few moments later, she added, "Before I met you, I had just broken off my engagement."

I wasn't sure whether to pursue that, but then I finally decided to ask. "Can you tell me why?"

"Yeah. I knew it wasn't going to work. I guess I really am a lesbian. I've always been attracted to females. I thought maybe it might work with him, but it really didn't."

I took some time to digest all of this. It was clear now what had happened. She guessed she was a lesbian, was afraid she was a lesbian, probably really knew she was a lesbian, but didn't want to be one. Oh, God, I didn't need this. I had enough of my own problems getting there. I decided that if anything more were to come of this, it would have to be up to her.

The weeks that followed were very strange. We sort of took turns avoiding each other. It was the most emotionally wrenching time of my life. I wanted her desperately. I loved her completely, yet I was afraid of her because she was afraid of herself.

The evening before Thanksgiving break, a friend and I stopped for pizza near the university. I spotted her as soon as we walked in. She was sitting with two guys and another girl. Her back was to me, but within minutes she turned around.

She told me later she felt me walk in. Amazing. Our eyes locked, and if we had white flags in our pocket, we would have raised them. There was total surrender in our eyes.

Her call came the Sunday after Thanksgiving. "I need to see you," she said. Since we both had roommates at home, we agreed to meet at a restaurant nearby. I drove there in a frenzy, almost missing stop signs and turns along the way. She was already there when I arrived.

"I want to be with you—whatever that means," she said.

"You know what it means."

"Yeah, I know," she sighed. "It's just that it's hard to give up on a regular life with a family and everything."

Those words stung. I knew I did not want this burden of sadness on our relationship. I felt if we could not move forward feeling happy about it, then we had no chance. I discussed these feelings with her. We talked until the restaurant closed.

We resumed where we left off before the kiss, spending as much time as possible together. We found ways to hold hands, to kiss, to hold each other. Our passion brewed like a ripe volcano, but we still had not made love. Then one Sunday afternoon at the ocean, she said, "Let's rent a cabin and spend next weekend there."

My heart raced at the thought. We had never spent a night together. "Sure," I said. "Great idea!"

That was the longest and shortest week I had ever spent. I couldn't wait, but I was nervous as hell. Friday morning before I left for school I packed my bag. I was to pick her up at her house after my last class. Along with the usual stuff—clothes, underwear—I found myself putting strange things in my overnight bag: some puzzles, several books and magazines, a sketching tablet, a deck of cards, and many other things I can't recall. It may take a Freudian analyst to figure that out.

The Bath

The cabin we rented overlooked the ocean. It was winter time, with cold air and a rough and stormy sea. We sat outside for a while and listened to the waves crash against the rocks. Then we walked to a little diner and had cheeseburgers and fries. I wasn't very hungry. My stomach was churning with anticipation and anxiety. She didn't eat much either.

Back at the cabin she took a bubble bath. I talked with her for a while from the bathroom door. Then for some inexplicable reason, I decided I had to take a walk. Even stranger, before I left, I brought some of the things I had packed to the tub. I have no explanation for that either.

I told her I had to get some cigarettes, and off I went. Actually, I found my way to a little tavern across the street and ordered a beer. I rarely drank, and I never drank beer, but I ordered a second. The bartender and I had a nice little conversation about rock formations on the Oregon coast. Eventually an hour passed. I couldn't believe I was still sitting there. Some guy at the end of the bar bought me a third beer. I knew I couldn't drink it without being noticeably drunk, so I thanked him and finally left.

"I can't believe this!" she said as I opened the door. "You bring me toys to play with in the tub, then you are gone for an hour!"

"I can't believe it either."

She looked at me and laughed and pushed me down on the bed. "You are nuts! But I love you."

All of the many months of desire and passion for her came flooding to the surface. I rolled on top of her. The terrycloth robe she was wearing fell open. She had nothing on underneath. Slowly I placed my hand on her stomach and let it slide up to her breast. My hand was trembling as it caressed the form of her breast and then finally her nipple. She began unbuttoning my blouse as I leaned over to kiss her. Together

279

we removed my clothes. The feel of her naked body against mine was awesome. Her pubic hair against my abdomen, her breasts against my breasts. We held each other like this for many minutes, applying pressure with our bodies, while my face was buried in her neck. She smelled so good, so female. Her hair tickled my ear.

Suddenly I wanted my mouth all over her. I wanted to devour her. I looked at her eyes; they were glazed with desire. I kissed her forehead, her nose, her cheeks, and her lips. A long, lingering, exploring kiss. My lips traced a path down her chest to her breasts. I circled her breast with my lips and tongue and took her nipple in my mouth. I felt her response: the pressure of her breast pushing into my face. I moved to the other breast while I let my hand slide down to her pubic hair. I felt her legs move apart, and in that moment I put my hand between her legs. She was wet and warm and soft and felt wonderful to touch. I stroked her slowly, gently, exploring her while my tongue caressed her nipple. She reached for me—her hand caressing between my legs, touching me as I had not been touched before. Our bodies responded together in convulsive passion and need. It was incredible!

That was a long time ago, but the memories remain. A first love is like that. A first experience is never repeated. Susan and I spent 11 years together. Quite frankly, that was about eight years too long. Neither of us was quite prepared for the pressures of a lesbian relationship in the early '70s. Neither of us entered the relationship in total peace with our sexuality. It couldn't help but fail.

Today it is different. Today I am in a relationship that is not a first, but it is my last. Today I understand what being complete with another woman is all about. Today—with her—I look forward to every tomorrow.

CHAPTER THIRTY-EIGHT
Chicken Lasagna with Ma and Pa
Jules Torti

*I*t wasn't the idyllic, breathtaking, earth-moving experience I had conjured up so many lonely nights before. I had imagined champagne kisses, chocolate-dipped strawberries, and bubble bath orgasms. She was to be the woman of my dreams, with skin like fine porcelain, long honey tresses, and a slick motorcycle we would ride topless into the hot desert. My goddess would recite Shakespeare and strum "Dust in the Wind" on her acoustic guitar under a midnight canopy of constellations.

Well, it wasn't August in Arizona with the cool metal of the bike between my thighs. There were no Shakespearean soliloquies, and she didn't know how to play the guitar (In grade three, however, she did learn to play "Hot Cross Buns" on a plastic recorder that she still had in a cardboard box in her closet if I was interested). She didn't ride a motorcycle or even a bike, for that matter. What she did have was two subway tokens, half a bottle of tequila, and a smile that easily lured me under the covers.

This woman was no stranger; we went to high school together. Jess was convinced in ninth grade that I was a boy until I tried out for the midget girls' volleyball team. I moved out West after we graduated, and I hadn't seen Jess since high school. I heard through a mutual friend that she was at York university, majoring in English, minoring in lesbianism.

I came home for Christmas a year later. I bumped into Jess's mom, who was eating pineapple chicken balls in the food court at the mall. She immediately gave me her daughter's new number. "Jess would be absolutely thrilled to hear from you," she smiled. "Gosh, it's been so long since you two have seen each other. What's it been, two years now? A year? Jeez, you kids grew up so damn fast."

Sure enough, Jess was thrilled, insisting I hop on the next train to Toronto. She'd show me "the neighborhood." She lived on Church Street, the gay ghetto where she and her Siamese cat had found a quaint little apartment above a bakery that made the best pecan butter tarts and lemon poppy seed bread. Before Jess hung up, she said in excited breath, "Emily told me. I know. I am too."

Apparently, I had made the prestigious and much-discussed "Guess Who's Gay?" list that had been formulated by hetero high school chums since I left the province. So Jess knew where I was at. I pegged her a long time ago—the Martina and k.d. lang shrine in her bedroom was a strong indication. Her apartment on Church Street confirmed it. I jumped on the train to Union Station, curious—not about Jess but about what the night would bring. New Year's Eve, 1993.

I arrived early in the afternoon, welcomed by Jess donning a new lesbian hairdo and accompanying "pride attire." Her long locks were cropped short. She had replaced her usual black Gothic ensemble with rainbow gear and scores of fluorescent pink buttons that announced her sexual orientation. She said I hadn't changed a bit, which was true. I still had my long hair in a braid, the silver nose ring she hated, and the thighs she lusted after.

Inside her apartment I chuckled to see the Martina shrine again, even larger than before. We sat on vinyl beanbags, while '80s music pumped from the next-door apartment. Apparently the '80s music was a pleasant alternative to the neighbor's daily threesome grunts.

The retro tunes led to reminiscing, mostly about how much we had hated high school. Of course, we too fell prey to gossiping about new additions to the "Guess Who's Gay?" list that we despised so much. In between bites of poppy seed loaf and swallows of chamomile tea, Jess told me about her infatuation with my thighs and that she'd been in love with me all through high school. She still was. *Whoa.* The poppy seeds stuck to the back of my throat. I felt naked on that beanbag, undressed by the bedroom eyes she gave me. Skin and vinyl. I grabbed one of the fatter butter tarts on the plate in front of me and occupied myself with eating generous mouthfuls of it.

I had never thought about Jess that way, even though she was the only lesbian I knew in high school—and my whole hometown. I fell in love with the dykes on *Oprah* and *Geraldo* and fantasized about my 12th-grade English teacher: the way she'd unbutton that creamy silk blouse she wore every other Thursday to reveal just an inch of her cleavage.

I suggested to Jess we take a stroll to the ghetto, get some fresh air, a beer, something, anything. Of course, the bedroom eyes were still on my thighs, and I worried about my safety in her one-bedroom apartment. One bed. One couch. No door in between.

Church Street was alive with drunken revelers, and within a block Jess met up with two fag friends she knew from the theater and their three wiener dogs. This led to a pit stop at the Soho for chocolate martinis. The fag friends thought I was Jess's girlfriend and insisted on batting their eyelashes and winking at her throughout the duration of the martini. They loudly whispered to each other about what a gorgeous couple we were. A woman selling long-stem roses swept passed our table, and—much to the joy of the boys—Jess bought me a rose and kissed the back of my hand with her pouty mouth.

We moved on since one of the wiener dogs had to rush home to take medication for an intestinal problem. The guys left us with a persistent bartender who insisted we try the drink she had just concocted. Sexy Grasshopper? I can't remember, but I recall the crème de menthe aftertaste in the morning. We had three each, and a headache to boot. A shot of tequila? OK.

By 10 o'clock I was sufficiently drunk and actually enjoying Jess's caresses under the bar counter. Her hand slipped between my thighs. "You still want to sleep on the couch tonight?" she asked, smiling.

Earlier I had made the sleeping arrangements quite clear, but now I hesitated in drunken lust. The beautifying qualities of tequila had suddenly turned Jess into my topless motorcycle babe. I gave her a sloppy kiss she said gave her goose bumps. We slid onto the dance floor, hips hugging, our breasts pressing firmly into each other. We laughed at the height difference: I hovered seven inches above her, and my breasts were practically in her mouth. I can't remember the songs, whether they were fast or slow or if there was music at all. I had already hopped on the back of her motorcycle.

We did the countdown to 1994 and staggered back to her place. *I'd sleep on the couch? What was I thinking?* My virgin vulva screamed this was the moment, the long awaited night of Romeo and Juliet-esque love. Jess gave me no choice, no time to think about hesitating. She playfully wrestled me onto my back and pinned me down, her pelvis grinding into mine. Her tongue darted into my mouth, as her hands slipped under my shirt and undid my bra in one quick swoop. Fingers found nipples, squeezing gently. Her tongue slid down my neck with the silent grace of a snake in long grass. She pumped her hips into mine, rocking back and forth, denim separating our wet pussies. I could faintly hear the '80s tunes next door. *Duran Duran?*

I watched as she undid my belt buckle with one hand, yanking my jeans down to my knees. "No underwear?" She smiled devilishly at the prospects. My clothes were soon heaped in the corner with a week's worth of her laundry. The only item I was left with was my socks. Jess warned me that her cat would bite my toes if I moved my feet around too much and that sometimes she got jealous. Ignoring the cat's tail whipping against my leg, I felt Jess's body on top of mine, her hot breath on my neck; she whispered that she had two clitorises. *What*?

Yup, two clitorises. It was hereditary; her mom also had two. Suddenly I had a vision of her mother's crotch in my head. Jess was no longer on top of me. She had transformed into her mother, complete with pineapple chicken ball breath. Any feelings of arousal I had came to a screeching halt. At the same time, I was painfully curious. *Two clits?* I had never heard of such a thing. I quickly turned Jess onto her back, spread her legs, and dove in—like Indiana Jones on a mission—to find both clitties. She had cute names for them that I've since forgotten.

I licked, slurped, and searched with a blind tongue. The clock radio beside the bed said 4:36. The cat who was supposed to be biting my toes was now asleep on Jess's chest. Jess was now asleep too. Her nose was whistling, and by the rise and fall of her chest (and her cat on top of it), I could tell she was in a deep sleep. I promised myself I'd look for this other clitoris for another four minutes, then crawl up beside Jess and go to sleep. Guess I got tired in the search. The mission was a failure.

A knock on the door woke us up a few minutes after 9 o'clock. Jess still had the cat on her chest, and my was head between her legs. It was either her parents or her girlfriend. *Girlfriend?* She said she'd explain later. I wasn't sure what was going to be worse. Parents? Her mother with the two clitorises? Did she have cute names for them too? Jess pushed me into the bathroom where I threw on my smoky, beer-stained clothes. I smacked my head on the sink while trying to quickly pull up my jeans. I brushed my crème de menthe teeth with her toothbrush (Maybe it was her girlfriend's. I don't know), and came out to greet Mom with two clits and Dad, sitting on the edge of the unmade bed with a newspaper under his arm. Whew, no angry girlfriend with black Docs up to her knees and a Grrrl Power T-shirt! Her parents were definitely the safer option.

Jess's mom had brought chicken lasagna, Jess's favorite. I exchanged polite conversation about sports and other father-ly topics with her dad and searched for coffee in the herbal tea-filled cupboards. Finally Jess directed me to the jar of in-stant Taster's Choice behind the orange floral tea cozy and canister of oatmeal.

We enjoyed the lasagna and Taster's Choice for breakfast. I packed up my stuff—*wait, did I even unpack anything?*—and grabbed a ride home in the cab of Jess's parents' truck. I phoned Jess before I flew back out West, and in half an hour we made no mention of the night, her girlfriend, or Sexy Grasshoppers. I asked her to send me her mom's lasagna recipe and haven't talked to her since.

My first encounter wasn't the hot, erotic night of tall ivory candles and melting ice cubes on skin. No Chopin, plump strawberries, or leopard-skin underwear. That only happens in the movies. Real life is the mother with two clits, chicken lasagna for breakfast, a cat who bites your toes while the owner bites your nipples, and falling asleep between your lover's legs in the heat of the moment.

CHAPTER THIRTY-NINE
Lady Killer
Cynthia Frazier

*O*ne feared Tess's arms, small and muscled, capable in sex. Her advances, often violent, were given to friends and strangers alike—if she liked them. Her taste ran from dark and denim-clad artists to obscure, small writers like me.

We met in the cafeteria the first semester of our sophomore year. Hunched over her food, Tess complained of being alone.

"My friends!" she cried, throwing up her hand in a gesture peculiar to her, fingers cupped together as though she was carrying a rock. "No one will eat with me."

I wanted to know why.

"Things last term. You know people too well; stuff happens. Misunderstandings."

"Yeah," I said glumly. I knew what she meant.

We began throwing food. I hit her with a kidney bean. She countered with another. I was in it for fun, but she must have been attracted. We told each other our astrological signs. She was a Sagittarius. My last boyfriend's stepmother had been Sagittarius—a very mean and intelligent woman. Tess said she wanted to marry a Libra. I am a Gemini.

"You should meet my brother," I said. "He's a Scorpio."

She seemed mean and intelligent. Her face was smooth, with sharp features: a pointed, upturned nose, full smooth chin, mouth spare in design—all gave her a look of direction. Her eyebrows were yellow slashes, and her eyes squinted at the outer corners according to the emphasis and outrage of her speech.

She always tilted her head three-quarters while talking, like a bird. Her hair was bountiful, gently frizzy, and covered her shoulders like a cloud.

She used to terrorize the young woman who roomed next to me by engaging her in mock fencing duels. Although Tess was half her size, Susan would end up brandishing an umbrella against her in real fear.

Upon entering our hallway, Tess would look into Susan's room, even before greeting me, and if she was present, strike the classic French pose.

Susan, a mild, attractive, civilized person, would stand in alarm and try to calm the approaching warrior with small smiles and jokes. This always failed. Delighting in the success of her stance, Tess, with a wild, crooked smile, would make small leaps into the room, engage in a brief tussle, and, her object completely terrorized, flee before the upraised weapon.

For weeks she tried to convince me that she loved me.

On late nights as I studied poetry she'd knock quietly on my door and enter, a small, almost sullen figure in winter hat and coat. At first I would be friendly, then immediately feel I shouldn't allow her to interrupt my study.

Tess would put a hand gently on my shoulder and look at whatever I was doing, but she wasn't really interested in that.

"How are you?" she'd ask in a husky voice. Bent slightly at the waist, she'd still have her hat and coat on. She wore a greasy, beat-up man's flannel hat of nondescript color, like the kind my dad used to wear mowing the lawn. It was pulled down rakishly on one side, not the way my dad would have worn his.

"I'm good. Doing Donne." I'd remain seated and offer her cookies or raisins. She scoffed at tea.

"What a night!" She'd begin to unbutton her coat, and I'd turn around on my chair. She'd sit on the bed after putting her hat and coat on another chair.

"Why? How come?" I found that I nearly always repeated myself when with her.

"We went drinking. I didn't drink anything. I just sang the blues."

Her friends mystified me. I had never met any of them. They lived on a goat farm in New York State, a kind of lesbian commune.

"God, I'm filthy." She'd shake her hair out on my bed. It was always full, so she said, of metal dust from the sculpture studio. "How can you stand me?" She'd laugh at herself for saying this, and I would smile.

"I like you very much," I'd say. Then she would rise and embrace me. I wouldn't know what to do. She began to consider me frigid.

She'd taunt me. "Haven't you ever been courted by a woman before?" I wouldn't answer; I eluded her.

One night we took a walk under the full moon as we held hands. It was a clear, cold night, and absolutely still. She wore a long, tailored, camel-hair coat with a belt and sharply upturned collar. The frizzy ends of her full, blond mane caught the moonlight. We stopped on the crest of a hill. She was beautiful.

"You look like Katherine Hepburn," I whispered. I began to feel masterful and turned her around by the shoulders to face me. We were the same height. For the first time, I noticed her eyes were nearly lashless.

I moved to kiss her, and we kissed with eyes closed. She had perfect lips. I put my arms around her, and she put hers around me. It felt like floating, holding and kissing her. In another moment, I had forgotten everything.

Then she turned her head.

"I can't love you," she said over my shoulder. "I'm still in love...with Joan."

"Oh," I whispered. She had mentioned that name a few times, as a friend with whom she had quarreled. I couldn't cry or protest. I simply should have known. I took my face away from where it had rested on her neck, dropped my embrace, and put my hands in my pockets.

"Cold, isn't it?" I said.

"I didn't mean to lead you on."

"No?" I was instantly ashamed of that remark.

"Don't be that way," she said dismissively.

"I know. I'm sorry." I knew there was something I should be sorry about.

"I'm walking back." She began taking big steps down the hill, like a Cossack. They sounded crisp on the frozen ground. I waited until the cold had stiffened my hands, took a gulp of frigid air, and followed.

CHAPTER FORTY
Extracurricular Activity
Nancy Hanson

*I*n late August of 1979, after spending a fun-filled summer of swimming and waterskiing with my family, I returned to the small Midwestern university where I had begun my college career the previous year. I arrived on campus to register as a sophomore, soon discovering that to sign up for classes I first had to declare a major. Since I hadn't a clue, I chose a generic communications major to assuage the powers that be until I could come up with something better. To this very day I don't know how teenagers are supposed to figure out what they want to do for the rest of their professional lives, and I admire the good fortune of those who choose correctly the first time.

At this stage of the game I was painfully aware of my sexuality but nowhere near coming out. Oh, sure, I had fantasized incessantly about women and always had a crush on someone or another. Still, I had continued to date and even occasionally sleep with guys to maintain the illusion of heterosexuality until a time when I had the courage to proceed with an honest personal life. I knew only one "out" lesbian and saw how she was treated, heard what people said about her, and even felt the prejudice firsthand when I was in her company. At that point in my life any relationship with a woman was all about the fantasy.

As I studied the catalog of available courses, I learned that Professor Sarah Miller taught several classes within the communications department. I knew nothing about her except she was supposed to be tough. Word gets around fast as to which teachers are easy, and as a rule their classes are snapped up in a heartbeat. I found myself in the position of taking either Professor

Miller during the day or an easy professor at night. At the ripe old age of 19, I preferred to party with my friends over being stuck for four hours in a night class, so I enrolled in Dr. Miller's 10 A.M. journalism class and readied myself for the challenge.

I knew I liked her right away when she breezed in the first day of class and presented herself as the tough, no-nonsense teacher her reputation had suggested. I suppose she acted tough to let people know they had to work hard if they wanted to do well in her class. But what won my loyalty that day was the discovery that if you paid close attention, a subtle and intelligent sense of humor permeated her conversation and lecture, and I realized I might actually enjoy this class.

Throughout the fall quarter I gleaned bits and pieces about her personal life, enabling me to create a portrait of the teacher. She was an accomplished journalist who had decided somewhere along the line to give up traveling for a teaching position. Although she taught at my university from fall through spring, during the summer she taught at another college located about 100 miles away in the town where she resided with her husband. She would brave the long drive home each weekend and during the week when she finished classes early or happened not to have any the following morning. She spent the balance of her weeknights at the home of a fellow university professor who had a wife and kids and plenty of room to spare in a big old country house about 20 minutes from campus.

She looked more like a student than a professor. She was a very youthful 39, with a tall, thin frame—I learned at some point that she swam for an hour most days, as much to justify the three packs of cigarettes she smoked every day as to stay in shape. She seldom wore makeup and preferred casual clothes. She had long brown hair and wore little round tortoise shell glasses that added an interesting dimension to her kind, pretty face. Her most striking features, however, were her intelligence and sense of humor.

By the end of the quarter, I grew to appreciate her so much that I found myself checking out the curriculum for the winter quarter just to see what classes she was teaching.

As fate would have it, however, I didn't wind up back in her classroom until spring of that school year. The first day of my second class with Sarah Miller, I walked in and was greeted with a smile of recognition that caught me off-guard, and to my great surprise, made me feel positively warm. I hadn't been pining away for her or even thought much about her in between our classes together, but her smile communicated to me that not only did she remember me, but maybe she also liked me just a little. Not romantic like. Just like. I was flattered. I smiled back and took a seat near the front. Once class started, I listened to a familiar "welcome but be afraid, be very afraid" spiel similar to the one that had initiated me into her journalism class. Much to my embarrassment, she pointed me out as someone who had not only survived a Sarah Miller course but had returned to wade through another one.

The quarter went well, and she made the very involved subject of communication law fascinating. She showed respect and appreciation for my work with kind notes and comments that always accompanied my papers and tests. About halfway through the quarter, I found myself showing up for class a little early just to chat. I soon figured out it was better to hang around after class because we both had the following hour free, and Professor Miller turned out to be quite generous with her time when she wasn't rushing off to swim or to drive home.

I looked forward to these conversations, but after a few weeks she seemed to be enjoying them just as much. I was into her being older and wiser, and it began to dawn on me that she was also kind of sexy. Even though at that point in my evolution I believed that her being married was a singular carved-in-stone situation, I let myself be attracted to her. I never considered the sexual energy I was feeling was coming from anywhere but me.

As the spring quarter drew to a close, I loitered after class one Thursday afternoon waiting for the two of us to be alone. We began our conversation as usual, expounding upon what had happened that day in class, when out of the blue she asked if I would "like to have a drink sometime at the flower shop?" a college hangout officially known as the Forget-Me-Not Inn.

I was far too thrilled at the invitation to be embarrassed by the immediacy of my response. I would have said yes to anything—but to spend time with just her? I could think of nothing I would like more. We agreed on meeting after classes the following Tuesday. Surprised, I could barely believe she enjoyed my company enough to see me outside of class. I was completely preoccupied over the weekend, and my friends kept asking me what was up. Of course, I couldn't express my odd excitement over having a drink with a professor, which most of us had done at one time or another, whether to gain an insight into a teacher's personality or to earn points socially that possibly would translate into points in class.

When she called my dorm room the following Monday to confirm that we were still on, some little voice inside my head was trying to tell me this was something out of the ordinary— she could have waited until class the next day to talk to me, and during our brief conversation she had invited me to call her Sarah. I was satisfied to let whatever it was nag at me from my subconscious and left it at that. My roommate, who had answered the phone, was teasing me about having a date with a teacher, and I laughed it off. She, of course, meant nothing sexual by her comment because the professor was female. I had decided to base my infatuation in reality and remain content to flatter myself that this woman simply enjoyed talking with me. When I discovered myself wondering what to wear,

I stopped dead in my tracks. This wasn't a date. I didn't want to appear any differently than I did any other day. Although I was fine with the idea that she must know I admired her, I thought she might be a little clued in to my crush if I showed up for drinks at the flower shop in an evening gown.

Tuesday afternoon finally arrived, and we met outside the administration building at 4 P.M. as planned. When she saw me I noticed a kind of sheepish grin on her face, and my heart immediately fell because I thought she was going to blow me off. Instead she shocked me by asking if I would mind going to Professor James' house instead of the flower shop. I was elated she wasn't canceling but also a little disappointed because it seemed a public place would lend itself to more intimacy than being in the midst of a family. Once again, I would have said yes to anything, so we walked around to the parking lot at the back of the building, climbed into her car, and made simple "after-class" style conversation for the duration of the short drive.

In no time, we pulled into the James's winding driveway and parked in front of their big white house. As we climbed the steps to the porch, she picked up the newspaper, collected the mail, selected a key, and inserted it into the lock. I guess I was expecting her to ring the bell. I was innocently contemplating the level of friendship between her and the James's at the exact moment she turned to me and said, "Oh! Professor James and his family flew to London yesterday, so it'll be just the two of us." She hesitated for a moment as she looked me straight in the eye, and seeing no hesitation on my part, pushed open the door. For the second time there was something scratching at the back of my brain, but I still had no idea what to do with it, and again just left it there.

As we entered the foyer she dropped her keys on a long narrow table against the wall and tossed her briefcase casually underneath. She led me down the hallway and into the kitchen for a quick tour when I explained to her I had been there before. Professor James always had a cookout to end the fall and spring quarters, and I had taken classes with him the year prior. The centerpiece of the main floor was the spacious kitchen, which opened up to dining and living rooms on one side, and on the other side a long counter separated it from the family room. This, she said, was her favorite room in the house—cozy and warm with a beautiful fireplace and a sliding-glass door that looked onto the patio and gardens. The two doorways off the family room led to the garage and to the guest bedroom where Professor Miller stayed.

Professor Miller—Sarah—asked if I would like some wine. I said yes. She removed a bottle from the refrigerator and took two glasses from a cabinet. She opened the bottle, poured, and handed one glass to me as she raised the other and smiled. As we both took our first sip, I was amazed at how good it tasted, being used to the cheap alcohol typically consumed by college students. She asked if I was hungry, and even though I said no she apologized for being unprepared and quickly threw together a plate of fruit and cheese. We carried the food and our glasses into the family room and sat in chairs facing the garden view. She took off her shoes and sat cross-legged in her chair as we talked a little about school and what my plans were. She began asking me questions about my family and where I had grown up. Once again, I was so flattered she was interested that I didn't notice the shift in conversation from small talk to a direct line of questioning about friends and boys I had dated. She asked and I answered: I enjoyed my sorority life and preferred spending time with my friends; I had dated several boys in succession; they turned me off when they got too serious emotionally; sex didn't scare me but neediness did; my current boyfriend would be getting the boot as soon as finals were over so I would be free to do as I pleased over summer vacation. It was a plan.

By this time our glasses were empty, and without asking she retrieved the bottle from the kitchen and refilled mine, as well as hers. We continued to drink and chat as it grew darker, and we emptied the first bottle. She asked if I would open another while she locked the front door and turned on the outside lights. I stood at the counter between the kitchen and the family room as I worked on the cork and reveled in the elation I was feeling at being all alone with this woman I so admired. Although my back was toward her I was aware of her return to the family room and her subsequent actions—drawing the curtains on the sliding glass door, turning on a lamp, and lighting a fat candle on the mantle. I was beginning to pour her a glass when I heard footsteps coming my way.

She slowly approached me from behind, making soft small talk as if to make me aware she was coming closer. I placed both hands on the counter to steady myself—for some reason I felt I was going to lose my balance. I suppose I was feeling the wine, because she was still speaking, but I could no longer process her words. I felt the warmth of her body before I ever felt her touch. Everything was moving in slow motion, and I was beginning to have trouble breathing. She was directly behind me now, and I jumped slightly as she placed her hand gently on my waist, left it there for a moment, and slid it slowly forward onto my belly. As she pulled me into her I felt her other arm reach around me, and she had me in her full embrace, pressing her body softly against mine. I closed my eyes and hung my head because the weight of it was just too great. Only two of my senses seemed to be working properly. My world became nothing more than the feel of her body and the faint smell of her perfume. I wondered if she wore perfume that night just for me, or if I had never been close enough to notice it before. As I inhaled, her hands moved slowly back to my hips, and she gently turned me around.

She asked quietly if I was all right, and I nodded as I struggled to open my eyes. She very cautiously leaned down and
placed her lips on mine. For the very first time in my life I felt
the feeling. In my years of dating guys, kissing always felt
good in a generic way, but it had never felt like this, even
though I had tried to imagine a million different times what
kissing a woman would feel like. I heard a rushing sound in
my head, and my whole body grew hot. Now it was my turn
to melt into her, and when she felt me respond she began
kissing me passionately. She wrapped her arms all the way
around me again, and her hands began exploring my body,
running themselves carefully up my back and down my sides,
as if she still wasn't sure I wanted her to touch me.

Then she stopped, almost abruptly, took me by the hand,
and led me to the couch. She leaned over and scooped all the
pillows onto the floor just before she placed her hand on my
chest and pushed me down. As I leaned back into the hard
corner of the couch, I felt awkward, but she grabbed a pillow
from the floor and shoved it behind me as if reading my mind.

I surprised myself by leaning forward to initiate the next
kiss, and I swear my heart stopped when she sat on the edge
of the couch and began to unbutton my shirt. I had a moment
of panic, because surely she must expect something from me,
and I had absolutely no idea what to do. Guys were easy, but
the bottom line with them was I never really cared. Now I
was in a situation where I cared completely. *If she realizes I've
never done this before, will she stop?*

She forced me back into the moment by pulling the front
of my open shirt out of my jeans and unbuttoning them. Her
lips moved down my neck with tiny soft kisses and made
their way to my chest where she continued kissing me just
above the lace on my bra. She whispered that I was beautiful
as she unhooked my bra from the front and kissed my

breasts, first one, then the other, and gently sucked my nipples. We began soul kissing again, and I reached for her, but she whispered "Just lie back," leaning over me as she guided me down on the couch, gently pressing my arms down to my sides, and pulling the pillow beneath my head.

She leaned over and grabbed the top of my jeans on either side and worked them down my hips. I kicked off my shoes as she grabbed the ankles of my jeans, pulling them off and dropping them on the floor. She placed her left knee between the back of the couch and my body as she squeezed in to lie down next to me. She moved her left arm underneath my neck and placed her open hand on my chest as if to try to calm me. She started to kiss me again, as her other hand returned to my belly for a moment and then—so slowly it was almost painful—slid between my legs, stroking me gently back and forth again and again until my little white panties were soaked all the way through.

I was in such ecstasy I was almost afraid to move, but I turned my body toward her and somehow found the courage to look into her eyes. I was startled by her expression, and although I could tell she was excited by her breathing and the color of her cheeks, she almost looked sad or scared, and I wondered if she was mirroring me. I studied her face as I tentatively placed my hand on her waist, and she pulled me to her so we were facing each other. Her left arm was around my shoulders now, and her right hand was on the small of my back. She slid her hand down again, ever so slowly, as her fingertips slipped underneath the top of my panties, reaching down until her fingers were back between my legs, this time against my hot, wet skin. She resumed the stroking, gently at first, but soon the motion became more demanding, the movements becoming smaller and quicker, and with every change in direction my breathing came faster, and my heart pounded so hard I knew she could feel it inside her own chest.

I was vaguely aware of someone moaning, and then I realized the sounds were coming from me. I wasn't certain I had never had an orgasm before until seconds later when her touch made my entire body shake and shudder and the feeling was so intense I had to push her hand away. I pulled her as close as I could until I finally stopped shaking and drifted off into a reverie that wasn't quite sleep. I would have given anything to stay like this forever, but I slowly realized I had lost all sensation in the arm resting beneath Sarah's body and had no choice but to untangle myself. She kissed me and smiled when she saw the disappointed look on my face as she stood up, returning a moment later from her bedroom with a huge university sweatshirt and a blanket she draped over my exposed body.

I wriggled out of my shirt and bra, thrilled to get out of my creamy panties. I slipped into the sweatshirt as she walked over to the counter for our wine. When she came back she crawled under the blanket with me and helped massage the life back into my arm. We cuddled and whispered about nothing (although I do remember her laughing as she asked me what I thought Professor James would think if he knew what we just did on his couch). I eventually fell asleep and woke to find her still holding me.

I asked what time it was and she said about 11 P.M. I was torn when she asked me to stay. My thoughts became very clouded. We both had 8 A.M. classes the next day. I had no idea what she was thinking or what she wanted from me. *Can I carry on an affair with a married female professor while maintaining my busy college career? Does she have any intention of seeing me again? Will it be the same? Have I ruined the thing I like best about college—the conversations we have together after class?* Way too much, all at once.

I called my roommate and told her I had run into an old friend at the flower shop and was going to spend the night at her apartment. I pushed everything else out of my mind and went back to Sarah. We called the only late-night pizza joint in town, and when dinner arrived we finished it off with a second bottle of wine. We retreated into her bedroom afterward, and she made love to me again in much the same way. I figured by not letting me touch her she felt a little less guilty that she was married, but we never really talked about it. That second time though, as she touched me, I felt her moving against my body, and when I came I think she came too.

I woke up frequently during the night, and the feel of her next to me made me happier than I can explain. We rose early to shower and dress. I skipped the panties, which I couldn't find anyway. On Thursday, after class when I saw her again, I asked her about my panties only because I didn't want Professor James or anyone else to find them. She just smiled and told me not to worry. I looked at her expectantly, but she kept the conversation casual. I kept hoping she would invite me over again—and hoping she wouldn't. I knew she understood my sadness when she didn't.

When the quarter finally ended, I met her after class for what we both knew would be the last time that year, but as it turned out it was actually our last time altogether. We said good-bye, and right before she hugged me she shook her head sadly and said almost inaudibly, "There's so much I could teach you."

I realize now that just as I wasn't in a place where I felt right pursuing her, she wasn't in a place where she felt right pursuing me. She didn't return to campus the following year, and I made a half-hearted attempt to find out where she was but was soon distracted by other things. About 15 years later I saw her on CNN being interviewed. I only caught the end of it, but she looked exactly the same, and her words held the same wit and fire. The moments that came flooding back to me were just as vivid as the night we "met."

CHAPTER FORTY-ONE
Typecasting
Gina Perille

A circle of folding chairs. Isn't that how everyone meets? People rattled off their names and majors on the first day of acting class. Gross. I was a stage manager filling a requirement; Megan was an English major branching out. I scanned the room. She was the only one who seemed the slightest bit interesting. Mental note.

Monologues, scene work, ensemble work. Yeah, yeah. The whole class was put into one play. Megan and I were cast as feuding lesbians in a scene from *Balm in Gilead*. Unbelievably funny, looking back. I was a wreck at the time, but I wasn't sure why. While we waited for our lines, we were supposed to "improv." Oh, no. Surely that didn't mean I had to stick my tongue in her ear! Megan seemed to really enjoy the scene. *Isn't she straight? Aren't I?* Another mental note.

We became fast and furious friends. "Did you two know each other from somewhere else? Did you go to high school together?" No, no, we would laugh. We just fit so well that it seemed we had been doing it for a long while. There were walks, there were hugs, there were sleepovers. There were hundreds of phone calls. There were late dates after whatever dinner dates we had. There were letters. There were coded dreams.

"What?"

"What?"

"What are you thinking?"

"I don't know."

There were lots of stares and lots of sighs. There was hand holding. There was waiting. At least it felt like waiting. But for what?

The semester chugged along toward finals, and after a particularly grueling week, Megan and I decided to go out dancing. I thought it was going to be just the two of us, but she brought along some guy friend of hers. I was horrified; she apologized immediately. But there we were. The three of us. All right then. We danced for a while. Megan attached herself to my right hip. Later she pressed herself against my back as I leaned over the balcony. I stopped breathing. Was this really happening? I got scared and, as we filed out of the bar, I sped off across the quad with a quick nod to Megan and her friend. It was the first time I had ever *not* been the last person to say good night to Megan since we had met. Yet another mental note. This time a weary one. Back at my dorm I stared at the phone for what seemed like hours. She called. Thank God.

"Why did you leave?" she asked.

"I don't know."

"Can I see you, Gina?"

"I don't know."

"Gina..."

"Fine. Let's go for a walk," I agreed with trepidation.

We walked to the park. In silence. Our park. We sat on the bench. In silence. Our bench. I cracked first.

"What?" was all I could muster.

"What?"

"Megan, what are you thinking?"

"I'm actually not thinking right now, Gina. I'm waiting." More silence.

"Megan," I pleaded, "are you trying to make me kiss you?"

"No," she grunted quite definitively. *A lie?*

More silence. And then...I did it. I reached over and pressed my mouth against her mouth. Megan's mouth. God in heaven. So soft. Her tongue parted my lips immediately. I was startled at first but felt myself biting down and sucking hard. We were there for a while, our kisses growing more passionate, more confident, more startling. I don't remember leaving the park, but at some point we did.

We walked home. In silence. A few days passed, but I didn't see Megan because of final exams. Finally we were together for our final presentations in acting class. My scene partner was late; I was annoyed. The instructor, thinking she'd be doing me a favor, called out, "Why doesn't Megan just read the lines to you, Gina?"

"No thanks," I said. "Megan and I already had our scene."

People in the room snickered. I was referring to our lesbian scene together earlier in the semester, but it was clear from the look on Megan's face that she thought I was referring to our night in the park. After class, she left immediately. I still had to do my scene and then take a final.

I called Megan when I got back to my dorm and asked her over. Panic set in. *What am I planning to say?* I mindlessly munched Triscuit after Triscuit. We just sat on the floor without saying a word. But it was a different kind of silence for us. Megan suggested playing cards. I was furious. I thought we should be talking, but went along for the time being. Uno! *How could she have suggested Uno at a time like this?* Megan was chatting away, I couldn't believe it. I snapped and threw the cards down.

"You just take everything in stride don't you?" I bellowed.

"What? No! Gina—"

I stood and stormed out of the room. Megan was sputtering something, but I didn't stay to hear it. I marched to the bathroom and fumed for a while. When I came back Megan was still there. In the same spot. "Sit down," she said quietly. I did. I sat. I stared. This time I waited.

The next moment is lost somewhere in the recesses of my mind. The moment after that our knees were touching and she was kissing me. A long, slow kiss. A real kiss. Her tongue found mine. I marveled again at the feel of her mouth. Our tongues collided, growing more forceful. The inside of her mouth was dangerously warm. We got down on the floor, me on top of her. We were kissing, talking, and laughing as if we had done this every day. Her hands traveled along my back, under my T-shirt. My thigh split her legs apart. She played with the waistband of my boxers. I felt myself arch so she could reach more of me. *More of what?* I felt a throbbing, an ache for something. She slid her hand along my butt and then reached down underneath me. Not between us, but from behind. "God, you're wet," she whispered. I froze because I didn't know if that was good or bad.

Her fingers slipped easily inside me, and I shivered and came immediately. Yes. My body quivered above hers. And then she touched me again…and again…and again. I couldn't get enough. Megan wouldn't stop. We wrestled with each other, a jumble of intense power and intense fear. We lay there on my floor, sweating, spent, and amazed.

And so it began. And so it still is. That damn acting class gave me the "roll" of a lifetime.

CHAPTER FORTY-TWO
Unexpected
Jan Scott

My first experience? I had to think about that for a second, but only because we're talking physical; some of my *crushes* were just as passionate. I'd figured out what I wanted to do with a woman, but I just hadn't done it...and I'd almost come to terms with the label "lesbian."

All the annoying little giveaways in my life had finally added up. You know, the stuff you don't think about when you go through it? Hindsight is marvelous. I couldn't ignore them; I just loved the mystery of it all, putting the puzzle together. How many other 12-year-old girls were more smitten with Mary Poppins than the Beatles and *then* wrote erotic stories about her to entertain her best friend? Sure, it was from a pretty naive point of view, and definitely hetero, but at age 12 in the '60s, who knew? It wasn't until age 13 that I first heard the word. I had to look it up in the dictionary.

I didn't know why it was—or even if it should be—wrong. I just knew it excited me. The next year, I badgered my mom until she took me to *Torn Curtain*. She couldn't know it was because the character Julie had a sex scene, and I needed an adult to get in. Back then even my mom blushed. She's an Aries prude. Something about those Aries women.

I had crushes on a couple of my elementary teachers too. Their resemblance to Julie was spooky. In fifth grade one day, I refused to go to school because the teacher had embarrassed me in front of the class. Mom couldn't figure it out, "This isn't normal—you always loved school!"

That's the way I was, hiding these secret affections, afraid to admit them to anyone—until *Barbra*. Yeah, you know who. Why her? She didn't even look like Julie. I'd never paid any attention to her before, just thought she was one of those old Broadway relics. And by 17 I'd forsaken Broadway for Led Zepp and the Stones. But then Barbra dated our prime minister. Sure, I liked Pierre, the whole country was swept up in Trudeaumania. A guy as old as my mom? Cool! His famous "the nation has no right to be in the bedrooms of the people" statement told you something about the man. He led the movement to legalize homosexual acts between consenting adults. And naturally, being so focused on the affairs of the capital, I even heard a wild rumor about a sex ring involving boys in Ottawa. Of course, *that* fascinated me, but not nearly as much as the Jewish singer dating my idol!

It didn't take long for me to check her out, and then I was hooked. I started to collect everything I could find, plastering my walls with her pictures and writing to other fans. The discovery that most of the guys were gay and most of the women wanted to get her in bed was a wonderful revelation. It was what I'd been waiting to discover, that others had those same "secret" passions.

On A Clear Day's wine goblet scene made me feel like jelly. I thought I'd come in the theater. In the days before home video—before that glorious slo-mo and pause—I had to skip university classes and sit through two matinees to get my thrills. That scene! That dress! Those creamy whites! I'm sure the seat was wet when I left.

Sure, *The Owl and The Pussycat* was raunchier, but I'm a romantic. I even wrote a sexy sequel to *Hello, Dolly!* just to get

my fantasy down in words. It all stemmed from a drawing I
did of Dolly's bountiful breasts pouring out of that 1890s lingerie. The drawings were a hit with the pen pals...and I
shared the "sequel" with just a couple of them. One was a gay
writer who thought that with some decent editing she might
even read it, and the other was an apparently straight guy. I
had hoped some sexy license with our idol would turn him
on, but he only questioned my preoccupation with Dolly's
"fullness of figure," as he put it. Didn't everyone—male and
female—want to undo that corset and dive into that woman?
It was hard to focus on drawing when I was melting inside at
the thought of her body.

So how come no real-life stuff? Well, I was one of the
untouchables, a fat girl until age 19. My form of rebellion,
I guess. I didn't want to be "feminine." I was a tomboy. My
mother was a fashion plate, always eating cottage cheese
and melba toast. I didn't want to be her clone. My younger
sister was anorexic—*c'est la vie*—her escape. I finally did
one of those radical diets, but only when I was ready: a
coming out of sorts.

At age 21 I went to Los Angeles to meet some of my
more "interesting" pen pals. I stayed with a gay woman
and met her girlfriend, who was married. I'd been writing
to both of them, and the letters had gotten pretty juicy. It
was all so scary, yet exciting, for a closeted loner who was
still living at home and going to university. I went to a
party, and one woman asked me to dance! I did, because
I wanted to try it, but I got scared. I wanted to feel more
for the girl than I did...or maybe it was just too new. I had
never danced with guys or even had a boyfriend—that
would have scared me more. Anyway, apart from being
enlightened about Barbra's song "Guava Jelly," I returned home relatively unscathed.

By then I had graduated and had landed a production job at a weekly shopping rag. It kept me in motorcycles and gas, my ticket to independence. But when I got back from my trip to L.A., suddenly it was trying to be a *real* newspaper and had actually hired a proper editor! It didn't take too long before I was in love.

Patricia was Barbra and Julie all wrapped up into one svelte, exotic-looking English broad. I must have been like a pathetic puppy dog. I adored her! I drew her, wrote notes to her, immortalized her in drawings, cartoons, and other tributes. She was 46, but I didn't care; it made her all the more desirable.

Another Aries. They'll take your adoration by the truckload...and I had plenty.

As our "madame editor," she was strong, authoritative, and cut a stylish and dashing figure. Fashion-model tall, she was leggy and full-busted, with broad shoulders and the narrowest hips I've ever seen on a woman. I wasn't sure what sex I wanted to be around her, but I definitely didn't like it when she played femme to the owner or the salesmen. It wasn't right—I wanted to be the object of her flirtations.

The job became my haven and my heaven, for I worked really closely with her. We worked evenings a lot of the time, just the two of us putting pages together. I was the artist, she the mentor. I was jealous every moment she was out of my sight. So naturally I wanted to be her friend, be interested in everything she did. She'd just moved to town, and I set out to ingratiate myself with her family.

They were renting an *Addam's Family* sort of house not a mile from my parents' place, to my delight. And she had this third or fourth husband—a crafty, crusty, old drunk—whose only aim in life was to prove how much everyone was in love with the Ice Woman. "Hedda," he'd call her.

I'm sure I scanned the play by Ibsen after figuring out he wasn't referring to Hopper, but I wasn't looking for any flaws in my idol. Warning lights went off about her being married—and so many other times—but that just made her more of a challenge.

There was also an Oxford lawyer son in his late 20s, still in England, and a daughter who was kind of a gangly, strange thing at 15. Intuitively, I knew Emily adored her mother too. She was the at-home "son," defending Mom against drunken Dad, and any other potential interlopers. I tried to be a confidante to Emily, even though she was six years younger. She was a tomboy too. They spent a lot of time together. My envy must have been conspicuous—I'd even tail them on outings!

I suppose I'd be deemed a stalker by present definitions, but at the time all I wanted was to get another glimpse of her. Even the sight of her car became an erotic stimulation. I'd spot it around town, and my heart would palpitate if I couldn't follow. One of those old '67 Ford Galaxie fastbacks, it sure said sex to me. The better part of a year went by before I was eventually accepted into her inner circle.

Patricia must have known exactly what I was about, but she never let on. She'd let me get close and touch her when we worked and never put an end to my notes and all-out worship. You'd have thought I'd have gotten the picture when she dropped the "when my son comes out from England, I'll have to set you two up" line on me. This was not what I wanted to hear but, true to form, I ignored it. To take offense and get angry with her would only end the little contact and intimacy I'd achieved. I forgave her endlessly, always sure she knew exactly how I felt.

I even became the extra in an awkward relationship with another writer hired at the paper. Ken eventually succumbed to her charm as well and was enticed into the inner circle by her husband. Another drunk. I rounded out the pub evenings.

And then worse…her son arrived from England.

A generously proportioned, flaccid man, Richard would have been right at home in a stuffy men's club, puffing on his pipe, sipping port, and inhaling fatty meals. Like me, he went through the motions of a date just to please her, but dinner and the theater failed to compare to any time spent with Patricia.

I had a few male chums from my motorcycling, but I was treated as just one of the guys…or so I thought. One guy pressured me endlessly, so I told him I had a thing for someone else. And for good measure I threw in Patricia's name. I'm sure he was not surprised, but maybe a little disgusted. After all, the woman could be my mother. It, however, wasn't mentioned again, and he remained a friend. He even took my sister out.

I was convinced Patricia was giving me hints. She'd come up behind me, stroking my neck or arms as we worked. Maybe it was just her way of being familiar, but I got braver. I'd touch her more openly at work or caress her hair. It seemed she was content to absorb all my worship as if it were a given.

I looked for opportunities to be part of her life away from work. She was into astrology and reincarnation, so I took up with that too. I spent hours doing our composite chart, convinced we were destined to be together. Finally I wrote her letters, the kind of self-doubting deep shit everyone goes through.

Between pen pals, work, biking, parties, and pursuit of Patricia, about three years drifted by. I had a Danish pen pal visit me and stay with me and my family. I guess she liked my drawings of Barbra as much as I did. She probably should have been my first. She was smitten with me! We spent a lot of time together that summer.

It turned out she had run away to Canada to come out, away from her parents and expectations, figuring I was the logical ally. But I wasn't out. I wasn't quite ready to take that step. She spent her days writing and waiting for me to come home from work. I knew what she wanted, but I couldn't respond. I should have, should have tried anything physical just to get over that first time thing with someone who actually cared, but in my mixed-up way I had to be true to Patricia.

Finally one night my pen pal and I had a huge fight my parents couldn't figure out. They thought we were friends. Why else would they put up with a foreign guest for six weeks? She'd been tailing me—sound familiar?—and I got mad at her for trying to get between me and Patricia. She just wanted to make love to me. I wasn't totally immune; we tried kissing once, but like Barbra said about kissing a woman in *Yentl,* it was "like kissing an arm." I liked her, but I wasn't sexually attracted to her.

One night I was hanging around Patricia's kitchen with Ken, Richard, and her husband. I knew Emily was lurking close enough to hear any conversation. They got on the subject of homosexuality. I carefully offered no opinion, but it was clear what everyone thought about being gay, including my beloved. The conversation got pretty ribald, talk of cocks and juicy fucks, what a real man could do for a woman. I felt bewildered and betrayed as she flirted with Ken and sick over her next teasing comment.

"I'll take your six inches anytime, ducky!"

My expression of distaste gave her husband some ammunition.

"Come, come, Patricia, that's not something your little friend wants to hear about, your insatiable nymphomania."

To their collective laughter, I got up shaking and left. I jumped on my bike and tore off. Mad and hysterical, I rode for hours. Then a couple of old babes ran a stop sign in their Toyota, and I nailed their rear bumper. More furious than hurt, I railed at the women, who were really just concerned about me.

"I'm fine, but my bike's fucking wrecked!" I screamed.

It wasn't actually, but I had to blow off steam at something. I was lucky. I had a few bruises, and the handlebars were just twisted. Easy fix. But I told Patricia about it the next day, and that I'd been reckless because of her. Had she really meant what she said?

Yes.

I had nowhere to go. I must have looked pretty bleak.

With the veiled conviction she was doing the best for me, she wrote a letter to my mother. I was still at home, so I guess she felt she could stop me through my mother. She stated she was concerned about my misplaced affections and sexuality and was afraid I might do something serious like attempt suicide.

Well, my mom cried, reassuring me I wasn't "that word." She said she always thought Patricia was an odd woman. "I never did like her," she chided. I chickened out and told my mom everything was fine; I wasn't gay. So I gave in—I didn't want a dialogue with my parents. And Patricia was a fucking coward. Just leave me alone to grieve the loss of the love of my life. Didn't anyone understand? Even Barbra in lingerie couldn't bring me up.

I took a night shift at work. Patricia deferred to a new *male* editor, preferring feature writing and working days. That seemed to end it for a while, until her life changed, giving me fleeting hope. She and Emily had moved to the other side of town after she separated from her husband and her son had moved out of town.

One day I got an odd phone call from Emily. She wanted to talk to me about her mother and "other stuff." Did she have some news of Patricia, something to rekindle my tentative passion? I was afraid to get my hopes up.

Yeah, I'd also figured Emily was gay. It seemed inevitable. The dysfunctional family. Poor kid's been screwed up by Patricia too. Maybe she was curious to know if I ever got into her mother's pants. I agreed to see her.

She picked me up in front of my parents' place around nine one night…driving *the car*. I had to remind myself she was 18 now and would certainly be driving. But *the car*, the Galaxie? It got to me, all those years of feelings, all the unrequited desire. She was still a lanky, raw-boned blond, but she had filled out a little. Honestly, I could see a mix of both parents, but she'd sprouted her mother's bust.

We drove to a park by the ocean, lots of trees and private spots. Emily picked one and offered me a swig from a mickey of scotch. That didn't surprise me; she seemed quite mature. I was on pins and needles wondering what she wanted to say.

She abruptly flipped over the seat into the back and stretched out.

"I've always liked this car."

"Me too," I said, turning in the seat to face her.

"Yeah, it's sexual, don't you think—like Pats, herself?"

I was quiet. It was odd hearing her refer to her mother by her first name.

"So in all the years, did you and Pats ever…?"

"No…" I stumbled, "unfortunately." I had to be honest. "Gawd knows I wanted to."

"I know. I guessed," Emily replied.

"You're gay?" I took the dyke by the horns.

"Pretty sure. I feel it."

"But you haven't been with anyone?"

"No. Have you?"

"Yeah. Well, sort of," I didn't want to lie. "Um…actually, no." It was time to get to the point. "I always hoped it'd be… Do you think your mom ever…?"

"I don't know. But you were getting too close. She got scared."

"Of me? Or what she really felt?"

"I don't honestly think she's gay, but she was flattered by you. She liked your attention, until you pushed her. I think she stopped your friendship because of me. She never wanted me to be gay. She was scared she'd done it or somehow brought this out in me…and you."

I thought of my own mother then—these damned Aries women! When I get drunk and horny, they're always the ones who get my attention. I admired Emily for her honesty and her maturity.

"Your mother's an intelligent woman. She should know you're born to be who you are. I still think she's afraid to come out."

"And you're not?" Emily was a little sarcastic. "Remember, Pats is 50 and has been through five husbands. I don't think she ever had any intention other than being a tease. And she's an incorrigible flirt. She lives for the attention."

"And we let her drive us crazy." I thought of Emily's father, her most recent victim.

"Tell me about it!" Emily sat up and sighed.

I wondered if Emily had ever wanted her own mother. It wasn't such a wild idea—boys often have those feelings.

"She's a true Aries. She loves the idolatry, the flattery, the all-out worship," I said. "She never cares as much as she likes you to think. Sorry, but it's true."

"I know," Emily said, her face close to mine.

Suddenly she was holding my head, kissing me. I responded, helpless. An animal passion took over both of us — being in *the car*, talking about the woman we both loved. I was over the seat and into the back before I knew what I was doing. Someone alive and horny wanted me! I wasn't in love, and she probably wasn't either, but this was wonderful!

We didn't say anything; we just went at it like we'd known what to do since we were born. To actually feel flesh, to fumble with the bra hooks...the rehearsal was over. She was grinding on me as aggressively as I was on her, fumbling with clothing, wanting that first look and feel of another's breasts. Her young woman's body, the fresh and musky smell, was familiar, yet new and stimulating. I think I lost all sanity that night, all inhibitions. I just wanted everything I'd ever imagined. I went for her perky nipples, rubbing them between my fingers. My tits never seemed to respond like the stories suggest, but hers were the key to her lusty body. I was almost disbelieving when she moaned and pressed my hands on her breasts, her nipples hard under my palms.

Emily was just as crazed. I felt her tugging my jeans as I concentrated on her breasts. I pressed my face between them, my hands full of firm woman-flesh. *Where am I? What am I?* I put my lips to one and licked her hard nipple. She moaned again. I wanted to play her all night.

"Do you masturbate?" she whispered, as her hands dug into my tits. She was moving her hips, thrusting. We were ready to find those places that lived in our fantasies.

"Of course. Who doesn't?" I gasped, slipping my hand between her legs. I was amazed to feel another woman like this; she was awash with hot juice.

"Yeah, but it's not as good as this," she replied, pushing her mound into my hand. I knew exactly how to rub her, and she responded eagerly, thrusting my hand farther into her. I just kept massaging her, discovering her clit, delighting at how she'd gasp as she came over my fingers. I was thrusting too. I had to fuck her!

I struggled out of my pants and got my leg between hers, feeling her warm wetness on my thigh. She got her hand on my mound, and I thought my vagina was going to reach out and suck her right up! She copied what I'd done, and my cunt was on fire. Lying back on the seat, we got our mounds together and ground like rutting beasts. Was it Patricia I wanted to fuck, or Emily? I didn't care who *she* wanted to fuck.

It didn't matter at that moment. I felt like one huge, drooling pussy with her fingers in me. I wanted my cunt to envelop her, my clit to enter her and replace my damned, sexless fingers. She came in waves, never ending! We were gasping now, a marathon of pent-up passion. She was tireless. I thought I was going to pass out when she found my clit. How could it get more electric? I just went rigid and focused on that wonderful, elusive but imminent orgasm. I let her explore, holding back until I just exploded.

Every fantasy of making it with Patricia culminated in that intense, ferocious orgasm. I fell weakly onto her daughter.

We lay there, our ragged breathing the only sound. I warily listened for passing cars, and it struck me as silly.

"What are you laughing about?" asked Emily.

"*Now* I worry about headlights! There could have been an audience, and we wouldn't have cared."

Emily laughed. "You have no idea how long I've wanted to do this."

I was immediately guarded. Did she have a thing for me? I couldn't say the same.

"Why?" I asked, trying to be nonchalant.

"To see what Pats was missing…and maybe because I was jealous."

"You...jealous? My gawd, was I *that* obvious in front of you?"

"Yes and no. Pats played you too. She made me jealous. Isn't that funny?

And here we are."

"Fucked!" I laughed.

"*Finally* fucked! Bravo!"

Emily relaxed and started to pull her clothes on.

"You know, this wasn't why I called you."

"Oh?" I was surprised.

"No, I wanted to tell you that Pats is getting married...again."

I swallowed that statement. Somehow it didn't matter.

"You know what, Emily, I don't give a shit!"

"Good," she laughed. "Neither do I!"

So that was how my first time was probably the best time. Sounds corny, but it released two butterflies from their cocoons. Well, maybe just a couple of moths...from their closets. Emily went on to university and bought a motorcycle with her girl-friend. As far as I know, they're still together. And me? I just keep having those fleeting crushes, a couple as bad as the "Pats," but I've settled down quite a bit.

And I'm still riding!

CHAPTER FORTY-THREE
Unwritten Story
Claire Robson

Although excited by Maggie's letter of application, I was unprepared for the shock of her beauty and for renewed temptation. My metamorphosis was—I had thought—complete. I was a fully fledged matron, a grand beetle, sterilized, possessed of a dry sense of humor, and a retentive memory for trivia. I was not without humanity, but certainly without passion. I wore my crisp cobalt uniform as a sexless shroud, a winding sheet. All that remained was to make my little corner comfortable enough to die in, and that looked like a secure prospect.

Maggie was small, compact, close-knit. She radiated contained power and physical certainty. Despite her size, one did not patronize. Her eyes were Atlantic-blue, dark with gray changes and a flash of challenge. As I ran through my store of interview questions, I was already resolving to ignore the attraction. After her appointment I avoided contact, refused an invitation to the pub with her and the other girls, tried to seem distant when I could. She proved to be professional, obsessive, angry at imperfection. She was also suspicious of authority, quick to give and take offense. Covertly, I watched her establish herself in the ward—impatiently, forcefully, too aggressively—and warmed to her more and more. Now and again she'd knock on my office door and demand advice, accepting it with caution, if at all. It was like hand feeding a shy tiger.

In my dull, stupid way, I was falling in love. I became sharply aware when she entered the room and increasingly certain I could speak to her if I chose. One weekend she dropped by my house for directions, with a young man and his red car in tow. I felt sad but safe; I could dream quietly of passion, dulling embers in a quiet life. I did not even breathe on them, merely watched, and believed myself contented.

Maggie arrived at my house at 8 o'clock one weekday evening, driven to distraction by a married doctor. Her touching faith in my ability to help surprised me. She who had seemed so suspicious! How could I resist? I couldn't murmur a few platitudes, toss in some sound advice, and show her the door. She demanded humanity. Trusting to the self-control that rewarded years of celibacy, I resolved to be human — disinterestedly, of course, like a grand beetle divesting itself of armor but not tempted to swoop and soar!

But it worked. Although I was tempted to sit near her, to touch her shoulder, I merely listened, and only helped. She went off to deal with the doctor, double-quick. Two days later she returned, handed me a letter, and left. She wished to "confess" to an early encounter with a woman — unsatisfactory, she hastened to add. She'd told no one. Maybe I would prefer not to speak to her of the matter, not to speak to her at all, now that I knew the truth. She would be at home.

The world flipped over, and all the grayness drained out of it. I felt light and fine as I drove. There were no thoughts in my mind. She stood with her back to me. I put my arms around her. I made it clear she had nothing to fear from me. I had never had women as lovers. I liked her fine, but she was a chick under the wing. It seemed natural when she'd talked herself to a standstill, for us to stretch out on the guest bed, side by side, in exhausted sleep.

When I woke, the light was gray, and Maggie's eyes, dark and direct, were examining me in the dawn. It was a time apart. I stretched out over years of loneliness to touch, and it was like stepping off a cliff. She turned into my arms, and my hands slid around her waist, up over the strong arch of her ribs. Her breasts were soft and tiny, concealing the sharp surprise of nipple. Her arms came around my neck, and as our mouths met she pulled me into the kiss. She was slick with anticipation, smooth, and clinging. I was lost in an offering of passion, the curve of a tense buttock, the feel of her heavy hair, over breast, over bone. I cried out as she turned my head to watch my face, her eyes objective, sardonic, tender.

Short stories have a preamble, a climax, a denouement. At present, like you, I am stranded in the middle. We are holidaying in France, drinking wine, making love, getting wet. She lies on the beach before me as I write. She is listening to the BBC news.

How will it end? Who knows? I refuse to contrive; I doubt whether I could. I'm not going to sacrifice her on some altar, conclude her with a clutch of children, conjure up a man to whisk her neatly away. Instead I leave you marooned in France, forever with Maggie. Her transistor lies in the crook of her arm. Her eyes are closed. It is the last day of our holiday.

CHAPTER FORTY-FOUR
My Quest for Lesbian Sex and What I Found There
Henri Bensussen

*I*n 1983 at age of 46 and after 27 years of an increasingly unsatisfactory marriage, it suddenly enters my consciousness that lesbianism could be the way to a happier life. As is my habit, I start researching this idea at the library. Almost daily I check out armloads of books and read them overnight. Within a week I am convinced. By the following week I have begun a quest for lesbian sex, for it seems pointless to declare oneself a lesbian without testing it out as soon as possible.

First I try the classic approach by going to a lesbian bar I've heard about, but I am unsuccessful in gaining anyone's sexual interest. Next I try groups. My local NOW chapter newsletter carries information about a lesbian group called SOL. I call the number listed. The woman who answers the phone introduces herself as Marian.

"Slightly Older Lesbians is a discussion group for women over 30," she says.

"I'm certainly qualified," I say.

"It meets every Tuesday night; let me know when you come. I would like to meet you, and maybe we could go out afterward and talk." Her voice is pleasingly low and soft.

This is in early September. Our youngest child, who is 18, has left home for college. I tell my husband I'm a lesbian. He accuses me of having another of my crazy ideas and goes outside to throw darts. A few days later he says we should get divorced, and I agree. I'll have to find an apartment. My salary should just about cover expenses.

The next Tuesday night I attend my first SOL meeting. It's held at the gay and lesbian center, which is a small storefront next to a Hispanic bar in an industrial area. A pool table, desk, phone, and a broken couch take up the front room. The back room is fitted with more old couches, pillows, a rug, and some folding chairs. Only a few women are present when I arrive, but the room quickly fills. Feeling very shy, I listen quietly to women sharing experiences on whatever the topic of the evening is. I try to remember names. When we go around the room during "check out," a young-looking woman, heavyset and tall, with brown curly hair and a mischievous smile, turns out to be Marian.

After the meeting almost everyone drives to a nearby gay men's bar that also welcomes women. I follow Marian's car and then follow her inside. It is dark, with a little candle at each booth. On the other side of the bar is a dance floor and jukebox.

Marian shows me to a large booth; six women sit around the table, some of whom haven't been at the meeting. "Let me buy you a drink," Marian says. "What'll you have?"

"A beer, I guess—light." I watch as Marian walks toward the bar.

"You're new," a voice says from the far end of the table."

"Yes," I answer, peering into the dark.

"This your first time?" the voice asks. The women around the table seem suddenly quiet.

"First time at this bar," I answer. Someone laughs.

"Know Marian very long?" the woman sitting next to her asks. "By the way, my name is Mary, and this rude person next to me is Pat."

"Hi," I say, and introduce myself, thinking there are more Marys and Pats in the lesbian world than anywhere else. "Marian and I just met tonight at the meeting." Marian returns with my beer and a soda for herself, saving me from more intimate questions. She sits down across from me and looks directly into my eyes and smiles. Our knees touch under the table. "Let's dance," she says.

A slow song is playing on the jukebox. Marian takes my hand, and we walk onto the dance floor. Soon we're surrounded by couples tightly holding each other. Marian pulls me into her ample body. My head fits into the space just below her ear; I lick the pink earlobe lightly. I don't know where I got the nerve to make that gesture, but Marian doesn't seem to mind. Our arms circle each other's waists. I'm surprised that under the loose clothing Marian feels more hard than soft.

We move to the music's romantic rhythm. Marian's leg slides between mine, and her spicy perfume envelops us. When the music ends I want to continue for the rock song that comes on next, but Marian hooks her finger into my belt and leads me back to the booth.

"Ever played?" Marian asks me as we sit down.

"Played?"

"She's asking about whips and chains," Mary chimes in from across the table.

Marian is grinning at me, waiting for an answer; she has perfect white teeth. "What do you do when you play?" I ask.

"Better not ask," Pat interjects from the black pit at the end of the table, "or she'll be happy to show you."

"Leave it alone," Marian says to Pat. Her lips turn up in a little smile, she tosses her brown curls, and focuses her attention on me. In a low voice she explains she's involved in sadomasochism and tells me that because she's tall and big and used to being in control, she enjoys being forced to not be in control.

I busily peel the label off the beer bottle, not sure how to respond. Nothing I've learned at NOW has prepared me for this situation.

"I have to go," I say.

"I'll walk you to your car," Marian says.

At the parking lot Marian asks, "When can I see you again? Thursday night?"

"I have my NOW meeting that night," I say. "How about Friday?"

"I have a party to go to Friday. How about Saturday?"

"I can't make it Saturday."

"Sunday?" she asks, thumbing through the calendar she keeps in her purse.

"Yes, in the afternoon," I say.

"Your schedule is as busy as mine," she says with admiration. "I feel like I've won a tennis match."

"Come at 1 o'clock. I want you for a long afternoon and evening."

"I can manage that," I answer.

"And I'm looking for a relationship."

I tell her I am not; I describe my situation at home. We exchange phone numbers and addresses on bits of paper Marian scrounges from her purse; I find out she is a decade younger than I. We kiss good-bye, lightly but with a promise of more. As I drive home, shivering in the cold night air or from anticipation, I remember the luxurious feeling of being held close in Marian's arms. Sunday seems a long way off.

The day finally arrives, and I show up on Marian's doorstep at the appointed hour. Turns out we both had made alternate plans in case the other failed to show. Inside she draws me into her arms and asks, "Do you prefer a movie or a concert?"

"Lovemaking."

"You'll have to wait, so make a choice," she says.

I choose the concert, but it turns out it's been canceled, so we go to a Woody Allen movie. Marian holds my hand during the movie; I clutch her arm. Then we go out for Chinese, and I tell her bits of my story. We finally return to her place. Her condo has a long overstuffed sofa, big-screen TV, tall ceilings, a small kitchen, and two bedrooms upstairs. Her bedroom is in shambles, but after five hours of enticement, I care little about that. If she merely looks at me with her piercing blue eyes, I melt.

She takes me in her arms for a long, slow kiss, then holds me on her lap; we undress each other, and she begins stroking my cunt. My hand closes over her breast. In a few minutes great waves of sexual release shudder through my body as I have the strongest orgasm of my life. She smiles down at me, crossing her eyes to make me laugh. After a while I push her down on the bed and make love to her. The element of surprise is on my side. My hours of book reading are paying off. I catch her fast and bring her to a kind-of orgasm. She likes it and says she hasn't felt that good in a long time. She has beautiful, soft, perfect skin, and her hair is fine and silky, a halo of curls around her face.

Toward the end of the month Marian and some friends help me move into my new apartment. It's a one-bedroom ground-floor apartment in a huge complex, close to my job, with low rent.

Over the next couple of weeks Marian spends Tuesday nights and sometimes Wednesday nights at my place, and we trade off weekends at hers. Our lovemaking is satisfying for me, but I can tell her expectations in that area are lower than mine. S/M is a large part of her life; maybe she can only feel sexual release through pain and intellectual game-playing.

One Wednesday evening, as the hour approaches 9, Marian calls and says she'll be arriving soon, that she had to work late at her Silicon Valley start-up company but needs to be with me; she is always working late and on weekends. I sit in my wingback chair, feet resting on an upside-down packing box, and gaze upon the room's clutter. As I wait for Marian, I wonder how long I'll continue living here. There are two problems: the cockroaches that race across the kitchen counter at unexpected times, and Marian. The apartment manager says she will spray the cockroaches into oblivion in a few weeks. Marian says she's in love with me and wants me to move in with her. I've never lived alone till now, and I tell her I won't be ready to move in with anyone for at least five years.

She likes to sleep late, and I have to get up early for work. When she stays over she leaves me notes to find when I return at the end of the day: "Give me time, and I may learn to be awake with you; 20 years should suffice."

A week later, on a Friday night, I'm at Marian's condo. We play Scrabble, listen to music. She likes Sondheim. Her mother gave her a piano, and she plays some of the music for me from *Pacific Overtures*. Saturday evening Marian comes to my place. We're in bed after making love, but just as I'm falling asleep she begins to cry. She feels abandoned. She feels she can't continue as "just friends." She's in love with me.

"What is love?" I ask.

"Love is what I feel for you," Marian says in a tone defyingly definitive. "Love is having a relationship."

"I'm not ready for a relationship," I answer.

"I can't go on like this," she says.

As tears form in her eyes, she runs to the bathroom to take out her contacts. When she returns she says, "You touch me like someone who loves me, you like being with me, you say everything but that you love me. I'm leaving!" She throws on her clothes. "I'm sorry you're leaving," I say sadly.

Marian slams on her glasses over her beautiful blue-green eyes, shakes her brown curls, and walks out, carefully locking the door behind her. I'm left wrapped in constricting sheets. *Am I giving her mixed messages? Coming on too strong, too affectionate?* I think it's the end.

Sunday morning Marian calls and asks me to come to her place; she now wants me no matter what. I say I'll come if she can accept this way of noncommitted relating. We meet and go out for breakfast, then walk in the park, then back to Marian's to watch football and MTV. After a trip to the grocery store, Marian cooks dinner for us.

"I'm trying to figure out why you are so defensive about the idea of a relationship," she says, "and I think it's because of your long marriage."

"That's probably right," I answer.

"So what do you think of us being buddies?"

"I like that term."

"But remember, buddies aren't monogamous," she says, giving me this meaningful look.

I feel a great sense of relief, the lifting of a burden. I can now allow myself to love her, knowing there is no obligation of formal relationship. There is freedom for me to be open to other women.

Marian and I have worked out a schedule of our time together because we're both so busy. I stay active in SOL and NOW, go on Saturday morning hikes, attend every lesbian event. Marian has her S/M groups and often comes home from a "party" in the city with bruises, not just on her body but emotionally. I am there for her afterward and try to understand. She enjoys seducing women and systematically tries to see all her lovers on a regular basis, each of us meeting some specific need of hers, although she keeps coming back to her wish to set up something special with me as things fall apart with others. She says I am the only one who has brought her close to sexual fulfillment.

Two months later I succumb to her wish to try a monogamous relationship, but it lasts less than six weeks. Marian is like quicksilver, always changing her mind, making new resolutions, trying out new plans; she never seems content with any one person or situation. In the summer, when I meet and fall in love with a woman with whom I do feel able to commit myself, Marian gracefully wishes me well, as I launch myself into a life I had been trying so hard to avoid—that of a settled lesbian.

CHAPTER FORTY-FIVE
Three Women In A Tub
Remi Newman

I arrived early and took one of the plush easy chairs in the far corner. I had grown to love this room. It was a sanctuary within a large gray building. Every Wednesday starting at 7:30 p.m., it became home to the Bisexual Women's Support Group at my mostly homophobic university. Many of the words that filled that space had never before been spoken aloud. The intimacy that ensued created a fertile ground from which sexual tension would naturally grow.

As a bisexual femme, I felt very much on the fringe of the lesbian community. My looks conformed to the male ideal of women. I was slender, with long legs and perky breasts. I dressed to accentuate my shape, kept my nails painted, and darkened my lip color. My dark brown hair fell well below my shoulders. To make matters worse, I had never actually been with a woman, and although I was an ardent political activist, furious in my dedication to many feminist and queer causes, I had no intention of eliminating nail polish or men from my life.

I found two other women within the group with similar feelings—Danielle and Karina. They were both 19. I was 20.

Soon after the door was locked, we heard a light knock. Someone opened the door to a shy-looking woman. She offered a seat directly across from mine. The first thing I noticed was the red hair that fell the length of her back. Its vibrant hue abruptly contrasted with the two inches of her natural brown color she had let grow in. She smiled nervously. Her large eyes were opened wide as she searched our faces. I could only guess the shape of her body because it was well-hidden by an oversized coat. I was curious. I looked at Danielle and Karina. Their slightly tilted heads and subtle smiles told me they too were taken with this new arrival.

The meeting started. During the introductions the three of us eagerly awaited "the new woman's" turn. "I'm Jennifer..." she began, but then hesitated. Before she went on, she smiled at us, a little less nervous. She told us a story about being born on a commune to two hippie parents who "originally named me 'Meadow,' but just a few months later decided to leave their free-loving lifestyle for a steady job and a house in the suburbs and changed my name to 'Jennifer.'"

Each one of us considered Jennifer—her long auburn hair, her earthy complexion, and how she was wearing all green. She had removed her coat, revealing the rest of her wardrobe. Her large breasts sat comfortably in a baggy green sweater, while her wide hips fit tightly into faded green corduroys. Her soft dark green jacket was carelessly draped over the side of her chair. Danielle voiced what we were all thinking. "You're not a 'Jennifer,'" she said, "you're a 'Meadow.'"

Danielle, Karina, and I drew Meadow into our little clique. Karina and I had only recently begun consciously exploring the idea of sex with women. Danielle had already acted on it. I looked up to her as if she held some secret knowledge. She had pale skin, long bluish-black hair, and delicate features she adorned with thin black eyeliner and deep red lipstick. Her voluptuous body was usually draped in flowing silk and velvet. Deep purple and green blouses that she and her mother had sewn gracefully accentuated her form. She moved with assurance as if the world had reserved a place for her wherever she was. She had spent years cultivating a soothing presence that kept her safe and calm and was completely different from the unpredictable world she had inhabited as a child.

Karina looked like a pixie from a fairy tale. She was petite, with darting bright blue eyes and long yellow hair that she wore parted down the middle. Her wardrobe was a variety of multicolored skirts that fell to her ankles and soft, loose-fitting cotton shirts carefully decorated with embroidered designs. At the meetings she sat slightly hunched in her chair, legs pulled up underneath her body, fingers toying with the edge of her skirt, giving away her nervousness. Like me, she had only experienced sex with men. Yet her situation was intensified because she was currently in a committed monogamous relationship with a male lover.

I was attracted to both of them and developing an attraction for Meadow as well. I got a strong vibe the feeling was mutual. After each exhausting and emotional meeting, none of us felt like going home. Instead, every week the four of us went out for chocolate chip pancakes topped with extra whipped cream. At the diner we could continue our flirtatious discussion with mouths full of melted chocolate.

"So what do you think about what Monica was saying tonight?" Meadow asked as we took our table by the window.

"Power to her, if she can do it," I was the first to answer.

"I think it's exciting," Danielle said.

"So you would, then?" Meadow asked, one eyebrow slightly raised.

"Go to a sex party with Monica's fiancée?" Danielle laughed just as the waiter was approaching our table.

"No—just have sex with more than one person at a time?" Meadow leaned in. "Sure, I'd love to," Danielle answered easily.

"But you never have?" Meadow continued her questioning.

"No, but I'm sure I will—sometime."

"I would like it too. Actually, I think I would really like it," I continued the conversation after the waiter left with our orders.

"It could be hard also. What if you got left out? Like what if the other people got really into each other and just left you," Karina said, wearing a worried look.

"Then you watch and get off on that," I suggested.

Meadow cut in, "I've never been with anyone at all." There was a long pause.

"Really?" I asked. She looked like she needed encouragement to continue.

"No, never—well, one time sort of, but not really—it's been only myself and the showerhead."

I smiled inside, thinking about the image of Meadow and her showerhead. She looked uncomfortable, and I wasn't sure what to say next.

Danielle said, "I think when you do, when you decide it's time, it's going to be good. You know your own body better than a lot of people do when they first have sex." Meadow laughed a little at this. "Yes, I know my body very well," she said.

"Are you nervous?" I asked.

"Very. It's safe with myself. It's my own ritual. I make love to myself. It always feels good. I'm not nervous about making love to another woman. I will know how to pleasure her, but I am scared to let another woman make love to me."

"It is scary. You make yourself very vulnerable, but that can also be very exciting." Danielle grinned as the people at the table next to us glanced over to see what real-life lesbians looked like.

"I'm definitely nervous too, but I want it very badly—with a woman, I mean." Karina spoke softly to avoid further glances.

"What are you gonna do?" I asked referring to her boyfriend.

"I dunno. I love David, but I think about women more and more. I fantasize about women when I'm with him," she scrunched up her face in frustration.

"Oh, shit, that's bad," I said.

"But I don't want to leave him. It's hard to imagine not having him. I don't wanna talk about it now."

"You sure?" Meadow asked, looking concerned.

"Yeah, there's no point. I'm not ready to break up with him. I just get frustrated."

I said, hoping to lift Karina's mood, "Actually, I did have sex with a female before, and more than once."

"What? I thought you had never been with a woman?" she looked shocked.

I continued, "Her name was Rebecca Goldman. She had long dirty blond hair, and we went to school together—"

Meadow cut me off, "Why didn't you tell us?"

"Because I was in first grade. She used to follow me home after school and we would rub pussies in the top bunk of my bed. She was the husband, and I was the wife."

"Aw, that's sweet," Karina said.

"But that's it. Still, it was some of the best sex I ever had! I always came."

"You came in the first grade?" Karina asked wide-eyed.

"Fuck, I came in kindergarten," I grinned as the waiter decorated our table with platefuls of steaming chocolate and melting cream. I turned to Danielle. "Do you miss sex with Jen?" I asked, referring to her first and only-so-far lesbian fling.

"Sex...yes. Her...no." She laughed at the thought.

"You miss sex a lot?" I prompted her.

"Every day," she laughed again.

"Shit, I miss it every night. The days I can do without it, but at night—mmm." I ran my finger along the edge of my plate.

"I like the mornings," Meadow jumped in. "I always masturbate in the mornings."

"Hmm…sounds nice." Danielle licked chocolate from her pretty red lips.

Sex with each other was never directly spoken about. We were a foursome, and sex was something Karina couldn't do with us. But this didn't keep the attraction from growing.

One night we rubbed oils on each other's backs in Danielle's dimly lit dorm room. "Why don't you women come with me to the tubs?" she suggested coyly. Danielle had an expensive hot-tubbing habit. She would go alone, pay 25 bucks, and soak for an hour after classes. There were no objections.

The following Friday, the four of us put towels in our backpacks and walked along University Avenue toward the tubs. We paid our money to the bleached-blond woman behind the counter, and Danielle took the key to what would be our private room for the next hour. She led us down a long corridor and through the wooden door. The room was all wood with the tub in the center.

Meadow, Karina, and I fumbled nervously with our things, dumping backpacks, removing coats and shoes. We undressed slowly, not sure when—or if—to stop. Meanwhile, Danielle prepared the room. She lit candles and incense and put a cassette in the tape player. Then she stripped down to her T-shirt and underwear and made her way into the tub. We too stopped at T-shirts and underwear and followed her into the steamy bath.

Our bodies formed a square as we leaned up against the edge of the tub, arms outstretched, hands touching. My eyes moved from face to face, occasionally catching a gaze in my direction and holding it there until the tension forced a giggle out of me, making me look away. We moved closer, until our hands rested on each other's arms. We took turns experiencing different sides of the tub and letting the jet streams massage our backs. We moved closer until our arms rested comfortably around each other's shoulders and the edges of our breasts touched lightly. We stayed this way, breathing in the hot steam, until we heard the knock on the door, signaling that time was up.

We decided to go back the following Friday. This time Danielle took her shirt off before she stepped into the hot bath. Karina and I followed. Meadow waited until she was submerged up to her neck and then removed her faded yellow T-shirt. The light from Danielle's peach-scented votives was just enough to see the soft flesh that curved and formed our breasts. Ella Fitzgerald's husky voice came from the cassette player in the corner. I closed my eyes and lost myself in the steam. When I opened them I found we were each still occupying our own side of the tub. Having our shirts off created a distance between us.

The next Friday, Karina already had plans to spend the night with David. When she told us, it was as if she knew something was going to happen and she was giving her consent.

"We don't have to go, you know," I told her.

"I know. It's OK. You should go." She knew we wanted her there, but it was her decision to remain in her relationship. I didn't feel right about it at first. None of us did. But as Friday drew closer, I began to imagine the possibilities of a visit without Karina. When Friday came we met a few blocks away and walked down the hill together. We swung big bath towels carelessly over our shoulders, too proud and excited to care what the frat boys or sorority chicks would think of us. What was left of last night's snowfall decorated the tops of the cars parked on the street, and the cold wind hurried us along.

We finally reached the bottom of the hill and entered through the glass door where we were greeted by the familiar scent of chlorine mixed with wood. We gave our $25, signed our names, and this time I took the key. The bleached-blond behind the counter seemed uncomfortable with our repeated visits. I gave her a wink before gliding down the hallway, but she pretended not to notice.

Danielle set up the candles and incense and put her Ella Fitzgerald back in the cassette player. Meadow began to slowly undress next to the shower. I, being less shy, threw off my coat, sweater, shirt, pants, socks, and underwear until every goose bump on my body was revealed. As I dangled my toes in the hot water, I felt them look at my long, slim figure. Not wanting them to take their eyes away, I slowly lowered myself into the hot water. I closed my eyes and waited.

As I sat alone in the tub, anxiety began to replace my earlier feeling of euphoria. *What if I don't know what to do? What if I do it wrong?* I reminded myself what had always enabled me to act out my fantasies—that I had a woman's body, and I knew what I liked.

I smiled as I let go of the strands of hair I had been nervously twisting. Moments later I sensed movement in the water around me. I kept my eyes closed. I felt a hand touch my face and gently move it. As I was pulled closer, I smelled the familiar breath of Danielle. Her lips barely touched mine. I opened my mouth and reached for her lower lip, held it for a moment, and then eased my tongue inside the wetness. I put my hands on her shoulders as her arms encircled my waist. We held each other, savoring the sweetness of our first kiss. I had been with at least 30 men but never had a kiss felt so soft.

Danielle reached for Meadow, and I backed up to watch. Danielle put both hands on the sides of Meadow's face and closed her eyes. I noticed Meadow kept hers open as Danielle placed her wet mouth on her lips. Her slow movements gently invited Meadow's tongue inside. Meadow wrapped her arms around Danielle's neck, and I moved in closer to experience their kiss. Danielle pushed against Meadow's quivering body, and soon her fingers were squeezing the pink flesh of Meadow's nipples. I massaged my own breasts as the rushing water tickled my clit. Moments later Meadow turned and noticed me touching myself. I giggled nervously at being caught and took my hand from my breast. It was the first time I had ever touched myself in front of another person.

"No, don't stop," she whispered just loud enough for me to hear. I paused for a moment, still feeling self-conscious. I took a deep breath and closed my eyes again. I began massaging my breasts and squeezing my nipples between my thumb and forefinger. I knew they were watching me, and my breathing got louder as I pushed harder. After a while I stopped. I opened my eyes and grinned.

They pulled me toward them. The three of us put our arms around each other. We were kissing and laughing and rubbing breasts. Danielle looked at Meadow and then at me. I knew what she was thinking. This was Meadow's first time with anyone. Danielle moved behind Meadow and put her arms underneath hers. I got what she was doing and reached for Meadow's legs. Before she could protest, we lifted her. Her face, breasts, belly, and pussy were bobbing out of the bubbles as we kept her afloat on her back.

We each moved to one side of her body. A bit unsure, I watched Danielle first. She leaned down and took the tip of Meadow's right breast between her lips. I did the same with the left. I sucked, taken with the sensation of soft flesh and hard nipple at the same time. Her breasts were even larger than I thought. Danielle began to run her hand down Meadow's belly until she reached the top of her cunt. Meadow moaned as Danielle stroked her clit. I entered her pussy, pushing gently as the flesh spread to accommodate my finger. Her legs began to shake, and her body quivered with each stroke and entry, creating waves on the surface of the water. We worked Meadow's body until she let out a squeal, opening her eyes and motioning to be put upright again. We obeyed.

My right hand moved slowly down her still quivering body and grasped the underside of her ass. Now her own fingers were rubbing the surface of her cunt. I moved closer and my clit pulsed as I rubbed it into her thigh. Her tongue moved slowly up my neck, over my chin, and into my mouth. She turned to press her breasts and pussy against mine. She wrapped her mouth around the tip of my breast. I watched as she sucked my nipple and caressed the flesh surrounding it. I felt her excitement, and I pushed my chest out farther.

I was about to come. I wanted to yell but wasn't sure how soundproof our little room was. I rubbed harder, imagining fingers pushing up inside my cunt. I imagined being spread wide, my body on top of Meadow's as she sucked at my breasts, my ass in the air, while Danielle fucked my cunt. I breathed louder and dug into the flesh of Meadow's ass. My thighs squeezed tightly around her leg as I came. I shivered and started to breathe deeply, slowly recovering from my orgasm.

I was shaken out of my dizzy euphoria by a knock on the door. Our $25 hour was up.

We looked at each other for a moment and moved into a three-way hug. We placed little kisses on each other's foreheads before stepping out of the tub. We giggled under the shower as we washed the chlorine from our bodies.

I went home that night with the smell of Danielle's apricot-scented lotion rising from my skin and the sweet memory of two women's bodies meeting for the first time with my own.

CHAPTER FORTY-FIVE
Encountering Myths
Jean Stewart

*T*he cold January winds were blowing in Philadelphia where we had both grown up, when Judy and I just happened to settle on the floor side by side at a Super Bowl party. Although we were the only single women in the crowded apartment, neither of us suspected we were being set up by Deb and Michelle, our mutual friends.

I remember looking at Judy, noticing the long dark hair that fell down her back, noticing how blue her eyes were. I also remember being relatively unmoved when she leaned closer to me in an effort to be heard above the crowd noise.

Although I pushed myself to be sociable, telling her droll stories about my students at school, I only succeeded in making her laugh a few times. Her gaze often went inward and she would seem to drift away. By the time the football game was over, I was amazed to realize that here was someone even more introspective and reserved than I was.

My friends insisted on prolonging the evening, and for some reason I let them talk me into going downtown to Rainbows. I had to teach school the next day and had not intended to stay later than the football game, let alone go out clubbing afterward in the city. Someone whispered in my ear, "She likes you," and the next thing I knew I was riding in a car beside her, our blue-jeaned legs pressed together in the darkness.

To be truthful, I was a lesbian virgin. I was nearly 29, and I had slept with enough men to know that, for me, a man wasn't the E-ticket ride at Disneyland. From playing sports,

I had grown used to being surrounded by lesbians, and I gradually came to accept, mentally at least, that these women I felt so comfortable with also reflected my own identity. By then, however, I had developed a detached disbelief about romance and the realm of sensual pleasure. Since I had never in all my life encountered more than romantic friendship, it seemed to me that true love was another myth of modern advertising.

While my friends shook their heads over me, I was immersing myself in work. In addition to teaching high school, I went to grad school at night and throughout the summer worked on my master's degree. In-between I kept an intense fitness regime, either lifting weights, playing pickup basketball with the boys, or going for long solitary runs.

As far as I was concerned, my life was complete. I had convinced myself that if love were missing, then I really did not have time for it anyway.

That is, until I was sitting in a darkened booth at Rainbows in the upstairs game room. I was nursing a beer, half listening to a friend, when I noticed Judy from the corner of my eye. She was playing pinball across from my booth, her slim form leaning over the rectangular box of flashing lights. As she bent forward, intent on her game, her loose jeans accentuated the shape of her thighs and ass. Her faded rugby shirt snugged over her hunched back and shoulders, and the long dark hair moved with each subtle shove she gave the machine.

Something big and warm and solid rose inside me, pressing against my sternum, my ribs. I could barely breathe.

Shocked, I dragged my eyes away. I took another sip of beer, and within seconds my eyes took a will of their own. I found myself staring at her body, mesmerized. For the first time in my life, lust moved through me like an ocean wave.

A little while later she came over and sat beside me, but by then I was speechless. In fact, I moved away from her leg as she casually pressed it into my own. I wasn't sure what to do with this unruly sensation spiraling through me. And my domineering mind reminded me this woman was six years my junior and probably not the least bit interested in me.

The leg pressing, I assured myself, was because the booth was pretty small. That she kept seeking me out and talking to me throughout the night, I reasoned, was because everyone else was partnered off. So I simply watched her in stolen, covert glances, and when she came by to talk, I tried out of sheer self-protection to make her laugh. At last, the evening came to an end, and we all rode back to the apartment building where our cars were parked.

I found myself beside Judy, again staggered by my reaction to her.

I suspected what it might be, but I did not know enough then to be afraid of it. Before Judy left, she slipped a torn piece of yellow legal paper in my hand, then kissed me swiftly on the lips. In my car I unfolded the note and discovered her phone number. It had another area code in front of it. She lived in Washington, D.C.

And I, who loved order and discipline like a nun, was not certain I would ever dial the number.

A few weeks later, a what-the-hell mood came over me, and I picked up the phone. Another woman answered, asked curtly who I was, then called for Judy. An R.N. at Georgetown Hospital, Judy had rotating shifts, and my call had woken her out of a dead sleep. I think she was barely coherent for most of the conversation, but she wouldn't let me end the call and send her back to bed. I didn't think it was because she was so eager to talk to me; I sensed somehow that my call was going to give that other woman, the one who had answered the phone, something to think about.

Judy told me she was in the midst of leaving a three-year relationship. Her lover, Pat, had inexplicably moved a new girlfriend into the townhouse Judy and Pat shared. Hurt and bewildered, Judy was going to move out as soon as she found an affordable place close to the hospital.

She told me she thought Pat might be an alcoholic, and somehow, while being head-over-heels in love with her, she had become Pat's enabler.

I thought: *God, you've only just turned 23, and you're dealing with this?*

By the time I hung up the phone, I knew I'd do whatever I could to help this woman.

When you're a mess, talking on the phone to a near-stranger is sometimes easier than trying to discuss it with people who know you. I suppose that's why she phoned me later. As for me, I told her funny stories about teaching school or shared insights gleaned from the books I read with the voracity of a lifelong bookworm. I eventually confessed I wanted to be a writer, something I rarely talked about, and she fervently encouraged the dream.

A month or so later, my friends Deb and Michelle called me, accusing me of becoming a hermit and demanding I go out with them for a night on the town. Laughing, I acquiesced. I didn't dare ask if Judy would be up from Washington. While I liked talking with her on the phone, I wasn't certain how I felt about seeing her again. I felt in control, on the safe side of friendship when we related on the phone, but I had a feeling there would be no controlling myself around Judy in the flesh.

Judy was at my friend Deb's townhouse when I walked in; she greeted me with a smile. In the half hour before the rest of the gang arrived and we got organized enough to leave the house, I engaged my friends with my usual banter, a mix of amusing tales and intellectual bon mots from whatever I was currently reading. It was a well-disguised defense so I would not have to talk about myself, about what I was thinking or feeling. It was a barrier I had become adept at long ago, to keep people from seeing my innate shyness, my constant fear of rejection.

I caught Judy watching me once—her eyes intent—as if trying to see who I really was.

We went downtown to another club. We spent the evening buying each other drinks, playing pool and pinball, exchanging partners in fast dances. I had had a few drinks and was losing a pool game when a slow song came on and Judy approached me. She took the pool cue from my hand, laid it on the table, and led me away to the small dance floor.

I had never slow danced with a woman before.

She put her arms around my neck and pulled me in close, leaning against me so gently that my breath escaped in a long, shallow gasp. My hands didn't seem to know where to go, and flustered, I touched them tentatively to her shoulder blades, then let them slide down her back. Even through her navy blue blazer and oxford shirt, I felt the chords of her muscles moving under my palms. Her long hair brushed over the backs of my fingers, and I was engulfed in the floral shampoo scent of it. Meanwhile, the space between our bodies all but disappeared. That strange inner force pushed against my chest again, and my arms tightened involuntarily around her. She was so slim, so strong; her body fit into mine like a missing piece.

Midway through the song, Judy drew back a little and brushed my lips with her own. The kiss deepened until I was lost. When we gradually ended it and parted, I realized by the way other people around us stared, that we had just made a spectacle of ourselves.

For the rest of the evening I was in a haze. I had had crushes in college but nothing like this. I was in love.

I spent the next weeks devising a way to get her in bed.

This was not easy. Judy, despite her seeming pursuit of me, did not really appear to be interested in anything more than flirting. Also, she seemed most interested when I was shy or distant. In hindsight, I think she was restoring her self-esteem, her identity as a woman able to attract other women, through my increasing attention. However, at the time, it was mystifying. Judy would enchant me, kiss me, then evade any attempt I made to take things to another level.

"Stewie, you're so good," she told me. "You're the most generous person I've ever met. I don't want to hurt you."

I didn't get it then. She said the last thing she wanted was another relationship. I was a distraction, and that was all.

Funny how clear things become years afterward.

On sensual overload, I busily recruited my friend Karen, who lived in Bethesda, Md., into helping me with my plot. On the excuse of introducing Judy to a whole new set of friends (other than Pat's) in the Washington area, we invited Judy to Karen's house for a party. Of course, I'd be there for the weekend too.

After a night of socializing and beer drinking, I persuaded Judy to forego driving home to Alexandria, Va., and instead stay the night at Karen's. Meanwhile, Karen and I had earlier prepared the hide-away sofa bed in the rec room. When I led Judy down there, I could see by the look on her face that the alarm bells were going off like crazy. I, however, assured her I was tired and that we were just going to sleep together and not do anything. I sat down on the edge of the bed and pulled off my sneakers.

I don't think she knew how to get out of there without looking like a virtuous prude.

Once we were in bed together in the dark, we lay side by side, breathing quickly for maybe two or three minutes. I casually rolled over and began slowly running my hands over her.

She shivered and whispered, "I thought we weren't going to do anything."

I whispered back, "I have to touch you." Because it was true.

Never in my life, before or since, have I felt like that. A script was written somewhere for me long before that moment in time. I was fulfilling something as primal and overwhelming as the flight of a chevron of geese heading south for the winter.

It was in me, and there was no denying it.

I kissed her lips, her neck, pushed the collar of her T-shirt aside, and kissed her shoulders. Trembling, she whispered "Oh, God," but she didn't stop me. I caressed her arms, her legs, her stomach, her breasts, following the path of my fingers with the touch of my lips and tongue. When she began writhing under me, making helpless noises, I lifted her, coaxing her T-shirt and panties from her and then spread her legs with my knees. I, who had never made love to a woman, knew what she wanted, what she needed. I teased her and adored her and went down on her until she was shuddering, moaning, and arching into me for more.

I made her forget about Pat and want me, if only for that brief time.

She'd been battling insomnia for weeks, and after I'd taken her several times, she nestled into me, hardly able to speak. As I cradled her, whispering to her she was safe, to just close her eyes, I felt her breathing change. She slept all night in my arms. Although I eventually began to feel stiff and sore from not moving, I willed myself to stay still. Half dozing, I savored the feel of her lying against me.

The next morning we showered together, and in the daylight I could see how her ribs protruded. Following my gaze, she confessed she was having trouble eating, that her clothes just hung on her these days. I told her not to worry, that this ordeal with Pat would pass. I told her she was a beautiful woman and that Pat was a fool. I held her and told her that the rest of her life was ahead of her, just waiting for her.

I wish I could say that was the beginning of us, of our partnership, but that is not how the heart works. I was ready, but Judy was torn and damaged. And as I fell in love with her, she began to run. In the end, devastated by Judy's quiet request to be friends, I retreated into my own bewildered, damaged shell.

It never was a reciprocal sort of loving.

I immersed myself in work again, in pushing my body to its physical limits and keeping myself maniacally busy. I swore off love. I convinced myself I was an asexual creature.

Despite my best efforts, I could not regain the asceticism of my former existence. I had tasted the nectar of loving a woman, and I longed to taste it again.

Six and a half years after meeting Judy, I met Susie, the love of my life, at a party one night. She had dark hair and perceptive blue-green eyes, and boy was she ready for me.

I have since discovered that I am not asexual and that true love is not a myth.

Despite the paradox that I tried to love her, and only ended up hurt, I've come to understand I have Judy to thank for my current happiness. She opened a door in me I had not known existed, and afterward I was no longer sufficient unto myself. Perhaps being needed was the only way I could learn to need.

Now, I live in Seattle and Judy lives in San Jose, both of us happily ensconced in long-term relationships. I have talked to her twice in the past ten years.

But I think of her. Oh, I think of her often.

About the Contributors

Stacy M. Bias is a 24-year-old femme-type thingypoo living in the typical squalor of her generation in Portland, Ore.

Linda A. Boulter says, "I am a single mother of three in a loving relationship with another D.—not the one in the story—but one who accepts me and my children unconditionally. I continue to write stories, articles, and poetry, and have completed my first novel."

Henri Bensussen is a San Francisco Bay area writer. "My Quest…" is dedicated to her first lesbian lover—she knows who she is—who enlarged her experience of the nuances of pain and the need for personal integrity in our lives.

Margaret Bradstock has recently retired as a senior lecturer at the University of New South Wales in order to write and research full-time. Margaret has been widely published in journals and anthologies in Australia and overseas and has won national awards for poetry. She has cowritten/coedited nine books of poetry, fiction, and biography. Her work has appeared most recently *Cutting the Cord* (Random House, 1998).

Giovanna (Janet) Capone is a lesbian poet and fiction writer. She was raised in an Italian-American neighborhood in New York City. Her writing has appeared in various books, including *Unsettling America: A Multicultural Poetry Anthology* and *The Voices We Carry: Recent Italian American Women's Fiction.* She recently coedited a book of writings by lesbians and gay men of

Italian heritage, forthcoming from Guernica. She's also completing her first novel, *Olive & Lavender*.

Miriam Carroll, fast approaching 69, is loathe to let a day pass without filling it with creative purpose. After moving to Atlanta 14 years ago, she has reclaimed long-suppressed interests: She is exploring dance, acting, community involvement, outdoor activities, music, art, writing, and is a bat mom each spring.

Wenona Susan Church is a recent Midwestern transplant to western Massachusetts, where she works in a feminist bookstore. Her mantra is "without life there would be no writing, and without writing there would be no life."

Lisa E. Davis has lived for a long time in Greenwich Village. With a Ph.D. in comparative literature, she has taught in the state and city university systems of New York. Lisa has also has published writings—both fiction and nonfiction—in several anthologies and is completing the last draft of a novel about the Village in the 1940s.

Debra K. Dekker lives in Bowie, Md. She earned her Ph.D. in psychology from the University of Connecticut. She is a full-time parent to her four-year-old daughter and has published scholarly journal articles and book chapters, but this is her first personal piece.

Bleau Diamond was born in England and currently lives in Scottsdale, Ariz. She divides her free time between writing erotic poetry and stories and hiking in the mountains surrounding Phoenix.

Sara Eclevia is making her first foray into the world of erotic writing, where she hopes to delight in many more pleasures and demons in the near future. She works professionally in the service industry.

Zoey Edwards is an aspiring writer living in Los Angeles. Her style is to simply "be in your face, tellin' it like it is."

Jody Ekert lives in Queensland, Australia. She is a part-time writer, editor, and check-out operator, and a soon-to-be graduate with a bachelor's degree. She hopes one day to earn enough money from writing to stop working altogether.

Jill Fontenot is a professional poker player who lives on the West Coast with her partner, as well as a lab named Rupert and a cat named Clyde. Her hobbies include attempting to grow the perfect tomato and reading just about anything.

Cynthia Frazier is a "working journalist," novelist, poet, playwright, and cartoonist. She lives in Santa Monica, Calif., with her partner of 19 years. In addition to covering Santa Monica for a local weekly newspaper and writing a column, she is a contributing writer to the *Lesbian News*, a national magazine, and covers gay and lesbian issues for other publications.

Jane Eaton Hamilton is the author of a children's book, *Jessica's Elevator*, two poetry books, *Body Rain* and *Steam-Cleaning Love*, and *July Nights*, a volume of short fiction. Her short work, which has appeared in such places as the *New York Times* and *Seventeen* magazine, as well as in numerous anthologies and lit mags, has won numerous awards, including the Yellow Silk fiction award, the Paragraph fiction award, and the Event nonfiction award.

About the Contributors

Nancy Hanson resides in New York City with her partner of six years and is working on her first novel.

Juliana Harvard is a half-Filipino, all-lesbian computer professional who lives in the San Francisco Bay area with her partner of three years and a varying assortment of grown children and small animals.

Veronica Holtz lived and studied for several years in Salzburg, Austria. She has been involved as a writer and composer in video, radio, commercials, and performance groups. She has written two plays, a novel, and several short stories.

Taj James is a caustic-witted brooding type who resides in the beautiful Texas hill country. She has a degree in both theater arts and literature from Texas Woman's University and is an avid reader. An enthusiast of both contemporary and historic erotica, she plans to continue to test her hand at the craft.

Laurie Kay, mother to three boys, lives in northern New York. She has moved on to another beautiful soft butch and says she is "still finding out who I am."

Isabelle Lazar is a writer, actor, and feature film producer. Her work has appeared in numerous magazines, newspapers, and anthologies. She resides in Los Angeles.

Robin Lind is a musician and office manager who came out, after a 20-year marriage, as a lesbian. She writes from Alameda, Calif., where she lives with her domestic partner.

Jennifer Lindenberger says, "I graduated and returned to Pennsylvania for my MA. I'm living on my own with two

lizards (my Cuban anole is perched on the computer moni-
tor as I write) and working in accounting."

Quinn Lioe was born in China and first lived in the United
States when she was a boarding school student. After graduating with a Ph.D. in mathematics, she decided to remain in
the States with her partner. They live in San Francisco.

Stephanie Mahone came to the United States from Canada
to attend the University of Washington and after graduation
opened her own chiropractic clinic. She lives in Seattle with
her partner.

Mary Marin's erotic fiction has been published in *Pillow Talk:
Lesbian Love Stories Between the Covers*. Her stories have also ap-
peared in *The Loop* and *Moon Magazine*, both in the United
States and Canada. She is working on *Drink Me: A Collection of
Erotic Liquor Recipe Stories*. She lives in Los Angeles where she
works as a psychologist and wishes to dedicate "Kiss in the
Dark" to the memory of Jayne Beth Sacks, Ph.D.

Marti enjoys life on the West Coast with her partner of many
years. She is a cruise director in charge of fun and games. She
loves writing, mixed with generous amounts of time with Jill,
as they write and direct *their* fun and games.

Elana Mendelson was born and raised in Brockton, Mass.
She attended the University of Massachusetts at Amherst,
where she earned a bachelor of arts degree in English in
1998. Elana has been involved with the GLBT community
for two years. She would like to thank her family and friends
for their support through her journey and give a special
thanks to Danielle for making "Distant Thunder" what it is.

Bonnie J. Morris is a women's studies professor and the author of three books, including *Eden Built By Eves* (Alyson, 1999), a tribute to women's music festivals. When not in the classroom or working at festivals, she can be found touring the country with her one-woman play, *Revenge of the Women's Studies Professor.* Her work appears in more than 30 anthologies.

G.L. Morrison lives in Eugene, Ore., with her lover (L.S. Williams) and her son (D.P. Morrison). She's published many poetry chapbooks, including *The Erotic Alphabet: 26 Haiku,* and is the poetry editor of *New Attitude,* the newsletter of the Fat Feminist Caucus. Her writing has appeared in a number of magazines and in the anthologies *Burning Ambitions* and *Mom: Candid Memoirs by Lesbians about the First Woman in Their Life.*

Remi Newman is a freelance writer living in Mexico. She has answered phones, checked faxes, and occasionally been published in *The Philadelphia City Paper* and *The San Francisco Bay Guardian.* She is currently collecting data for a documentary on the "art of pussy smelling."

Patricia was born in England and has lived in North America since the early 1960s. She wants to thank the women of her poetry writing group (together now for 24 years) and the participants in the Feminist Women's Writing Workshop who have all helped and supported her in her writing endeavors.

Gina Perille was born in Chicago and now lives in Boston. Consultant-to-be by day, MBA candidate and theater reviewer by night, Gina is a horrible cook and has no pets.

Ashley Robbins lives in Maine and is a certified public accountant. She says, "I have always been a rebel—independent, with a mind of my own. I don't buy into the traditional corporate bureaucracy. I graduated from high school at 17 and worked my way through college. I was a bartender, a waitress, and a secretary before getting my degree."

Claire Robson is a British-born writer who currently lives in New England. She runs "Women Read," the Boston series, and runs retreats and workshops both there and in the White Mountains of New Hampshire. She has been published here and there and always feels the need to say so in these biographies. Now why is that?

Elisa Ross works and plays in Washington, D.C. She has published stories in the literary journal *Refractions* and in the anthology *Pillow Talk*. While drafting her first play, *Family Blessing,* she wrote *Star-crossed* as a form of regression therapy.

Sarah Russell is a writer who lives in Virginia and is propelled by the creativity and strength of women before and around her.

Amy J. Saruwatari says, "I am a writer of short stories and poetry who lives in Southern California. For the past three years, I have been a student of Terry Wolverton, who has been my writing mentor. I am working on a collection of short stories titled *Stories My Father Never Told Me.*"

Jan Scott continues to ride motorcycles with her partner of 19 years. She has worked as a motorcycle assembler, printer, freelance artist, copywriter/editor, and designer. Currently, she creates advertising and Web pages.

Lisa C. Stanton works as a freelance writer in Missouri and enjoys the fierce support of a slightly kooky and mostly queer writer's group.

Kyes Stevens is from a "little bit" of a town in Alabama. She now attends graduate school at Sarah Lawrence College in New York where she is working on an MA in women's history and an MFA in poetry.

Jean Stewart is the author of a series of feminist sci-fi/fantasy books (*Return To Isis, Isis Rising, Warriors of Isis*) and a modern work called *Emerald City Blues*. She lives near Seattle with her partner, Susie, two rowdy dogs, and two sweet cats. For those *Freeland* addicts out there, she's working on the next Isis book.

Ila Suzanne's poems have been published in lesbian, feminist, pagan, and literary publications. *Bones of My Dreams*, her chapbook, is a collection of ten years of her carefully crafted work. She lives with her lover at the See Vue Motel on the central Oregon coast. This is her first venture into prose.

Jennifer Terrett resides in suburban Rockland County, N.Y., with her partner, Sandy, and their seven cats. She is employed by Rockland Community College as a technical assistant and is pursuing a master's degree in social work. She and Sandy care for homeless cats, hoping to eventually establish an animal sanctuary for stray and abandoned felines.

Jules Torti writes erotica in bouts—between studying neuroanatomy and endocrine pathology. She's a painter, a baker, a candlestick maker, and she makes a lovely lasagna. The fruits of her labor have appeared in *Beginnings, Awakening the Virgin, Hot and Bothered*, and *The Mammoth Book of Erotica*.